HE BLEW IN WITH THE STORM

Miriam scurried inside and grabbed a sturdy chair from the nearest table. Part of her wanted to call the Brenneman boys—her Rachel's fiancé, Micah, would be here in two shakes of a tail—yet she craved some time alone with this stranger. She told herself she was giving him a chance to recover before anyone else saw him in this sorry state—

"If ya don't mind my drippin' on your floor, I'll just rest here for a few."

Miriam jumped. Why wasn't she surprised that the man had already stood himself up and come in without her help? He eased into the chair she'd pulled out.

"I'd ask what ya were doin' here at this crazy hour, in the pitch dark," he murmured as he looked around, "but I guess that's none of my business. I've got to tell ya, though, it smells so *gut* I must've passed through the pearly gates and into heaven."

Miriam laughed again in spite of her agitated state. "I'm bakin' pies and decoratin' cakes for the bishop's surprise party tomorrow. Gettin' the day's breakfast and lunch started, too," she replied. "Welcome to the Sweet Seasons Bakery Café . . ."

Also by Charlotte Hubbard

Summer of Secrets

Published by Kensington Publishing Corporation

AUTUMN WINDS

Seasons *of the* Heart

Charlotte Hubbard

ZEBRA BOOKS
KENSINGTON PUBLISHING CORP.
http://www.kensingtonbooks.com

ZEBRA BOOKS are published by

Kensington Publishing Corp.
119 West 40th Street
New York, NY 10018

ISBN-13: 978-1-4201-2170-4
ISBN-10: 1-4201-2170-7

First Printing: September 2012

10 9 8 7 6 5 4 3 2 1

Printed in the United States of America

For Aunt Ruth and Aunt Sandra,
who are every bit as spirited and adventurous
as the aunts in this story!

ACKNOWLEDGMENTS

All thanks and praise to You, Lord, for leading us from Missouri to Minnesota, and for being with us every step of the way. Once again You've put me in the right place at the right time.

Continued gratitude to my editor, Alicia Condon, and my agent, Evan Marshall. Your enthusiasm and belief in my work mean more than ever in these rapidly changing times.

Many thanks to Jim Smith of Step Back in Time Tours for his incredible assistance as I researched this book in James-port, Missouri—the largest Old Order Amish settlement west of the Mississippi River. It's a pleasure and a privilege to work with you, sir!

Much love to Neal, my husband of thirty-seven years. It's been an adventure, ain't so?

Who can find a virtuous woman? for her price is far above
 rubies.
The heart of her husband doth safely trust in her . . .
> She will do him good, and not evil,
> all the days of her life.
She stretcheth out her hand to the poor;
> Yea, she reacheth forth her hands to the needy.
Strength and honor are her clothing,
> and she shall rejoice in the time to come.
She openeth her mouth with wisdom; and in her tongue is
> the law of kindness.
Her children arise up and call her blessed;
Her husband also, and he praiseth her:
> "Many daughters have done virtuously,
> but thou excellest them all."
Favor is deceitful and beauty is vain,
But a woman that feareth the Lord, she shall be praised.

—Proverbs 31

Chapter 1

Lord, if this rain's gonna cause another flood like Ya sent Noah, I hope You'll give me a sign to get to higher ground. Can't have my bakery blowin' off the face of the Earth in this wind, either, as we're countin' on these pies and cakes for the big party tomorrow!

Miriam Lantz slammed the whistling window shut. When was the last time they'd seen such a fierce wind? Rain pelted the roof of the Sweet Seasons Bakery Café, not quite drowning out the troubling thoughts that had wakened her in the wee hours. Too often these past weeks she'd dwelled upon Bishop Knepp's vow to somehow get her out of her business and into his home. Ordinarily it wasn't her way to fret so, but Hiram Knepp could stir up more trouble than a nest of ornery hornets, if he had a mind to. It hadn't made him one bit happy, when an English fellow had outbid him to buy this building a month ago.

Miriam sighed. She didn't usually start the day's baking at one in the morning, either, but lately she'd felt so restless . . . as unsettled as the weather they'd had all during September. Now that she and her partner, Naomi Brenneman, wouldn't lose their building—or their booming business—she should be focused on her daughter Rachel's wedding, set for October 20. Such a happy time, because Naomi's son Micah was the perfect match for her daughter! But even kneading the fragrant, warm dough for the cornmeal rolls on today's lunch menu didn't settle her.

Miriam pushed the grainy dough with the heels of her hands, then folded it over itself and repeated the process time had so deeply ingrained in her . . . sprinkled more cornmeal and flour on the countertop, and then rolled the sleeves of her dress another fold higher. "Awful warm in here," she murmured.

The oven alarm buzzed, and she pulled out six thick pumpkin pies. As she replaced them with large pans of apple crisp, Miriam paused. Was that a horse's whinny she'd heard outside?

Not at this hour, in this storm. Who'd be fool enough to risk life and limb—not to mention his horse—travelin' the dark county blacktop that runs through Willow Ridge?

She inhaled the spicy aromas of cinnamon and cloves, imagining the smiles on folks' faces after tomorrow's preaching service at Henry and Lydia Zook's, when they surprised the bishop by celebrating his fifty-fifth birthday. These pies, made from her sister Leah's fresh pumpkins, would be the first to go—but their hostess, Lydia, had also ordered a layer cake and sheet cakes from the Sweet Seasons for the occasion.

And if Hiram gets the notion I baked all these things especially to impress him, he'd better just find somebody else to court. And to raise his kids, too!

Miriam chuckled in spite of her misgivings. If anyone could think of a way to dodge the bishop's romantic intentions, it would be she and her girls! It was no secret around Willow Ridge that Hiram's young wife, Linda, who'd died of birthing complications, had borne more than just the burden of being married to their moral and community leader. While Miriam believed she could live the more upright life required of a bishop's wife, serving as an example to their Old Order Amish community, she had no illusions about sharing the same house with Hiram and his rambunctious kids—not to mention his daughter Annie Mae, who was in the throes of a *rumspringa* no stepmother wanted to deal with!

A loud *crash* out in the dining room made Miriam jump. Glass tinkled over the tables and a sudden gust of wind howled through a jagged hole in the window before the power went out.

The bakery grew eerily quiet, what with the freezers and the dishwasher shutting off. This storm was a reminder of how her gas appliances at home had an advantage over the electric ones required by the health department and installed by the Schrocks, the Mennonite quilters who shared her building. Miriam was no stranger to the darkness, as she usually started her baking at three every morning, but this storm had set her on edge. And when had she ever seen a huge tree limb on a table?

"Lord a-mercy, what's next?" she murmured as she warily made her way through the darkness, between the café's tables. "Better have Naomi's boys clean this up before folks come in for the breakfast—"

Again a horse neighed, right outside the window this time.

"Whoa, fella! Easy now!" a male voice coaxed.

A bolt of lightning shot across the sky, to backlight the frightening silhouette of a huge Percheron rearing up, frantically pawing the air. The horse's handler stood near the damaged tree, struggling with the reins, still talking as calmly as he could while dodging those deadly hooves.

"Pharaoh, take it easy, fella! We'll wait out the storm right here, so—"

But another ominous flash filled the sky and in his frenzy, the horse tipped forward to buck with its powerful back legs.

Miriam heard a sickening *thud* as those hooves connected with a human body, and then a cry of pain and another *thud* when the fellow struck the café's outside wall. The huge Percheron galloped off, whinnying in terror, its reins flapping behind it.

Things got very quiet. Only the patter of the rain and some rapidly retreating hoofbeats punctuated the darkness. Miriam rushed to unlock the café's main door, afraid of what she might find. Her husband, Jesse, had been trampled to death by a huge stallion that spooked while Jesse was shoeing him, so frightening images rushed through her mind as she stepped outside.

The poor man lay sprawled against the foundation of her building. She considered herself a fairly stalwart woman, able to heft fifty-pound bags of flour and such, but for sure and for certain she wouldn't be moving this stranger.

Best not to shift him around anyway, she reasoned, noting that his head was up out of the puddles. Should she find something to cover him, and then call for help? Or hurry straight to the phone shanty behind the building? *Best to call 911 and then . . . but what if he got kicked in the head? What if he's not gonna come around?*

Miriam hesitated but a moment. If the fellow was unconscious, at least he wasn't in pain, and if he was already gone, well, the paramedics had better come to make sure of that. She started back inside but before she reached the door, the man groaned loudly.

"Don't try to stand up! Ya got kicked mighty hard, by the sound of it." Miriam sensed that he, like most injured fellows, would ignore a woman's instructions, so she hunkered down beside him. The cold rain soaked through her kapp and the back of her dress, but that was a minor discomfort compared to what her visitor must be feeling. "Where'd he kick ya? A horse that big—and that scared— could've killed ya, easy."

The fellow winced, shifting. "I should've known better than . . . just wanted to get one town farther along, ya know?" he rasped. "Should've just stayed with my wagon instead of thinkin' Pharaoh would get over bein' spooked by this lightnin'. Smarter than I am, that horse is."

Miriam looked all around but saw nothing. She moved closer, under the eaves where she wouldn't get quite so wet. "What kind of wagon are we talkin' about?" she asked. Maybe this man was half out of his head after being kicked so hard. He had the nicest voice, though. And even if he was in horrible-bad pain, he was thinking of his horse's welfare.

"Smithy wagon. I'm a travelin' farrier." He looked at her then, gingerly rubbing his chest. "Lookin' to find some reasonable land for a mill, so's I can settle down. I came to these parts on account of the rapids I heard about on the river."

Miriam's heart played hopscotch in her chest. "A travelin' blacksmith?" she asked in a thin voice. "We've got an empty smithy right behind the café buildin' here. Belonged to my Jesse, but he's passed now, and . . ."

Had she said too much? It wasn't like her to speak of her widowed state to strangers, yet this fellow seemed willing to reveal his own hopes and dreams to her. So what could it hurt?

"I'm sorry to hear that, ma'am." He inhaled, testing the pain in his chest. "Ya know, I think if I could sit up against the buildin'—"

"Here, let me help ya!"

"—and draw a few *gut*, deep breaths to clear my head—"

"Don't try to stand up just yet!" Miriam knew she sounded like a mother hen clucking instructions, but she didn't want him falling over. "If ya can wait here, I'll call the ambulance and—"

"You'll do no such thing!" He grabbed her arm, and then managed a tentative smile despite the rain that soaked him. His other hand remained on his chest, massaging the spot where the horse must've kicked him. "A fella in my line of work gets some sense knocked into him every now and again. Probably a *gut* thing."

Oh, but that smile and his touch set the butterflies to fluttering inside her! Miriam drew back, and he released her arm. She chuckled nervously and he joined her, a happy sound, even though the thunder still rumbled around them. "All right then, since you're a man and you'll do as ya please anyway, can I at least bring ya out a chair to pull yourself up with?" she asked. "Better than sittin' in this puddle, ain't so?"

"Right nice of ya to look after me this way."

Miriam scurried inside and grabbed a sturdy chair from the nearest table. Part of her wanted to call the Brenneman boys—her Rachel's fiancé, Micah, would be here in two shakes of a tail—yet she craved some time alone with this stranger. She told herself she was giving him a chance to recover before anyone else saw him in this sorry state—

"If ya don't mind my drippin' on your floor, I'll just rest here for a few."

Miriam jumped. Why wasn't she surprised that the man had already stood himself up and come in without her help? He eased into the chair she'd pulled out.

"I'd ask what ya were doin' here at this crazy hour, in the pitch dark," he murmured as he looked around, "but I guess that's none of my business. I've got to tell ya, though, it smells so *gut* I must've passed through the pearly gates and into heaven."

Miriam laughed again in spite of her agitated state. "I'm bakin' pies and decoratin' cakes for the bishop's surprise party tomorrow. Gettin' the day's breakfast and lunch started, too," she replied. "Welcome to the Sweet Seasons Bakery Café. Can I get ya some coffee, or—"

"Seems Pharaoh knew more about where to drop me off than I gave him credit for." Her visitor leaned toward her, smoothing the wet hair back from his face. "I'm Ben Hooley, by the way, originally from out around Lancaster County. I appreciate your takin' a chance on a wayfarin' stranger."

"And I'm Miriam Lantz. So I guess we're not strangers now, ain't so?"

And where had such boldness come from? Here they were in the dark without another soul around, chatting like longtime friends. At three in the morning, no less!

Oh, the bishop's not gonna like this! Not one little bit!

The fellow extended his hand, and as Miriam shook it the kitchen lights flashed on. The refrigerators hummed, and for a moment she could believe it was the little spark of electricity passing from his hand to hers that had restored the building's power.

Ben's laugh filled the empty dining room. "Well now. What do ya think about that?" He looked around, smiling. "The Lord's watchin' over me for sure and for certain, bringin' me here to your place on such a nasty night. A port in a storm. Just what I've been needin' for a while."

Miriam smiled at that . . . at the sound of his mellow male voice and the way it seemed to make itself at home in her little café. Then she blinked, remembering the reality of this situation: she knew nothing about this Hooley fellow, except that his clothes and speech announced he was Plain and that he'd been kicked by his horse. But now that he was recovering, and the power was back on in her kitchen—

"If you'll point me toward a broom, I'll clean up this mess and get that branch back outside where it belongs," he offered. "It's the least I can do, seein's how ya got me in out of the rain."

She'd been so busy following the lines of his clean-shaven face when he talked, she'd made a fool of herself; there *was* a huge section of maple tree covering two of her tables and she'd all but forgotten it. "Oh, but ya surely must be too sore to be heftin'—I can get a couple of our fellas—"

"Comes a time when I can't move that tree limb or push a broom, ya better just bury me." Ben scooted to the edge of his chair and slowly stood up, testing his balance. "See there? I'm *gut* as new. A little soggy, but movin' around's the cure for that, and a way to keep from gettin' stiff, too."

Miriam didn't know what to say . . . didn't think it proper to examine his chest, even if he probably had a huge, hoof-shaped bruise where his horse had kicked him. It was the first time she'd been alone with a man since Jesse had passed—except for Bishop Knepp, and she'd ducked out of his embrace—so she felt acutely aware of Ben's broad shoulders and how his wet shirt clung to them. He was a slender fellow but muscular—

And what business do ya have gawkin' at him? He can't be thirty yet. More Rhoda's age than yours!

Thoughts of her grown daughters—how they'd be here with Naomi in a couple of hours to prepare for the breakfast shift—steadied her resolve. She smiled at Ben but stepped back, too. It wasn't proper for an Amish woman to behave this way, even when no one was watching—except God, of course. "If you're up to that sort of work, I'd be grateful, as I've got my bakin' to get back to," she replied. "But if ya feel woozy or short of breath, like ya need a doctor—"

"Your kindness has already worked a miracle cure, Miriam. Right nice of ya to set aside a few of the Old Ways to help me out."

Had he read her mind? Or did he just know the right things to say? A traveling blacksmith surely knew all sorts of ins and outs when it came to making deals for what he needed . . . And what sort of fellow, in a trade every Old Order Amish family relied upon, didn't settle in one community? And if Ben knew about the rapids in the river, what else had he checked up on? What if he was making up this story as he went along, to gain some advantage over her— or whomever he met up with—in Willow Ridge?

And what if you're spinnin' all this stuff out like a spider, about to catch yourself in a web of assumptions? Sure, he's got a nice smile, but—

He did have a nice smile, didn't he? Miriam quickly fetched a broom and dustpan from the closet, relieved that Ben had already stepped outside to see about pulling the big tree branch from her window. She set the tools where he would find them and then returned to her kitchen, where the lights were brighter and the serving window acted as a barrier between this good-looking stranger and her work space.

Jah, he is gut-*lookin'. And that's not his fault, is it?*

Miriam laughed at herself. No, Ben Hooley's looks and manner were gifts from God, same as the way Rachel, Rhoda, and Rebecca favored their handsome *dat*.

"And what do ya think of all this, Jesse?" she whispered. Every now and again she asked her late husband's opinion, or thought about how he would have handled situations she found herself in, even though her confidence had increased a lot during these past months of successfully running her business.

Miriam stood quietly at her flour-dusted work table . . . just letting the hum of the appliances and the aroma of spicy pumpkin pies keep her company.

Wait for the promise of the Father.

She blinked. Was that still, small voice she relied upon for guidance—be it Jesse's or God's—implying the heavenly Father might have made a promise to her? And that He was about to keep it? As glass tinkled onto the café floor and that tree branch disappeared out the gaping hole in the window, she wondered if this had been a providential morning. Meant to be, for both her and Ben.

For sure and for certain, this stranger was giving her a lot to think about.

Chapter 2

Ben squatted to center the tree branch over his shoulder, wrapping his arms around its girth. It said something about Miriam Lantz that she'd left the huge old maple in place when she'd built her bakery, which looked to be only a couple of years old. The dull ache where Pharaoh had kicked him throbbed back to life with the effort of shifting the limb from her window, but the pain kept him focused on the job at hand rather than on the woman he'd just met.

Ya know nothin' about her! Got no business sayin' flirty things nor gawkin' at her, either. Every unattached fella in the district's got his eye on Miriam, no doubt.

But just as the storm hadn't stopped him from driving farther down the road, common sense wouldn't keep his mind from lingering on the café owner who'd rushed into the storm to help him . . . whose deep-set brown eyes and gentle laughter were already working on him. He gave the tree limb one last heave so it would clear the building's front wall.

Miriam Lantz, was it? Ben peered through the jagged window glass, inhaling the spicy sweetness of her pies as he observed the quick efficiency with which she handled her rolling pin. Every Plain woman he knew was a fine cook, industrious to a fault. And plenty enough younger ones had tempted him with their pies and whatnot from the oven, trying to win his favor, yet this woman with a few streaks of silver in her rich brown hair made him sit up and pay close attention. She'd no doubt opened this business to support herself and her family—

Jah, probably has a passel of kids!

Yet Ben sensed no desperation in Miriam. No attempt to size him up as husband material, even though she'd taken a few long looks, same as he had. Was it providential that Pharaoh had abandoned him to this woman's care . . . especially considering the empty smithy she'd mentioned? She wouldn't notice if he went around back to check out the forge and equipment while she was busy baking, yet something made him wait. Better to have Miriam show it to him of her own free will, in her own good time. He knew all too well how older Amishmen believed their desires were more important than a woman's. And that was the wrong foot to start off on.

He inhaled the yeasty scent of rising bread . . . the cinnamon goodness that hinted of apple pies to join the six pumpkin ones cooling on the countertop. His stomach rumbled. Ben smiled and made himself go inside for the broom. Sweeping up broken glass was a better way to please Miriam Lantz than hanging around like a puppy with his tongue lolling out. After breakfast he'd look for Pharaoh and find a way to replace her window, but meanwhile it felt downright cozy just to be here, in her presence.

Maybe it's time ya got off the road . . . parked your wagon and put down some roots instead of roamin' the roads like a lost dog.

A startling thought, that one! Ben cleared the café floor of its broken glass, stealing glances at the cook in the

kitchen. She wore a simple rust-colored dress, the shade of
the bittersweet and sumacs he'd seen last week, changing to
their fall colors. Miriam was fully filled out from having
babies, but she was by no means fat. Her brows formed
gentle arches above eyes as homey as hot cocoa . . . eyes
that told him she found him as *interesting* as he found her.

But why lie to himself? When she'd fussed over him out
in the storm, Miriam brought to mind his favorite aunts,
Nazareth and Jerusalem—wonderful-*gut* women, but not
the type to have romantic notions about!

"Know where I might find a tarp to cover this window?"
he asked over the rumble of her big mixer.

Miriam flipped off the switch, thinking about her answer.
"Most likely you'll find some in the smithy, out back. Got
a lantern here by the door, if ya care to look."

When she looked at him straight on, Ben recalculated her
age in a hurry. Here in the glow of her kitchen, Miriam was
far more appealing than his aunts and nowhere close to their
age. That put a whole different spin on things—but Ben set
aside his wandering thoughts. Here was his invitation to
check out the forge. And to think more about whether he'd
want to be the town's next blacksmith, or get back into his
wagon and roll on out of here. He entered the café's kitchen,
in awe of the gleaming stockpots and utensils hanging from
hooks, and realized how hungry he was when he saw large
metal pans of hash browns awaiting whatever heavenly stuff
Miriam would layer over them.

As he made his way to the door, he struck the wooden
match against the box. Ben lit the lantern, considering how
best to express his concern. "Won't bother ya if I need to poke
around to find that tarp? That bein' your husband's shop—"

"We've been in and out a lot. Micah—my Rachel's
fella—just remodeled the upstairs so Rhoda and I can live
there after they get hitched next month." Miriam's smile

wavered a little, probably when she thought about her man who'd passed, but she didn't change her mind. She went back to stirring eggs in a big cast-iron skillet on her stove.

Ben dashed across the parking lot through the rain, wondering if he'd need a key. The smithy door swung open when he unlatched it, however, and by the light of his lantern he recognized the familiar shapes and shadows of a blacksmith's domain: the forge, the bellows hanging neatly nearby, and other pneumatic equipment that ran just fine without the electricity Miriam required for her kitchen. A doorway painted springtime yellow most likely led to that apartment upstairs, and Ben dared to picture himself living there rather than bedding down in his wagon . . .

Keep your silly notions to yourself! She's got plans for those rooms and they don't include you!

Still, it felt good to inhale the masculine scents of steel and sheet metal. Jesse Lantz had kept a right clean shop before he died, or else somebody had cared enough to redd it up in his memory; all the welders and tools were in their places, ready to be picked up and used again. He spotted a bin with a couple of tarps stacked on it and grabbed them, along with a hammer and a bag of tacks. Best not to linger too long, he thought, picturing the sturdy Belgians and the sleek carriage horses folks would bring here so he could shoe them. It would be a true pleasure to ply his trade in all this well-planned space instead of working from the back of his wagon . . .

Ben jogged back through the rain and around to the front of the café. It didn't take him long to tack the heavy tarp to the window casement. He returned the tools to the smithy then, inhaling the sense of security—the sense of already *belonging*—he felt when he stood in Jesse Lantz's shop.

But it was too soon to think he'd be settling here. He didn't even know the name of the town yet! And it was too soon to give in to his cravings for home-cooked meals and a church service that would be as familiar as his favorite shirt.

Tell me if I'm barkin' up the wrong tree, Lord, he prayed as he returned to the back door of the bakery. *And don't let me be misbehavin', or makin' fools of this fine woman and myself. She deserves better than that.*

It was a nice step back into happiness, having Miriam smile at him over a huge mound of dough she was covering on her countertop. "Ya might as well join me for a bite of breakfast before my partner and the girls get here. We always sample what we're puttin' on the menu, to make sure it's fit to eat." Miriam raised her eyebrows in a way that made him hold his breath. Was she flirting with him?

"Best idea I've heard all day," Ben replied as he moseyed around the kitchen. "Mighty nice place you've got here. I'm thinkin' those are Amish-made tables and chairs in your café—"

"*Jah*, the fella my Rachel's gonna marry built them in his wood shop."

"—and I can't help but notice your electric appliances." Ben looked at the big freezers and refrigerators along the back wall, as well as the sleek new ovens, stoves, and a dish-washer Old Order women could only dream about. "Not that I'm findin' fault. Just curious as to how ya talked your bishop into allowin' that."

Miriam smiled while she dished up large servings from a glass casserole and put them alongside thick slices of toast on two plates. "Here in Missouri we've got to have electric-ity to run a café, so I partnered with a Mennonite gal who makes quilts in the shop next door. The land's mine, and I put up the buildin', but Mary, Eva, and Priscilla Schrock got us on the grid—to run their sewin' machines and my kitchen equipment.

"Back in August, though," she continued with a shy smile, "the bishop got a bee in his bonnet about how all this success must surely be standin' in the way of my salvation. So he said I was to sell the buildin'."

Miriam paused to fill two mugs with fresh coffee. "It nearly broke my heart, thinkin' I'd lose this little place and the business I've come to love—but God had His way about it! An English fella—who, bless his soul, raised the baby daughter I lost in a flood eighteen years ago—offered the bank a lot more money than Bishop Knepp had."

As they carried their plates out to sit at a finely crafted oak table in the dining room, Ben grinned. "I love hearin' about folks who find a way to succeed . . . to do the work God's put in their hearts while still followin' the Old Ways." After they shared a silent grace over the food, Ben closed his eyes again in sheer bliss over his first mouthful: bacon and sausage and onion, layered with bread and lots of cheese, with crunchies on top. "And it's no secret you were born to cook for folks, Miriam. Goodness, woman, this is the best food I've had since—well, since I left my *mamm*'s table!"

Her face turned a pretty shade of pink. "It *is* my purpose, feedin' people," she stated quietly. She studied him over her toast, as though considering whether she'd share her private thoughts. "Truth be told, Hiram Knepp wants me to be feedin' him and his houseful of kids—"

Ben's fork stopped halfway to his mouth. "Your bishop wants to hitch up with ya? *That* would put an end to this place right quick."

"*Jah*, there's that," Miriam agreed as she rose from her seat. "His second wife—lots younger than he is—passed on about nine or ten months ago. He's got a daughter, Annie Mae, lookin' after the household, but she's more interested in her *rumspringa* than in bein' a stand-in wife for her *dat*.

Can't say I blame her, either," Miriam added, shaking her head. "Tough enough just bein' a bishop's kid."

"*Jah*, lots of us traveled hither and yon, smokin' and drinkin' and whatnot durin' our runnin'-around days. Somethin's to be said for growin' up and growin' out of that phase, though." Ben watched the way Miriam walked into the kitchen with quick efficiency to fetch a pumpkin pie and a big knife. Her dress fell a few inches below her knees . . . still short enough to reveal shapely, sturdy legs in black stockings.

"But here I am yackin' your ear off, when you're more likely wonderin' where your horse got off to and wantin' to get back to your wagon." She turned to grin at him. "I'll have to watch myself or when Naomi and my girls get here, they'll think I've been actin' right sinful, entertainin' a young fella we've never seen."

"*Jah*, I'm a real shiftless sort. Got a string of broken hearts for a hatband, ya know," Ben teased. He tried not to be obvious about looking her over as she returned to the table. "So . . . this Bishop Knepp with the need for a wife. Gettin' a little long in the tooth, is he?"

"Matter of fact, we're surprisin' him with a birthday party tomorrow after preachin'. Why not stay for the services and join us for the meal?" she suggested cheerfully. "Hiram's turnin' fifty-five. Not all that old, as bishops go—"

"But way too old for *you*, Miriam!" Ben's eyes got as wide as hers did, at the forceful way he'd spoken. "What I mean is—it's not for me to say, ya understand—but the last thing a woman like you needs is a fella on his third wife, set in his ways—"

"Like a fence post in concrete, *jah*."

"—and expectin' ya to fit into a family that's already got their habits. Not to mention mixin' your girls in with the

bishop's youngsters," Ben added. "And you'd be givin' up
your own home . . . this nice café and your bakin' business."

Miriam considered him carefully then; really *looked* at
Ben. He could only gaze back, his breakfast forgotten.
"Now how'd ya know about such a thing?" she murmured.
"That's exactly what I told my Rachel and Rhoda—twins
they are, and twenty-one now—about why I wouldn't consider courtin' Hiram. They're all grown up—and with
Rachel marryin' later this month and livin' in our big house,
mixin' them with the Knepp kids isn't such a concern. But
jah . . ." She sighed as she cut two huge wedges of that
pumpkin pie. She plopped a big spoonful of real whipped
cream on them, too. "Hiram's not a man to take no for an
answer."

Ben inhaled the spicy scent of cinnamon and cloves as he
cut off the tip of his piece of pie. He dragged that bite through
the whipped cream and then took his time about closing his
mouth over it . . . savoring its thick sweetness and the dense
texture. "Miriam," he finally said.

She looked across the table at him, her fork still in front
of her mouth. "*Jah?* Did ya get a taste of somethin' that
didn't mix in just right? Or—"

"Not hardly. Never in all my days have I tasted such . . .
mighty fine pie."

Miriam's eyes widened. So sweet and dark brown they
were, like fudge sauce. And even though she'd not taken the
time yet to pull herself together for the day—hadn't expected anyone to drop in at this hour, after all—Ben
couldn't stop gazing at her chestnut hair . . . which probably cascaded well below her bottom when a man plucked
out the hairpins . . .

"You'd be givin' up a lot more than ya got, Miriam," he
stated softly—and where this advice was coming from, he
hadn't the slightest notion. "Not just hitchin' in with this old

Hiram fella, but havin' to live as a bishop's wife instead of bein' the fine cook and companion ya were born to be."

Miriam's face lit up like the sun. "Well now. Ya might be just a pup, Ben Hooley, but you've got an old dog's wisdom about ya."

He chuckled, finding his appetite again. After another mouthful of that incredible pie, he quipped, "*Jah*, probably best to keep my nose in my own bowl instead of pokin' around in another dog's chow," he remarked carefully. "But don't believe for a minute I won't mark my territory and defend it. It's better to be a wise old dog at home than actin' like a lost pup alongside the road, ain't so?"

Chapter 3

Rhoda Lantz came through the Sweet Seasons back door into the kitchen, inhaling the heavenly aromas of apple crisp and pies and the cheesy-bacon scent of the casseroles her mother had already made for the breakfast menu. She was a little later than she'd intended to be, but hungry as she was, it was best to eat some breakfast before she helped her sister set up the dining room.

"Mamma, ya must've been starvin'! Half of this casserole's missin' from the pan!" she teased as she filled her plate. Then she glanced at the lineup of pies set aside from those that would go in the glass case out front. "And ya cut into one of the pies for the party, too?"

"I've been here a while, child. Bakin' pies. Decoratin' these cakes for the bishop's birthday," came the reply from the other side of the kitchen. Mamma was focused on the bottom edge of a tall white layer cake, squeezing on frosting in a scalloped design with a pastry tube.

"*Jah*, your *mamm* already had the goodies made for tomorrow's party and this big pan of crisp for today's lunch buffet by the time I got here," Naomi Brenneman chimed in. "And to think she was here by herself durin' that storm, too. That was some kind of wind we had, to toss a big limb through the front window! Lucky that's all the damage we got."

"Blew so hard into my room, I slammed the window down," Rhoda's sister Rachel remarked as she loaded the dishwasher. "Sure hope this rain's all passed through before the preachin' service tomorrow, or Zooks' basement'll smell damp."

Rhoda took in their chatter as she quickly ate her breakfast, but she didn't miss the way Mamma had passed off answering about that pie and why so much of the casserole was gone. When she looked out into the café's main room to see what Naomi was talking about, her jaw dropped. Didn't anyone else see the obvious? "So how'd ya get that tarp up over the hole in the window, Mamma?" she quizzed.

Her mother quickly swished her hands in the dishwater. "Just a sec—that's the phone ringin'," she chirped before she bustled to the shanty out back.

Rhoda raised her eyebrows at Naomi. "Has she told ya how that big tree limb got taken outta the dinin' room? It's for sure and for certain Mamma didn't heft it outside by herself!"

Her mother's partner shrugged. "It's life's little mysteries that keep things interestin', ain't so? I'm bidin' my time. She'll fill us in when she's *gut* and ready."

Her sister Rachel loaded a tray with plates for the buffet, and then Rhoda followed her twin into the main dining room. "Ya don't suppose Hiram saw the lights on and came over to—"

"Mamma wouldn't be steppin' so lively or wearin' that kitty-cat grin for *him*, Sister! I'm thinkin'—"

The loud whine of a chain saw cut into their chatter, so they both went to the window to see who was revving it up. Outside, the dawn was veiled in mist and the crimson leaves of the maple tree out front still dripped from the morning's downpour—except where the storm had left a raw, jagged edge after ripping off one of its thickest main branches. The road glistened a shiny black. Rachel's beau, Micah Brenneman, grinned at them before he started slicing the downed tree limb into pieces.

Rachel blew him a kiss and then shrugged at Rhoda; no sense in trying to talk above the racket of that saw. And no reason to believe their mother was keeping any secrets. Micah came here nearly every day to see to any maintenance work before he and his brothers sat down to their breakfast in the Sweet Seasons Café. He might have come in to clear away the broken window and hang that tarp when he heard that big piece of tree snap in the storm . . . or he might not have.

With a frustrated sigh, Rhoda wrapped silverware in napkins and then stacked the white bundles in a dishpan, the same as she did every morning, while Rachel checked the condiments and put place settings on the tables. Her mother had returned to the kitchen and was chatting with Naomi as they filled a roaster with sliced apples, which would be simmered with butter, brown sugar, and cinnamon for the morning's buffet. Maybe Micah's mother could wait for the solution to the little mystery that surrounded them, but Rhoda wanted answers!

"So ya were here when that tree branch came through the window, Mamma?" she called in to them. "Must've scared the livin' daylights out of ya. I know it sounded mighty scary at the house, with all that crashin' thunder."

"*Jah*, and if we'd known you'd already sneaked over here," Rachel chided, "we'd have grabbed ya between us and hauled ya back home, too! Ya need your sleep, Mamma!"

Mamma and Naomi turned from their work, their knives going still in their hands. "One of these days, you'll be old enough to wake up wonderin' about things. Or there'll come a time when ya sleep alone after havin' a husband," their mother pointed out. "Then you'll understand the comfort of keepin' your hands busy."

"Amen to that!" Naomi agreed. "I can't recall the last night I slept clear through without bein' pestered by some bothersome thought or another—or Ezra's achin' and painin'. Better to be up and doin' instead of lyin' there stewin'."

"And what would ya be frettin' about, Mamma?" Rachel asked. "Thanks to Bob Oliveri and Rebecca, ya kept your restaurant. Ya surely can't be worried that nobody'll eat your pumpkin pies tomorrow!"

"Puh! Pies're the least of my worries," Mamma replied. She went back to slicing those apples as though that would help her think of what to say next. "Seems like when I shed my black dresses for color, I switched one problem for another."

Rhoda exchanged a look with her twin. "*Ach*, now, Mamma. Didn't Rachel and Rebecca and I promise ya there'd be no hitchin' up with the bishop?"

Naomi let out a laugh. "Ya think Hiram knows about that?"

"Or cares?" Mamma blurted. "And don't you girls be spreadin' it around, what we're talkin' about right now! We'll be takin' on trouble for sure and for certain."

"*Jah*, nothin' Hiram Knepp likes better than to be told he can't do somethin', or can't be in charge," Naomi agreed. "Wouldn't surprise me one little bit if he got right personal with your *mamm* tomorrow at his party. With a birthday like fifty-five, a fella gets more . . . determined to go after what he wants. Before time runs out on him."

Rhoda rolled her eyes at her sister. "All right then, our lips're sealed. But we're keepin' watch over ya, Mamma.

Now what's the breakfast menu—and what lunch specials are we servin', so I can write them on the whiteboard?"

As she waited for her mother and Naomi to discuss what they had in the fridge for today—and what would make best use of the potatoes, pumpkins, and all those apples Aunt Leah and the neighbors were bringing in, Rhoda realized they'd had this very same conversation yesterday. And the day before. And the day before that. And while she considered herself as patient as anyone she knew, she wondered when things would ever be different for her. With Rachel marrying Micah at the end of this month, and moving into the big white house they'd lived in all their lives—not to mention Mamma being hounded by Hiram Knepp, and being gawked at by a few other fellows—it seemed as if she was the only one standing still. Stuck in a rut.

"We're havin' the usual stuff on the breakfast menu, along with fried apples, this breakfast sandwich casserole, and pumpkin-blueberry muffins on the buffet," Mamma finally called out to her. "Lunch buffet's gonna include ham balls, baked yams and apples, and loaded potato casserole. We've got apple crisp and fudge ripple cake for dessert, along with whatever pies we put together by that time."

"*Jah, jah*," Rhoda said with a sigh. Again, as she carefully wrote on the whiteboard, it occurred to her that even the menu didn't change a lot from day to day—but then, the locals who ate here didn't seem to mind that, and the English tourists didn't know the difference.

"And why's that serious look puckerin' up your face, Sister?" Rachel had found some bittersweet in the woods and was tucking it into the table vases along with silk mums they'd used last fall. "You're goin' to the singin' tomorrow night, ain't so? Hopin' to match up with Jonah Zook or Seth Brenneman afterwards?"

"Most likely." Rhoda shrugged. Here again, she'd known

Jonah and Seth all their lives and *they* hadn't really changed, either. More like part of the landscape, they were—fellows she took for granted, rather than anyone who made her heart pound the way Rachel said Micah's kisses did.

Kisses. Now there was a topic she wanted to know more about! At twenty-one, what girl didn't? If too many more autumns passed her by, day after day the same—even though she'd be living in the new apartment above Dat's smithy with Mamma—folks would be whispering about poor Rhoda Lantz becoming a *maidel*.

She finished writing on the whiteboard and then glanced at the window covered by that blue tarp . . . a mystery she knew better than to ask about anymore this morning. "We should probably have Micah or one of his brothers board that up, in case we get more rain," she remarked.

"*Jah.* He'll be measurin' for new window glass after his breakfast, no doubt," Rachel replied.

That was Micah: dependable and efficient when it came to anything about carpentry or repair. Predictable to a fault.

That's what it was—everything had become so *predictable*! Not that finding the precise word behind her bleak mood made her feel any better. Rhoda gazed out at the autumn mist, which filled in the low spots across the pastures and floated above the river in the distance . . .

And then she stood at attention. The tallest, blackest Percheron she'd ever seen was coming down the county road, hauling an enclosed red trailer behind him. Most folks in Willow Ridge farmed with Belgians, so this horse looked mighty different from any she'd seen around these parts.

No, this animal looks like somethin' out of a fairy tale— bigger than life! And who's that drivin' him?

Rhoda smoothed her kapp, not taking her eyes off the horse, the trailer, or the driver as they came closer to the café. She couldn't yet read the lettering on the side of the tall, enclosed rig—not that she cared about the business it advertised. That fellow in the seat, holding those reins and sitting tall as if he were on a throne, now *he* got her attention! Who *was* this man with the light brown hair blowing back in the breeze beneath a broad-brimmed hat that announced him as Plain? His suspenders shifted with the movement of his muscular arms, and as he drove closer Rhoda gazed out the window for as long as she dared.

He was stopping here! Right out front!

"Rachel, get a look at this fella," she murmured as she backed away. No sense in being caught like a little kid with her nose pressed to the window. "He can't be from around Morning Star or New Haven, not that I know of."

Her twin raised an eyebrow. "Let me finish with these vases."

Rhoda had no inclination to help her so Rachel would finish faster. Instead, she went to the buffet table as though to check the plates and baskets that awaited the breakfast Mamma and Naomi were cooking. From there, she could peer out through a different window without being seen.

The driver hopped down from his seat and went behind the enclosed trailer to open its back doors. HOOLEY'S HORSESHOE SERVICE the yellow lettering on its sides proclaimed. And the rig was painted bright red, like a circus wagon! Now didn't that beat all? Did this fellow realize Willow Ridge had been without a smith since her *dat* had died? And of all things, he was carefully sliding a large pane of glass from the back of his wagon. Meanwhile, Micah had already loaded that cut-up tree limb into a farm trailer and taken off.

Rhoda pushed through the door like the place had caught fire. "Here—let me help ya with that!"

The man turned with a smile, almost as if he'd been expecting her. Then he paused for the slightest moment. "That's right kind of ya. It would be a shame, for sure and for certain, if this big piece of glass slipped before I got it into your window frame."

And how did he know their window had been broken? This early, hardly anyone had driven past the bakery yet, and locals were most likely tending to any damage at their own places before stopping for coffee or breakfast. Even if Mamma had called for somebody besides Micah—which she wouldn't think of doing—why would a total stranger in the farrier business be pulling in as though he knew they needed a new window?

One of those little mysteries Naomi was talkin' about . . .

Rhoda steadied the heavy, awkward pane of glass while the mystery man guided it toward the wall of the café. He was tall and lanky, but strong . . . had a summer-bronzed face and an easy way of moving . . . a smile that made her heartbeat pound in her ears when he focused on her with sparkling golden-brown eyes. "Ya must be one of Miriam's girls. Ya look a lot like her—and that's a fine thing, too."

Rhoda's face went hot. She caught herself blinking too much. "*Jah*, I'm Rhoda!" she stammered. "We're settin' up for breakfast, so we'd be pleased to feed ya—free!—for takin' care of this window so quick!"

"That's mighty generous, Rhoda." He rummaged for tools in a big metal box. "*Gut* as that bacon and sausage smell from out here, I'd be crazy not to take you up on your offer, ain't so?"

"How'd ya know our window was broken?" Rhoda blurted. "And—and how'd ya know my *mamm*'s name?"

Oh, that wasn't a gut *way to impress this fella*, she chided herself. *You're soundin' as silly as a girl about twelve years old.*

As he deftly popped the tacks out of the blue tarp with his claw hammer, he smiled as though he knew things he wasn't telling. "Just happened by the right place at the right time, I suppose. I'm only doin' what any fella would, after seein' how a tree limb had crashed through the café's window."

"So that's your tarp, too? *Denki* for helpin' us, by the way."

The fellow looked at her with another one of those friendly yet . . . secret smiles. If he were female, she'd think of it as a kitty-cat grin like Rachel was so good at hiding behind. But this was no girl she was standing beside.

"Your *mamm* told me where to find it. Stand aside now—and ya might want to tell anybody inside I'm about to break out the rest of this jagged glass."

Rhoda stepped inside as he'd told her to and headed straight for the kitchen. "Well, Mamma, your little *secret*'s come back!" she announced, as much to Naomi and Rachel as to her mother. "And he called ya by name! He's out front now, fixin' that window! Takin' down the tarp ya told him to fetch from Dat's shop!"

She planted her hands on her hips, noting the way Mamma's blush spread up her neck and all over her face—as well it should! "And just what were ya doin' here alone with this fella, in the wee hours, while we were still sleepin', Mamma?"

Chapter 4

Miriam's heartbeat took off like a shot. Ben was back! And while she wanted to rush out front to see what he was doing and how he was feeling now, her daughter's unspoken accusations rang in the kitchen. And it wasn't as if Naomi or Rachel were going to stop staring at her until she answered.

Her lips twitched with a grin even though it was clear Rhoda wanted to whip up a scandalous situation. "Ben Hooley happened along in the thick of that storm—"

"Oh, it's *Ben*, is it?" Rhoda interrupted. "He wasn't sharin' his name with me."

"—and after his horse spooked and kicked him in the chest—"

"Probably so, considerin' how it wasn't fit weather for neither man nor beast!"

"—he was kind enough to put up that tarp from your *dat*'s shop, to keep more rain and broken glass from blowin' in." Miriam cleared her throat, determined not to let Rhoda's tone upset her. "And this was after he hefted that tree limb out of the café. It was better than gettin' Micah out of bed at that hour, ain't so? And certainly better than tryin' to do such things myself—not that I could reach the top of that window. *Now*," Miriam said, mimicking Rhoda's assertive stance, "what else do ya want to know?"

Rhoda's face curdled, an expression Miriam recalled from when this daughter had been challenged as a child and didn't much like it. "What I want to know," she echoed in a rising voice, "is why you're gettin' so sticky-sweet on a fella who's young enough to be your"—she threw up her arms in exasperation—"well, he's *my* age, Mamma! Ya don't know a thing about him, but he's already got ya blushin' like a bride!"

Rhoda had said a mouthful there, hadn't she? Miriam felt a little stunned at how she must be wearing her heart on her sleeve, if Rhoda had picked up on so much from just talking with Ben for a few minutes. But there was a limit to how many questions a mother had to answer . . . and to how much sass she could take.

"Don't be so sure about that age difference, missy," Miriam replied in a tight voice. "Right now you're actin' about twelve. Readin' wayyyy too much into a *gut*-hearted fella helpin' us out—after he got himself kicked, no less."

To see how this response was going over, Miriam glanced at Rachel and Naomi. Their eyes were wide, but they were staying out of it—and rightly so! Some of the regulars—like Naomi's boys, Seth and Aaron, and her sister Leah's sons, Nate and Bram—were coming in to eat, and they were bringing Ben Hooley with them, already chatting him up the way men did. So she relaxed. No sense in letting anyone else see the two of them going nose to nose.

"It's time to load up the buffet table," Miriam said, nodding toward the fellows coming inside. "We'll take up this conversation later."

Rhoda's impatient sigh told her they *would* be having more of this talk, and that she'd better have her answers ready. Her girls knew to set aside the personal stuff when they waited tables, because the men settling into those chairs out front had no time to waste before they went to their day's work. Naomi was filling a metal steam table pan with crispy bacon, so Miriam grabbed a big basket and filled it with fresh, warm pumpkin-blueberry muffins. There was nothing better than getting into the café's routine to smooth over ruffled feathers.

"How are ya this mornin', boys?" Miriam asked her nephews, Nate and Bram Kanagy. "Will your *mamm* have a wagonload of veggies for us later?"

"*Jah*—yams and acorn squash," Bram replied. "She's been diggin' lots of potatoes, too."

"And pickin' apples!" his younger brother, Nate, crowed as he removed his hat. "Between your apple trees and ours, the orchard's puttin' out the most fruit we've seen in a long while."

"And they're nice and firm, too," Miriam said as she picked up a carafe of coffee. "I made apple crisp for the lunch buffet, and we'll no doubt have some apple walnut coffee cake for tomorrow mornin'."

"No pies?" Micah had settled at his usual table with his two brothers, and had invited Ben Hooley to sit with them.

"When have ya ever come here and not had pie?" Miriam teased. Then she smiled at Ben, who looked right at home amongst these younger locals. "These boys belong to my cookin' partner, Naomi. Their *mamm*'s here workin' early every mornin', so we feed Seth and Micah and Aaron before they open their cabinet shop."

"And ya still turn a profit?" Ben's eyes glimmered . . . an interesting shade of golden-brown they were, now that it was daylight. "Looks to me like this bunch could clean ya out before anybody else had a chance to eat and pay ya for it!"

"We do our best!" young Aaron said with a laugh. "I'm

gonna be the first to load up on that casserole. It's the kind
with bacon and sausage and cheese stacked up and baked in
eggs, ain't so?"

"Better get movin', runt," Seth Brenneman threatened as
he scooted his chair back. "You'll get trampled on your way
to the trough if ya stand here jawin' about it."

The bell above the door jingled and Tom Hostetler, the
local dairy farmer, came in with Reuben Reihl, his neighbor to the south. Both wore muddy trousers, from clearing
away storm damage on their farms, no doubt.

"Say, who belongs to that blacksmithin' wagon out
front?" Reuben asked as he looked around the crowd. "I've
got some horses needin' shoes and no time to take them
clear to Morning Star, what with the harvest still goin' on."

Ben turned to wave at him. "I'm the fellow you're
lookin' for. Ben Hooley. I can head to your place as soon as
I eat breakfast—or whenever ya want me to come."

"Appreciate it," the bulky, redheaded farmer replied.
"The name's Reuben Reihl, and I'm on the gravel road just
east of here, past the Brenneman boys' carpentry shop."

"I've got some milkin' machines that need repair, too,"
Tom said as he stepped up to shake Ben's hand. "Do ya do
that kind of weldin'?"

"For sure I do. I'll load the smaller pieces into my trailer
for later, and work on the bigger stuff in your barn while I'm
there," Ben replied. "We'll do whatever it takes to keep ya
up and runnin'. This afternoon be all right?"

Tom chuckled. "Can't ask for better service than that!
I'm Tom Hostetler, just on the other side of Reuben's place."

Again the bell jingled, and this time it was the bishop.
Several English travelers had taken seats and were ordering
their breakfast, but Hiram Knepp spotted Ben right off, as
the only Plain fellow he didn't know. "That farrier wagon's
an answered prayer," he said as he approached Ben's table.

"Welcome to Willow Ridge. I'm Hiram Knepp, the district's bishop—and I breed Belgians. I've got a whole stable of fine horses, some of them going to auction in a week or so. It'll probably take you the better part of a day to shoe them all."

Ben rose to shake the older man's hand. Was it Miriam's imagination, or did Ben Hooley look Hiram over pretty close, as though considering whether he'd take the job he'd just been offered? She moved around the room then, filling coffee mugs and taking a few orders from the menu. Thank goodness Rhoda had been waiting on another table of two English couples, passing through on vacation by the looks of their big RV out front. The last thing they needed was any silliness from Rhoda while Hiram Knepp was here.

"Need a couple cheese omelets with ham and hash browns," Miriam called over to Naomi as she returned to the kitchen. "Everybody's showin' up at once this mornin'. They've probably done a day's work already, lookin' after their livestock and fences since the storm blew through."

"Looks like that Hooley fella's linin' up his work for a *gut* long while." Her best friend's brown eyes sparkled as she plopped butter into two omelet pans. "No question in my mind about the sort of man he is, either, if he fixed up the window without ya havin' to ask him."

"*Jah.* And I have no idea how he got his horse back, or how he fetched his wagon or got that pane of glass here so quick, either," Miriam said. "Closest place to get glass cut is over in New Haven, at the hardware store." She took two more long metal pans out of the warming oven, knowing their breakfast casserole would be mostly gone by the time the Brenneman boys and her nephews ate their fill. "Some fellas just have a way of makin' things work out right, and he impresses me as one of them."

"Right nice to look at, too. Not that ya would've noticed that, Miriam."

Miriam glanced up quickly to see how her partner had meant that—and then they giggled together like a couple of girls. "So ya picked up on that part, Naomi?"

"I've got eyes, don't I?"

"Eyes like a potato and ears like corn. Ya don't miss much." Miriam glanced out into the dining room, where her twins were clearing away plates while Naomi's boys went to the steam table for seconds. "So tell me straight-out honest," she said in a lower voice. "Was I out of line, puttin' Rhoda in her place awhile ago? It never dawned on me she'd be gettin' her nose outta joint over—"

"Ben's gonna cause a stir amongst all the single women. That's just the way of it in a little town like Willow Ridge." Naomi tipped the skillets to allow her egg mixture to spread around the edges of the pan so the omelets would cook faster. "No doubt in my mind Rhoda's set her cap for him, but Ben Hooley might be just the kind of sugar you're wantin' in *your* tea, Miriam. I don't know one thing about him, but he'll make ya happier in a heartbeat than Hiram Knepp could dream of doin' in a lifetime."

Miriam blinked. It wasn't Naomi's way to say things she didn't truly believe. "I hope ya don't think I was crossin' the line, actin' interested in Ben so soon—"

"You've got eyes, too. And a heart needin' the love of a *gut* man, after two years without your Jesse." With an expert flip of her wrist, Naomi slid one folded omelet onto a plate, and then the other. "A daughter Rhoda's age won't understand that, even if she knows, in her mind, that you're awful young to be a widow for the rest of your life."

"It's no secret, either, that Rhoda wonders what she's gonna do with herself once Rachel and Micah get hitched," Miriam said quietly. "She and I've got that little apartment above the smithy, but things'll change fast for both girls when Rachel's keepin' a house and a husband, startin' up a family."

"*Jah*, they're close, even for twins. Does Rhoda have her eye on anybody that ya know of?"

"Who can say? She talks a bit about Jonas Zook, but he's not the type I see her settlin' down with."

"I can't see that match strikin', either," Naomi agreed. "The older boys have teased Aaron when he's paired up with Rhoda after singin's, but I think he mostly drives her home so he won't be the only man without a date."

Naomi arranged thick slices of ham and helpings of hash browns alongside the omelets and then took them to the window. "Here ya go, Rachel," she called above the chatter in the dining room. "How's that buffet table holdin' up?"

"We're *gut* for a few minutes yet." The slender girl rolled her eyes and chuckled. "Or at least we're *gut* until my sister trips over her own feet from gawkin' at that Hooley fella."

"*Jah*, there's that!" Naomi agreed with a laugh.

"Rhoda's already asked him over to shoe our four horses."

Miriam's eyebrows rose. "That's probably a *gut* idea," she said after a moment's consideration. "It's been a while since their hooves were tended, and winter will slick up the roads before ya know it."

"The men seem to like him. Every fella in the room's got him doin' some work these next several days." Rachel lifted the steaming plates of food and hurried back to the table of English travelers.

"Ya can't argue with that. Word'll get around quick, about how he handles horses and whether he works for a fair price," Naomi remarked.

Miriam smiled. "Not that either of those things matters to Rhoda."

"So what'll ya cook him for dinner that night after he shoes your horses, dearie?"

Once again laughter bubbled up from deep inside Miriam and she slung her arm around her best friend's shoulders. "What would I do without ya, Naomi? Always makin' me laugh and see things from a different angle, even when life leaves me a little out of kilter."

The blond cook in the brown dress smiled as only a long-time friend could. "I can't tell ya how I liked watchin' the roses bloom in your cheeks when you were givin' Rhoda what for about Ben Hooley. I'm happy for ya, Miriam. It's *gut* to see ya grinnin' again. Livin' again."

While Miriam basked in her friend's encouraging words, it seemed a little . . . *early* to be talking as though she and the handsome blacksmith would get together. She sighed and then looked toward the countertop, where the cornmeal rolls she'd shaped earlier had risen in their large metal pans. "I'd better tend to my bakin' instead of moonin' over Mr. Hooley. He's got his work, and I've got mine. We'll just see what happens next, ain't so?"

And meanwhile, Lord, I'm askin' ya to guide my heart and my head—and my mouth—when it comes to Rhoda. Ya know how we love each other, so help us remember that part if things get prickly between us.

As she took the towels off the pans of rounded, golden dinner rolls, something made her glance into the dining room. How was it that Ben Hooley stood up, right then? And lo and behold, he winked at her!

Chapter 5

Sunday morning, Miriam sat on the wooden pew between her sister Leah and Reuben's wife, Esther. Was it her imagination, or did Preacher Tom seem windier than usual during the first sermon? *Lord, Ya know why I'm so wiggly today and I hope You'll forgive my foolish ways.*

She tried to focus on Tom Hostetler's message about steadfast love for God and family, because she truly admired him for taking on such a topic. His wife, Lettie, had left him for a fancy man last spring. He'd been a dear friend since before her Jesse had passed. But truth be told, the dairy farmer wandered along his sermon's paths like a cow that had strayed through a hole in the fence: still eating grass, as was its intention, but not too clear about where it was going or where it wanted to end up.

So she gazed at the back of Lydia Zook's black *fer-gut* dress . . . *and maybe, Lord, You'll help me find a way to suggest—nicely—that she should be cuttin' her seams about an inch wider on each side.*

And wasn't *that* a judgmental thought? It wasn't as though she was getting any thinner as the years passed, either. Sighing, Miriam straightened her spine, willing her stomach not to rumble . . .

Ben Hooley sat directly across from her on the men's side. And he was looking between Matthias Wagler's dark brown mane and Seth Brenneman's haystack of blond hair, right at her!

Miriam sucked in her breath, and then met her sister's glance straight-on to keep Leah from asking too many questions about her lack of attention to the service. She let her gaze wander back . . . and yes, the handsome Ben Hooley was still focused on her as though he'd chosen that exact spot on that very bench so he'd have a way to study her without anyone being the wiser. His light brown hair looked clean and shiny, combed slightly back over his ears instead of looking like he'd used a mixing bowl and dull scissors to trim it, like some of their men.

And who cuts his hair for him? Where did he stay last night? How did the rest of his day go after he left the café yesterday?

She'd last seen him midmorning yesterday, rolling onto the county road, Pharaoh hauling his big red farrier wagon—with at least two weeks' worth of blacksmithing to do in Willow Ridge. It was a testament to Ben's easygoing smile and willingness to accommodate the local men's schedules that he'd found such easy favor with them . . .

Or had he lined up all that work so he could stick around town for a while, maybe to call on *her*?

Miriam shifted on the bench, daring to meet Ben's gaze again, for a little longer this time, knowing full well such distracting games had no place in a preaching service.

She thought back to yesterday's storm and the way this man had appeared out of nowhere . . . hadn't said much about who he was or where he was from, much less about why he'd never settled into a Plain community with his own shop. Or a wife.

And does he have a bruise the shape of a huge horseshoe on his chest? Did he get hurt worse than he was lettin' on? The thought of peeling back his clean white shirt to check for blood blisters or places where the skin had broken made Miriam squirm before she could catch herself. Too long she'd gone without a man's presence, a man's company—

And those are the last thoughts ya should be thinkin' right now!

Everyone shifted into place, kneeling on the floor for prayer. Miriam swore she felt Ben peering at her over the other bowed heads. Did she dare peek over at the men's side?

Leah elbowed her. Miriam tried with all her might to focus on more godly thoughts. And as though Bishop Knepp knew her weakness today, his sermon lit into a forceful interpretation of the twenty-sixth verse in Matthew 16, about what a man profited if he gained the whole world but lost his soul. Hiram's sermon left no room for doubt: those who walked the wayward path of worldly pleasure and success lost all chance at salvation.

Has Ben been baptized into the faith? Or is he just driftin' from town to town with work that will always be in demand?

Again Miriam let her gaze wander . . . Ben had his head bowed as though he might be praying for serious help. His face was tight. And why would that be? Why did Ben Hooley seem so friendly with all the fellows at breakfast, yet study Hiram Knepp as though . . . as though he didn't trust him?

But that was a silly idea, wasn't it? Bishops were chosen by lot because God had already decided who should be a community's leader in the faith. Even Plain folks from other settlements would understand that and show Hiram the respect they felt for their own districts' bishops. Maybe she was reading her own history with Hiram into the look she saw on this new fellow's face.

Lord, if I can ease Ben's doubts—set aside my own judgment—lead me along the way You'd have me go. It's for sure and for certain Rhoda and Hiram and maybe other folks won't see any gut *comin' of my acceptin' Ben's attentions.*

At last the service came to an end, and a welcome thing it was that no one had any confessing to do or any business to bring before the district in a members' meeting. Lydia Zook, their hostess for the day, popped up from her place before anyone left the basement.

"Let me be the first to wish ya a happy birthday, Bishop!" she sang out. "We've been plannin' a little somethin' special for the common meal today, on account of how we appreciate your leadin' us along the upward way. So if you men'll scoot along outside, we'll be settin' out the plates and the food."

Miriam chuckled and placed her hand on Lydia's shoulder. "*Gut* for you, herdin' the fellas out so's we can get things goin'. I saw baskets of fine fare in your kitchen, so it's gonna be a tasty afternoon!"

"And the perfect day for eatin' outdoors and visitin' afterwards, too. We're not likely to have many more Sundays like this before winter kicks in," she replied. Then, as the other women filed out of the benches around them, Lydia leaned toward her. "And what's this I hear about that Hooley fella gettin' kicked by his horse, yet still fixin' your café window? He stopped by the market yesterday afternoon for some cold cuts and bread," she confided in a low voice. "Said he'd been to Reuben Reihl's, and then out to Preacher Tom's repairin' machinery, and that he was on his way to the bishop's tomorrow—buyin' food as though those two men without women weren't gonna provide him any meals."

"He ate a couple of heaped-up plates at the café yesterday mornin' and we were pleased to feed him, too," Miriam confirmed. "There wasn't any way the girls and I could've moved that big limb, never mind fixin' the window."

Miriam bustled upstairs to Lydia's kitchen with the other women and began cutting her pumpkin pies as well as apple, cherry, and rhubarb pies other women had brought. Tom Hostetler stuck his head into the kitchen with a grin. "I stashed a nice supply of homemade ice cream in your deep freeze at the store, Lydia. Come time folks're ready for dessert, I'll fetch it for ya."

"*Denki*, Tom!"

"*Jah*, your cows' milk makes the best ice cream, Preacher!"

The outdoor common meal began with a silent prayer. Because Amish women weren't to cook or work on the Lord's day, the congregation usually ate sandwiches, pies, and foods that were prepared the day before. Miriam smiled when her Rachel set out platters of sliced meat loaf she'd made herself, along with cheese and fresh oatmeal bread, sliced thick. Her sweetheart, Micah, was no fool; he claimed a seat within reach of that platter of meat loaf—and then looked through the crowd that milled around among the trees.

"Ben, you've gotta sit with us!" he said, waving the farrier over from the cluster of older fellows he'd been visiting with. "I want to talk to ya about some ornamental metal work at a historical place we're rehabbin'. How are ya with garden gates and wrought iron balconies?"

"*Jah*, I do that."

Ben headed for the seat Micah had saved for him, yet he looked—until he found Miriam. He grinned apologetically at her, as though he was sorry so many fellows had already crowded around to sit at his table. *See ya later?* he mouthed, his eyes wide in a question.

Miriam's heart skipped in double time. She nodded happily and then turned toward a table where Leah and her mother-in-law, Essie Kanagy, sat alongside Naomi and her daughter, Hannah, with Rachel and Rhoda. Was it silly to feel lighthearted because Ben had asked to see her later? As Miriam took a seat among the women and girls who'd gotten her through a couple of tough years as a widow, she felt their curiosity . . . their speculative thoughts . . . not to mention some resentment on Rhoda's part. No doubt her daughter had seen the way the handsome stranger had gawked at her during church.

And the best way to handle everybody's assumptions is to hold your head up and be who ya are. It's not like you've done one thing wrong. And it's not like you've got to explain anythin' to anybody.

Miriam smiled sweetly as she reached for the platter of sandwiches in front of her. "Do ya think the bishop had any notion of his birthday surprise before Lydia announced it? He didn't give any hint of it during the service."

Essie Kanagy, well into her eighties, stabbed a slice of cold country ham. "It's not our way to go celebratin' such things, if ya ask me. Not just because it's callin' attention to one person above the rest, but because Bishop Knepp does a perty fine job of doin' that for hisself."

Rachel and Hannah snickered, while the older women around them bit back grins. "It's a *gut* excuse to eat some of Miriam's fancy bakery cake, though," Leah remarked. She often tried to steer her mother-in-law's crabby remarks toward something happier. "What flavors did ya make, Sister?"

"I baked the bishop's cake from my favorite coconut cake recipe, and there's fudge ripple pound cakes and strawberry cream cakes, too—Rhoda and Rachel's favorites, those are," Miriam replied. "The chocolate and strawberry ones started from a box mix, but you'd never know it after I doctored them up."

She looked at Essie then, nodding in agreement. "It was Lydia's idea to celebrate the bishop's birthday because the service was here at her place, or I wouldn't have made cake for more than a hundred people."

No sense in givin' Hiram the idea I was seekin' his approval and attention, she added silently. *I'd make him birthday cakes until Kingdom Come if he'd leave me be.*

A few moments later, their hostess clanged a spoon against a glass water pitcher. Speaking above the crowd, she said, "While we're all still at the table, I thought we'd share a little surprise—a way of showin' our appreciation to Bishop Hiram for his *gut* work and guidance—and his fifty-fifth birthday today! We've got special birthday cake for dessert, and here comes Preacher Tom with the ice cream he's made, too!"

Faces all around them brightened. Josh and Joey Knepp, Hiram's five-year-old twins, ran down the lane to pull Tom Hostetler's cart so they could have their ice cream faster. Applause erupted when Lydia came out with a round triple-layer cake studded with candles, decorated in white cream-cheese frosting. By the time she took a match from the box, little Sara and Timmy Knepp had squirmed away from Annie Mae to race up front where their *dat* was now standing.

"Don't be lightin' all of those candles or we'll have to call the fire truck!" one of the fellows called out.

Laughter erupted around them as Hiram smiled. The bishop was no doubt thinking up an appropriate response to this surprise; while the *Ordnung* said he wasn't to encourage such celebrations, he seemed pleased that Lydia and Henry Zook had honored him. As Lydia was lighting the last candles, Sara Knepp chirped, "Don't forget to make your wish, Dat!" Timmy, barely three, squawked and raised his arms to be picked up so he could see what was going on.

Hiram glanced impatiently at his youngest children and then glared at his eldest daughter, Annie Mae. The slender girl slipped up to grab the children by the hands.

"This is indeed a surprise," the bishop said as he stood before his cake with its flaming candles. "It's my privilege to serve as your bishop, and to do the work God has called me to, here in Willow Ridge. It's also a fine time to express a wish before all of you, so you'll know my intentions are sincere and . . . visible, rather than hidden."

When Hiram looked around the tables until he found her in the crowd, Miriam swallowed hard.

"Miriam Lantz, I confess before God and the People that I love you—and that it's my sincerest wish you'll be my wife."

Gasps sounded around her, and Miriam's face went hot. This was even worse than she'd feared! Hiram kept gazing at her, too, as though he expected her answer right then and there.

"Mamma, ya don't have to say a thing," Rachel rasped.

Across from her, Naomi leaned forward. "If that don't beat all!" she muttered beneath the crowd's chatter. "Tryin' to embarrass ya into sayin' yes, he is!"

"*Jah*, he couldn't buy our buildin' so he's trappin' ya this way," Rhoda blurted.

Miriam clasped her hands in her lap, her head bowed to avoid Hiram's gaze. *Dear Lord, I'm askin' for a graceful way out of this—or just grace to behave the way You'd want me to. This has to be the most humiliatin'* . . .

"Well, we all know how it goes with birthday wishes," a

male voice spoke up. "If ya say them out loud, they don't come true."

The place got so quiet that Lydia's cake knife made a racket when she dropped it. As everyone looked to see who'd said that, Miriam's heart pounded for an entirely different reason: Ben Hooley rose from his seat, his face tight with disapproval.

"Where I come from, we keep our courtin' private," he stated tersely. "'Husbands, love your wives,' the *Gut* Book tells us, yet you're makin' a mockery of Miriam—and here in front of everybody, too!" With that, Ben edged between the crowded tables and walked quickly down the lane toward the road.

The crowd buzzed like Leah's bees, while Hiram stood as silent and still as a pillar of salt. Miriam felt like invisible walls were closing in on her—and she didn't like it one little bit that two men were pressing her between them.

"Dat, blow out the candles!" Hiram's little Sara called out. "You're gettin' wax all over that perty cake!"

The Knepp twins, Josh and Joey, returned with Tom's clattering wagon, which was loaded with large tubs of ice cream. Katie Zook had fetched scoops and a tall stack of paper cake plates, so Hiram stopped staring after Ben. He leaned down, closed his eyes, and blew mightily across the candle flames. When every last one of them went out, several of the men roared their approval and clapped.

Why is Hiram doin' this to me, Lord? And doesn't Ben realize he's only makin' it worse, fannin' the flames?

She hadn't seen the end of this episode, for sure and for certain, so Miriam was glad her two girls and Leah stayed close around her while folks ate their cake and then got up to visit. Sunday afternoons were a time for staying in touch with neighbors they didn't see during the week, and on such a warm October afternoon a lot of them would stay at the Zooks' place well into the evening.

"Let's head on home, Mamma," Rachel suggested quietly. "We can fetch your cake pans tomorrow. I've had enough of the bishop's shenanigans for one day."

"*Jah*, me too." Rhoda gazed toward the road out front, as though looking for a less obvious way to walk home. Or was she watching for a certain someone?

Miriam sighed. Would that certain someone still want to see her later today?

Chapter 6

You've gone and done it now—caused even more problems for Miriam by standin' up for her! Move on down the road before ya make things worse.

Ben turned in front of Zook's Market, where he'd parked his farrier wagon. Pharaoh was still tied to a shade tree where he could graze on grass growing along the roadside, but Ben gave his horse no sign they'd be going anywhere soon. He had a lot of praying to do—a lot of frustration to walk off, as well. He'd watched how Hiram behaved yesterday at breakfast, in Miriam's café; and after the bishop's disgusting display of power today, it burned him even more that Knepp thought his position should get him anything he wanted.

But Ben was the outsider here. He'd bucked Amish tradition by spending his life mostly on the road . . . had told himself land was too expensive in Pennsylvania and Ohio. And the Indiana towns he'd worked his way through didn't have the right feel to them—or a woman he could love. Yet now that he'd reached Missouri and Miriam Lantz, he had to face the truth: he was almost thirty-five, with not a lot to show for it. At his age, most men had a wife and a houseful of kids, not to mention a solid place in a community where folks counted on his good work.

It felt like the right thing to do, Lord, Ben prayed. *I thought I was followin' where Ya led me, and yet . . . why would Miriam see my unsettled ways as anythin' she should rely on? How can I prove I've been seekin' out Your place for me rather than rollin' along on a string of excuses?*

On he walked, his head lowered as he prayed. As Ben strode down a lane farther along, however, he focused on a well-tended apple orchard . . . white, stacked beehives in the background . . . rows of hoed garden where all that remained were pumpkins and some acorn and butternut squash.

Ben blinked and looked around him. Without even noticing, he'd walked past the vacant smithy where he'd found the tarp for Miriam's window . . . which meant his feet had taken him to her place—and a right pretty spread it was, too, where the trees gloried in their autumn finery and a white two-story house basked in the afternoon sunlight. The windows sparkled. The porch swing swayed in the breeze, inviting him to sit . . . with Miriam.

She'll have all sorts of questions now. Maybe she won't trust ya, now that you've shot off your mouth to the bishop. A four-year-old would've known better!

Ben strolled more slowly, interested in the Lantz place for many reasons. The well-equipped farrier shop tempted him even more now that he saw it in the daylight. And yes, this home with its sense of cleanliness and order called him to do more than sit for a spell on that sun-dappled front porch where the clematis and morning glory vines sported the season's final blooms. He wanted to be a part of this family—this thriving little community—

Way too soon to be thinkin' that way! Cool your heels . . . clear your head before ya make any more stupid moves.

Ben strolled across the driveway to sit against a sturdy old apple tree. As a kid, when he'd needed quiet time away from his brothers and sisters, the orchard behind the house had been his favorite place to let his mind wander . . .

Clip-clop, clip-clop!

Out on the road a carriage was turning in, and he saw three white kapps inside—which meant Miriam, too, had left the Zooks' rather than linger where Hiram might press her for an answer to his proposal. While Ben wanted to talk things over with her—clear any suspicions she might have about him—he didn't care to bare his soul in front of her girls. It was easy to see young Rhoda was smitten, and he didn't want *two* Lantzes peeved at him!

So he would wait for them to unhitch the horse and go inside . . . give them time to unpack the picnic hampers before he knocked on the door—

Clip-clop, clip-clop!

Ben swiveled his head as another carriage turned into the gravel driveway. That distinctive broad-brimmed hat and long beard belonged to the one man he didn't want to see right now. Should he stand up and show himself?

There might come a moment when Miriam's glad you're here. But the bishop doesn't have to know just yet . . .

"Most women would be pleased to live in my home, which I remodeled for my dear, departed Linda." Hiram Knepp gazed at Miriam with those compelling dark eyes as he leaned closer. "I would update the place for you, too, to make it feel like *your* home. I would do anything you asked of me, Miriam, for I've chosen you to be the mother of my children."

Miriam closed her eyes, praying the bishop had just offered her a way out of this bramble bush of a dilemma.

He'd followed her home from the Zooks'—had brought along that coconut cake rather than sharing it at the common meal, or even letting his own children devour it after he'd left them there with Annie Mae.

But this was no time to think about cake.

"Hiram, ya know full well I can't give ya any more children," she said earnestly. She'd convinced the bishop to walk with her outside so they'd have some privacy—but where she'd be in full view of the house. "It's like I told ya this summer after my long-lost Rebecca returned to us. When she got washed downriver in the flood all those years ago, I lost the baby I was carryin' then. Couldn't conceive again," she reminded him, although such personal details were none of Hiram's business. "It was a sadness that came between Jesse and me and he took it to his grave."

"We'll see the best specialists, Miriam. We'll go to fertility clinics," he insisted as they strolled between the driveway and the orchard. "I'll do everything in my power—and God's—to fulfill your purpose as—"

"Beggin' your pardon, Hiram," Miriam interrupted. It was impolite—went against all the Old Ways—but then, this man wasn't her husband and she never intended for him to be. "I've got my three grown girls and you have six kids of your own—"

"God commands us to be fruitful and multiply." Hiram stepped around to face her. He quickly set the cake on the ground and reached up, grasping tree branches to block her path. His beard was mostly silver, but his hair remained coal black. He worked with draft horses every day, so the bishop was fit and strong for his age. Miriam recognized the hunger in his probing eyes, and it had nothing to do with the cake he'd brought. "Miriam, my thoughts of you burn so intensely I must either marry you or risk committing sins no bishop wants to confess. You're in your prime. Certainly not beyond having such . . . longings. Such *needs*."

Oh, but this man irritated her! Wrangling his own desires around to make her appear ungrateful for his attention! There was no other way to handle this but honestly.

Miriam looked him straight in the eye. "I'm sayin' *no*, Hiram." She ducked from under his arms then and started for the house. "You're not listenin' to me. What you want and what I want are—"

"Immaterial," Hiram stated. "I'm following God's will for my life. And yours."

"*Jah?* Then you're hearin' a different voice—marchin' to a different drummer—than I am!" Miriam walked faster, angling into the orchard to pick a large Jonathan apple in case she had to throw it at him. "My Jesse would *never* have cornered me, nor called me out in front of the whole town like you did today! I won't put up with that from you nor anyone else, Bishop Knepp."

Hiram grabbed her shoulders and turned her around to face him. His cheeks were flushed and he was breathing like an enraged stallion. "I thought we cleared away this obstinate streak—this willfulness—when we were selling your building," he muttered tersely. "Have you been listening to Ben Hooley, Miriam?"

The apple dropped from her hand. Fear shot through her, along with that urge to fight or flee, neither of which would solve her problem. This whole conversation became thornier when Hiram brought up the man everyone was speculating about, because all of Willow Ridge now knew how Ben had repaired her window after she'd taken him in during the storm.

Were Rachel and Rhoda watching from the house? Would they come outside if they saw she was losing ground to Hiram Knepp?

The bishop took advantage of her hesitation to drive his point home. He leaned down, so close she could see her reflection in his large, black pupils. "Are you falling for an unbaptized man who makes himself out to be one of us, Miriam?" he demanded in a coiled voice. "The way I hear it, things between you and Hooley flared like wildfire—while you were alone in that bakery at an ungodly hour."

Miriam almost retorted that since God created all the hours of the day and night, surely none could be ungodly. But she remained silent. He was digging a conversational pit so she'd slip into it, because if Ben Hooley hadn't been baptized into the faith, she had compromised her own status in the church.

"Do you really think he can make you happy, Miriam?" Hiram continued with a sneer. "Would you throw away your salvation—be shunned by your family and friends—for a faithless man destined for hell? Jesus tells us to let the dead bury their dead, and that 'no man, having put his hand to the plough, and looking back, is fit for the Kingdom of God.'"

Hiram reached for her shoulders again but stopped short of touching her. "You've set your sights forward, Miriam," he whispered. "You've buried your dead and you're moving toward the Kingdom. Don't let a total stranger get you off course."

She swallowed hard, wishing a good biblical reply would fly off her tongue.

"And it's just a few verses earlier in the book of Luke where Jesus says 'foxes have holes and birds of the air have nests, but the Son of man has no place to lay his head.'"

Miriam jumped at the sound of another voice, yet the sight of Ben Hooley standing beside an apple tree in the next row sent a surge of relief through her. She didn't even care how he'd gotten there, or what he'd heard. Hiram stepped aside and his focus shifted away from her—and away from a conversation that could have no good ending.

"Don't you dare compare yourself to the Son of man, Hooley!" the bishop snapped. "Adding sacrilege to the wrongs you've already done—"

"I would never pretend to be at Jesus's level, Hiram. But my passage lends itself to this situation every bit as much as yours does." Ben's voice remained low, but his face was tight with anger. "Some fellas have no place to call home because they're out seekin' what God's been tellin' them to find."

"Well, you won't be finding it here in Willow Ridge!" Hiram blurted. He drew in a deep breath, trying to regain control of himself—and their conversation. "I strongly suggest that you complete the farrier work you've promised, and then move on."

Ben shrugged. "If you'd rather I didn't shoe your Belgians tomorrow—"

"This is ridiculous!" Miriam looked from one man to the other, peeved by this flare-up of temper. "'Wherever two or more are gathered in Christ's name, there He'll be also,' ain't so? Yet I think the *gut* Lord's none too happy with the way you're actin' like boys pickin' a fight in the schoolyard. Or two dogs scrappin' over the same bone."

Hiram raised one imperious eyebrow. "I believe you and I were having a serious conversation when this man, who was obviously hiding—eavesdropping on us—had the audacity to—"

"No, Hiram, I told you this conversation is over. And my answer is *no*." Miriam's heart pounded. Ben's presence had given her the confidence to speak up, but nobody talked back to the bishop without apologizing or asking his forgiveness. She had nothing more to say to him, however.

After a tense silence, Hiram looked pointedly at Ben

Hooley, gesturing toward his carriage. "All right, I'll go. But you're leaving, too, Hooley. I can't in good conscience let Miriam be alone with you while—"

Desperate for a solution to this situation, Miriam turned toward the house—and then grinned. Rhoda and Rachel were coming down the steps. One of them carried a pitcher of lemonade and an old quilt while the other gripped a picnic basket. As they smiled and waved, Miriam thought they'd never looked more like angels.

"The girls are home with me, Bishop. At twenty-one, they're watchin' after their *mamm*'s welfare, keepin' an eye on Mr. Hooley—and on you, as a matter of fact," Miriam added pointedly. "Go and do what ya need to do, Hiram. I see no point in you and Mr. Hooley discussin' your differences in front of my daughters."

Had she really dismissed the bishop? Miriam's chest tingled with discomfort at her brazen behavior. And had she just given Ben Hooley a chance to further beguile them with his serpent's tongue?

The bishop's chin stiffened. He glanced at the girls, who were still several yards away. "We'll talk again, Miriam. You'd better think about what I've told you." He turned and strode toward his carriage.

"My answer'll still be no, Hiram," she called after him.

"Bishop!" Rachel called out as the two of them approached. "We were just bringin' out a little picnic supper. Can't ya stay for a bite?"

Hiram turned, his frown souring. He hopped into his carriage and then steered his horse in a wide circle so he was pointed toward the road.

Miriam shielded her eyes from the sunset, walking back the way she'd come. "Well, here ya have it—the bishop's cake, full of holes on top, like maybe we spoiled his birthday." She picked it up, chuckling now that the storm had passed—for the moment, anyway.

"*Gut!*" Rachel proclaimed. "After the way he's been actin', well—we don't want him gettin' ideas about hitchin' up with ya, Mamma. He'd probably expect ya to make a coconut cake for your own wedding, too."

Chapter 7

"Why, Ben Hooley! What're *you* doin' here?" Rhoda gaped at him until Ben wondered if she might drop her pitcher of lemonade. "We thought Mamma was alone with the bishop—"

"And we're mighty glad she wasn't, no matter how ya happened along," Rachel joined in. "We whipped up an excuse—and this basket of food—as fast as we could, but even with the two of us showin' ourselves, I'm not sure he would've let up. And it's gettin' outta hand, I can tell ya."

"Obnoxious!" Rhoda agreed as her sister spread the quilt on the grass. "He might be the bishop, but it's time somebody took him down a peg or two, after that stunt he pulled at the Zooks'."

Ben heard his own distaste echoed in the sisters' remarks. He was pleased they were watching out for their mother, but they were right: their presence might have delayed Hiram Knepp's advances, yet the bishop impressed him as the type who never gave up until he got what he wanted. And wasn't that a sorry thing to say about a leader in their faith?

"I left the common meal to think things through," he

explained as Miriam returned to them with the tall coconut cake. "I blew in with the wind yesterday, so I realize ya have no reason to believe—"

At the *clip-clop! clip-clop!* of approaching carriages, Miriam turned toward the road. "Let's see who's comin' before ya go on with—"

"It's Micah!" Rachel popped up from the quilt to wave her arms at him. Then she smiled at Ben. "Micah Brenneman's my honey, and we're gettin' hitched on the twentieth," she gushed like a girl in love. "He's the one who fixed up the apartment above Dat's smithy for Mamma and Rhoda. A wonderful-*gut* carpenter, he is!"

"Is everythin' all right here?" Micah called out. He stopped the carriage and hopped out. "I wasn't any too happy about that scene at the meal, Miriam. I was guessin' the bishop might come over here to—"

"*Jah*, he did," Miriam replied. "And *denki* for thinkin' of us, Micah."

The burly blond nodded, removing his felt hat to smooth his hair. He looked back toward the road. "Preacher Tom had the same idea, comin' to see that you were all right— except the bishop stopped him, to talk. Hiram's little trick's got everybody stirred up, for sure and for certain." As Tom's buggy rattled down the driveway toward them, Micah parked his rig and put his horse in the pasture.

After they all settled onto the quilt, Ben accepted a glass of lemonade from Rhoda, noting again how her blue eyes widened as she looked at him . . . wondering just how many fires he'd started by coming to Willow Ridge. Clearly Miriam Lantz and her girls were being watched over by men who cared about their welfare, so maybe they didn't need him here, shaking up their daily lives.

Don't believe that! Ya feel things for Miriam and she sees somethin' when she looks into your eyes, too. Let this play out. Don't assume ya have nothin' to gain by stayin'. Ben took a long sip of sweet, cool lemonade as Preacher Tom stepped down from his buggy.

"Well now! Looks like I'm bargin' in on a little picnic—"

"Got plenty for you, too, Tom. Glad to see ya." Miriam scooted over to make room for him. "Seems we've got a lot to chew on—besides this cake Hiram left behind."

"Oh, there'll be some chewin', all right. Before I left the Zooks', Gabe Glick and Reuben told me we needed a meetin' about this, and just now the bishop was sayin' he wants to call a meetin', too," the preacher replied with a shake of his head. "But I can tell ya, *our* agenda's a lot different from Hiram's, if he thinks we're gonna go along with the way he's treatin' you, Miriam."

He looked over at Ben then, his lips twitching. "Why am I not surprised to see *you* here, Hooley?"

Ben smiled. Preacher Tom Hostetler wasn't a very fiery, fascinating speaker, but he was a genuinely nice fellow. If Old Order ways allowed it, the dairy farmer would probably be courting Miriam Lantz himself. He'd poured out his story in the milking barn, about how his wife, Lettie, had left in the night with an English fellow in a fancy car. Lettie had divorced him, but according to the *Ordnung*, he couldn't remarry until she died.

"I was mighty upset when I up and left the Zooks'. Sounds odd, maybe, but I was walkin' off my temper," Ben explained. "Got so caught up in my thoughts I didn't realize my feet had brought me to this orchard. Just as well, too," he added with an emphatic nod. "Nothin' goes right in the heat of risin' voices and pointin' fingers."

Ben smiled at Miriam. She was cutting that fancy coconut cake while her girls went after more glasses and plates. It was just as well they were headed for the house, considering what he wanted to say. "Maybe I'm out of line, but I can't see where Hiram's servin' the higher *gut* by tellin' Miriam it's God's will that she marry him."

"That's horse hockey," Tom agreed. "It's been a case of sour grapes with Hiram ever since the banker let an English fella buy Miriam's bakery buildin' instead of goin' along with the bishop's plans to own it."

"It's all about ownership," Ben agreed, "and nothin' about love. That I could see."

He paused, wondering if his next thought might backfire. "I've got no business tanglin' with your bishop, but I suspect that'll keep happenin' as long as I'm in Willow Ridge. Am I wrong to stay here?" he asked quietly. "Should I forgive and forget, and move on?"

The way Miriam's face fell—the way her wounded eyes sought his—was all the answer Ben needed. He held her gaze for as long as he dared, here in front of Micah and the preacher. He sensed these men wanted him here, no matter how Hiram Knepp felt about it.

"Could be ya found your way here to Willow Ridge for this very reason, Ben." Tom smiled at Miriam as she handed him his cake. "Sometimes we're left to struggle with things, bein' led all kinds of places and not knowin' for sure where to go—or why. But we're not fightin' the *gut* fight alone," he added confidently. "If it weren't for my faith—and friends like the Lantzes and the Brennemans here—I'd have reached the end of my rope long ago and hung myself with it."

Ben smiled, enjoying the way Miriam's face softened as she sliced off a large wedge of cake and handed it to him. "A little somethin' to sweeten up your day," she murmured. "I spent too much time on this coconut cake not to share it with my family and friends. Especially if Hiram's gonna leave it beside the driveway!"

"*Jah*, I'll have a big piece of that cake, Mamma!" Rhoda

called out as she returned. She handed her mother more plates and then squeezed between Ben and Miriam to tighten their little circle on the quilt. "So what're we gonna do about this bishop situation?"

"Folks all over Willow Ridge are already talkin'," Rachel remarked as she took her place beside Micah. Then she smiled at Ben. "Ya maybe didn't know what ya were gettin' into when ya fixed Mamma's shop window. You're kind of settin' this little town on its ear, ain't so?"

Ben couldn't help chuckling as both twins forked up huge bites of cake and stuffed their mouths at the same time. Amazing how they finished each other's sentences and behaved so much alike, yet their distinct personalities came shining through their sparkling blue eyes as they looked him over . . . assessing him more closely, now that he'd taken a stand on behalf of their mother.

"Like I was tellin' your *mamm* after I blew into her bakery with that storm," Ben began, "I've been lookin' for better-priced land than can be found farther east. Wantin' a place of my own for my farrier business and maybe to set up a mill on the rapids for my brothers, alongside the river near here." He paused to cut a forkful of the moist white cake. "With all the corn and wheat I'm seein', a mill could be a *gut* outlet for local farmers—and a way to branch into some of those specialty flours and whole-grain cereals that're sellin' so well these days."

"*Jah*, that organic stuff's all the rage now," Tom agreed. "If I switched over to feedin' certified organic grains, so my Holsteins could give organic milk, it'd sell for a pertier penny at that new whole foods place over past Morning Star."

"*Gut* as your homemade ice cream is, ya ought to be sellin' that, Tom!" Rhoda said with a grin. "I was real sorry we left the Zooks' so early. I was lookin' forward to some of that ice cream with a piece of strawberry cream cake."

Micah moved the tines of his fork over his plate to catch the last moist crumbs. He was a big, brawny young fellow but gave a lot of thought to things before he said them. "Ben, it seems to me a farrier like yourself would have full-time work here in Willow Ridge without the mill. I saw that right off over breakfast yesterday, the way fellas were linin' up to have ya come to their places."

"There's that," Ben agreed. "I never run out of horses to shoe in Plain settlements, no matter where I go. My wagon might not look like much, but I've made myself a right nice livin' over the years." He paused then, to close his eyes over a mouthful of the most luscious dessert he'd ever tasted. "Miriam Lantz, I don't know what kind of wand ya waved over this cake, but it's nothin' short of magic."

When Miriam leaned forward to smile at him from the other side of Rhoda, her face glowed like a pink rose. "The secret is usin' the best brand of coconut and a lot of oil and eggs—not that you'll be tryin' out the recipe anytime soon, ain't so?"

Ben laughed. It was a sudden outburst, totally unexpected, and when everyone else joined in, he felt indescribably wonderful . . . like he *belonged* here. All the controversy and conflict with Hiram Knepp lifted, like an autumn fog that dissipated from above a river when the sunshine struck it. How long since he'd sat among friends, on a blanket beneath a tree? How long since he'd talked about his dream of a mill . . . branching into a new and different enterprise?

Sunshine . . . that's what Miriam Lantz reminded him of. Never mind all this business with the bishop; the woman who looked at him with those wide, doe-like eyes and smiled from deep in her heart was taking his breath away, right here in front of all these other folks. There was nothing secretive about her. No petty games or pity parties or playing up to win his attention.

How long before ya ask Miriam to meet ya out here alone, in the moonlight, when there's nobody else around and no tree limbs to pull out of windows? Just you and her, cozy and close . . .

"If ya want a place to work on some of that equipment, Ben, you're welcome to set up in Jesse's shop." Miriam's voice sounded clear and confident. No wavering over the fact that her late husband had built that business, and no asking her girls what they might think of the idea, either.

Ben's eyes widened. Tom, Micah, the twins, and Miriam were all waiting for his answer. Their faces differed in age and complexion, but their expectant expressions and suspended cake forks told him his reply *mattered* to them.

"That's quite an honor," he murmured, returning Miriam's gaze as though no one else were there. "And I'll take ya up on it, too."

Chapter 8

"And where will ya be sleepin', Ben?" Rhoda asked later that evening when they'd come in to sit on the porch. She realized then how odd that sounded, for her to be asking such a question of a man, so she added, "I mean, if you're usin' the forge and Dat's equipment, it seems only sensible that ya sleep upstairs in the new apartment."

Ben Hooley's eyes widened. He looked over at Rachel and Mamma, who sat in the porch swing. "I don't want to take somebody else's bed, but—"

"Rhoda and I'll be stayin' here in this house until Rachel and Micah get hitched," Miriam clarified. "And if you've been sleepin' in your wagon all this time, a real bed—and a bathroom—might be to your likin'. That was a *gut* idea, Rhoda!"

Rhoda grinned. High time she got recognized for something, on account of how crossways she'd felt ever since Mamma had spent all that time alone with this handsome fellow when the storm blew him in. Was it wrong to want to prove to Ben Hooley that *she* was the woman he'd be happier with? While it was the man's place to do the courting, surely it was the woman's place to put good ideas in his head about where and when . . . and how that might come about.

"I surely do appreciate your kindness," their guest replied. In the light from the lanterns, his face took on the soft shadows of the autumn night as he smiled at them. "With the cooler weather—and considerin' how I'm to be at Hiram's place first thing tomorrow—a *gut* night's rest will be to my advantage."

"And ya won't have far to go for your breakfast, either!" Rachel smiled. "That's one more thing the bishop won't like so much, but then, we're offerin' hospitality like Jesus said we're to do, ain't so?"

"Hiram aside," Mamma remarked—as though *aside* was exactly where she wanted to put him—"we're happy to let ya stay there, after the way ya repaired the café's window. I'm still goin' to pay ya for that—"

"And I'm still refusin' your money, Miriam. You're feedin' me all this *gut* food and now puttin' me up for the night," Ben pointed out. "A man can't ask for better than that."

Rhoda gazed into the evening, smiling. She imagined escorting this fellow to the little nest above the smithy . . . being the one to make sure he was up and around in time for breakfast . . . cooking his favorite foods and pouring his coffee in the morning. Tomorrow might be a fine day to wear the new burgundy dress she'd made last week.

"We end our days with a Bible passage, Ben," Mamma said, interrupting Rhoda's thoughts. "Would ya be so kind as to read for us tonight? Always *gut* to hear the Lord's word in a man's voice, considerin' it's just us girls here now."

Rhoda stopped short of rolling her eyes. Why was Mamma seeing herself as a girl, when she was forty? "I'll fetch the Bible," she said, rising from the chair beside Ben's. "Anybody want more of that cake, or maybe a cup of tea?"

Mamma and Rachel shook their heads, but when Ben held her gaze with a mischievous grin, Rhoda laughed. "Catchin' up on all the bedtimes when ya didn't have a little somethin' sweet?"

He chuckled and looked away. "You could say that, *jah*. I'll be pleased to read from the Lord's word tonight," he added. "Are ya followin' a certain book? Wantin' to hear anythin' in particular?"

"You pick!" Rachel said. "We do like Dat did, lettin' the *Gut* Book fall open and puttin' our finger down with our eyes shut. Seems our Bible's so cracked and creased, we do a lot of repeatin', though."

As she caught the screen door against her backside, Rhoda's mind raced. Now that Micah and Tom—and the bishop—were gone, it felt so nice and cozy to be on the porch with Ben. Soon the chill of the October nights would drive them inside again for their evening devotionals . . . and by then, who knew what might become of Ben Hooley? Would he finish his jobs and drive on down the road?

She intended to see that he did *not* leave them. Why couldn't she be the one who gave this fellow the best reason of all to stay?

Rhoda put a thick slab of the coconut cake on a plate, with a fork. She ran her finger quickly through the gooey part that stuck to the cake platter, closing her eyes over the sweetness of sugar, butter, and coconut—cake as only Mamma could make it, and far better than the bishop deserved for his birthday. More like the wedding cakes they'd been baking for a lot of brides around the district, and soon for Rachel and Micah . . .

And why not for me? I got baptized years ago. Have traveled these back roads in many a rig after singin's, and still haven't found a fella I want to live with . . .

She picked up the big Bible from the table in the front

room and returned to the porch. "It's up to you what ya do first, Ben—Scripture or cake," she teased.

"And all these eyes are followin' my every move, watchin' for things like that, too, aren't they?" Ben countered with a laugh.

Rhoda laughed with him and resumed her seat. She placed the Bible on the little table between her chair and Ben's, watching his face in the flickering light of the lantern. Without his hat, his light brown hair fell around his temples and then flared back slightly over his ears, like soft, glossy bird's wings . . . such a nice contrast to the way most of the men in Willow Ridge combed their hair down and got it chopped straight across their foreheads and along their shirt collars.

"My *dat* used to say that life was short, so ya should eat dessert first," Ben replied. "But I feel bad bein' the only one to give in to this temptation."

Ya think Mamma's cake is a temptation? Just you wait, Ben Hooley!

Rhoda smiled to herself and glanced at her mother. She wasn't surprised that Mamma was watching the way their guest's fine mouth closed over his forkful of cake. "We don't decide on our breakfast menu most mornin's until we get to the Sweet Seasons," Rhoda remarked as Ben's eyes closed over his first bite of dessert. "Sometimes—for special occasions—we take requests. And your goin' to Hiram's tomorrow seems like a *gut* time to fortify ya with all the stuff ya love best. What would you like?"

Ben swallowed, thinking about it as he savored another bite of cake. "I don't think a fella ever gets enough *gut* bacon and sausage," he said in a dreamlike voice. "Especially if it's butchered local."

"Our meats come from Zook's Market, and Henry himself does the butcherin'," Rhoda assured him. "He makes the best—"

"Apple sausages!" Mamma joined in gleefully. "This time of year, he can't keep his sausage links with little chunks of ground apple in stock, but his boy, Jonah, delivered us a case yesterday. We'll cook some up tomorrow!"

"Makes the whole café smell wonderful-*gut*," Rachel agreed.

"And I make mighty fine French toast, too, topped off with fried apples, all sweet and spicy with cinnamon!" Rhoda leaned on the arm of her chair closest to Ben, determined not to let her sister and her mother steal her thunder. "Or those fried apples are tasty with oatmeal pancakes—"

"Or how about that apple walnut coffee cake ya made a couple weeks ago?" Rachel suggested. "Once Micah and the Kanagy boys got into that, it was gone before any other customers got a chance at it."

Ben laughed as he took the final bite of his cake. "I can't possibly eat all that! But I'll do my best to devour whatever you're cookin', because for sure and for certain it's better than what I'd grab at a convenience store like I usually do when I'm on the road."

When he handed her his empty plate, Rhoda saw how lean and strong his hands were, with occasional scars, like Dat had gotten over the years, when sparks had jumped from the forge. To keep from staring at his long, slender fingers, she patted the Bible. "Pick us out somethin', Ben. I'll be right back."

As she entered the dim kitchen, Rhoda's thoughts spun like tops. Oh, but she'd wanted to keep Mamma out of their menu planning! Wanted to ask Rachel whose side she was on, too, giving Ben ideas about what their mother baked best! It wasn't like she herself fell short on the cooking end of things!

*Don't be a little kitty cat, mewin' for attention! You'll hear
no end of it!*

Rhoda took in a deep breath. Reminded herself that Ben
Hooley would be in Willow Ridge—in the little apartment
above the smithy—for at least a couple of weeks yet. Plenty
of time for him to see how he'd be better off marrying a
younger girl like herself, who wasn't already used to running
her home a certain way, and wasn't tied down to keeping a
café open, either. Mamma had always made it clear that her
daughters had their own lives to live when they got hitched,
and that Naomi's girl, Hannah, would most likely be working in the café when she turned sixteen in November.

*Jah, Ben, it's gonna be you and me . . . God brought ya
to my doorstep for a* gut *reason, and together we'll explore
why your comin' here is the best thing that ever happened to
both of us.*

More settled, Rhoda returned to her chair and saw that
Ben had picked a passage and raised the wick of the lamp
so he could read the dark, crowded columns on the pages of
the old Bible. Mamma and Rachel had stopped swinging
and sat with their hands folded on their laps, ready to hear
the Word, so she sat the same way. Ben needed to see that
while she might be younger than he was by a few years,
she'd been raised in the faith to show proper respect and
attention when God spoke to them through these evening
readings.

"This was one of my *dat*'s favorite passages," Ben began.
His expression turned wistful in the flickering lamplight.
"He was a smart fella who understood all the difficult lan-
guage in our King James version—would've made a *gut*
preacher—and he put the Scriptures into words we kids
could follow, so we'd know more about what was goin' on
when we heard the verses in church."

"He must've been a mighty *gut dat*," Mamma remarked with a nod.

"*Jah*, and I miss him somethin' fierce sometimes—but don't get me yackin' about that," he added with a chuckle. "It's late and we've all had a . . . day that needs finishin' out on the right note."

Ben drew a breath and found his place with his finger. "I'm readin' from the Proverbs, in chapter thirty-one," he said in a low voice. "Sayin' the verses like I recall hearin' them at home, when my family gathered around just like this to listen."

Rhoda closed her eyes to better focus on Ben's mellow voice . . . even though she wasn't paying as much attention as she should to the message itself.

"Who can find a virtuous woman—a truly *gut* wife? She's worth more than precious jewels. Her husband trusts her with all his heart and he'll never lack for anythin' while he's with her."

Rhoda's heart thumped faster. Ben had not only chosen a passage about a good wife, but he sounded as if he was saying the words directly to her! She leaned back in her chair, allowing his low voice to ease all the worries of this day . . . all the doubts in her own mind about finding the right man.

". . . She does *gut* things for him all her life long," Ben went on in that dreamlike rhythm. "She spins wool and flax and works with willin' hands . . . she's up before dawn providin' food for her family and settin' up everybody's chores for the day. She knows good land when she sees it and she plants vineyards and gardens with her own hands . . ."

Rhoda peeked between her slitted eyelids. Mamma and Rachel, too, sat in the shadows with awed looks on their faces, as though Ben Hooley wove some sort of magical spell around them.

". . . opens her hands to the poor, and she helps folks who need it."

This was a world apart from how Bishop Knepp and the preachers read the Bible: the Old Ways dictated that members not stray from the exact wording and never hazard a guess at interpreting the verses for themselves. Rhoda sighed, drifting along on the pleasant rhythm of Ben Hooley's voice.

". . . pays attention to what goes on with her family and the household, and she's not idle or wastin' her time," he went on earnestly. "Her children grow up and say she's blessed—and a blessin' to them—and her husband does, too. And he praises her for all the things she does to make his life so fine."

Ben paused then, sighing with satisfaction as though he'd reached the happy ending of a story. "Many women have done well and lived excellent lives, but *you* surpass them all. Charm is deceitful and beauty makes ya prideful and vain, but a woman who loves the Lord is to be praised."

After a moment of absolute silence, when the world around them seemed to hold its breath in wonder, Rhoda sighed. So did Mamma and Rachel.

"Well, now," Rachel said in a low voice. "It's for sure and for certain we'll never hear the preachers readin' it that way—"

"And while Hiram's preached on this passage a time or two, mostly tellin' us women how hard we're to be workin' to make life *gut* and prosperous for our men," Mamma added, "it does my weary soul a real favor to hear this passage in our own everyday words. Especially after the way Hiram spelled out his expectations for a wife today. *Denki*, Ben."

"*Jah*, Ben, that was wonderful-*gut*," Rhoda murmured.

Truth be told, she shimmered inside from seeing herself in the circumstances Ben had described: working hard, planting the garden and cooking the food, tending the house and taking care of her husband and their children. And hadn't he intended this message—chosen these verses—just for her? "We're blessed yet again by your comin' here, Ben. I—we— hope you'll decide to stick around for a *gut* long while."

His smile softened, his face tanned by riding in the wind and the sun. "Mighty nice of ya to say that. I haven't had anybody to share my faith with these past few years on the road, and there's preachers a-plenty who'd shake their fingers at me for messin' with the way our Bible reads." He shrugged, making his pale ivory shirt ripple across his shoulders. "'But as for me and my house', Dat used to quote from Jeremiah, we served the Lord by learnin' His book in a way we could understand even when we were kids. That way, there's no excuse for not knowin' or followin' Jesus."

"Amen to that," Mamma murmured. She rose from the swing then, stretching like a contented cat as she yawned. "Hate to see this evenin' end, but mornin' comes early when ya bake for a livin'. You girls can show our guest to his rooms. I'll see ya for breakfast, Ben."

"*Jah*, get a *gut* night's rest, Miriam," Ben replied, standing to open the door for her. "*Denki* for a right fine day, all things considered."

"I'll be callin' it a night, too." Rachel picked up the big Bible and then followed Mamma into the house. "Mondays Rhoda and I do the wash, and we like to get a *gut* start on it before we show up to wait tables and help Mamma. 'Night, now."

"You, too, Rachel."

Ben closed the screen door so it wouldn't slam. Then he

turned to Rhoda, smiling at her in the lamplight. "Guess that leaves just you and me."

Rhoda's heart throbbed so hard she wondered if he could hear it banging in her chest. "*Jah,*" she whispered. "Just you and me."

Chapter 9

Ben gestured for Rhoda to precede him down the porch steps, hanging back to collect his thoughts. All during their time on the porch he'd felt this young woman watching his every move, hanging on his every word . . . gazing at him like a love-struck puppy. And a sweet, lovable puppy she was, too, but he couldn't let Rhoda follow him around with that moony-eyed look on her face. Couldn't let her friends in the Sweet Seasons make fun of her for doing special things for him. Couldn't let her believe he was the answer to all her prayers.

At twenty-one, Rhoda Lantz must feel her clock ticking, especially with her twin sister getting married soon. He'd watched a couple of his younger sisters go through crushes like this—love at first sight for fellows who had no intention whatsoever of loving them back, if they even had a clue about how Gracie and Bess felt about them. Boys could be so heartless . . . even when they got to be Hiram Knepp's age.

But Ben set aside all thoughts about the bishop. Plenty of time tomorrow to deal with that man. As he strolled along the gravel driveway toward the dark smithy and café, he prepared himself for whatever might happen.

*Lord God, help me be the man ya created me to be . . .
honorable and kind and up-front about situations like this.
And if I'm behavin' this same lost-puppy way toward
Miriam, not readin' her right, will ya please give me a* gut
swift kick before I do somethin' stupid?

"It's mighty nice of you gals to let me stay in your new
apartment," he said to break the awkward silence as they
walked. "Right kind of you to ask me what I'd like for
breakfast, too. You're a sweet girl, Rhoda. Very thoughtful."

Her smile beamed up at him and then she focused on the
pale gravel path with the strip of grass down its center.
Rhoda walked closer to him then, with her head lowered
shyly, so that Ben saw how the moonlight glimmered on her
kapp. Someday, when she filled out, she'd be as attractive
as her *mamm*.

When they reached the side door of the blacksmith shop,
Rhoda fumbled beneath a flowerpot for the key. "We didn't
lock this place when Dat had his business here," she remarked. "But what with all the traffic on the county road,
and the way word got around about Micah fixin' us rooms
where the loft used to be, we just figured it to be safer."

"Three women alone have to be careful," he agreed.

"Come on up. Will ya be all right on the stairs, or shall I
fetch the lamp from the bakery?"

Ben stepped inside the blacksmith shop and allowed his
eyes to adjust to the dark until he could make out the shapes
of the big forge and the bins full of horseshoes and tools.
"I'm *gut* in the dark if you are."

*Wrong thing to say! You've got to do better than that,
Hooley!*

"Oh, I'm fine. I know my way around down here, and the
stairs have a handrail," she pointed out as she took hold of
it. "Rachel's Micah did a real nice job of puttin' this place

together for us, and I'm excited about movin' in after they get hitched."

"Even though you've had a room next to your sister's all your life? It'll be different, livin' here in this little place with your *mamm*."

Rhoda turned on the stairs to face him. "How would ya know about that, Ben Hooley?" she whispered. "Ya seem to understand so much about me even though we just met."

He cleared his throat. Any more little honeybee remarks like that one would swarm him if he didn't swat them down—gently—from the start. "I have sisters myself. And since there were only two of them amongst us six boys, they were thick as thieves, too," he remarked. "When Gracie got married, Bess wandered around the place for days lookin' like she'd lost her best friend."

Rhoda turned the key in the door at the top of the stairs and they stepped into a set of rooms that still smelled of fresh paint, varnish, and new wood. "I'll light the lamp now, so ya can pick which room ya want and see what-all Micah's rigged up for us," she said proudly. "A couple months ago, on our birthday, we unveiled this little place and he got a lot of orders for wall systems like he built here."

When the flame caught and the lamp revealed a tidy, simply furnished set of rooms, Ben smiled. "It looks better than the back of my wagon, for sure! And you're pullin' that wall forward on a track!"

Rhoda chuckled. "*Jah*, that's the amazin' part. Durin' the day you've got a nice sittin' room and the kitchen nook, and when ya shift this wall forward, ya make a bedroom with book cases along the wall. And the beds pull down when you're ready for them, too."

Ben ran an admiring hand over the glossy oak woodwork. It was hard to believe how many room combinations

could be made in this cozy nest by shifting segments of the
walls across the main space.

"So . . . which bedroom are ya takin', Ben?"

He chuckled. "That's another one of those questions that
says a lot about a fella, ain't so?"

"I already know all I need to."

Ben closed his eyes. Rhoda was getting bolder . . . standing close enough that her skirt brushed his pant leg.

"Pale green walls or light blue?" Ben murmured, stalling
until he figured out how to set Rhoda straight without hurting her feelings.

*And how will ya do that? She's been seein' all these perty
pictures in her mind and it'll be a big letdown, no matter
how ya go about it. Watch out, now!*

Rhoda had grasped a handle on the side of another set of
shelves, to lower a Murphy bed into place. Sheets and all.
Surely Miriam Lantz's girl wouldn't play the jezebel with
him . . .

"The green room's yours, ain't so?" he murmured. "I can
find my way around now, Rhoda. Everythin' a man could
possibly need is here—"

"Ben, you're the fella I've been waitin' for all my life,"
she murmured. "I'd almost given up ever findin' somebody
who can make me as happy as Micah makes Rachel, but—
but here ya are!"

He slowly let out his breath. "Rhoda, ya have no idea
about—"

"Don't be goin' modest on me now, or gettin' shy!" She
came up to stand in front of him, mere inches away, with her
face lifted up for a kiss. Her eyes sparkled in the dimness.
"I've been courted by my share of fellas—"

"That's no surprise, but—"

"—but none of them come close to bein' the man *you*
are, Ben Hooley," she continued earnestly. "Ya probably

think it's too soon for me to be sayin' this, but nobody's ever made me feel this way!"

Ben groaned inwardly. "Ya don't know what you're—"

"I'm twenty-one, Ben. Plenty old enough to know a lot of things." She stepped closer, smiling so sweetly it broke his heart.

He reminded himself how crushed Bess and Gracie had been; for days after each of them had been ignored or ridiculed by the men they'd set their hearts on, there was no living with their red eyes and long faces. And their brothers had shown them no mercy, either—nor had their *dat*, who'd told them all along they were headed for heartbreak.

When Rhoda stood on tiptoe to brush his cheek with a kiss, Ben stepped back. He took hold of her arms before they wound around his neck and gently pushed her away.

"Rhoda, you've got to hear me out now," he said firmly. "Ya don't want to fall for me on account of—"

"It'll be so perfect, Ben!" she insisted. "Mamma thinks you're gonna be *her* fella, but she's way too old for ya! Folks'll squawk about her makin' a fool of herself—"

"How old do ya think I am, Rhoda?" He hadn't intended to sound so gruff, but it was the only way he knew to make her pay attention.

Her brow puckered. Oh, but Ben could believe she'd given a few of the local fellows the what for! Rhoda Lantz was so far ahead of them in so many ways, they didn't know how lacking they were. "Why does that matter?" she demanded. "Older fellas marry younger gals all the time."

"Like the bishop wantin' to hitch up with your *mamm?*"

"That's disgustin'! You think so, too!" Rhoda retorted. "Why are ya tryin' to—"

"If Hiram's fifty-five and your mother's forty, that's fifteen years between them," Ben calculated aloud.

"It's not so much his age as his *attitude* that makes Hiram Knepp an old goat!"

Ben tried not to laugh at the disrespectful remark she'd just made. He hated to burst this pretty girl's bubble, but she needed a strong dose of reality. "So that means if you're twenty-one and I'm well into bein' thirty-five," he countered, keeping his voice as kind as he could, "what's that tell ya?"

Rhoda's eyes looked the size of salad plates. "You're just sayin' that to get rid of me!" She backed away, her lip quivering. "That's the meanest—Ben Hooley, any woman with eyes can see you're not more than twenty-five! Ya can't be!"

Ben sighed sadly. A tear had trickled down each of Rhoda's cheeks and he didn't dare wipe them away. "I wouldn't lie to ya, Rhoda. My *mamm* and *dat* fooled a lot of folks into thinkin' they were newlyweds well into their marriage—and *jah*, part of it was their attitude, their ability to enjoy life even though they had to work from sunup to sundown to keep us all clothed and fed."

Rhoda planted her fists against her hips then, challenging him with another frown. "I don't believe ya! You're sayin' that on account of how Mamma sweet-talked ya first, and—and ya think she's got money—you're hitchin' your wagon to her star!" she blurted. "Is that how it goes?"

Ben removed his hat to sweep his hair back from his face. "Do I impress ya as a fella who'd chase after a woman so he could live off her?" he demanded in a low voice. "That hurts, Rhoda, to think ya see me in such a way."

He stepped farther away from her, thinking fast. Trying to remain rational . . . knowing Miriam and Rachel would eventually be hearing Rhoda's version of this story. "Ya better leave now—or I will. There's gettin' to be too many reasons for not stayin' in this wee little room together."

Rhoda swiped at her face, fighting a crying spell. "I'm

sorry! I didn't mean to—ya got me all *ferhoodled*, sayin' ya were thirty-five." Her voice sounded raw with disappointment as the truth settled over all the dreams she'd been weaving. "I can't believe you're only five years younger than Mamma! She's so much older than you in so many ways—"

"We always see our parents as old, Rhoda," Ben replied with a rueful smile. How could he prove his point without making her feel even worse? "I know how it hurts to have somebody turn ya down," he murmured. "When I was about your age, I was courtin' a girl—real serious about settlin' down with her because she was just perfect for me. Next thing I heard around town, she was marryin' a fella who'd come into some farmland and a house when his *dat* died." He shrugged, not knowing what else to do.

Rhoda turned away, covering her face with her hands. "I'm soundin' like a biddy hen, peckin' at ya," she said in a ragged voice. "I didn't mean to—oh, I'd best be on my way before I do anythin' else stupid. What would a fella like you possibly see in me?"

Rhoda hurried down the stairs then, the sounds of her sobs echoing in the shop below before she slammed the outside door.

Ben slumped, wishing he'd said kinder, more comforting words . . . wondering what Rhoda would tell her *mamm*, and if there might be any backlash from this little conversation.

Here less than two days and already ya broke somebody's heart. You've got to do better if ya think Miriam'll turn down other fellas, more established, in favor of settlin' for you.

Miriam gazed into the moonlit night from her upstairs window, not really chaperoning Rhoda from afar yet watching, all the same. What a day they'd all had! She was

exhausted and three o'clock would come too soon—not to
mention a big order for breakfast rolls and pastries to be
served at a retreat for some of the department heads at the
college in Warrensburg. If Hiram had any idea how much
the Sweet Seasons business had expanded beyond the Plain
communities of Willow Ridge, Morning Star, and New
Haven, he'd be taking her down a peg or two.

*Puh! His own business depends on buyers from all over
the country! Don't be thinkin' ya have to remain such a
small, local shop—especially with winter comin' on, cuttin'
down on the tourist business.*

No doubt in her mind the bishop wasn't finished coming
after her, finding ways to steer her toward his own upkeep
and family concerns. Had Ben not been resting against that
apple tree, what might Hiram have done? Her shoulders still
felt sore from where he'd grabbed her this afternoon.

The sound of sobbing came through her closed window,
and here came Rhoda down the driveway, mopping her face
while she walked at a fast, stiff gait toward the house. What
had Ben Hooley done to her? Had he gotten caught up in
Rhoda's big blue eyes and the wishful look she'd worn ever
since she'd met him? Had he behaved in a way that dishon-
ored her daughter—

Just as Hiram's behavior dishonors you!

Or had Rhoda been the one to start the sparks flying?

Miriam sighed, knowing this night wasn't nearly over
yet, even though she needed her sleep. It broke her heart to
see her girl as upset and unsettled as she'd been of late. She
headed down the hallway, praying for words of comfort to
come out instead of anything that might sound judgmental
or nosy.

"Rhoda!" she murmured as her daughter topped the
stairs. "What's happened, honey-bug? Can ya tell me about
it so's we both won't lie awake all night?"

Rhoda stepped away, her bitter expression clear even in the shadowy hallway. "Ben says he's thirty-five, Mamma! Does that make ya happy?"

Before Miriam could figure out the story that must have led to such a sharp-edged remark, Rhoda slipped into her room and shut the door. The lock snicked.

Ben must've given her a talkin'-to about bein' too old . . . even though we all know couples with fourteen years between 'em.

And if that's what had happened, Rhoda would someday realize Ben Hooley had done her a big favor, setting her straight with tough talk. She, like every other person on God's green Earth, had to learn the hard way that life wasn't always fair. Things didn't always work out the way you saw them in your dreams. Goodness knows she herself had learned that lesson plenty of times over the years.

Miriam chuckled. Why was she smiling in the darkness? *Thirty-five! Who'd have thought* that?

Chapter 10

Early Monday morning, Miriam scraped the sides of the crockery bowl she held, stirring the dense, dark batter of the Boston brown bread she was making for that breakfast retreat at the college. Those academic folks tended toward anything healthful, but they liked their sweets, too. Along with her Danish pastries and sticky buns she was making whole grain breads and bran muffins studded with raisins and walnuts. Nothing smelled nicer than the earthy scents of whole wheat flour, cornmeal, and the molasses that gave this bread its rich sweetness and color.

She stopped stirring to listen. Was someone tapping on the door? Or did a branch from the sweet gum tree out back need pruning? Miriam stepped toward the kitchen window for a better view.

When Ben Hooley pressed his nose to the glass, his smile made her heart skitter.

"Come on in!" she called out.

As he stepped into the bakery's kitchen, Ben inhaled deeply . . . yeast and cinnamon . . . butter and sweet cherry filling . . . scents he'd enjoyed as a boy in his *mamm*'s kitchen. The warmth in this room came from the ovens, yes, but it was Miriam's smile that took the chill off the windy autumn morning. His mother had never looked this fetching wearing a puff of flour on her nose!

Ben grinned, and then reminded himself of his mission. He fished a ten-dollar bill from his pocket. "Whenever you're ready for a break, I'll buy ya breakfast so we—"

"I'm not takin' your money, Ben!"

"*Jah*, you are, Miriam. I've got some talkin' to do and I'm interruptin' your work time," he replied firmly. "It's best that folks know I'm a payin' customer so there's not so much talk."

"Puh! The tongues're already waggin' about us."

"Never let it be said that Ben Hooley doesn't pay his way."

Miriam stirred the raisins into her dough. It might be best to let him say his piece and save her from asking some pesky questions.

Ben watched her divide the brown dough into four loaf pans. Why did this woman's café kitchen feel like such a fine place to clear his mind? Or was it the cook who set him at ease with her presence? "I'm sorry about upsettin' Rhoda last night," he began, leaning against the back counter so he could face her. "I didn't want any passersby seein' her in the apartment alone with me, and—well, there's no easy way to explain this, Miriam. When Rhoda expressed . . . romantic notions, I told her I was too old for her. She didn't like it one little bit."

Oh, but that grin on her smudged face played with him! Miriam cleared her throat.

"Not much you can do about bein' thirty-five, Ben."

"Ah. So she talked to ya."

"Mostly she cried and carried on like it was my fault ya turned her down."

"Rhoda's a nice girl. Smart and perty, like her *mamm*. I s'pose that's your fault, too, Miriam."

"*Jah*, and if it weren't a sin, I'd be right proud of it, too—Rhoda bein' smart and perty, that is."

She'd kept a straight, serious face, but then she chuckled. The kitchen rang with their laughter, and Miriam got to giggling so hard she couldn't stop. Her whole body shook with laughter, and Ben liked it that he'd made her give in so completely to a moment of happiness.

"I—I felt awful bad for her, Ben," she admitted when her laughter settled down, "but I thank ya for spellin' it out instead of lettin' her go on with hopes and dreams that weren't gonna work out."

"And how did ya know that?"

"Know what?" She looked up from smoothing the batter in the pans, eyes wide, as though she had no idea what they'd just been talking about.

Once again Ben felt fluttery inside. How did this woman make him laugh so easily—make him feel so alive and vibrant? "How'd ya know I wouldn't go along with Rhoda's plans for my life? She's a *gut* catch, ya know."

"I raised her that way."

It was Ben's turn to chuckle when she stuck her pans in the oven as though they hadn't been discussing something important. "You're a tease, Miriam."

"*Denki*, Ben. It feels *gut* to have a man tell me that." She cocked one eyebrow as she ran water into her dirty mixing bowl. "But I can't lie to ya. While I felt all crushed and hurt inside for my girl, I was happy for me. And mighty grateful for the way ya stood up to the bishop yesterday, and—"

"I was just doin' the right thing." Ben shrugged, crossing his arms. "And I wanted Hiram to know straight-out I wasn't gonna go along with his plans for your life, either."

"And why would that be, Ben?" Miriam nipped her lip. Had she gotten too forward and presumptuous? This fine-

looking fellow had only been in town forty-eight hours and
already he'd shaken up a lot of lives.

"I like puttin' that smile on your face of a mornin',
Miriam. If it's the only thing I accomplish all day, makin'
you happy makes me happy, too."

Miriam felt the color creeping up her neck. Oh, but this
man was a smooth talker! In all their years together, even
when they'd been young and courting, Jesse Lantz had
never been so flirty or quick with a quip.

*Your husband was somber and serious, but he took gut
care of ya. Have ya forgotten that part?*

Where had that prickly thought come from? The *ding-
ding-ding* of an oven timer gave her something to do as she
considered the questions that had whirled in her mind ever
since Ben Hooley blew in with the rain. But she hated to
spoil this fine mood they were in.

Ben watched her pull out one pan and then another of the
biggest, puffiest cinnamon rolls he'd ever seen. The cinna-
mon-raisin filling bubbled out between the pinwheels of
dough and filled the air with the promise of sweetness . . .
*Sugar and spice and everythin' nice. That's what Miriam
Lantz is made of!*

"I'd like to think that little grin's somethin' I put on your
face, too," she replied quietly. "But we've got things to talk
about." She avoided his gaze now . . . began to drizzle white
frosting over the hot rolls.

"What do ya want to know, Miriam? I whooshed into
Willow Ridge and we haven't had a chance to talk about—"

"Are ya baptized into the Old Order faith, Ben?"

His eyebrows rose. "*Jah*, I am. Took my kneelin' vows at
seventeen."

She nodded, satisfied for the moment. It didn't take
her but half a minute to finish squirting squiggly lines of
frosting on the first pan of rolls, and she started the second

pan without missing a beat. He'd always enjoyed watching experts at work—the way they moved so smoothly, as though their tools were extensions of their hands.

"*Gut*," she finally remarked. "Hiram said ya weren't."

"And how would he know?" Ben challenged her.

Miriam's lips curved. "Because he's the bishop? Got divine connections?" she replied with an apologetic smile. "But all teasin' aside, I've got to wonder why a fella would take his vows so young and then set off across the country. Ya didn't take much time for runnin' around and whoopin' it up durin' your *rumspringa*."

Ben eased closer to her worktable. He laughed out loud when she smacked the hand heading for one of those cinnamon rolls that smelled so outrageously delicious. "I was settin' myself up to marry the little gal I'd been sweet on all through school—Polly Petersheim," he explained. "She was takin' her instruction to join the church, so I did, too. For her, I would've stuck around home."

Miriam looked up, the obvious question in her dark brown eyes.

Ben sighed. It just didn't seem right to spoil their good mood, so he didn't go into all the details. "Seems she fell for a man from down the road who'd just come into a nice piece of ground when his *dat* died."

"So she followed the money? I'm sorry to hear that, Ben," Miriam said in a low voice. "It couldn't have been much fun to find out your honey was sweet on somebody else."

He shrugged and thought back to that time of heartache and disappointment . . . and realized his life on the road had been leading him to Willow Ridge the whole time. He just hadn't known it. "We all take our turns at gettin' our hearts broken, ain't so? If it's not one thing, it's another," he ventured. It was too soon to gush about how his life's purpose had just come into focus as he stood in Miriam's kitchen, talking to her.

"*Jah*, it's true." The way she said it told him another question would follow close behind. "So . . . your girl turned ya down? And you've been runnin' the roads ever since?"

Ben smiled ruefully. "No two ways about it, Miriam. With six boys in a family, some of them have to take jobs that aren't tied to the family land. I'd already apprenticed with the local smith and become a journeyman farrier, so—"

"So if you've been a smith all your adult life, why are you lookin' to start up a mill?"

There it was again, her direct way of getting information she needed to make informed decisions. Miriam Lantz was obviously a woman of faith—lived the life God gave her every day—yet she took nothing for granted.

"I've got a couple brothers in the millin' business, and they're itchin' to expand—which is all but impossible to do there in Lancaster, what with such high property prices. And most of the *gut* land passes from father to son."

Miriam nodded; he had mentioned those brothers before. With the sticky buns finished and the dough on the rise for her next pastries and bread, it was a good time for a break . . . a good time to feed this fellow who'd already given her more to be thankful for these past two days than he would ever know. "So you'd be bringin' family out this way to run that mill, then?" She leaned down to grab a cast-iron skillet.

Ben crossed his arms tighter. He should be focused on their talk instead of on the way Miriam moved in her kitchen. "That's the plan. Of course, I have to latch on to the land first," he remarked. "Who would I talk to about buyin' up some ground near those rapids on the river? I'd have to look the whole area over, of course, before I made up my mind to—"

"You're already talkin' to her."

Ben swallowed. Had he really met this funny, fabulous woman as well as the owner of the land he was most interested in? "This is almost soundin' too *gut* to be true, ya know?"

"That thought's crossed my mind." Miriam melted butter in her skillet and then cracked five eggs, one after the other, and dropped them into it. Salt, pepper . . . even a sprinkle of dill and paprika to color them up. Seasoning food was second nature to her, even more than for most Plain women.

"If it's the right place for the mill, I'd pay ya cash up front, top dollar for—"

"*Jah*, ya will. I know just the banker to write up the sale, too." She smiled at him and then expertly flipped the eggs with her spatula. They crackled in the hot butter as she turned off the gas. "Not because I don't trust ya, understand, but because Hiram would be all over me for lettin' ya have anythin'—"

"It's the right way to do business, Miriam. No matter what happens between you and me as a man and a woman, I don't want bad business spoilin' a *gut* friendship."

One eyebrow rose. She flipped two eggs onto a plate, three onto another, and then lifted a hot, frosted cinnamon roll onto each plate, as well. "Friendship, is it?"

That tone in her voice made him chuckle. He liked the way Miriam teased him yet let nothing important pass her by. "It should start as that, *jah*. Too many folks get hitched for the wrong reasons and then they find out they don't much like each other," he mused aloud. "I'm a man of my word, but I don't want to spend the rest of my life with somebody only because I made a promise to."

Miriam's heart hammered so hard she wondered if maybe the doctor should check on her; her parents had both passed young, from heart problems.

You're a silly goose, ya know it? This fella's sayin' all the things ya wished Jesse would've said . . .

She turned toward the stools she and Naomi sat on while they peeled veggies—but Ben had already grabbed them. He put them at the back counter . . . close together, yet not so close that he'd be touching her, should Naomi or her girls show up early. "Shall we pray on it?" she whispered.

"*Gut* idea. Even if God's already workin' all this stuff out for us."

Miriam bowed her head, yet the nearness of this man had her too *ferhoodled* to feel very prayerful. *Sorry, Lord, if I'm feelin' all giggly instead of bein' respectfully grateful for all You've brought me—*

"I thank Ya, Lord, for this fine food, and for the woman who cooked it, and for the way Ya led me here to meet her. Amen." Ben peeked at Miriam through half-open eyelids, savoring the way her lashes brushed her cheeks. Whatever her silent prayer was about, it seemed to be making her awfully happy. And again, that left him feeling like a kid who'd found the first girl he wanted to kiss—even though he and Polly had kissed a lot, those years he'd courted her.

Miriam opened her eyes and then glanced at the clock. "If there's anythin' else ya want to say before Naomi and the girls get here, we've got about half an hour," she remarked as she unwound the edge of her cinnamon roll. "Not that I'm expectin' big, important announcements."

Will ya marry me, Miriam? Will ya let me be a part of your life here in Willow Ridge?

Ben chuckled to cover the twitch of nerves that thought had caused him. If he wasn't careful, he'd be blurting out such things before it was a good idea. "If ya have suggestions about workin' for the bishop today, I could use them. Not that I'm nervous or—"

"Hiram loves to make everybody squirm a little." She smiled at Ben as she cut into her eggs. "He raises the finest draft horses around. Sells them at a premium price to folks all around the country, too."

Ben's lips lifted. "You'll never convince me a Belgian's better than a Percheron—but that's all a matter of what you're wantin' a horse for. A personal preference," he added matter-of-factly. "I'll give Hiram his money's worth of work, but he'll be gettin' no discounted prices just because he's the bishop—nor because I want to curry any favor with him."

As Ben caught the end of his cinnamon roll between his teeth and uncoiled it, an inch at a time, Miriam held her breath. Her sticky buns were an everyday thing here in the bakery, yet this man closed his eyes as though nothing had ever tasted so good.

He caught her watching him. "I've got to tell ya straight-out," he murmured, "that this warm, fresh roll will be the best thing that happens to me today."

"Puh!" Miriam wiped the yellow yolk from her plate with a section of her roll. "And here I thought *I* was gonna be—"

Ben crooked his arm gently around her neck to bring her face within inches of his. "I want to kiss ya silly right now, woman," he said under his breath. "But if I do that, there'll be no keepin' my concentration while I work at the bishop's. If you'll save me some kisses for later, though . . . maybe when we take a look at that land along the river?"

Miriam could only gaze into his hazel eyes and nod. It wasn't smart, the way she already wanted him to have her land—and much more than kisses. She cleared her throat, fighting the urge to taste that dab of frosting on his upper lip. "Unless I miss my guess, Hiram and Tom Hostetler and Gabe Glick'll be havin' a little get-together this mornin', considerin' the way the bishop behaved at his party," she murmured. "Usually they eat their breakfast here after Tom's milked his herd. Then they mosey over to Hiram's office in his barn to talk over any church business."

Ben considered this. He backed away from Miriam and the kiss he craved so they could finish their meal, even though his insides still rumbled like a storm about to blow in. "For your sake, it might be best if I'm not here when they come to eat. So I'll arrive at Hiram's bright and early," he said in a low voice. "He told me he had a full day's work . . . but I've got ideas about how to spend my evenin', and they don't include shoein' horses nor steppin' in anythin' he spreads around."

Miriam chuckled. "I like your attitude. Fightin' fire with fire."

Ben wiped his plate clean with the last chunk of his roll and then popped it into his mouth. He grinned at her, chewing . . . looking like a little boy scheming something up. "Ya might've been married to a farrier, Miriam," he murmured as he scooted his stool back, "but you've never known fire the way I'm gonna stoke it up. Can ya handle that?"

Miriam swallowed hard. Had she gotten herself in too deep by flirting with this handsome newcomer she knew so little about? "*Jah*, I can," she heard herself reply in that same low, smoky voice.

"I thought as much. See ya later, perty girl. Nothin' I like better than a stroll along the river at sunset."

Oh, but that smile told her things about Ben Hooley— and about herself. She stared in his direction long after he went to fetch his wagon, and then roused herself just in time to put on a fresh kapp and apron. She was mixing a new batch of sweet dough when Naomi came in.

Her partner's brown eyes went immediately to the sink, where two plates had been rinsed. "Hmmm," she said in a rising voice. "Bet I know who put that kitty-cat grin on your face, don't I, Miriam?"

"Get used to it!" Miriam replied as she playfully widened

her eyes. Then she chuckled—at herself, mostly. "But if I shut myself into the fridge or I forget to take these pastries out of the oven, smack some sense into me, will ya?"

Naomi chortled. "Look busy, now! Your girls were startin' down the lane when I got here."

Chapter 11

"All right, big fella, I've finished with your buddy, Saul, so it's just you and me. Savin' the best for last," Ben murmured as he tethered the stallion to a ring in the barn wall. "And we're gonna get along just fine."

Goliath had been watching him with those alert brown eyes ever since Ben had entered Hiram's barn this morning, and rightly so: every Belgian here knew he was a stranger, rather than a trainer or a stable hand. Ben had begun by shoeing the youngest horses, soon to be sold, and worked his way through the five mares, to get the two majestic stallions accustomed to his scent, his voice, his presence. Hiram's horses lived better than a lot of people he knew: the large barn was warm and the air smelled of sweet, clean straw.

Ben eased around the massive Belgian, admiring his conformation and size. At nineteen hands and probably twenty-six hundred pounds, this stallion demanded his respect. Ben rubbed the sore spot on his chest, recalling when his Percheron had spooked. If Goliath nailed him with a swift kick, it would bring all his plans to a halt for a long while—and Ben didn't want the bishop getting the best of him through his horse's hooves. Not when he was already planning out the new mill and his evening with Miriam . . . and more.

Ben stroked the stallion's lustrous sorrel neck, running his hand down its muscular shoulder and leg. Then he placed a massive front hoof on his thigh. "You're a *gut* boy, Goliath," he said in a low, singsong voice. "Doin' just fine now, fella."

Goliath stood quietly, as he'd been trained to do. It was peaceful here in the barn—a prosperous place to be a horse—and the stallion seemed to know how good he had it. Ben quickly rasped the clinches from the outside of the hoof and then positioned himself with the hoof turned up between his thighs. His lap and farrier's chaps acted as a tabletop, giving him a flat surface as he pulled the nails and popped off the old shoe. With his hoof knife, Ben cut away dead tissue and then trimmed the edges with his nippers.

The stallion shifted but stood calmly. "*Gut* boy, Goliath," Ben repeated as he grabbed his rasp. "We'll get this leveled off for ya . . . now put your foot on this stand and we'll file away the flare so's that perty new shoe'll fit ya just right."

Goliath stood loose and relaxed, his breathing smooth and even. He was a wonderful horse to work with, and Ben made a mental note to compliment Hiram Knepp on his training staff.

A side door swung open and then a burst of boyish laughter and rapid-fire footsteps echoed inside the barn. The horse shifted and shook his mane. Ben stepped out of the way just as a badminton birdie flew into view and pinged against Goliath's haunch.

"Hey there! You boys know better than to—" Ben swatted at another birdie fast enough to keep it from striking the horse, and then strode toward the two young intruders as they came after their birdies. Despite the bandannas they wore as bandit masks beneath their stocking caps, he recognized the bishop's twins, Joey and Josh—surely spitting images of Hiram at that age. "There'll be big trouble if I have to fetch your *dat*."

The boys stopped and gawked at him. "What're *you* doin' here?" one of them challenged him.

"And who are ya, to be in the barn when Pop won't let us near his horses?" his twin chimed in.

"I'm the farrier your *dat* hired. Ben Hooley," he said, extending his hand.

The boys kept their distance, looking around him to see where their birdies had landed.

"And why aren't you boys in school?" he demanded.

"Puh! Too little for school!"

"Puh! Not goin' until next year—but they'll have to *make* us go!"

Ben looked sternly at them, wondering how Hiram or any of the other Knepps told these two apart. Boys would be boys—and a bishop's kids were no different—but Ben wondered why he was hearing such sass. Had he smarted off that way, his *mamm* would have washed out his mouth with soap and then reported to his *dat*, who would have adjusted his attitude out back of the barn later that day. Ben knew better than to chase after these two and discipline them himself, however. "Are ya gonna go along now? Or do I have to let your *dat* know how ya spooked Goliath so's I had to waste time settlin' him down again?"

"Pop don't scare *me!*"

"Can't whack us if he can't catch us!"

The boys darted around either side of Ben to retrieve their shuttlecocks, oblivious to how close they got to Goliath's huge back hooves, before sprinting away. The stallion shifted from foot to foot, tossing his head. With the *bam!* of a door farther back, Ben went to check on the ornery boys while the horse settled himself. What these young fellows needed was closer supervision and more chores . . . tasks like his aunts, Nazareth and Jerusalem Hooley, had been quick to assign him even before he sat in their classroom.

Down the aisle between the stalls he strode, noting fine workmanship that might well have been the Brennemans'. From what he'd learned during his breakfast conversation with Seth, Micah, and young Aaron, they turned out a lot of cabinets in their shop and did on-site construction, as well. Just the sort of help he'd need soon if his ideas about a mill worked out.

Ben quietly opened the door the two boys had slammed and peered around a large tack room, but the twins had already disappeared through another door in the back. It smelled of fine leather in here, and the walls were lined with glistening black collars, hames, and traces that were definitely for showing and parades rather than farm work. From what he'd seen in a catalog for the upcoming Belgian sale, where the prices had widened his eyes, most of Hiram's horses were sold to breed and show rather than to haul Plain farmers' plows and hay wagons.

Ben looked up and blinked. Mounted on a crossbeam at the back of the room was a screen, somewhat smaller than most televisions he'd seen. The picture was divided into quarters, and when one of them flickered, there he was, standing in the doorway of the tack room!

He closed the door behind him, shaken yet intrigued. He'd worked for a good many English breeders who had sophisticated security setups, but such electronics were surely not condoned on Old Order farms . . .

But when you're the bishop, who's to say ya can't have such contraptions?

Ben decided not to challenge Knepp about his discovery. Hiram had seemed pleased when he'd arrived so early to work, and that he was making good progress before the bishop left for breakfast at the Sweet Seasons—as though their confrontation in Miriam's orchard had been set aside. Ben's rumbling stomach told him it had been several hours since he'd enjoyed his eggs and that sticky bun in Miriam's kitchen, but he wanted to finish with Goliath before he got something to eat.

From across the large barn, he could hear the stallion still stomping his foot. Ben slowed his pace and his breathing so he'd be calmly in charge before he approached the horse tethered at the far end of the aisle. While he wondered at Hiram's naming both good-natured stallions after Old Testament villains, he had no doubt that such massive male animals could put him out of work quicker than he could duck or jump away. It was well worth a few extra minutes to stand here, out of the horse's sight, while Goliath calmed down.

Ben gazed up into the barn's sturdy crossbeams . . . admired the majestic heads of the horses he'd already shod, waiting . . .

"I'm tellin' ya, Hiram, that move ya made on Miriam on Sunday's been causin' quite a stir! Not your best idea to force her hand in front of everybody!"

Ben's jaw dropped. That sounded like Tom Hostetler, but his voice was far more insistent than when he'd been delivering Sunday's sermon. Ben realized then that the large glass windows he stood beside, where the blinds were shut, probably formed a wall of Hiram's office.

"*Jah*, what were ya thinkin'?" came another man's voice. "Next thing we know, some younger fella from the membership'll be tellin' ya to get a room! That's not what we need at a church gatherin'."

Ben's lips twitched, even though this topic still raised his dander. It was surely talk the bishop didn't want him to overhear, yet there was no point in returning to Goliath's stall yet.

"There comes a time when a man must behave in an unconventional way to make a woman see the light."

Ben frowned. Once again Hiram Knepp was assuming his will should override anything Miriam Lantz wanted or believed. Ben had hoped to be out of here by three, but this loud talk was a way to get a feel for what he might expect if he and the bishop had words again—and Ben figured they would, indeed.

"Ya didn't score any points back when ya tried to sell her bakery buildin'," an older fellow pointed out. "Seems to me Miriam's got even less reason to hitch up with ya now that you've made a fool of yourself—"

"Oh, ye of little faith," Hiram replied, in such a tone Ben could well imagine the smirk on his face. "That Hooley fellow from off the road'll be the one to take the fall, mark my words. He's thinking to settle here—and catch Miriam while he's at it—but he's playing right into my hands."

Ben's heartbeat sped up. What sort of a preachers' meeting was it when a bishop—the spiritual leader of Willow Ridge—said such a thing about a potential new resident? It wasn't like he was an aimless drifter living off the goodwill of these local folks. He would provide farrier and welding services that had died with Jesse Lantz, and he was about to build a mill that would bring a whole new market for their farmers' grain, and provide new products that would create more sales for several of the local shops. And if his younger brothers settled here, it would also add a fresh bloodline to the local population—something to be considered in small Plain settlements like Willow Ridge, where the same families lived and intermarried generation after generation.

Ben almost banged on the office door to let Hiram know just what he thought—

Return not evil for evil . . . love thy neighbor as thyself . . .

forgive not seven times, but seventy times seven . . . His *dat*'s voice reminded him of Jesus's teachings about how to handle folks who provoked his temper. Better to let the preachers take Hiram to task while he finished his own work, for the sooner he finished with Goliath the sooner he could spend time with Miriam at the river.

Quietly Ben strode down the center aisle again, toward the stallion. He hummed a tune from the *Ausbund*—not that the massive Belgian would recognize a hymn about grace when he heard it. Goliath pricked up his ears and stood more quietly as Ben walked up to stroke his head and neck, drawing his hand down the horse's muscled shoulders. "You're a fine, fine fella," Ben murmured. "You and me, Goliath, we'll finish our job if ya just forget all about those ornery boys, ain't so?"

On he chattered, in a low, soothing cadence that kept the stallion listening . . . cooperating. Ben finished in about half an hour, and as he was leading Goliath back to his stall, the office door opened at the other end of the barn. Tom Hostetler and the men Ben recalled as Gabe Glick, another preacher, and Reuben Reihl, the deacon, walked out ahead of Hiram. Seeing him with Goliath, they waved and went on their way.

The bishop came toward him, watching the way he handled his prize stallion. "My boys give you any trouble?" Hiram asked, gesturing at Goliath and over toward Saul, down the row.

"Not a lick. Fine animals you've got here." Ben paused, considering how to word the rest of his response. "Your twin boys, though, nearly got themselves kicked when they came runnin' through the barn, hittin' badminton birdies at Goliath while I was shoein' him. It's a credit to your trainers that we didn't all get hurt."

Hiram scowled. "I've told them repeatedly that they're

not to come in here. Annie Mae lost track of them again—"
The bishop's tone told Ben that Annie Mae would catch
more of a talking-to than Josh and Joey, but then he smiled
and pulled an envelope from his pocket. "Glad you stopped
in Willow Ridge when you did, Hooley. Safe journey to you
after you finish your work here."

Ah, but ya know nothin' about the work I'm about to do!

Ben nodded, his thoughts whirling around what he really
wanted to say . . . but he followed the bishop's script—for
now. "Pleasure doin' business with ya, Hiram. Have a *gut*
rest of your day, now, and a real successful sale."

Ben loaded his tools into his wagon, clucked to Pharaoh,
and then rolled on down the road. His stomach rumbled, but
he had no doubt that Miriam would soon feed him wonderful-
gut food—and feed his soul, as well.

That evening, along about five, Miriam's heart was soar-
ing; Ben Hooley was carrying her picnic basket and holding
her hand as they strolled past the apple orchard toward the
back acreage of the Lantz farm. Pharaoh and her own four
horses nickered from the corral as she and Ben strolled past,
while cardinals and mourning doves called to their mates.
Even though the autumn breeze was brisk now that the sun
was descending over the western hills, Miriam had never felt
warmer. Ben had asked about her day at the café and had
told her about his run-in with Hiram's twins . . . and for the
first time since Jesse had passed, Miriam was sharing moments with a man who cared about her and her world. Even
though Rachel and Rhoda were her constant companions
and Naomi Brenneman knew her inside and out, Miriam
hadn't realized how much she'd missed the company of an
adult . . . a male who didn't expect her to follow his rules.

"I feel bad for poor Annie Mae," she remarked, "because

there's no way a girl of seventeen can keep track of those two wild boys as well as little Sara and Timmy, all while cookin' the meals and tendin' the household chores, what with Nellie still bein' in school. Truth be told, Hiram's wife Linda didn't have much better control over their behavior."

Ben chuckled under his breath. "I've no doubt Hiram intended to give Annie Mae a piece of his mind—but enough about the bishop, Miriam. I've never laid my eyes on such a wondrous sight."

As they reached the ridge, Miriam held her breath. Ben was gesturing toward the panorama of the river and the trees in their autumn glory, and at the farmland spread before them like a patchwork quilt of greens, golds, and browns— but he was looking at *her*. "This is one of my favorite places on God's *gut* Earth," she murmured, drawing her gaze away from his. She smiled and pointed toward a hillside that dropped down to the flowing water, just upstream from the rapids. "And right there's where I watched my other little girl wash away when a storm made the water rise faster than I could climb away from it."

Ben's face reflected his horror. "And how can ya stand here so calm-like, tellin' me about such a tragedy—"

"The story has a real happy endin'. No doubt you'll meet my Rebecca one of these days and we'll tell ya all about it," Miriam replied, still amazed at how the whole surprise had worked itself out. "It's nothin' short of a miracle, how she survived the ride down that river and got raised by a nice English couple—and then came lookin' for her real *mamm*." She smiled up at Ben, squeezing his hand. "But enough about the girls. Do ya see anythin' here that suits ya?"

Miriam gestured toward the land and the river, and just that quickly Ben set down the picnic basket to slip his arms around her. "Everythin'," he murmured. His eyes had a shine like honey, deep and sweet, as he lowered his face to hers. "But enough about this place bein' the perfect site for my brothers' mill."

Her heart beat so frantically Miriam thought she'd faint—but the gentle pressure of Ben's lips on hers revived her. It was her first kiss in more than two years and it ended too soon. Yet she knew she was marked forever.

"Miriam," he whispered, "I'm sorry I couldn't hold back—or wait for a more proper time to—"

"So help me, Ben Hooley, if you apologize for kissin' me, you'll not get a chance to do it again."

He raised his head to look at her, a smile lighting his face. "Ya won't have to warn me twice, perty girl. Shall we walk along the river while I tell ya what I've got in mind? It's a big decision all around—you sellin' the land, and me tellin' Luke and Ira to pull up roots and move to Missouri on the strength of my word."

"Your brothers would do that, without comin' to look for themselves?"

Ben chuckled as he took her hand again. They resumed their walk toward the river and a picnic on its banks. "They're thirty and twenty-eight, champin' at the bit to find a life for themselves, knowin' the Hooley spread in Lancaster won't support them. Even if a place came up for sale thereabouts, the price tag would stop your heart."

"*Jah*, I've heard Missouri's still one of the most affordable places for folks to live, Plain or otherwise. Guess I take it for granted, after bein' here all my life." Miriam stopped at the top of the bank where she'd lost her grip on Rebecca that fateful day more than eighteen years ago. Downstream a little ways, the channel narrowed and the water rushed over a series of natural dams and boulders, sending up a fine spray above its white foam as it sang a bubbly, burbly song. "Not puttin' ya off, understand, but I've got no idea how much I should be askin' for—"

"We'll let the bank decide that, after we have the area appraised. For everyone's sake, we've got to handle this as a business proposition, fair and square, Miriam."

She nodded, respecting Ben all the more. "We can call Derek Shotwell, the loan officer who handled the sale when Hiram tried to buy my buildin'. He'll do the job right."

Ben slipped an arm around her shoulders, gazing at the flow of the river and the trees dressed in autumn reds and golds that sparkled as the sunset struck them. "I can wait as long as ya want, Miriam. This doesn't have to be settled until you're ready."

"I'm fine with it, Ben." And as the words came out of her mouth of their own accord, Miriam knew them to be true, no matter how other folks might tell her she was thinking with her heart instead of her head. "This part of the farm has always been so rocky and the soil so shallow, it's not been *gut* for crops. Jesse ran a few cows here years ago, but the river was a hazard to them. So fishin's about the only productive thing we've done here. A lot of Missouri land's mostly just nice to look at."

"*Jah*, it's perty in a different way from Pennsylvania. Less cultivated . . . less crowded." Ben cupped his hand over his brow to keep the sun out of his eyes. "We'd need access to the road. Can't have property locked in by other folks' land—and that's the blacktop runnin' in front of your café, ain't so?"

"*Jah*, and since Lantz land goes across the river a bit, and the road is the boundary on the north, the access ya want is no problem at all." Was this conversation—this business proposition—going too smoothly? Was there anything she should consider before agreeing to what Ben wanted? Four days ago, she'd not even met this man. "Tell me again what sort of mill you've got in mind," Miriam said. "How will it turn a *gut* enough profit so your brothers can put up the buildin' and buy the equipment and still make a livin' for themselves?"

Ben turned to gaze at her. "Miriam Lantz, talk like that tells me you're not just another perty face," he murmured. "And I like it that you've got some business smarts!"

Once again her heart hammered with joy. "My ledger kept me from cavin' in to Hiram's plan to buy me out a couple months back. He'll think this land transaction is more monkey business than *gut* business."

"When Luke and Ira write up a business plan for the banker, it'll include the kinds of grains they plan to mill—basics like wheat and corn and oats, but also the organic grains for cereals and baking mixes like you find in whole foods stores," Ben explained. "The mill wheel can run on water power from those rapids, or it could be horse drawn or have a diesel engine," he added. "And since Luke and Ira could grind feed for the local farmers' livestock, as well as pay those fellows to grow the specialty grains for these new products, a lot of folks in Willow Ridge stand to profit from diversifyin'."

Miriam nodded, already certain Derek Shotwell would approve of this forward-thinking idea. And wasn't it a bonus that Ben Hooley's brothers were single? Years of the same families intermarrying was a concern as more Old Order children were being born with genetic disorders.

"But enough about my brothers," Ben quipped. "I'm so hungry I could eat this whole picnic plus the basket ya brought it in."

"Well then." Miriam took an old quilt from the basket, and they spread it on a large, flat rock overlooking the rapids. Ben was lifting out foil packets, inhaling each one with an ecstatic grin.

"Let me guess," he murmured. "Ya fried up a chicken . . . and this flat one is sliced bread, buttered and still warm . . .

and this bowl is"—he lifted the edge of the aluminum foil—
"green beans cooked with potatoes! How'd ya know what
all my favorite foods were?"

Miriam laughed. What a joy to have a man get so excited
about everyday dishes. "Ask Rhoda. She was in charge of
dinner tonight—and I stashed away the last couple pieces of
that coconut cake, so you and I could share it. I know you
men like pie better, but—"

"It never pays to quibble with the cook. And your Rhoda's
a fine one, too." Ben watched her take out two plates and the
silverware. "Is she still peeved at me for sayin' I'm too old
to court her?"

Miriam shrugged. "She and Rachel were headed to my
sister's for a carvin' party. Leah grew some huge pumpkins
for jack-o'-lanterns and she's donatin' some for a benefit
auction this weekend."

"Hmm. If any of those scary Halloween faces look like
mine, I guess we'll know how Rhoda feels, ain't so?"

Miriam giggled, loving the way Ben's laughter blended
with hers in a duet that lingered among the trees. He took
her hand then, bowing his head. Miriam closed her eyes,
which made her aware of how her pulse rushed like the
rapids . . . and how warm and strong Ben Hooley's hand felt.

*Lord, I thank Ya for this fine time . . . for this man who's
givin' me so much to be happy about. Is this the promise You
were talkin' to me about the other day, Father?*

What a pleasure it was to sit beside this man and watch
him enjoy his food. How soothing, to talk in low voices
about farmers around Willow Ridge who might grow grain
for his brothers . . . downright intoxicating, to bask in the
last rays of daylight as Ben Hooley gazed at her, obviously
as smitten as she was. Too soon the food was gone. They
packed up and headed back to the house hand in hand,

strolling across the fields of evening as a nearly full moon lit their way.

When they were within sight of the house, Ben cleared his throat. "I have a couple of favors to ask, Miriam. And *no* is a perfectly *gut* answer to either one."

She gazed up at him, wondering if she could possibly deny anything he'd ask for. "I'm listenin'."

"May I use your phone to call my brothers? If I let them know I'll be comin' East for them when I finish the work I've promised here, they can be packed up and ready to roll by the time I get back to Pennsylvania."

"Of course ya can use my phone, Ben! I—"

He caught the side of her face in his hand. "One more kiss before the girls might see us." With that, he eased his lips over hers, lingering longer this time. When they finally separated, they sighed together.

"And now for the bigger favor," he continued. "When I get here with Luke and Ira, they'll be needin' a place to stay while they build the mill—"

"We live in a six-bedroom house, Ben. The girls and I would be pleased to clear out one of the spare rooms for them."

"Actually, scoldin' those Knepp twins today gave me another idea." He grinned at her in the moonlight, as though he were about to suggest something outrageous. "If it's all right with you, my brothers could bunk with me above the smithy and . . . I might bring a couple of aunts back, too— more for an extended visit to help us out, rather than to make their home here. They're *maidels* who used to teach school. Might be more proper for *them* to stay in one of your rooms at the house, ain't so?"

Miriam's eyebrows rose. "Of course your aunts can stay with us, Ben! And why do I think you're up to somethin'?"

He chuckled richly, stepping away from her as they

emerged from the orchard. "See there? Ya already know me so well I won't be gettin' away with much."

When they reached the steps, Ben looked at Miriam with an expression she couldn't read. "Might be best if I go now, Miriam, in case your girls come—"

"I've got nothin' to hide from Rachel or Rhoda. They need to see me with a man again." Miriam let out a short chuckle as she preceded him to the kitchen door. "Hiram doesn't count, ya know."

Ben's chuckle followed her inside the house. He stepped in behind her, waiting as she lit the lantern nearest the door and then the one over by the sink.

"How about a cup of coffee? Or tea?"

"Sounds like the perfect endin' to a wonderful-*gut* walk along the river." As he hung his hat on a peg by the door, his boots made a solid, sturdy sound on the plank floor.

"Make yourself at home, Ben. I'll just be a minute." Miriam's fingers trembled as she filled the teakettle under the faucet, set it on the burner, and lit the gas flame beneath it.

This felt mighty bold. If her girls came home from Leah's to find her cozying up to Ben Hooley, she'd have no end of questions to answer. It had been so long since they'd had a man in their kitchen, except for Micah, coming to fix some little thing.

When Miriam turned to ask Ben more about his aunts, the bottom dropped out of her stomach. Ben sat in the chair at the end of the table, always her husband's place. For a fleeting moment it was Jesse's face she saw: the weathered skin, pale across the top of his forehead from wearing his hat; the dark hair with gray at the temples and the wavy black beard with threads of white.

Jesse's blue, blue eyes looked through to her soul. Those eyes had missed nothing, and at times Rachel and Rhoda's expressions—those same direct eyes—called up Jesse's memory.

What do ya think you're doin' with this strange fella in my house? And who gave ya the right to sell off my land?

Miriam's hand flew to her mouth. That was Jesse's voice asking those questions. His disapproval made her heart skitter as though one of the preachers had called her out in church for falling asleep.

"Miriam, are ya all right?" Ben rose from the chair.

And then the mirage disappeared. The spell cast by a moment's memory dissipated as quickly as it had come. But Miriam's heart still raced while her husband's voice echoed in her mind. The teakettle whistled, but she paid it no mind. "I— I'm sorry, Ben," she rasped. "I don't know what's come over me. There for a minute, it was Jesse sittin' at the table—"

He stepped quickly to her side. "I wasn't thinkin', Miriam. Sat down at the end as though I was at—at home."

"Ya have to go now, Ben." Miriam backed away from him. "I—I'm havin' second thoughts about that land—"

"It's all right, Miriam," he murmured. "We can talk it over—"

"Just go. Jesse's tellin' me this is all wrong, and I—I have to listen."

Ben sighed. He took his hat from the peg and put it on, gazing at her sadly. "I'm sorry, Miriam," he whispered. "Maybe this'll all look better come mornin'."

Miriam bowed her head, knowing that if she maintained eye contact it would be easier for this man to charm his way back into her heart.

The door closed quietly. The kettle whistled, loud and shrill like a siren, but for the longest time she didn't have the strength to turn off the burner.

Chapter 12

Across the yard Miriam strode, wrapping a shawl around her shoulders as she hurried toward the Brenneman house. She shivered when the wind kicked up. What on Earth had she been thinking, sitting on the riverbank in October without a wrap, eating a picnic dinner with a man she hardly knew? Naomi's lamplit windows were a welcome sight as Miriam hurried past the garden plots her sister Leah tended for farmers' markets.

Up the gravel driveway Miriam rushed, as though the Devil nipped at her heels. Had that same serpent been whispering in her ear, tempting her to fall for a sweet-talker none of them had seen before last Saturday? All along she'd wondered if things between her and Ben Hooley had been going too smoothly. Why hadn't she listened to her instincts and put on the brakes?

Miriam raced up the Brennemans' porch steps to pound on the door. Through the glass she saw Ezra at the head of the table in his wheelchair, with Micah and Seth seated across the table from Aaron and Naomi. Naomi motioned Miriam inside with a wide smile.

Miriam swiped at her eyes. She hadn't thought about it

being dinnertime—had lost all track of normal activity, it seemed—because Ben had beguiled her. It wouldn't do to weep and wail in front of the boys, and Ezra wouldn't tolerate her crying, either. The poor man had fallen through a rotten roof on a construction job and lost his legs; his constant discomfort colored his entire outlook on life.

Bless her, Naomi came to the door as though she sensed a crisis. "Miriam!" she whispered, drawing her in out of the chill. "I thought ya were goin' for a stroll with—did Ben not show up, dearie?"

"Oh, it's not that!" Miriam whimpered. "It was all goin' so well—too well. We were talkin' about his brothers comin' here to start up a mill—but then Ben came into the kitchen and"—Miriam gulped hard, catching her breath—"oh, Naomi, I've made a horrible mess of things. Thank goodness my Jesse stopped me. Scared the daylights outta me, but it scared some smarts back into me, if that makes any sense."

Glancing at her sons and husband, who were watching them with curious expressions, Naomi grabbed a barn coat from a peg by the door. "I'll be back in a few," she said. "Your pie's on the sideboard, all cut and ready."

Miriam felt better as Naomi guided her to the front porch. She trusted her dearest friend to answer her questions honestly and point out details she might have missed. And Miriam had a sinking feeling she had missed a *lot* of pertinent facts these past few days while she'd been basking in the glow of handsome Ben Hooley's smile.

"So what's this about Ben?" Naomi slipped an arm around Miriam's shoulders and they started down Ezra's ramp together. "I thought you two were hittin' it off—"

"All too well!" Miriam exclaimed. "I—I can't explain it. Deep down, I sensed things with Ben were kickin' up too fast, yet I didn't stop and think! And I've all but sold off a parcel of land along the river so his brothers can come here and start up a mill—"

"*Jah*," Naomi remarked, her expression taut as she followed along. "Seems reasonable enough to me, as long as ya get everythin' drawn up nice and legal-like."

"But then—then we were walkin' back from the river, and I invited him into the kitchen for a cup of—" Miriam shuddered. "Oh, Naomi, I can't describe it. When I turned from settin' the kettle on to see Ben sittin' at the head of the table, it was suddenly *Jesse* lookin' back at me! Askin' me why I'd let that stranger into his home! And what right did I have to sell off some of his land!"

Naomi's eyes widened. "That would startle anybody, for sure and for certain."

As they walked slowly along the edge of the Brennemans' cleared-off garden, the sight of the neatly tilled earth, glimmering with a hint of frost in the moonlight, gave a sense of order to Miriam's chaotic thoughts.

She stopped and took a deep breath to clear her head. "Am I goin' crazy, Naomi? I thought I had myself all settled, where Jesse's concerned. Thought Ben Hooley came along at just the right time, with just the right smile—"

"Can't argue with that. Ben's smile could dazzle ya into doin' just about anythin'."

"That's what I'm sayin'! I've lost all sense of priorities, thinkin' I could just sell off a piece of Jesse's farm—and *that* after I already let Ben use Jesse's shop and sleep upstairs in the new apartment!" Miriam turned to face her friend, imploring her to figure out the riddle of her recent behavior. "Is it any wonder Hiram's warnin' me to—"

"Let's leave the bishop out of this. It's got nothin' to do with what Hiram wants or thinks." Naomi held Miriam's gaze for a moment. "Seems to me that while you and Ben were at the café . . . and while ya were out amongst folks at

the Zooks' . . . and while ya were walkin' along the river, the
two of ya were gettin' on as fine as pie. But once Ben
seemed to be takin' Jesse's place—"

"*Jah*, nobody's sat in that chair since he passed."

"—somethin' in your mind backfired." Naomi gazed in
the direction of the dark café and the smithy, where a lamp
flickered in the upstairs window. "Seems like as long as Ben
is with ya where Jesse never was—like in the café—you're
fine and dandy. But when he slipped into that one spot—into
the house where ya were Jesse's wife for all those years—"

"I see what you're sayin'." Miriam let out another long
sigh. "But if that's the case, why could I stroll along the
riverbank agreein' with every suggestion Ben made? I don't
know this man from Adam, Naomi! Just met him last Saturday!"

Naomi raised her eyebrows. "Did you and Jesse go for
walks along the river?"

Miriam blinked. "Truth be told, we didn't walk anywhere
except to your place when ya hosted preachin' Sundays.
Didn't have . . . time for walks."

And why was that? Something pricked at her heart and
Miriam began to cry again.

Naomi wrapped an arm around her shoulders. "Anybody
would be upset, Miriam, seein' her husband the way you did
and hearin' his voice. Especially when a new fella steps
in—which was bound to happen sometime—and moves
amongst the rooms you'd only shared with the man who
built them for ya. Am I makin' sense?"

"*Jah, jah*, you are." Miriam shook her head to clear it.
"But what if Jesse was warnin' me? What if he knows
things about Ben Hooley, as he's lookin' down from heaven,
and I haven't asked all the questions I should?"

Naomi's eyebrows rose as she thought about this. "Was

Ben tellin' ya he wanted that land right away? Pushin' ya to say yes, or—"

"Ben's been nothin' but patient and considerate." Miriam relaxed . . . felt the shock of that vision in the kitchen losing its grip on her. "But somethin' warned me to put on the brakes before I did things I couldn't undo."

"Nothin' wrong with that. Think of how excited we were to be startin' up the café and then one of us would hit an invisible wall, an obstacle we couldn't see our way around," Naomi recalled. "For me, it was believin' Ezra wouldn't allow me to work away from home—even though the Sweet Seasons mailbox is right beside ours."

"*Jah*, you were afraid he'd haul ya out of the kitchen the day we opened," Miriam agreed fondly. "Yet after he stewed about it, sittin' home alone while the boys kept the construction shop goin', he got that job at the hospital. It gave him somethin' to think about besides his disability, and it was an income for him."

"So it worked out the best for all of us." Naomi smiled kindly. "It's just plain ole *fear* you're dealin' with, Miriam. You're scared, not knowin' what'll happen next—or what changes might come along without you agreein' to them first."

Miriam nodded, pondering this. Ben Hooley had lots of new ideas, yet he'd never once forced any of them—or himself—on her.

"I think it's the *permission* idea that's givin' ya the most trouble, dearie. Even though you've been makin' your own decisions since Jesse died, ya still want to know you're not goin' against everythin' ya honored and believed in while ya were his wife."

She smiled, just a little. "Ya said a mouthful there, Naomi."

"Have ya ever known me to keep quiet?"

Miriam thumbed away her tears. As she looked across Naomi's dark garden to where the boys' custom cabinet shop was . . . along the county road leading over to the café and quilt shop . . . up the lane to Jesse's blacksmith shop and then up to their home, she realized that her world was still intact, despite her ominous vision of Jesse. Logic told her it was Ben sitting there in her kitchen that had triggered one last, poignant memory of the man who'd shared his name and his life with her for nearly twenty years.

Would Jesse really have questioned her so harshly?

Maybe. Jesse Lantz hadn't minced words or spared anyone's feelings. And while he'd fished many a time in that river, he'd never invited Miriam to join him. She'd had her girls to watch and her chores to do, after all.

Ben Hooley was created from a different recipe altogether. Fresher. Spicier. He was a man who cooked things up on the spur of the moment, confident he could make them turn out right. And didn't she concoct some of her best café meals that way?

"I can't thank ya enough, Naomi," Miriam murmured. "Sorry I pulled ya away from your dinner."

Her partner laughed as they turned back toward their homes, now outlined in the moonlight. "I could stand to miss a meal or two. Truth be told, my gooseberry pie didn't set up right and Ezra's most likely complainin' about what a gooey mess it is."

"There won't be a speck of it left. I bet the four of them ate the whole thing, thinkin' gooseberry wasn't your favorite, anyway."

Naomi chortled. "There's that, *jah*. I should thank them for takin' away the temptation of eatin' pie just because it's there." She rubbed the center of Miriam's back as they reached the spot where they would part ways to go to their own homes. "Will ya be all right, Miriam?"

"*Jah*. The girls'll be back soon. And it's not like Jesse was really in that kitchen chair, nor like I've had trouble bein' alone in the house since he passed." Miriam smiled. "I can reason it all out now, this situation with Ben. Thanks for seein' things I missed, Naomi."

"Happy to help. See ya tomorrow, bright and early."

Chapter 13

Miriam busied herself with baking biscuits, sticky buns, and several apple walnut coffee cakes before the rest of her crew arrived at the Sweet Seasons the next morning. It felt good to be surrounded by her kitchen equipment, in the hum of the refrigerators, after a night of not sleeping well.

How could she explain to Ben what had happened at her kitchen table? After such a perfect evening with him, feeling so happy as they enjoyed their riverbank picnic, Miriam wondered if Ben would even talk to her. It must have seemed that another woman had taken over her soul, and certainly her mouth, in those moments when she had abruptly told him to leave.

Naomi entered the kitchen, smiling brightly. "Feelin' better this mornin', Miriam?"

"*Jah*, but I must've seemed like a mighty black cloud last night when I—"

"You can cry on my shoulder any time ya need to, dearie." Naomi gave her a quick hug and then took a package of bulk sausage from the fridge to make breakfast patties. "Ya did so well after Jesse passed—kept yourself so busy startin' up this café—it's only natural for memories to pop up when a new fella gives ya the eye, ain't so?"

Miriam got out the cast-iron skillets for bacon and Naomi's sausage. "Is it? I was feelin' so *gut* about sellin' that section of land by the river—"

"Did he give ya anythin' besides the eye, Miriam?" Naomi's brown eyes sparkled. She always knew just what questions to ask, didn't she?

Miriam glanced through the back window to be sure Rachel and Rhoda weren't coming. "Oh, *jahhhh* . . . Ben kissed me a time or two, and we ate our picnic on—"

"And how was it?"

Miriam stopped laying strips of bacon in her skillet to meet her partner's gaze. The answer to that question made her heart sing . . . just as those kisses had. "Truth be told, I felt like a girl gettin' her very first kiss. It was . . . so fresh and sweet and—"

"Better than Jesse?"

Miriam blinked. She'd loved her husband dearly, and he'd provided well for her.

"That part would be normal, too, I'd think. Not that I would know," Naomi added quickly. "But after all these years with Ezra, we're not the lovebirds we were as newlyweds. All those years and kids take their toll on that mushy stuff."

A grin spread across Miriam's face. "The same was true with Jesse, especially after we lost Rebecca in the flood, and I lost the baby I was carryin' and couldn't have any more."

"So now it's all new again, with a fella who seems to be a wonderful-*gut* worker and who can't stop lookin' at you as though he'd found himself a miracle. And the men all respect him, too."

Was it true, what Naomi said? Did Ben really gaze at her

that way? Again Miriam glanced out the window. "Here come the girls. I'd just as soon they didn't know how upset I was last night."

"They'll have their share of heartache, and it's your turn for some fun with a fella. You were a *gut* wife, Miriam," Naomi insisted. "Faithful and lovin' to Jesse until the day he died."

Miriam flushed and turned on the burner under the bacon. "Don't remind Hiram of that, all right?"

They laughed, and as her daughters set up the tables and the first fellows came in for their breakfast, Miriam found herself glancing toward the dining room . . . looking for that light brown hair and easy smile, hoping Ben would still have a smile for her.

And there he came, with Naomi's boys. Micah Brenneman and Seth, the oldest, were holding quite a conversation with Ben as they sat down at their usual table and waited for Rachel to pour water and take their orders. It seemed like a business proposition they were discussing—and then Ben looked up and his eyes met hers.

Miriam held his gaze. Smiled shyly.

He smiled back, thank goodness. Then he and Aaron Brenneman led the way to the steam table. Tom Hostetler and the Kanagy boys came in, as did Preacher Gabe and a few English fellows who farmed nearby.

Miriam relaxed. It was a new day, and she was feeding people—surrounded by her friends and family—and for that she was grateful. Last night's startling vision of Jesse had lost its power to make her second-guess all that had been going so right . . . so very sweetly with Ben Hooley.

She started rolling out crust for the eight fruit pies Lydia Zook wanted for the market.

"Hi, Mamma! Do you have a minute?" Her daughter Rebecca stood in the doorway between the kitchen and the tables out front. She went by Tiffany Oliveri, as that was the name she'd been given by the English couple who'd rescued and raised her, but there was no mistaking that she was Rachel and Rhoda's identical sister.

"*Gut* to see ya, Rebecca! And don't ya look perty in that shade of turquoise!" Miriam said with a grin. "Come on in, honey-bug. My hands're all floury from makin' these pies, but I've got all the minutes ya want."

Rebecca grinned at Naomi and perched on a stool where Miriam worked. "So . . . how many pies are you making there?"

"Well, the Zooks want to restock their supply for the store, and that's usually eight at a time. And while I'm at it, I'll make about that many to have for our lunch shift, too."

Her daughter's jaw dropped. "Sixteen pies? At one time? That's, um, fifteen more than I've made in my entire life."

Miriam saw that Rebecca was unfolding a square contraption that had a keyboard and a shiny screen, setting it up on the counter. "You've got other talents, for sure and for certain. And you're about to show me one of them, aren't ya?"

"This is my laptop computer," Rebecca explained as she tapped a few keys. Pictures came up on the screen then, and Miriam could only gawk at that sort of magic. "I'm taking a graphic design class at Missouri Western—"

"And what would graphic design be?" Miriam asked. "I don't know a thing about what ya do, honey-bug, but I'd *like* to know."

Rebecca smiled as though that remark pleased her. Her face—the exact expression Rhoda wore when she was intent on frying chicken just right—glowed with health and just a trace of makeup. What a huge improvement over the way she'd looked the first time she'd come to the Sweet Seasons last summer! "Graphic design is where you create signs and logos—like people use for their stores or their letterhead," she explained. "Or these days, it's mostly putting together websites and ads people will see on their computers."

Rebecca looked at her then, her blue eyes sparkling. "As a class project, I have to launch a website I've designed. I hope it's okay if I set up a site for your bakery, Mamma."

Miriam blinked. The screen showed a pan of sticky buns and SWEET SEASONS BAKERY CAFÉ in bold, homey-looking lettering. "That's us! That's this place!"

"It is!" Rebecca said with a chuckle. "I know you Amish ladies can't design websites for your shops—"

"*Jah*, there's that," Naomi remarked as she peered over Miriam's shoulder.

"—and I'd like to put a photograph of your café on here, and maybe scan in your menu," she went on. "I know some of that stuff's against your religion, so I *don't* want to get you in trouble with that Hiram guy."

Miriam wiped the flour from her hands to wrap her arms around Rebecca's shoulders. "*Denki* for thinkin' of that, child of mine. As long as *my* picture's not on there, and as long as I don't own a computer, you can do whatever ya need to for your class."

Rebecca smiled. "It would be a great idea for you to advertise online, anyway. Plenty of people around central Missouri would *love* to come to Willow Ridge for your good food, and to see the other shops here. And you know what? A few other people here have already established an online presence."

Miriam's lips curved. "We probably could use some advertisin' in places besides the billboard on the county road," she agreed. "Micah got his idea for the movin' walls in the apartment from studyin' a little movie on your computer, after all. He's doin' a right *gut* business installin' those, too."

A movement at the pass-through window caught her eye:

Ben Hooley was leaning on the counter, smiling at them. "Nearly all the places in Lancaster advertise online," he remarked as he studied Rebecca. "Some of the Mennonites have started designin' websites and such for the Amish folks. That's the way English customers would rather shop now, too, and it's how tourists know what places they want to visit when they're on vacation."

Miriam smiled, thankful he'd come to say hello. "Ben, this is that washed-away daughter I was tellin' ya about—my Rebecca, who goes by the name Tiffany Oliveri now. Her *dat* bought my buildin' in August . . . so Hiram couldn't. Rebecca, this is Ben Hooley."

Ben came into the kitchen, grinning as he looked her over. "*Jah*, you're Rachel and Rhoda's sister, all right. And your *mamm*'s still mighty excited that ya came back to find her." He studied the computer screen then. "Now ya know, Miriam, she can make that Sweet Seasons lettering any color ya want, or change things all around on the page. But I think it looks right nice the way it is."

"*Jah*, it's fine with me. And if it brings more English business once winter slows things down—oh my. Would ya looky here."

The screen had changed. The wording at the top now said BISHOP'S RIDGE BELGIANS and showed photographs of two stallions, Goliath and Saul. There was also a list of awards and the details about the lineage of the two registered champions who were standing at stud.

"I put shoes on those fellas yesterday," Ben remarked in a low voice. "That's an impressive place the bishop's runnin'."

"Yeah," Rebecca murmured, "but here's what I thought was even more interesting." She made the screen move up a few inches.

"Why, that's Hiram!" Miriam exclaimed. Then she clapped her hand over her mouth.

"No mistake about it," Naomi murmured. "He's smilin' at the camera full-on, like he's mighty happy to be havin' his picture taken, too."

Ben cleared his throat. "Ya know, I saw a fancy security setup in his barn, like the ones the big English horse breeders use to keep track of who-all goes in and out of their barns."

"And it's all perfectly legitimate," a familiar male voice replied from the doorway.

Miriam's skin prickled. Hiram Knepp had been eating his breakfast out front, as he usually did, and her outburst had attracted his attention. Now here he was in the kitchen, and Tom Hostetler and Gabe Glick were standing up as though the topic of conversation had piqued their interest, as well. Rebecca had somehow moved the screen so the bishop's photograph didn't show up. Only the name of his business and those two fine stallions were visible.

"Ya know, Hiram, I had no idea there was such a place as Bishop's Ridge," Naomi remarked.

The bishop stood behind Miriam to look over Rebecca's shoulder. "The English fellow who designed my website thought that would be a catchy advertising hook. We Amish are respected for the horses we breed, you see." Hiram turned as Preacher Tom and Preacher Gabe came into the kitchen. "I could see where your dairy farm might benefit from a website, too, Tom."

"Got all the business I can handle, keepin' up with orders from Central Dairy and the local folks wantin' my fresh milk and cream," Tom replied. "If I advertised like that, I'd have to buy more cows and hire more help. I'd need a new barn, too."

Miriam was barely breathing. Here she stood at her counter, with pie crust rolled out, while the bishop, two preachers, Ben, and Naomi were gathered around Rebecca's computer . . . and it wasn't just curiosity that thrummed among them. Hiram stood very stiffly, as though to keep her and Ben Hooley apart. But Miriam also sensed the bishop was on the defensive about the photograph he didn't want Tom and Gabe to see.

"Well! Now that everyone knows I advertise online like any intelligent businessman," Hiram announced, "we should get out of Miriam's way so she can make her pies! And if you'd put together a peach pie for me, I can pick it up later, Miriam."

Miriam cleared her throat. "*Jah*, I can do that, Hiram."

"And you should consider what Tom has just said," the bishop added, letting his hand rest on her shoulder. "If your bakery gets any busier, because folks all over the world see your website, you, too, might have to expand beyond what we Old Order Amish consider self-supporting. It would be such a disappointment if your business became so commercialized and worldly that you'd have to give it all up when you become a bishop's wife."

Miriam bit her lip to keep from blurting out the answer that popped into her mind.

Rebecca went into a coughing fit and then, as though by magic, the screen shifted. There was Hiram's photograph again, smiling at them all. The preachers inhaled so suddenly, they seemed to suck the air out of the kitchen.

Gabe pointed to the forbidden image on the screen. His finger shook, maybe from age but also from the dismay that was making him go pale. "Hiram." The older preacher stepped away from the group standing around Rebecca's computer, as though he needed to separate himself from what he'd just seen. "Here's another example of what Tom and I were tellin' ya yesterday, about how you've pushed the limits. And now, with this graven image, you've plain and simple crossed the line, Bishop."

Hiram looked ready to knock Rebecca's computer off the countertop. Instead, he became very, very calm.

"No two ways about it," Tom joined in quietly. "Ya just told Miriam all the pitfalls of advertisin' on the computer, and meanwhile you've been lookin' right at the camera— right at the folks you wanna sell your horses and your stud service to. And that's wrong, Hiram. It's just wrong."

Miriam's temples pounded. At the sound of the girls coming to place orders, Naomi excused herself from their gathering. Thank goodness someone was running the café while this very serious matter was being discussed in the kitchen. Rebecca squirmed slightly, but she knew better than to leave that stool. Miriam suspected her English-raised daughter might have hoped for just such a reckoning all along, even before she had come here this morning.

Hiram remained silent, waiting for others to say what they would. Miriam knew this was not the time for her to express her objection to the way their bishop had gone against the age-old rules of the *Ordnung*. He must have thought none of his members would see his photograph because they didn't own computers.

Gabe cleared his throat. "I see no way for you to sidestep the same sort of discipline ya ordered for Miriam a couple months ago, when she confessed at a members' meetin'. And that was just a matter of reunitin' with her daughter, the way any mother would, and makin' a livin' now that Jesse's gone," he added in a voice that shook with anger. "Preachin' will be at the Kanagy place in a couple weeks. If the members say you're to be shunned—"

"Don't be ridiculous," Hiram snapped. "I'll have my webmaster remove the photo—"

"But it's been there for all the world to see. And now we've seen it, too." Ben stepped away from the group, his face somber. "And the *gut* Lord knows what your intentions were when ya stood in front of that camera, Hiram. It's not like ya were puttin' your hand in front of your face, or gettin' snapped by an English tourist who didn't know our ways." His brow clouded over as he controlled his rising anger. "It's mighty hard to respect a bishop who punishes folks for their sins—makes them go through the confessin' and repentin' in public—when he acts as though the *Ordnung* doesn't apply to him, too."

Miriam's heart hammered. Hiram would no doubt retaliate for the way Ben had said that, and for the way her daughter had gotten him in trouble.

Their bishop looked out into the dining area, which seemed awfully quiet considering how many folks were out there eating breakfast. Rachel, Rhoda, and the Brenneman boys, along with Nate and Bram Kanagy, were looking toward the kitchen, wondering what was going on.

"This is not the time or the place for such a discussion," Hiram said to Tom and Gabe. "We'll take it up later in my office. And Miriam," he added, narrowing his eyes, "you should question this man Hooley about his past dealings with other women who have found him . . . irresistible. He has quite a list of them in his wagon." With that, the bishop strode purposefully from the kitchen and out the back door.

He doesn't want to answer to the folks out front. And he's nailin' a checkered past on Ben Hooley, to make himself look better after Ben criticized him, Miriam thought.

Tom Hostetler let out the breath he'd been holding. "So where's that leave us? If the bishop's to be shunned, right before Miriam's girl gets married—"

"We'll talk with the bishops in New Haven and Morning Star," Gabe replied. "It's not Hiram's place to do that, and most likely he'll wiggle out of it if we leave this up to him. And that's a sorry, sorry thing to say about the fella God chose to lead us."

Tom let out a snort. "Seems Hiram left without payin', too. I'll pick up his meal and—"

"You'll do no such thing, Tom." Miriam grabbed a towel to wipe her hands. "I'll go out front and ring you fellas up. I'd appreciate it if you'd let me know about the wedding situation, too—especially if we need another bishop to perform Rachel and Micah's ceremony."

"I'll do that, Miriam." Tom nodded, and he and the older preacher went back through the dining room with her.

She hated it that Hiram had cast suspicion on Ben Hooley's past and what was inside his big traveling wagon . . . but Tom would give her an honest answer. "So . . . do ya suppose Hiram was blowin' smoke about a list of women in Ben's past?" she murmured. "It's not my place to go pokin' around in his private life—although Hiram obviously has. That wagon's his home on the road."

Tom shrugged as he fished out his money. "While I've never known an Amish fella to run the roads the way Ben has, he seems like a truly nice man—sincerely interested in Willow Ridge and in you, Miriam. Only way to know about that list is to ask him, now that Hiram's tossed that idea out in front of everybody."

"Seems you and your English daughter—and now Hooley—have brought on a lot of new situations we've never had to deal with in Willow Ridge," Gabe remarked. His wrinkled face reflected concern, yet perhaps a touch of amusement, as well. "But it was Hiram fannin' the flames when Rebecca came back to ya, and his own fault—not hers—that we've seen his advertisin' now. Sorry this is all landin' in your lap, Miriam. It's easy for everybody—except Hiram—to see that ya want no part of him or his shenanigans."

"Ya got that right, Gabe. Every day I pray that God'll lead me out of this pinch I'm in."

After she totaled up the two preachers' meals, Miriam

returned to the kitchen, hoping her dough wasn't all dried out by now. Bless her, Naomi had rolled the pastry into a ball, wrapped it in a damp towel, and put it in the fridge. It was good to see the way Rebecca was talking so easily with Ben, as it gave her another chance to assess this man she knew so little about.

"Just out of curiosity," he was saying as he looked at Rebecca's computer screen, "is there a way to find out who designed Hiram's website? I'm wonderin' if Hiram could make that photograph disappear before the other bishops hereabouts see it."

Rebecca moved the screen very quickly past that photo of Hiram and more shots of the stables and his horses, to a little note in small print. "I know this guy," she remarked as she pointed to the little wishing well beside the copyright notice. "Tristin Wells does the design work for a lot of businesses in Chillicothe and St. Joe. He'd be the one to take that photograph off the site—unless Hiram's more web savvy than he's letting on."

She smiled ruefully at Miriam then. "Mamma, I didn't come here to cause *you* problems, and if you don't want a website, I'll design one for another place for my class project. The last thing I want is more trouble for you with Hiram."

"Don't you go worryin' about that, honey-bug." Miriam slung her arm around her daughter's shoulder. "Thanks for thinkin' about me and the café, but maybe now's not a *gut* time to do that website. Maybe after Rachel's wedding, when things settle down a bit. I like it that ya asked me first instead of just doin' it, too."

Ben smiled, looking from Miriam to Rebecca. "It was a real pleasure to meet ya, Rebecca. I'd best be gettin' over to the Schrock place for that weldin' work Zeb wants."

Miriam brightened. "Schrocks! Ya could design a website for the quilt shop next door, Rebecca! Those gals are

Mennonites—you know the ones. Ya met them at your birthday party."

As she folded her computer shut, Rebecca grinned. "I like the way you're thinking, Mamma. I'll ask them. And when you feel better about this whole thing, we'll see if Dad wants to put up a website for the two businesses in his building. Hiram couldn't say a thing about that, ain't so?"

Her exaggeration of that Amish phrase made them all chuckle. "I like the way you're thinkin', too, Rebecca." Miriam glanced toward her two other girls as they cleared tables out front. "How about ya come to supper, Rebecca? And you, too, Ben, so we can make our final preparations for the wedding."

"I'd love to come, Mamma! What with my college classes taking so much time, it's been too long since I saw everybody."

"Can we do it tomorrow night? It'd be *gut* to have everybody around the table," Miriam said with a smile for Ben. "And you'll be shoein' our horses one of these days, so it's only fair for me to feed ya."

"I wouldn't miss it. It'll be a real pleasure to be there with your family."

As Ben strode from the kitchen to fetch his hat in the dining room, Rebecca let out a low chuckle. "Now, Mamma, who is that, really?" she teased.

Miriam fetched her pastry dough from the fridge, considering her answer. This daughter had friends who were a little rough around the edges, so Tiffany Oliveri was wiser to the ways of the world than Rachel and Rhoda—and what a blessing, that her Rebecca had gotten past all that black hair dye and heavy makeup, and that she kept her tattoo covered now.

"Ben Hooley blew in with the wind the other day, when a tree limb took out one of the café's front windows,"

Miriam replied, her eyebrows rising. "And it seems he's been whippin' up a storm here in Willow Ridge ever since."

"For sure and for certain he has." Rhoda smiled at Rebecca, a hint of mischief on her lips. "Ben's just the sort of fella I've always wanted to latch on to . . . but when he said he was thirty-five—"

"No way!" Rebecca blurted.

"—I decided to let Mamma have him."

Rebecca's eyes were wide as she considered this information. "Well then, you did me a big favor by telling me, sister, because I was thinking Ben was *my* type. I might have followed him home like a puppy and made a fool of myself."

An expectant silence filled the kitchen—until Rachel started giggling. Once again the laughter they loved to share was contagious. Oh, but Miriam felt relieved that Rhoda was laughing the loudest of them all . . . except it meant her feelings for Ben would be open for discussion, or speculation, from here on out. But she could live with that.

Rebecca snickered, kissing Miriam on the cheek. "You're so cute when you get that kitty-cat grin on your face, Mamma. And Ben Hooley, he's cute *all* the time, ain't so?"

Miriam laughed. She watched Rebecca stop out in the dining room to chat with the strapping young Brenneman and Kanagy brothers before she left. *It's another case of how I have to trust Ya, Lord, to lead me to the things I need to know—and to the truth about Ben—just the way Ya did when we found out about Rebecca bein' alive and raised English. Ya made me a promise, and I know You'll keep it.*

Chapter 14

Later that day, when Ben had finished welding Zeb Schrock's hay baler, he drove past Hiram Knepp's place. The barns looked immaculate, as did the bishop's home, perched on a rise—the "ridge" in the name on his website, no doubt.

He grinned. It seemed pluck, love, and justice ran in the Lantz family, and he couldn't wait to hear the whole story of Rebecca's miraculous return. For a moment though, he slowed Pharaoh for a closer look at the barns, the corrals, and the other outbuildings. From all appearances, Hiram Knepp was the most prosperous man in Willow Ridge—not that there was anything wrong with making a good living from the talents God had given him. It just seemed that Hiram Knepp basked in his own glory more than other bishops he'd met during his travels.

But maybe ya think that because he's after Miriam. And it makes ya mad, the way he treats her—and the way he hints to her about your way with the ladies and your shadowy past.

Ben clapped the reins lightly on his Percheron's broad

black back. Even without his red wagon he was a marked man here because he preferred a different breed of horse than Hiram bred and sold—not that most farmers in Willow Ridge could afford the bishop's purebred champions. Ben clattered down the road and turned onto the blacktop, toward the Sweet Seasons. Miriam should be closing up by now . . .

And as he compared her place to Hiram's, a smile warmed his face. Here, the garden plots took up every available space along the lane and beyond the house, and the bakery and the smithy shone in the afternoon sun. Miriam's apple trees swayed in the breeze as he recalled his walk with her . . . those kisses he'd been so eager for. Ben hoped that whatever had come over Miriam Lantz when he'd heedlessly sat in her husband's chair was behind them now. He prayed for a way to prove that his feelings for her were sincere. And permanent.

Only one way to do that.

Ben pulled in between the café building and the smithy. He unhitched the wagon and tethered Pharaoh to a big sweet gum tree so the horse could graze in the shade. Then, on inspiration, he opened the hinged doors on the back of his wagon. He stepped past his farrier equipment to the chest of drawers where he kept his clothes and belongings, and took out the notebook. Oh, but it galled him to think Hiram Knepp had snooped inside his wagon while he'd been shoeing the bishop's Belgians!

He left the wagon, peeked in through the kitchen's back window, and tapped on the glass when he saw Miriam draping wet towels over a drying rack.

Her smile made his stomach turn somersaults. "Come on in, Ben!" she called.

He opened her door, enveloped by the sweetness of fruit

pies and the lingering aromas of the lunches they'd served. "Still here?" he mused aloud. "What's this make ya, a twelve-hour day? And ya start and end it alone?"

Miriam chuckled. "That's my own choice, ya know. The quiet before and after a day in the café helps me settle myself. And meanwhile my girls are doin' the laundry and reddin' up the house—and cookin' my dinner!" she added happily. "Can't ask for better than that."

Ben spied a pie box on the counter. And, always astute, Miriam read his thoughts. "That's the peach pie Hiram ordered, so we'll leave it be," she remarked as she opened the closest fridge. "But I've got a slice or two left from lunch. Blackberry, there is . . . and cherry . . . and apple with a streusel toppin'."

"Pick one and share it with me."

Miriam's eyes widened. That playful look he loved returned to her face, and for that Ben was grateful. "First, though, have a look at that list of women Hiram was talkin' about. I can understand how that might make ya wonder about me—which was his intention, of course."

Miriam frowned. "So that means he dug around in your wagon while ya were workin' for him?"

Ben nodded, turning to the page of phone numbers he kept in his notebook. "And he's right: it's mostly women's names ya see, because it's mostly women who answer the phone." He ran his finger along the column of names as he read them. "Jerusalem and Nazareth Hooley are those aunts I've told ya about, and below that are my older brothers and their wives—"

"Ben." Miriam stilled his hand with hers. "I don't need to see them. I feel horrible that Hiram's tryin' to dig up dirt on ya when he's got secrets of his own."

Ben gazed into her doe-like brown eyes. It scared him,

how much he wanted this woman to trust him—how much he wanted to make a home with her. She was still vulnerable, still feeling the presence of her husband and maybe missing Jesse Lantz more than she realized. And maybe he would never measure up to Jesse, in Miriam's eyes. "I hope ya didn't feel like I was pushin' that mill idea past ya before—I didn't intend to get ya all upset by sittin' in Jesse's chair, and—"

"And now that I've had a chance to think it through, I'm back to our original plan, Ben." Miriam came toward him with a glass pie pan that held a slice of the apple streusel and a slice of cherry. She plucked two forks from the silverware drawer. "I think we should call Derek Shotwell at the bank and get things started on this end, while ya call to see if your brothers are willin' to pull up stakes to get that mill goin'. If those three fellas think it's a *gut* idea, I'm all for it, Ben. Partly because it means ya might stick around Willow Ridge awhile."

Two somersaults and a handspring his stomach did, while she stuck the pie in a toaster oven. Yet while he was ecstatic that Miriam had worked her way past last night's vision of Jesse, these plans would indeed mean he needed to stick around Willow Ridge. For the first time, he wondered how he would handle that. Would putting down roots be confining, compared to the freer life he was used to?

"That's the idea, *jah*." He sat on the tall stool beside the one Miriam perched on and took the fork she offered. Her face looked damp from working in the steam of the dishwasher, yet this rosiness showed him how she must have looked when she was Rachel and Rhoda's age.

Before he could cut into the apple pie, Miriam sneaked her fork beneath his to section off a large part of its tip. Ben laughed—and then opened his mouth to accept that first big bite from her. "So what did ya think of my Rebecca?" she asked.

"I like her a lot." He chewed that bite of warm pie, closing his eyes over the cinnamon and buttery crumb of the topping . . . sweet-tart apples and a moist crust. "And I'm glad she's come back to ya and wants to be your daughter. Could've happened a lot different, I suspect."

"Oh, she looked like a ghoulie-girl that first day! Witchy-black hair spiked like a porcupine. Black-painted fingernails and little chains between her wrists and her finger rings." Miriam shook her head as she opened her mouth for the bite of cherry pie he'd forked up for her. "She got Hiram and Gabe all stirred up, comin' here—but after her English *mamm* passed, she'd found the little Plain pink dress she was wearin' the day she washed away. She wanted to know where it came from . . . what sort of family she was born into."

She paused to take another bite of pie from Ben's fork. "And then, at the girls' twenty-first birthday party in August, she wanted to dress like Rachel and Rhoda! Oh, it was a sight for this mother's eyes to see my three girls together in their new blue dresses and fresh kapps, so happy to be sisters."

Ben's eyes misted as he listened. He took a bite of cherry from her fork this time, and then cut a bite of the apple for Miriam. What a treat it was to sit so close to her, holding a pie plate between them, talking about things that fulfilled them. It seemed the best form of forgiveness, having Miriam share herself with him again.

"Luke and Ira are that way. Not twins, but they're real close because they came along later than the rest of us," he reflected. "They gave our *mamm* and *dat* fits as they were growin' up, but this chance to start fresh where there's *gut* land will help the folks accept their settlin' so far from home."

"And they'll be with their brother Ben. Who also left home at a young age."

"But none of us left the faith." Ben playfully snatched up the last bite of their pie and held it a little way from Miriam's mouth. "And we never lost faith in followin' our own talents, doin' what we believed was the Lord's work."

She fixed her huge brown eyes on him. "And is it the Lord's work you're doin', teasin' me with that last bite, Ben? Well, I'll have ya know, I don't want it! It's yours."

"Nope. I can tell the cherry's your favorite, so it's yours, perty girl." He leaned in as close as he dared, craving the way her lips would taste right now, all sweet and moist and fruity.

The loud jangle of a phone made them both jump. Miriam laughed and waved it off, saying, "We've got the phone wired so when it rings in the shanty we can hear it in here over the sound of the dishwasher and exhaust fan. Most likely it's—"

"You'd better answer it. Could be orders for ya."

"—Lydia Zook or somebody else wantin' pies, but the message machine'll catch it. Or Eva, next door at the quilt shop, will get it."

Ben nodded, but when the phone stopped ringing and then rang again, their moment of closeness was lost, anyway. "I'll wait at the wagon while ya take that call," he suggested. "After Hiram's remarks today, I thought ya might be curious about my home on wheels but too polite to ask about it."

Miriam hurried out the back door to answer the phone behind the building. Ben ran some water in the pie plate, gazing around the kitchen . . . the world where Miriam and Naomi Brenneman and the Lantz girls had made a new life for themselves after Jesse passed. Good, solid women, they were. Their love for their work showed in every pie, every pancake that got plated here each day.

Ben sighed, pulled in different directions: if he got the itch to move along again, after he settled his brothers into their mill business—or even when he finished his two weeks' worth of work in Willow Ridge—Miriam would have a fine life without him hanging around to complicate it for her.

He ambled out past the shanty toward his wagon. Why now, when he'd run across such a wonderful opportunity to settle down like any good Amish fellow would, was he having doubts about wanting to stay? Ben shook his head. He went to his wagon and sat on the back end of it, waiting for Miriam to finish her call.

Miriam gripped the receiver, closing her eyes as the female voice on the other end chattered on.

". . . so when my bishop, John Knepp, called me to say Ben Hooley was there in Missouri, and gave me this phone number, I—I just wanted to call and say hello!"

"And what did ya say your name was again?" Miriam murmured. She watched out the shanty's window as handsome Ben walked to his wagon.

"Polly Hershberger—Polly Petersheim Hershberger," she replied brightly. "And isn't that somethin', that your bishop's name is Knepp, too? But then, there must be a hundred John Knepps here in Pennsylvania alone, so it's really not such a coincidence, but . . ."

Miriam's head was spinning. Had Hiram really called a bishop—named Knepp—in Lancaster County? And how had he known that Polly was Ben's former fiancée? With Polly talking her ear off, it was difficult to think about such connections, and as she saw the way Ben was looking at her, waiting for her, Miriam's heart felt like it was beating out of rhythm. "So tell me this, Polly," she began, sensing it was an impertinent question, but necessary. "When ya married your husband all those years ago, instead of hitchin' up with Ben Hooley—"

"Oh, that was all Dat's doin', ya know. He insisted Ben wouldn't settle down—would never amount to much on account of how he was travelin' around with his blacksmith work instead of lookin' for land and a house. So he told me I was to marry Homer Hershberger instead."

Miriam blinked. Maybe it was best to play along with this chatty woman who was so free with her talk. "And how did that work out? Ya don't hear so much about arranged marriages nowadays."

Polly sighed. "Homer passed about a year ago—he was quite a lot older than I, ya know. The two daughters who've survived—I lost four little babies over the years—are joinin' the church so's they can get hitched by the end of November. What I'm gonna do in this house all by myself is beyond me—"

"I—I'm sorry about your husband. I've lost mine, too, and it takes some gettin' used to," Miriam replied quietly. Oh, but her heart was beating hard. The rise in Polly's voice could only be leading to one thing.

"So, is Ben still workin' there in Willow Ridge?" she asked. "Sure would like to talk to him—catch up on what-all he's been doin', and whether he's still travelin' around shoein' horses, or—"

"*Jah*, he's still doin' that."

"Would ya tell him I called? Here's my number—got a pencil?"

Miriam pressed her lips together to keep from screaming. "*Jah*," she rasped—but she copied the number, figuring it might come in handy. "Okay, I got it, Polly. I'll tell Ben ya called."

The click on the line ended the call, but it was just the beginning of the race her imagination was about to run—unless she told Ben what had just happened, and watched how he reacted. Hiram Knepp had set this ball to rolling, but his insinuations might well be her saving grace, when it came to answering questions about who Ben Hooley was . . . and what sort of husband material he'd make.

She stepped outside into the bright autumn light. At this time of the afternoon, the sun hit her right in the face, so she had to squint and shield her eyes with her hand. *Wouldn't it be somethin' if, while you're bein' blinded by this light, you really see Ben Hooley for the first time?*

Ben smiled as she approached the back end of his red farrier wagon. "Must've been quite a conversation. *Gut* thing ya answered."

"Polly Petersheim wants ya to call her," Miriam murmured. "I left her number on the scratch pad in the shanty."

Ben's face was a kaleidoscope of emotions. His brow furrowed, and then his eyes widened, and then his jaw dropped, and he looked, well—completely *ferhoodled.* He was swallowing so hard his Adam's apple bobbed above his shirt. "How on God's *gut* Earth did Polly know I was here?" he rasped.

"Best I can tell from that flurry of chatter, Hiram called her bishop. His last name just happens to be Knepp, too."

Ben speared his hand through his light brown hair. He replaced his hat and then stared at something taped on the inside of his wagon door. "Oh, this is gettin' too . . . Bad enough Hiram was in here snoopin' amongst my things, but he had to have read this piece from the paper and made some connections. Look, Miriam, what do ya think?"

Miriam approached, to see a yellowed clipping that had

a photo of a wagon. It was a blue wagon, with HOOLEY'S
HORSESHOE SERVICE on the side, and it was hitched to a
different horse, but it was clearly Ben's business at an
earlier stage of his life.

Ben jabbed a paragraph of the article. "This was written
up in the *Lancaster News* on account of how I was so unusual, travelin' with my trade. Hiram must've read this part
about the district I was from—"

His breath left him in a rush. "Polly's *dat* was the bishop
then. So if Hiram called out there askin' for Bishop Levi
Petersheim, he might've talked to Polly's *mamm*—"

"And gave her my phone number."

Ben's mouth clapped shut. "Miriam," he murmured,
"I'm sorry this is gettin' so twisted around, all because
Hiram got so nosy and—" His arms dropped limply to his
sides. His eyes filled with regret. "I was just a kid when I
was engaged to Polly. It's been a lot of years and miles—"

But Miriam had heard the hopeful tone in Polly's voice.
Maybe Ben was saying he'd left his old fiancée behind, but
the widowed Polly had *not* forgotten about the fellow her
dat wouldn't let her marry.

"—and I was hopin' if ya looked around in my wagon,
you'd understand a little better about the life I live," he went
on in an earnest voice. "And I hope this fluke phone call
won't make ya doubt my intentions about buyin' that land
for my brothers—nor doubt my feelin's for you, either,
Miriam."

Her heart wasn't completely in it, but when Ben pulled
down the little steps so she could climb up, Miram went inside
the wagon. As her eyes adjusted to the dimness, she recognized safety masks, farrier aprons, tool carts, welders, and
other equipment Jesse had used in his shop . . . everything
in its place, and neatly arranged so Ben wouldn't waste time
finding what he needed. As she stepped farther back, she

saw a few shirts hung on hangers . . . more pegs on the walls for hats and galluses, and an old washbasin and pitcher with a small mirror, on a shelf fitted into the wagon's front corner. A hammock hung from hooks in the ceiling.

Ben stepped up behind her and slid a section of the ceiling aside to reveal a small window. "What do ya think? Not as homey as your place, but it's everythin' a fella needs to do his job, wherever he might be."

Miriam was secretly fascinated—impressed—with Ben's tidy little quarters, yet the questions remained. "So . . . if Polly's *dat* made her marry that Hershberger fella because ya weren't likely to settle into a home—"

"The bishop wanted all his girls livin' close by. Some of the older Petersheim girls had had a chance to settle a new community with their husbands, but their *dat* forbade them to go," Ben explained. "Levi suspected they were gonna start up a Beachy Amish town—freer, ya know—or even join up with the Mennonites thereabouts. Bishop Petersheim felt like his religion—his version of the *Ordnung*—was the only true faith."

"Ah. Ruled with a heavy hand, did he?" Miriam asked with a rueful smile. "Guess we know another bishop who likes to have that sort of control, too."

Ben stepped closer to her, beseeching her with his eyes. "That's another reason I didn't want to stay around home," he admitted softly. "I'm as faithful to the Lord as the next fella, but I'm not much for bein' told how to live every little detail of my life. And—like everybody knows—there was just no practical way to buy land when I was that age. So I took off down the road, and I only go back now and again to see my family."

"And will that change this next time?" Miriam felt she might as well ask, since all these difficult questions were popping up now. "Polly's husband passed last year. And if the bishop's name is Knepp now, that means her *dat* has passed, too."

Ben's gaze didn't waver. "Too much water under the bridge—and I'm not in the habit of lookin' back," he replied in a low voice. "I felt at home here the minute I walked into your bakery, Miriam . . . the minute ya helped me in out of the storm and got so worried about Pharaoh kickin' some sense into me."

"And did he? Kick some sense into ya?"

Ben chuckled and framed her face in his hands. "Miriam."

She swallowed hard. In the light from his little ceiling window, Ben's eyes took on a shine and his hair glowed. "*Jah?*"

"I believe Willow Ridge is where I've been drivin' to all along, and I finally got here—to find you. And I believe we can make this work out for the both of us, even if our life looks unconventional to some folks, or downright un-Amish to others," he added with a smile. "We've both done our best life's work by followin' what God put in our hearts instead of listenin' to what other folks told us we should do. Ain't so?"

"*Jah. Jah*, there's that."

"We don't have to hurry this along, Miriam. If ya don't want to sell that land—"

"No. I'm fine with that now. For sure and for certain I am."

Ben's smile widened. "Then let's settle first things first. You can focus on gettin' Rachel married, and I'll get my brothers started in their business. Then we'll decide what happens for you and me. Make sense?"

Miriam smiled in spite of the misgivings that had plagued her during Polly Petersheim's call. Ben made a valid point: now that she'd lived without a husband and had supported herself and her girls, she wasn't one to follow anyone else's rules about how she should practice her faith or live her life. "It does make sense, Ben. Is this what came of Pharaoh kickin' ya, then?"

He looked at her for a moment before opening his pale blue shirt between his galluses. "He left his mark, *jah*."

"Oh, Ben—" Miriam couldn't help touching the dark purple bruise, feeling an edge where he'd bled and a scab had formed. "Ya should've let me put on some—"

"Doctored it myself, with some peroxide and salve," he insisted as he pressed her palm against the injury. "This happens every now and again, as ya know. Occupational hazard."

"*Jah*, I'll never forget how that spooked stallion trampled Jesse," she whispered.

"But if ya look close, you'll see why I think of it as a sign—on account of its shape and location."

Ben lifted her hand. Miriam couldn't help smiling even though the bruise was surely as painful as it was colorful; it was centered on his chest, in the shape of a heart. Ben placed her palm on the wound again, resting his forehead against hers. His pulse beat steadily . . . tamed her own rapid heartbeat into his more controlled rhythm as they stood together for several moments, silent.

Ben sighed and kissed her cheek. "Please be patient with me. No matter how the evidence might pile up while Hiram's diggin' his dirt, I . . . I love you, Miriam."

Miriam closed her eyes. Her thoughts raced ahead in joy even as his words made her more nervous and scared than she'd been in years.

"Don't say that back to me just yet," he added. "I know you're not ready. But I sure hope ya will be someday. Fair enough?"

Miriam blinked back sudden tears. "*Jah*, fair enough, Ben."

They stood there in the silence for several moments,

breathing together . . . just holding each other, with her hand over his heart. Finally she sighed; sooner or later someone was bound to peek inside the wagon.

"It's probably a *gut* time to call Derek in his office, to set up the appraisal and the survey we'll need," she finally suggested. "Would ya like to call your brothers after that?"

"Sounds like a plan, perty girl. And we'll make it work out, too."

Chapter 15

The next afternoon, Miriam wiped down countertops and took time to redd up the fridge as she waited for Derek Shotwell from the bank in New Haven. Once again her pulse quickened as she considered what it meant to sell part of the Lantz land to the Hooley brothers. Jesse's *dat* had farmed here, and Jesse had built his farrier shop before he'd even courted her. Miriam hoped her husband was pleased with the decisions she was making in his absence; it wasn't as though they had sons to pass the land to, and Rachel and Micah would live in the house next door to the one the Brennemans had grown up in. So much history here . . .

"Miriam, good afternoon! It smells awesome in here!" a familiar voice called from the dining room.

She closed the fridge door and greeted Derek Shotwell. "Can I get ya somethin' while we wait for Ben? A fruit muffin, maybe, or a slice of fudge ripple cake?"

The loan officer rubbed his stomach. "Thanks, but I need to weigh in at the doctor's office tomorrow for my physical."

Miriam smiled, glancing out the window to see if Ben's wagon was in sight. "It's *gut* you're takin' care of yourself regular-like. Can't say that about most of the fellas I know."

Derek tilted his head slightly, smiling. "So what's going on with your land along the river, Miriam? No disrespect intended, but I hope it's not Hiram Knepp's idea that you're selling this property."

Miriam laughed. "No, not this time—but *denki* for askin', Derek. I'm doin' this of my own free will, and Hiram doesn't know about it yet . . . but meanwhile, I've got a favor to ask."

"And what would that be? This transaction could change things in Willow Ridge, if your buyer builds a gristmill—especially because land doesn't come up for sale all that often among the Amish."

"*Jah*, but this is a different sort of situation." Miriam looked again to be sure Ben wasn't coming. "I like the idea of bringin' a new business to town, and I . . . I like the fella who asked me about that possibility. But he's from out East, and all I know about him is what he's told me. When ya do your credit checkin' and all those other things that go into drawin' up the papers, I hope you'll let me know if somethin' doesn't seem right to ya. These fellas'll be my close neighbors, after all."

Derek nodded as he made a note on his legal pad. "I can call our bank's affiliates in Pennsylvania. As part of the loan process we do thorough credit checks—although I must say that as a rule, Amish transactions are among the lowest risk we see. You folks don't believe in defaulting on loans, and lots of times you pay them off early."

"*Jah*, my Jesse was that way, and I am, too." She glanced outside, gesturing toward Ben's approaching wagon. "This fella who's goin' to the river with us . . . let's just say he's interested in more than settin' up his brothers with a mill."

"Are you, um, *interested* in the same things Ben is, Miriam?" Derek's smile brightened his face. "Seems to me, any man would be very, very lucky to latch on to you or any of your girls. But if you're asking me to give you my opinion of him—confidentially, of course—before the transaction takes place, I'd be happy to do that."

She clasped her hands, grinning. "*Denki*, Derek! I can't tell ya how glad I am that you and I usually think along the same lines." Miriam went to the door to swing it open for Ben. "Come in and meet Derek Shotwell, Ben! He's a *gut* friend and he watches out for me and my money."

"*Gut* to meet you, Derek. Ben Hooley—and I appreciate your comin' so soon to help us with our mill idea." Ben and Derek shook hands and sized each other up quickly, and when they'd all stepped outside, Miriam locked the café's door.

The stroll to the riverbank was a good opportunity for the two men to discuss particulars of the mill in a way Ben hadn't shared with her—man-to-man but businessman-to-businessman, as well. Miriam listened closely, especially as the two of them spoke about the potential for the mill's profitability and the opportunities for other Willow Ridge residents to benefit. She felt confident that Ben was presenting himself and his brothers honestly—a key point, once Hiram Knepp challenged the loan officer about this transaction. Because the bishop was still peeved that Derek had allowed an English fellow to buy her building, he *would* protest it.

It was also good that Ben and Derek talked about how Willow Ridge's farmers depended upon water from this section of the Missouri River for their livestock. Anyone who used the river's water to operate—as a mill would—affected water quality and availability for everyone downstream, after all.

As they came to the ridge where the rapids were first visible, Derek paused. He stood silently for a moment, taking in the adjoining hayfields and pasturelands that belonged to Tom Hostetler. As the river curved around the back side of her land, it marked the boundary for Leah and Daniel Kanagy's farm, as well.

"What a beautiful place," Derek said, a sense of awe evident in his voice. "Working in an office all day, I forget that some folks have this for scenery instead of a parking lot or the strip mall across the road." He smiled at them both. "And where do you foresee this mill, Ben? Do you have any idea of dimensions, or building costs, or how much Ira and Luke will want to borrow—?"

"Oh, they're puttin' down cash," Ben assured the banker. "They've been savin' up for this opportunity, waitin' for the right place to come along. I knew this would be a *gut* spot as soon as I saw it."

Derek glanced at Miriam, and then back to Ben. "You realize if we're talking about twenty-five acres of bottom land, along with the costs of the survey and the appraisal, that we're tallying up to more than a hundred fifty thousand dollars before you even build the mill."

"My word, that's a chunk of money," Miriam remarked.

"At six-thousand an acre, it's a lot more than Jesse paid for it," Derek agreed. "But the going rate in this area's running between five and six thousand, so I figured you should ask on the high side, Miriam. That way Hiram Knepp can't say you sold it for less than you should have."

Ben nodded. "To a fella from Lancaster County, that sounds like a real bargain, Derek."

The loan officer jotted a few more lines in his notebook. "So how did your brothers make their money? You said they were only around thirty."

"They're already growin' the grains they want to mill here, and they've gotten into organic feeds the last couple of years, too," Ben explained, "so they can bring along their own seed to start some farmers out with. They've marketed these grains to regional mills, but they've always wanted to mill it themselves."

Ben extended his arms, gesturing at the farmland around them. "It could give the farmers in Willow Ridge a real *gut* advantage, bein' among the first to grow these specialty crops in Missouri. And it's a procedure to rotate away from the wheat and corn they've always planted, to replenish their soil."

Derek was nodding, looking at Miriam as he replied. "Sounds to me like your brothers have the know-how to really make a go of it, Ben. I'll call the surveyor and get the appraisal done, and meanwhile, if you and your brothers can present a blueprint of the mill design and a business proposal, we'll be on our way to making this work."

The banker smiled at her then. "Does that sound reasonable to you, Miriam? I know you want to do the right thing with your husband's land, and the right thing for Willow Ridge."

Miriam inhaled deeply. Derek Shotwell seemed genuinely impressed by what he'd heard, so she felt better already about making the gristmill a reality . . . and more confident about Ben, too. "This sounds like the most excitin' thing since—well, since I opened my bakery!" she replied. "I want to ask the girls, though, and we can talk about it tonight when all three of them are together. Ben's gonna join us. You can come, too, if you'd like, Derek."

He extended his hand and she shook it. "My family's expecting me home for soccer games and dinner on the run tonight," he said apologetically. "I sometimes envy you Amish, because your kids aren't involved in so many activities that keep us English parents running the roads."

As they walked back toward Derek's car, Miriam felt a real sense of satisfaction: not only was she moving forward, rethinking the use of Jesse's land, but she had progressed beyond those overwhelming feelings of dismay she'd felt when she'd talked to Polly Hershberger. And after that, Ben had said he loved her. Recalling that moment in his wagon made her flush with a pleasure she hadn't known since she was a girl Rachel's age, preparing to marry Jesse Lantz.

Yet she still needed to be cautious. Things were happening much faster, on the business front as well as the personal side, than was common for Amish folk. Change happened slowly—sometimes not at all—when it came to some aspects of their Old Order life, and the sameness of their faith made a good measuring stick when fellows like Ben Hooley blew in from out of nowhere, claiming to be guided by God.

Such gratifying thoughts changed when they came in sight of the Sweet Seasons. A carriage was parked there, with a familiar figure standing beside it. "Well now, do ya suppose Hiram's somehow gotten wind of this mill proposal?" she asked quietly. "We've not mentioned it to him yet, Derek, so be ready for a burst of bluster."

Indeed, as the three of them came down the lane toward the café, Hiram was watching them with a scowl. "I came by for my pie, Miriam, but the door was locked," he said in a testy voice.

Miriam reminded herself that women were to be respectful and submissive. "We close at two, ya know," she replied sweetly. "And you're always tellin' me I stay too long after hours, ain't so?"

"Good afternoon, Hiram. Good to see you again," Derek said as he offered his hand. "Ready to take your horses to that big sale?"

Ignoring the loan officer's etiquette, the bishop looked from Ben to Derek to Miriam as though he suspected them of conspiring against him. "I load them up tomorrow. My webmaster has passed along several inquiries from prospective buyers, so I'm expecting top dollar for the yearlings and the mares I'm selling. And what might you be discussing with Miriam and our guest, Mr. Hooley?"

Ben took the bait rather than let the banker get caught in the crossfire between him and the bishop. "I've got brothers wantin' to build a mill. We're buyin' a parcel of Lantz land along the river for it, as soon as we get the plans drawn up."

The bishop scowled, gripping his suspenders. "If you think I'll grant you permission to electrify this business—"

"We're usin' water power. Or, if the river runs low, we'll hitch horses to the machinery—as the Amish and other civilizations have done for centuries." Ben reached for his wallet then, turning to Derek. "And here's money for that survey and appraisal you're arrangin'. Will this cover it?"

Miriam's eyes widened. She didn't get a close count, but as Derek spread the bills between his fingers, she was pretty sure that more than fifteen hundred dollars had just changed hands.

"This is more than enough, Ben—"

"And as I told ya, my brothers'll be payin' cash for the land. The Brenneman brothers'll be paid as they buy the lumber and supplies, so the mill will be paid in full by the time they finish."

The color rose in Hiram's face. "You both know better than to transact such business behind my back," he said in a tight voice. "Miriam, you're making a big mistake, allowing men you've never even met to start up a business on land that's been in your husband's family for generations! What are you thinking?"

Miriam assumed the most polite tone she could, considering the sins the bishop had recently committed on the sly. "This is better use of that rocky, thin soil than Jesse ever made of it," she replied quietly. "And if ya believe for one minute that havin' Ben's old girlfriend call me is gonna scare me away from Ben or this sale," she added pointedly, "ya haven't paid much attention to the way my faith—and my God—guide me when I make decisions. Seems we'll have a lot of business to discuss at the members' meetin' when ya come forward to confess, like Tom and Gabe have requested."

Hiram's nostrils flared, but when Derek Shotwell's face registered his concern at this information, the bishop didn't respond to it. His gaze remained on Miriam, as though he were seeking out the next soft spot beneath her spiritual and emotional armor.

"We'll be discussing your lack of respect, as well, Miriam. Some matters are not meant to be discussed before people who don't follow our faith." Hiram cleared his throat stiffly. "Now, if I can have that pie, I'll be going—to discuss this mill proposition with the preachers. Without their consent, you've done a lot of business that will need to be undone—as you're surely aware."

Miriam quickly fetched the boxed pie from her countertop. The talk among the men outside sounded anything but cordial, but it was better than having the bishop follow her in here to impress his dissatisfaction on her personally . . . physically. And at least the subject of the mill had been brought to his attention now, in the presence of the banker who handled Hiram's Belgian business.

As she handed the bishop his box, he nodded curtly. "Hooley, I've advised you to move on after you've completed your farrier work this week," he remarked. "I suspect you're constantly on the road, because every bishop along your path has seen you for the undesirable influence you are—especially among Plain women—and has sent you on your way."

Neither Miriam nor Ben nor Derek replied to that as the bishop got into his carriage. As the *clip-clop! clip-clop!* of his horse's hooves faded in the distance, the banker cleared his throat.

"That man continues to annoy and astonish me." Derek pulled a small form from his notebook and quickly wrote out a receipt for Ben. "We'll keep in touch, of course. If this mill proposition goes sour, rest assured you'll get your money back, Ben. And if that happens . . . and other investors from outside the Plain community wish to build a mill in such a perfect spot," he added with a purposeful smile, "don't be surprised if they want your brothers to manage it."

Miriam grinned. "*Jah*, the Lord has worked in such mysterious ways before, ain't so?" she asked. "*Denki*, Derek. It's a pleasure to work with ya."

As the loan officer drove off in his silver SUV, Ben looked after him. "And what did he mean by that? Derek seems like a trustworthy fella—interested in expandin' Willow Ridge's horizons, which, of course, will make his bank some money in the meantime."

Miriam nodded. "Neither he nor I were expectin' it when my Rebecca's English *dat*, Bob Oliveri, bought the Sweet Seasons buildin' by outbiddin' Hiram. It's just another example of how things work out for the *gut* of them that love the Lord, ain't so?" She smiled up at Ben, pleased with how their meeting had gone, all in all. "Shall we see what the girls have cooked up for dinner? We've got a lot of plans to discuss tonight."

Chapter 16

As Ben sat in the large, cozy kitchen that rang with the Lantz women's laughter, he recalled his *mamm*'s kitchen, where his two sisters had worked every bit as efficiently as Rachel and Rhoda. He realized how much he missed them . . . felt a little sad that he'd left them behind. While Plain folk had welcomed him wherever he went, it wasn't the same as being home.

He shifted in his chair, which he'd taken mostly to stay out of their way. The girls had set places for him and Miriam across the table from theirs, leaving their *dat*'s seat empty, and for that he was grateful. When a red sports car roared up the driveway and Tiffany Oliveri—Miriam's Rebecca—climbed out, Ben felt warm all over. What an excited, noisy welcome this English-raised girl received! She hugged Rachel and Rhoda as though she felt honored to be included in the wedding plans—and in their lives.

"Isn't that a sight to behold?" Miriam murmured as the triplets all chattered at once. "It makes those eighteen years, when we assumed Rebecca had drowned, a reminder of how God works in mysterious, miraculous ways even when we don't have the strength to believe that."

"*Especially* when we can't believe," Ben clarified. He took in the pale yellow walls and modest oak cabinets . . . the pedestal table that had probably belonged to Jesse's parents. "All the more reason to keep the faith, concernin' this mill. Though if your girls object to the idea, I'll not even call my brothers to tell them about this place."

As Miriam removed two beautifully roasted chickens from the oven, he noted deepening lines between her brows, like parentheses.

"That's *not* to say I'll leave ya to keep lookin' for property," he added quietly. "Truth be told, Ira and Luke have been keepin' an eye out, too, and they might've found a place closer to home."

"And if bein' close to home is where they'll be happy, that's the most important thing." Miriam flashed him a grateful smile that made his insides quiver. After the long day in the café, she'd changed to a dress in a shade of lavender that brought out a velvety, roselike freshness to her cheeks. As she turned toward her girls, her sleek profile, mature yet fit, teased at him.

He felt mighty blessed that such a woman as Miriam Lantz would go along with his business plans, as well as his dream of their life together.

"Shall we set everythin' on the table, girls?" she asked after another outburst of their giggling. "We've got lots to talk about besides Rachel's big day."

Rhoda raised an eyebrow as she carried the buttered beets and a yam casserole to the table. "Sounds like things have been simmerin' in places besides the café," she remarked playfully. "And I'm *gut* with that, too, Ben. I didn't mean to come between you and Mamma, or act like my feelin's mattered more than—"

"Honey-bug, it was a natural thing to do," Miriam remarked with a loving smile.

"I'm glad it didn't turn ya against me, when I asked ya to leave the apartment," Ben remarked. "There's another fella out there waitin' to find ya, Rhoda—even if he doesn't know it yet. Sometimes it takes us men a while to figure out who'll make us happy."

"Well, your bishop wasn't any too happy with me when I showed you his website." Rebecca grabbed pot holders to carry the platter of steaming chicken Miriam had cut into pieces.

Miriam glanced at Ben with a subtle smile. "*Jah*, well, Hiram's not been happy with me since long before your *dat* bought the café buildin', Rebecca—and now he's peeved at Ben, too." She shrugged. "I've learned to see the situation for the challenge it is—and to believe God's teachin' me to stand up for what I believe instead of assumin' Hiram's right just because he's the bishop."

Rachel brought a bright yellow gelatin salad from the refrigerator, and a prettily arranged plate of fresh vegetables. "Here's the last of the tomatoes from the garden, and some of our carrots, and celery with peanut butter—and we've stashed so much celery in the root cellar for the wedding! Creamed celery is one of the dishes ya just have to have for the feast, ya see. You're comin', ain't so, Rebecca?"

"I wouldn't miss it!"

"And you, too, Ben?" Rachel grinned at him, alight with a special glow that graced every bride-to-be. "Micah's glad ya happened along to work on that wrought iron railin' for the historical home they're restorin'. He says ya might have another project for him and his brothers to build, too, but he won't tell me about it!"

As they sat down, Ben hoped the girls would see his

brothers' mill as progress rather than a takeover of their family's land. When they bowed their heads to pray, he wanted her wedding plans to be the priority for their dinner-time discussion. "So will the ceremony be here?" he asked as he took some of the yam casserole. "How many do ya think might be comin'?"

"Upwards of a couple hundred, maybe," Rachel replied happily. "Which means we'll be as busy as Leah's bees reddin' up the house for the ceremony and linin' up folks to help with the meal."

"The dinner'll be served in the Brenneman's big shop," Rhoda continued as she helped herself to the chicken. "Those fellas have a *lot* of reddin' up to do. But once they move their big saws and wagons and what-all, we're hopin' we can feed everybody in two sittin's."

Rebecca was listening with wide eyes. "You'll have the wedding here in the house? How on Earth can you seat everyone?"

Miriam and her girls chuckled. "You'll see how all the wall partitions between these downstairs rooms lower to make room for the pew benches—"

"And we'd love it if you'd help us cover the tables and set the places, a couple of days before," Rhoda added. "It's lots more fun when a bunch of us girls do it."

"So, Mamma, are you making all that food? My English mom would've freaked at the thought of so many people cramming into her house—and at having to feed them, too!"

Miriam laughed. "I've helped with many a wedding. And I bake a lot of the local girls' cakes now—but, bless her, Naomi has taken charge of the food. She and the Schrocks from the quilt shop will be cookin' in the Sweet Seasons kitchen. We're closin' the café for the Wednesday before the Thursday of the wedding, and the Friday after," she explained. "Usin' the café's ovens and fridges and dishwashers'll make it easier for all the helpers."

"And we're gettin' sixty-five chickens from Reuben Reihl," Rachel added, her eyes aglow. "He'll have them all butchered and ready to cook—"

"Better him than me," Rebecca remarked with a grimace.

Rhoda laughed. "*Jah*, I'm a lot better at eatin' chickens than killin' them. We've got apples from the orchard set aside to make the applesauce ahead of time. And along with the celery for creamin', Aunt Leah planted us an extra row of potatoes for mashin'."

Rachel was nodding happily, spooning more beets onto her plate. "Mamma's sister—our aunt Deborah—makes wonderful-*gut* breads and jellies, so she's bringin' those when they come in from Jamesport. Mamma's makin' the pies, of course," she added as her grin widened. "But best of all, she's makin' us one of her tall, perty coconut cakes!"

"And it'll be a special privilege, too." Miriam smiled and then focused on Rebecca again. "So ya see how lots of hands will make light work of all that cookin'? And I'm so glad you're wantin' to join us, Rebecca, on account of how many of my Raber family and the Lantzes have heard about ya comin' back to us. They can't wait to see ya again after all these years! Ya weren't even three when ya washed down the river, so they've got a lot of catchin' up to do!"

They ate for a moment and passed the platter of chicken around. Ben closed his eyes over the tender, seasoned meat, once again grateful to be included in this family's meal—and in their future plans. "Sounds like the whole town's been preparin' for your wedding for months now, Rachel. It'll be the biggest day of your life, and I know you and Micah'll be real happy. He's a *gut* fella."

Rachel nodded, but then looked at him and her mother. "What was I hearin' when Hiram and the preachers were back in the kitchen the other day? Somethin' about havin' him confess on the next preachin' Sunday . . . maybe bein' put under the ban just a few days before our wedding?"

Although Ben had plenty of opinions about Hiram's actions of late, he let Miriam answer that one while he savored a bite of sweet, buttery yams that had been layered with apple slices.

"Don't ya worry about that, Rachel. Preacher Tom'll make sure your big day goes on, even if the bishop from New Haven or Morning Star comes to perform the ceremony." Miriam smiled at her daughters, all three of them seated across the table: Rebecca, wearing jeans and a T-shirt, between her Plain sisters in their cape dresses, aprons, and kapps. "He's a *gut* friend and he thinks the world of you girls."

Rhoda grinned. "Do ya suppose he'd make ice cream for the supper that night? Nobody's ice cream tastes like Tom's!"

Miriam's laugh had a sly edge to it. "Maybe I've already asked him about that. If my Rachel gets her cake, my Rhoda should have her favorite treat, too."

Rebecca was following this conversation closely as she ate, fascinated by how this big Amish celebration would take place. "So, do you have a wedding party, and flowers, and music?"

"Well, some of that. For side-sitters—those are the *gut* friends who sit up front with us during the ceremony— we're havin' Rhoda and Aaron Brenneman, and Katie Zook and Bram Kanagy," Rachel explained. "But no bouquets, and no wedding rings. We sing some hymns, on account of how this is a regular church service along with the wedding. But there's no organ or piano, ya know."

"*Jah*, it'll be three hours or more by the time the preachers deliver two sermons and the bishop does the wedding ceremony," Rhoda chimed in. "And what with folks stayin'

after the main meal to visit—on account of so many comin'
from a distance—it's an all-day party."

"And first thing Friday mornin', Micah and I clean it all
up—with help, of course!" Rachel laughed at Rebecca's
amazed expression. "Then, on weekends for the next month
or two, we visit the aunts and uncles and other kin who live
out and around, to collect our wedding presents."

"No honeymoon?" Rebecca looked from Rhoda to Rachel.
"This is a big switch from my friends' destination weddings,
where everybody flies to some exotic beach or an island in
the Caribbean."

Miriam passed Ben the fruit salad. "It's a family gatherin', first and foremost, because to us, family means everythin'," she remarked. Then she shook her head. "Sounds like
a lot more fuss, arrangin' for so many folks to fly off hither
and yon."

"It's expensive, too." Rebecca sighed. "But I've got no
wedding in my future, so I'm glad you want me to come to
your big day, Sister."

"Oh, it wouldn't be the same without ya!" Rachel exclaimed.

"You've got a lot of cousins to meet!" Rhoda added.

Rachel and Rhoda embraced the girl between them . . .
affection such as Ben had rarely seen displayed in his own
family. He reached for Miriam's hand under the table, grat-
ified when she squeezed it. She, too, was visibly affected
by the sight of her three daughters enjoying each other so
much: her eyes softened and she quickly thumbed away
a tear.

"Oh, Mamma, did we upset ya with somethin' we said?"
Rhoda asked, which made all three girls focus on Miriam,
wide-eyed and concerned.

"Puh!" Miriam waved them off, chuckling. "It's such a
wonderful-*gut* thing to see you girls gettin' on so well. But

it'll take some gettin' used to, callin' Rachel Mrs. Brenneman and not havin' her under my roof anymore."

"Which makes me wonder if I should bunk in my wagon after I get back from Lancaster so you and Rhoda can have that apartment, like you'd planned." Ben figured it was a good time to set that matter straight; he didn't intend to inconvenience Miriam—or to intrude upon the newlyweds, either.

Rachel and Rhoda's eyes widened. "You'll be leavin' us?"

"You're not comin' to the wedding?"

Ben chuckled at the way the two sisters responded as one person without missing a beat. "Well, I let a cat out of the bag there, didn't I?" He gazed at Miriam, whose slight nod gave him the go-ahead to reveal his plans for the land along the river. "First off, *jah*, I'll be leavin' but I hope to be back for the wedding. And I'll have my two younger brothers, Ira and Luke, along if you ladies approve of an idea your *mamm* and I have been discussin'."

The girls all looked at each other, their blue eyes alight with speculation.

"Ben's been lookin' at some of our land along the river," Miriam began in a low voice. "Right at the spot where Rebecca got washed away, truth be told. He thinks the rapids would make a fine place to build a new gristmill for specialty grains."

"My brothers have always wanted to start up a mill, but back home there's no property available," Ben continued. He looked at the two girls in matching blue dresses, so much like their mother must have been at that age. "So, if it's all right with you that we buy a parcel of your *dat*'s land, I've been talkin' to Micah about constructin' the mill. Take your time and think about it, because I want ya to believe it's a *gut* idea before I call my brothers. It means you'll have new neighbors right close."

"Does it mean you'll be stayin' in Willow Ridge, too, Ben?" Rhoda's gaze passed between him and her mother, gauging what he might be saying between the lines.

"*Jah*, I see a real *gut* future for my smithin' business here," he replied with a sidelong glance at Miriam. "And maybe a fine future on a more personal level—but I'm not rushin' your *mamm* on that one."

When Miriam looked away to hide a grin, all three girls began to giggle.

"And just so you'll know," Ben continued, still grasping Miriam's hand beneath the table, "we've already managed to irritate Hiram Knepp with this mill idea. He's sayin' he won't allow it, while Derek Shotwell has agreed to work with us on the legal details, handlin' the money so it's all done fair and square."

"So there ya have it," Rachel replied with a firm nod.

"*Jah*, it's history repeatin' itself," Rhoda remarked with a chuckle. "Mamma makes one little plan that wasn't originally Hiram's idea and the bishop pounces like a cat on a mouse."

Seated between her sisters, Rebecca considered what she'd heard. "Does Hiram really have the power to tell you what to do with your land, Mamma? Or to tell Ben he can't bring a new business to Willow Ridge?"

Miriam smiled at her English-raised daughter's astute question. "Bishops have their own way of doin' things, from one district to the next. I see Hiram's attitude as a reaction to the way Ben has already made so many friends here so fast—"

"Especially you, Mamma."

"*Jah*, he doesn't like it one little bit that another fella's lookin' ya over," Rachel declared.

Rachel, Rhoda, and Rebecca all looked thoroughly peeved at this new example of Hiram trying to box up Miriam like a carryout pie and take her home for himself. "Those things aside, nothin' about this mill's gonna happen unless you girls are all right with it," Ben repeated.

As Rachel and Rhoda pondered his request, Rebecca began to smile. "From what I've seen of Willow Ridge, a new mill sounds like an opportunity for other local folks to work there—"

"*Jah*, there's that," Ben confirmed.

"—but it's also a great way for Mamma to expand her bakery menu," she went on, thinking aloud. "Sure, Amish bakeries are known for their pies and sticky buns, but not many of them offer whole grain breads or the healthy alternatives lots of people want these days. If customers can indulge their sweet tooth or eat something that's good for them—or both—you'll have something for everyone. Folks'll come to the Sweet Seasons knowing they'll feel good about whatever they choose."

"Well now, would ya listen to my college daughter! I hadn't even thought of such a thing," Miriam said with an excited grin. "The Sweet Seasons would be a perfect place to sell bags of the mill's whole grain flours and cereals, too. And we could point out which grains we use in our menu items each day."

"That's such a *gut* idea!" Rhoda exclaimed. "Just this week I was thinkin' how, week in and week out, I write the same menu specials on the whiteboard. I like it!

"And ya know what?" she went on, her blue eyes a-sparkle. "The specialty grains would be a *gut* thing to advertise on a website, too. If that's Hiram's way to keep his Belgian business goin', why shouldn't we have one, too, Mamma? It's not like any of us owns a computer or knows how websites work—except Rebecca here," she added emphatically. "So we'd not be goin' against the *Ordnung*. We'd be followin' our bishop's own example. Ain't so?"

"And a mill would be somethin' for people to *see!*" Rachel continued in a voice rising with her excitement. "Think how many folks would visit Willow Ridge, curious about the new mill, and then eat at our café, and see the furniture the Brennemans make, and look at the Schrocks' quilts next door, and shop at Zook's Market. So Ben's brothers need a website for the new mill, too!"

Rebecca was following her sisters' remarks with a dreamlike smile on her face. "The Mill at Willow Ridge," she murmured. "Now *that* has a ring to it. We'll call their flours and cereals *artisan* grains—and Mamma's new recipes will be artisan breads, too. Nowadays they're all the rage in high-end grocery stores. Amish artisan bread . . . now there's a new angle to your product line, Mamma!"

Ben's heart had swelled with every new idea, while Miriam's pulse had accelerated as he kept hold of her hand. "All I needed to get this business off and runnin' was to turn you girls loose with the idea. So it's all right to call Luke and Ira?"

"Oh, *jah!*"

"It sounds wonderful-*gut*, Ben!"

"I'll have those websites mocked up for you by the end of next week," Rebecca said with a nod. Then a grin flickered on her lips. "So, Ben . . . are Luke and Ira single? And do they, um, look anything like *you?*"

Miriam and her girls burst into laughter that rang around the walls of the kitchen, and Ben laughed, too. What a fine feeling, to be included in this family's fun and to know his brothers would be a welcome addition to Willow Ridge. He couldn't wait to get to the phone. He hadn't been this excited about a project since he'd had his special wagon built to carry his smithing business wherever he wanted to go.

And wasn't it God's doing that his travels had brought him *here*?

Ben smiled at the three identical, beaming faces awaiting his answers. "*Jah*, Ira and Luke are single—unless
somebody's caught their fancy since I last talked to them a
couple of weeks ago." He glanced at Miriam, who was still
chuckling. "And as for looks? Well, I'm no expert on what
makes girls gawk at a man, but my brothers have the same
sort of hair . . . faces similar to mine. Twenty-eight and
thirty, they are. They'll always be my pesky little brothers—
more trouble than they're worth, I tell them. But maybe you
girls can change that."

"Now Ben, how can ya think we'd ever try to change a
man?" Miriam teased. "We've been taught to say *jah*—to
submit and obey the fellas who marry us. And we do that,
too. Mostly."

Again the Lantz triplets got the giggles and their *mamm*
chortled right along with them. Ben knew of so many
Amish homes where laughter and displays of affection were
rare . . . where family members stoically bore their burdens as the will of God, without seeking help or confiding
in one another. And while that was one way of living the
Plain faith, he was glad the Lantzes had learned to make
their own way—depending upon each other rather than accepting a man's decisions for their futures. Maybe such notions smacked of New Amish beliefs, or even crossed the
line into Mennonite ideas, yet Ben sensed he would never
meet a more devout, inspired woman than Miriam Lantz.

He eased his hand away from hers. "Shall we have the
evenin' Bible readin' before I call my brothers?" he asked.
"I'd be pleased to read, or just as happy to listen."

"I'll read!" Rhoda popped up from her chair. "I'll decide
which verses while ya clear away the dirty dishes and such."

Rachel rolled her eyes as she began to stack plates. "Sounds
like a *gut* excuse to get outta reddin' up, if ya ask me."

"Puh!" her Plain sister teased. "Ya just wish you'd thought of it first!"

When Ben started to carry the half-empty bowls of food from the table, Miriam stopped him. "Go pick whichever chair in the front room suits ya—won't take us but a few minutes to finish here. And it's *gut* to see Rhoda actin' like her bubbly self again, ain't so? Whatever ya told her must've done the trick."

Ben, too, had noticed Rhoda's improved mood, and as he left the kitchen he considered how best to mention that to her. She sat on the end of the sofa where the lamp lit the dense printing of the big Bible in her lap, and as he eased into the platform rocker across the cozy room from her, she looked up at him.

"It's *gut* to see ya smilin' again, missy," he remarked. "I feel better about bein' here now, knowin' you and your *mamm* won't be at odds because of me."

Rhoda's winsome shrug soothed him. "Mamma and I would've worked it out, one way or the other. I've decided that *jah*, your bein' thirty-five—fourteen years older— might make a difference, down the road. A couple of my friends hitched up with fellas who were older and more established," she explained, "and they found out right quick, even after knowin' the fellas most of their lives, that those old bachelors were used to doin' things *their* way. I wanna be happy when I start up a home, ya know?"

Ben smiled. "Your *mamm* didn't raise any fools, Rhoda. And it's the Lantz *happiness* that makes ya stand apart from most families I know." He leaned back in the old rocker, savoring the way it creaked when he rocked. "A lot of Plain believers get so caught up in avoidin' hell after they die— livin' along a straight and narrow path—that they miss the slice of heaven they've got right here on this Earth."

Rhoda flipped the thin pages of the Bible, then ran her

slender finger along the columns to find just the passage she wanted. As Ben considered his two younger brothers' personalities, he hoped that either Ira or Luke would find Rhoda compatible. Rebecca would be a good catch, too, but it was doubtful she'd give up her computers and schooling to join the Amish Church—and that was fine. Each of the Lantz girls had a strong sense of her own talents and worth, and that seemed so much more appealing than a woman who fit herself into the mold of her husband's expectations and beliefs.

Miriam and her other two girls joined them a few minutes later. Rachel settled on the sofa beside her sister, while Miriam chose the upholstered armchair with the ottoman and Rebecca slipped into the beautiful carved, cane-seated rocking chair beside him. Ben smiled at the way this comfortable room wrapped its arms around them. The glow of the two flickering lamps colored everything with a softness he missed while he traveled in his wagon.

Rhoda cleared her throat. "I picked a Psalm for tonight— one of the first ones Rachel and I set to memory when we were kids. I liked it then because it was about makin' noise," she added with a chuckle, "but while we were at the table laughin' together, the passage came back to me, on account of how joyful we were."

She glanced down at the page, but it was merely a formality; soon they were all saying the words silently as Rhoda recited Psalm 100. "'Make a joyful noise unto the Lord, all ye lands. Serve the Lord with gladness; come before His presence with singin'.'"

And indeed Ben's heart was singing. When he glanced at Miriam, the depth of her soulful brown eyes drew him in until they were mouthing the familiar words to each other. "'Enter into His gates with thanksgivin' and into His courts with praise; be thankful unto Him and bless His name.'"

As they came to the end of the Psalm, with the promise of God's mercy and truth enduring for every one of them, Ben closed his eyes in gratitude. *Surely, Lord, You're tellin' me this is where I belong. But Ya know what a change it'll be for me, settin' down roots . . . and I ask Ya to guide me. I don't want to mislead this fine woman or break her heart.*

"*Denki* for sharin' that, Rhoda," Miriam murmured. "It's *gut* to be reminded of whose sheep we are, and that we're in God's constant care—even when the bishop seems to have his own ideas about how things should be." She smiled at Ben then. "And I'm at peace with Ben's bringin' his brothers here to build a mill. I think your *dat* would've been pleased about puttin' that land to *gut* use, too."

What better benediction did he need? Ben rose from his chair. "I'll give my brother Luke a call before I turn in for the night. Soon as I hear back about their decision, I'll let ya know—and *denki* for a wonderful-*gut* evenin'. It's a blessin' to be included here amongst ya."

Chapter 17

The next week and a half before the wedding sped by for Miriam. She was filling orders for several homecoming events at nearby colleges, so she felt grateful that Naomi, the Schrocks, and Lydia Zook were taking charge of the wedding meal. Ben was finishing the farrier work he'd promised to nearly every family in Willow Ridge, so she didn't see as much of him as before. Had he called Polly Petersheim, or at least taken her phone number? That piece of paper was no longer in the phone shanty.

She felt a little blue when Ben was ready to leave for Pennsylvania, the Saturday before Rachel's wedding. He'd hired a local driver, Englisher Gregg Hatch, to take him back to Lancaster so he could return to Missouri with his brothers and their belongings. Along about two thirty, after the café had closed, Ben slipped into the kitchen with his duffel bag. His smile seemed as hesitant as the one she felt on her own face.

"Sure appreciate you keepin' Pharaoh while I'm away," he murmured. "If it all goes like clockwork, I'll be back with Luke and Ira by Wednesday mornin'. Lookin' forward to the wedding on Thursday, ya know."

Miriam smiled, wiping her hands . . . or was she grabbing her towel to keep from clutching at Ben? "It'll be *gut* to have your brothers here—and to have ya back, Ben," she added quietly. "We'll keep ya in our prayers for a safe journey."

A horn beeped outside as Gregg's van pulled up. When Miriam went to fetch the bakery box she'd set aside for him, Ben was right behind her. He turned her in his arms, kissing her full on the mouth. "I love ya, Miriam," he murmured. "Not even gone yet and already I miss ya. Take care while I'm gone."

He snatched the white box and headed for the door without looking back, as though he felt just as bereft as she did. Miriam waved to Gregg from the café door and then watched the white van disappear down the county blacktop.

When she turned, Mary Schrock was standing in the doorway between their two shops, where the shared restroom was. "So Ben's off to Lancaster, is he? Pretty excitin' to know he'll be back with a whole new family business for Willow Ridge."

"*Jah*," Miriam agreed. She blinked back unexpected tears—chalked them up to the wedding being so close now—and returned to the haven of her kitchen. "Ira and Luke are supposed to have all their seed stock loaded, along with their clothes and everythin' else they're bringin', by the time Ben gets there," she said. "They're gonna put it all in a long livestock trailer so they can bring a few horses, too. I guess their driver's got a big pickup."

"It's quite a move for them, halfway across the country. But then, younger fellas think of that as an adventure." Mary joined her in the kitchen, taking up a towel to dry the few dishes in the drainer. "So where do they figure to live once they get here? If they need rooms, Zeb and I have some to spare."

"They're gonna bunk with Ben above the smithy for

now," Miriam replied. "Rachel's invited Rhoda and me to live at the main house for a while, like maybe that feels more comfortable to her until she and Micah get used to each other."

"That won't take long! They've known each other all their lives."

Miriam smiled. Mary had married her Zeb even before Jesse had brought Miriam to this homeplace as his bride, so her Mennonite friend had long ago forgotten how strange it felt to be living with a man for the first time. "Rachel's mighty close to Rhoda. It'll be different for her, answerin' to Micah's needs instead of havin' her mother and sister to take up where she leaves off," she remarked. "But she'll be workin' here for a while yet. At least until the kids start comin'."

Mary smiled, gazing around the kitchen. "Priscilla and Eva are mighty excited to be helpin' with the wedding dinner. We haven't had one of those in Willow Ridge for a while." Her expression turned speculative. "Of course, they see Ben Hooley comin' and goin' and they predict we'll be havin' another wedding not so long from now," she said with a sparkle in her eye.

Miriam couldn't help smiling. "We'll see about that, won't we?" she hedged. "Ben's got a lot to do, helpin' his brothers set up their new mill—"

"He's awful nice, Miriam. All of us wish ya the best." Mary hung up the tea towel and smiled at her. "If there's anythin' at all we can do—"

"Oh, it's plenty enough that you're pitchin' in on the food and the servin' for us." Miriam waved as Mary went back over to the quilt shop. When the silence of the bakery's kitchen settled over her, however, she immediately wondered how Ben was. Were he and Gregg finding things to

talk about? The drive would take them better than fifteen
hours, all told.

*And why are ya worried about that? Ben can talk to any-
body. What ya really want to know is whether Polly Petersheim is watchin' for him, hopin' he'll take up where they left
off before she married that other fella.*

The phone jangled, making her jump—and wasn't that
silly? Miriam sensed she was making more of Polly's call
than she should. As she stepped out the back door she reminded herself that it was Hiram who'd set that whole ball
of wax to rolling. If he hadn't contacted Polly, she wouldn't
be any the wiser about Ben's working in Missouri now.
Miriam got to the phone just before the message machine
kicked in.

"*Jah*, this is the Sweet Seasons Bakery Café, and this is
Miriam," she said in her usual phone voice. "How can I help
ya today?"

"Well, I'm wonderin' why Ben Hooley hasn't called me
yet. Ya *did* give him my number?" the woman on the phone
demanded.

Miriam closed her eyes, willing herself to remain cool
and detached. "So this is Polly Petersheim, is it?" she asked
quietly.

"Well, *jah!* Who else would it be?"

Oh, but she wanted to blurt a few random female names!
But it was best not to take the bait . . . best to listen and learn
what she could about this woman Ben Hooley had almost
married. "This is my bakery and café," Miriam answered
politely. "I confirm my callers' names out of habit, takin'
orders for caterin' and cakes and what-all. And *jah*, I left
your number for Ben. What he did with it is his business,
ain't so?"

"So is he there? Can I talk to him?"

Miriam scowled. Such a tone this woman had in her

voice today . . . not sounding nearly so chatty or nice-as-pie as she was last week. "No, I'm sorry, ya can't. He's—"

"Tell him I called then, will ya? I'll try him again later." *Click.*

Miriam gaped at the receiver before she hung up. She hadn't figured the mill was a topic of conversation to share with Polly, even before she got so snippy. But she'd almost asked if Hiram Knepp had called her again.

Not that it mattered. Miriam was far more interested in whether Hiram would be confessing his website sins after the church service tomorrow. While it was wrong to hope their bishop would receive the same sort of penance he'd dished out to her, the congregation would have plenty to say about his recent behavior. And she was mentally preparing herself for whatever Hiram Knepp might do now that Ben was headed to Pennsylvania.

Miriam sighed and closed the kitchen door behind her. She needed to hear her girls chattering as they sewed their new blue dresses for next Thursday's wedding. They were also making a matching dress for Rebecca, who wanted to dress Plain for this occasion, even if she wasn't in the wedding party.

On her way up the lane toward the house, Miriam paused in front of the smithy. Ben's wagon was parked beside it, but otherwise it remained the same—at least on the outside—as when Jesse had been alive. Inside, of course, the upstairs was a totally different place . . . a new home and a new beginning for her and Rhoda once Rachel married, and once the Hooley brothers were housed elsewhere.

And isn't it the same for you? Hasn't a change been happenin' inside ya for a while now? Ben Hooley has shown up to take that change farther along. Most everybody thinks he's gut *for ya, so it's best not to worry about what that*

Polly Petersheim wants! God's gonna take care of all the details.

And no matter what happened with Hiram or Ben, she had her family—and she had her faith in Jesus. And for that she was ever so thankful.

Miriam headed toward the house with hope in her heart, ready to rejoice in new blue dresses and the girls who would look so precious and heartbreakingly lovely in them. Now there was a vision for her to get by on until Ben returned!

Sunday morning, as Miriam sat beside her sister Leah, she felt the thrum of curiosity in the women who had packed themselves closely into the pew benches: Would Hiram call a members' meeting? And would he come before them to confess about his photograph on the website, or to admit he'd displayed arrogance that defied the humility called for in the *Ordnung*?

Willow Ridge was a small, tightly woven community, and word had gotten around about what Preacher Tom and Preacher Gabe had seen on Rebecca's computer screen. The question in everyone's heart concerned more than just gossipy anticipation. It was about Hiram Knepp's integrity as their spiritual leader . . . about whether he could admit his mistakes, the same as the rest of them were expected to, and then accept the discipline voted upon by the members.

As Deacon Reihl read the Scripture passage for the day, Miriam shifted on the seat. Had the backless wooden benches become more difficult to sit on because she was getting older? Beside her, Leah muffled a sigh. Larger than Miriam, and more inclined to physical work in her vegetable gardens, Leah Kanagy was no doubt thinking of a dozen other things she'd rather do than listen to Gabe Glick's main sermon. Their eldest preacher was long-winded, and he was getting short of breath to the point they had to sit forward, barely breathing, to hear what he was saying.

"While Reuben has just read us the passage the lectionary sets forth for today," Gabe began, "I wish to depart from that, to better illuminate the most relevant subject of humility . . . the ability to set aside the desires of one's own heart to submit to the public good—and indeed, to submit to God's will rather than our own," he declared. "We Plain folks believe our accomplishments don't deserve attention or praise because all glory goes to God, who created us, and to Jesus, who died to save us."

Everyone in the crowded room sat straighter. Leah and Daniel's house wasn't as large as some of their homes, so even after Daniel and the boys had taken down the partitions between the rooms, the Willow Ridge members sat like sardines in a can turned upright; they could tell what everyone around them was thinking by the way they sucked in air or laughed to themselves—or sighed wearily.

And at this moment, all the adults in the room were focused on Gabe Glick. Because he habitually spoke his mind, they trusted him to name sin for what it was, even when it was their own shortcomings he discussed. The old preacher paused to gaze at them—men on one side and women on the other. Hiram, Tom, and Reuben were sitting on a bench behind him.

"It's in the sixteenth chapter of Proverbs where we learn that pride goes before destruction and a haughty spirit before a fall," he continued, "while in the New Testament, Peter says in the fifth chapter of his first letter, 'yea, all of you be subject one to another and be clothed with humility: for God resisteth the proud and giveth grace to the humble.'"

Miriam glanced at Hiram Knepp. As always, he sat straight and tall, his black hair in contrast to his long beard spangled mostly with silver. He met no one's eye, yet he showed no sign that the preacher might be addressing *his* pride, either.

"Yet it is in the tenth Psalm where we see an even more unsettlin' description of pride, which is equated with wickedness—and I beg your indulgence while I read from the Bible rather than risk leavin' anythin' out."

Eyebrows rose. Preachers were expected to deliver the message prompted only by God's Holy Spirit, without depending upon notes. Yet who could point a finger at Gabe Glick? He was admitting to age and imperfection, rather than succumbing to the same pride he had denounced.

"These thoughts come from verses two through eleven," he went on, his gnarled finger planted on the page. "'The wicked in his pride doth persecute the poor; let them be taken in the devices that they have imagined. For the wicked boasteth of his heart's desire and blesseth the covetous, whom the Lord abhorreth. The wicked through the pride of his countenance, will not seek after God; God is not in all his thoughts.'

"And then we have this image," Preacher Gabe went on, sounding sad and sorry about the task he'd undertaken. "'He sitteth in the lurking places of the villages; in the secret places doth he murder the innocent. His eyes are privily set against the poor. He lieth in wait secretly as a lion in his den; he lieth in wait to catch the poor . . . he croucheth and humbleth himself that the poor may fall . . . He hath said in his heart, God hath forgotten, he hideth his face; he will never see it.'"

Gabe gave the big Bible back to Reuben Reihl, sighing. He looked a hundred years old, like Miriam imagined an Old Testament prophet, delivering a message from God even as he knew the people would not like it—and might not listen. "How well we know the pitfalls of believin' that just this once, we can get away with somethin' wrong and

God won't notice," he went on. "It grieves me to say that one among us closely resembles that lion lyin' in wait, crouchin' to pounce upon those he considers beneath him— condemnin' them for their trespasses while remainin' blind to his own."

Miriam glanced at her sister. Leah looked as wide-eyed as the other women seated around them. Without naming names, Preacher Gabe was calling a spade a spade, saying Hiram Knepp had condemned others while believing his position as bishop set him above the need for confession. Never mind that she could see herself in the role of that "poor" soul being pounced upon.

Gabe went on at great length, asking them to ponder their tendencies to place themselves above punishment— above the law—and to humble themselves by falling on their knees to confess and repent. Miriam wondered how Hiram must feel, being so overtly called upon to submit to the will of God and the People . . .

Yet the bishop showed no sign of discomfort or displeasure. For a moment during the long sermon, Hiram met Miriam's gaze, yet he showed no inclination toward that humility Gabe was expounding upon. After the singing of the final hymn, when Hiram asked the children and nonmembers to leave, it surprised them all that the members' meeting he called was about a totally different topic from what Gabe had preached about.

"A situation that demands our full attention has arisen," the bishop began in a ringing voice, "involving the sale of property along the river, on the Lantz place. I understand Ben Hooley is bringing two of his brothers to Willow Ridge to open a new gristmill. He's had papers drawn up and a survey done, and Sister Miriam has agreed to sell him this land without consulting any of the preachers or me about it."

"I think a mill would benefit every one of us," one of the

men declared. "And after havin' Ben over to my place weldin' a baler and shoein' my horses, I'm pleased such a fella wants to live here."

Miriam and the other women stretched to see who had spoken so boldly. Hiram turned to study the men's side of the room. "Please stand so we know whom to address," he said in an extremely polite voice.

After a few tense moments, Daniel Kanagy—Leah's husband—rose to his feet. He stood a bit taller than the bishop, and his life of farm work had muscled him out and burnished his skin like fine leather. Beside Miriam, Leah murmured, "Oh, I hope he knows what he's lettin' himself in for."

Hiram smiled stiffly. "Several among us have done business with Mr. Hooley; myself included. But until I called to speak with the bishop of his home district near Lancaster County, I was unaware of the sort of person we're inviting among us," he continued in an ominous voice. "Ben has never settled down—keeps his wagon rolling down the road—because he jilted a young woman to whom he was engaged, dishonoring both her family and his own."

Hiram paced a few steps in his confined area between the male and female sides of the crowded room. "Is this the sort of man you want to do business with, my friends? And more importantly—is he a man our sister Miriam should be associating with?" he asked in a rising voice. "Ben might be a fine farrier, but I don't trust him. And I fear for Miriam's soul when she's alone with him."

"Beggin' your pardon, Hiram, but you're pouncin' on Miriam yet again, just like that lion in the Scripture." Of all things, Leah stood up. She clasped her work-worn hands in front of her, nervous, but she didn't waver. "You're the leader God chose for us by the drawin' of the lot, but I'd respect ya a lot more if you'd go down on your knees to admit you've stepped outta line, the same as you decide for the rest of us. And it's time ya stopped houndin' my sister in front of the whole town, too," she added staunchly. "Miriam's made it clear she wants no part of marryin' ya."

Miriam groaned inwardly, yet she was grateful that her sister had stood up for her. It compensated for the way Leah had tattled to Bishop Knepp last summer, when Miriam had gone to meet Bob Oliveri, her daughter Rebecca's English *dat*. Across the room from them, heads nodded while the women's kapps bobbed in agreement.

"Sister Leah, you're changing the subject," Hiram informed her. "We were discussing the sale of Miriam's land—"

"*Jah*, well, Moses thought he could get away with killin' that Egyptian slave driver who was beatin' up on one of his kin, too. Thought nobody saw him—but Pharaoh got word and Moses was banished from the palace." Henry Zook, the storekeeper, stood up a few benches away from Daniel Kanagy. "After that, Moses had to hide out in Midian, keepin' sheep—and *my* concern is for *your* soul, Hiram. Seems to me you're ignorin' your need to confess before God—and ignorin' what most of us think is a *gut* opportunity for expansion here in town."

Then, lo and behold, Henry's wife, Lydia, stood up a row in front of Miriam. "King David wanted Bathsheba for his wife, too, so he sent her husband to the front lines of battle, knowin' he'd be killed," she began in a nervous voice. "But God took David down a peg or two later on, for behavin' like he knew it all and didn't need to listen to his Lord. How come you're not willin' to confess like the rest of us, Hiram? Are ya better than we are, just because ya raise those fancy Belgians and ya can't be voted out of your position?"

The roomful of people got deathly quiet. What an unprecedented situation it was, when two bold couples stood

together to denounce Hiram Knepp. Miriam closed her
eyes, praying that this matter would come to a positive solution before Ben returned from Pennsylvania. Why would
Ira and Luke Hooley want to stay in a place that was in such
an uproar over their mill, before folks had even met them?

"Ah, but I have indeed confessed to Bishop Shetler of
Morning Star and to Bishop Mullet of New Haven." Hiram
pressed his palms together, the vision of a man about to
pray. "I admitted my guilt to those in a position to hear and
accept my plea for forgiveness. The offending photograph
on my website has been removed, and I'm sorry those of
you who saw it—"

"*Jah*, see there? Just like the fella in the Scripture, ya figured nobody would know any better about that picture."
Preacher Tom stood up then, and Gabe rose beside him.
"Gabe and I, in your best interest, asked you to show some
contrition. Callin' a members' meetin' to point a finger at
Ben Hooley's long-ago past and to shut him down without
lettin' us have our say about it—now that's a horse of a different color altogether."

Tom shook his head as he gazed out over the gathering.
"For all we know, Ben confessed and was forgiven for
breakin' his promise to that gal so long ago—if indeed that's
the way it happened. We can't judge him, because we
weren't there."

Again the room went silent. Hiram Knepp's face furrowed as he looked at the two preachers and the two couples
who still stood, challenging him. Miriam's insides felt un-
bearably tight. When the bishop glared at her, she sensed
Hiram believed she had rallied her friends in Ben's best
interest, circumventing his authority. And she knew, too,
that he still intended to marry her—was perhaps even
more determined now that a younger fellow had shown an
interest in her.

After what seemed an eternity, during which no one moved or spoke, Hiram let out a disgusted sigh. "All right then, we shall vote upon the matter of Ben Hooley and his brothers opening a mill on the river," he proposed tersely. "And should time prove me correct—should misfortune occur in Willow Ridge because we invited this family into our midst—we shall remember this day when we ignored the counsel of one who tried to steer us away from consequences we'll regret."

He turned to Mahlon Zook, Henry's father, who sat on the end of the front pew with the church's oldest members. "The vote will be aye or nay, in favor of the mill or against it," the bishop stated. "As always, we strive for unanimity so the will of the People shall prevail."

"Aye," Mahlon said.

"Aye," stated Wilbert Reihl beside him.

And on it went, until all the men had voted in favor of the new mill.

Hiram's face remained a stern mask as he turned to the women's side. Leah and Lydia had sat down, but their speeches had inspired confidence among their sisters in the faith. Never in any of their lifetimes had members so openly challenged a bishop's leadership, yet when the eldest— Daniel's mother, Essie Kanagy—said aye, the room rang with her conviction. And down the rows it went. Miriam grasped her sister's hand in triumph as the vote proceeded to the back of the room where the youngest members sat.

This time the silence that followed felt entirely different; the People had spoken, unanimously, and only the bishop had taken a negative stance. Hiram quickly ended the meeting with a prayer.

The October day had a chill to it, so the men set up long tables for the common meal indoors, using the pew benches as seats. They chattered excitedly as they discussed the potential a new mill offered to each of them.

In the kitchen, the women bustled about unwrapping the pies and other dishes they'd prepared beforehand to go with the platters of ham Leah had prepared. Miriam had fried several chickens in the café on Saturday, for cooking on the Sabbath was forbidden.

And oh, the quiet comments from her friends as they put out the place settings and poured water into the glasses.

"Such a nice fella, Ben Hooley is," Reuben's wife, Esther, remarked. "A real pleasure it was to talk with him while he ate his dinner at our place last week. And he spoke so well of *you*, Miriam."

"*Jah*, it'll be *gut* havin' another family here and another business," Hannah Brenneman joined in. She was Naomi's youngest, and she'd taken over most of the household chores for her mother. "And it can only be *gut* if Ben's brothers are hardworkin' and lookin' to start families, ain't so?"

"Been needin' some new blood for a long time now," Gabe Glick's granddaughter Millie agreed. "Seems like all the older kids have married and moved down the road to Morning Star or—"

"But with Rachel marryin' Micah next week, that'll start a whole new generation here," Rhoda pointed out.

That inspired a flurry of conversation about the wedding details, and Miriam's heart swelled. She felt blessed to be living among families who had supported her in her darkest days after Jesse had passed. Her parents were long gone and her older sisters and brothers had scattered to Plain settlements in Bowling Green and Jamesport.

"So are ya ready for the big day? Thursday's not far off," someone behind her asked.

Miriam turned to smile at Annie Mae Knepp, the

bishop's oldest daughter still living at home. She had a harried look about her, as usual, yet she was making an effort at conversation among older women who had outvoted her father's wishes. "I've got the cake to make yet," Miriam replied, "but otherwise we've made progress on the cleanin' and preparin' at the house."

"*Jah*, there's always that," Annie Mae replied with a shake of her head. "At our house, I no sooner get one chore done—the floors scrubbed, say—when in come the twins, trackin' mud from the creek bed, or—"

As though her brothers had known they were the topic of conversation, Josh and Joey Knepp came racing through the front room, down the narrow aisles between the tables, in hot pursuit of little Sara. Fifteen-year-old Nellie, holding toddler Timmy against her hip, tried to corral the twins as Sara gleefully ran behind Annie Mae's skirt, grabbing her knees and laughing at the ruckus she'd started.

Then it was Hiram entering the kitchen, his expression stormy as he looked at his two older daughters. "Time and again I've told you to take better charge over the twins and Sara," he warned in a tight voice. "Where else will they learn proper behavior if not from you?"

The kitchen got quiet. Every woman there had an answer to the bishop's question, but none of them expressed it.

Miriam said a quick prayer for Nellie and Annie Mae, who surely missed their *mamm*—and probably even missed Linda, Hiram's second wife and the mother of the four youngest Knepps—whenever their *dat* scolded them this way.

As they carried the last of the food to the tables, Naomi Brenneman stepped up to the bishop. "It's none of my business, maybe, but Linda told us—more than once—that her doctor insisted she should be havin' no more babies or it would do her in," she murmured.

Although they were startled that Naomi dared to bring up this subject, the women around her nodded.

"Yet ya refused to go along with that, Bishop," Naomi went on in a trembling voice. "So now the twins and Sara and Timmy are runnin' wild because their *mamm*, Linda, died of complications birthin' a stillborn—"

"You're right. That's none of your business." Hiram's dark eyes bored into Naomi's until she looked away, mumbling an apology. He scattered the rest of the onlookers with a disapproving gaze. As he approached Miriam, it was obvious he'd had enough of folks finding fault with him.

"The longer you defy my intention to marry you, Miriam, the higher the price we'll all pay for your obstinance," he murmured tersely. "While your friends might voice their support, you have forgotten the Scripture Gabe read from Peter, who tells us to be accountable to one another, clothed in humility . . . living honorably in marriage, as God intended. This won't happen if you encourage the attentions of Ben Hooley."

Miriam clutched her platter of chicken to keep from dropping it. "I'm leavin' it up to God, as far as what's honorable and what He'd have me do with the rest of my life."

She sensed the sympathy of the women around her . . . felt Rachel and Rhoda—and even Annie Mae and Nellie Knepp—supporting her in their silent witness. So she dared to pick one more bone with the bishop. "I'd appreciate it, Hiram, if ya wouldn't call Ben's former fiancée out in Lancaster anymore," she said quietly. "You've got Polly all stirred up—hopin' Ben'll come back to her now that her husband has passed—the man her *dat*, the bishop back then, made her marry. It's not one bit honorable, the way you're twistin' the facts to suit your purpose. And my answer is still *no*."

Miriam stepped around him with her platter while Leah, as the hostess, informed the men that the meal was ready. Was it her imagination, or did Naomi and her daughter Hannah—and even Annie Mae and Nellie—move in around her as they headed to the tables to sit down? Once again, Miriam was ever so grateful for her friends and their daughters.

And once again, Miriam wondered how Ben was doing. She prayed that he and his brothers and aunts would get an early start to Missouri tomorrow morning—and prayed she could hang on until Wednesday when they were to arrive. With Hiram in such a foul mood, it was anyone's guess how he'd behave come Thursday, at Rachel and Micah's wedding.

"Oh, but the bishop irritates me!" Rachel muttered as she stepped outside with Micah after the common meal. She felt so fired up she didn't bother to grab her shawl or bonnet. "The way he's been badgerin' Mamma about marryin' him has gone beyond embarrassin'. What if he acts this way at the wedding? What if he—"

Micah kissed her, trying to settle her down. Then he slipped an arm around her waist, steering her toward the dozens of carriages that were parked off to the side of Aunt Leah and Uncle Daniel's long lane. "Rache, that's a whole 'nother ball of wax," he remarked in his low, unruffled voice. "And I suspect the other preachers'll be watchin' Hiram pretty close, now that so many folks have pointed out his refusal to confess."

"*Jah*, but what if he keeps after Mamma in front of all our kin and the friends who're comin' from far away?" she continued in a rising voice. "Seems like we Lantzes can't make a move lately but what the bishop doesn't aim Sunday mornin's Scripture at us like an arrow."

Micah laughed quietly. "Far as I can see, he's only pointin' up how you girls and your mamm are standin' strong. Every time he throws up a barrier—like tryin' to buy the café, or sayin' ya shouldn't be sellin' land to the Hooleys—you gals find a way to get past his bluster and do the right thing. Folks all over Willow Ridge are cheerin' ya on, too."

They strode past the corral, where dozens of horses pricked up their ears. Once they were behind the cattle barn, Rachel threw up her hands. "Micah, you just don't get it!" she blurted. "Our wedding's the biggest day of our lives. Years from now, I don't want to recall how Bishop Knepp ruined it by making a spectacle of Mamma yet again. If someone doesn't—"

Micah took her face between his large hands, which were callused from his carpentry work yet ever so tender. "Years from now," he repeated in a low, purposeful voice, "you and I are gonna look back on our wedding as the start of a wonderful-*gut* life together, Rachel. We'll gather our kids around the table every day and give thanks for all the things God's blessed us with, and by then Hiram Knepp's carryin' on'll be somethin' to laugh about."

Rachel stared up at him, ready to protest yet again . . . but Micah's deep green eyes held her captive. "*Jah*, but—"

"No buts, Rache. No more what-ifs or gettin' all upset, makin' up problems where they don't exist." He leaned down to kiss her softly, once . . . twice . . . until she couldn't help but kiss him back. The tension she'd felt all morning eased from between her shoulders.

"Seems to me," Micah went on as he pulled her close to shelter her from the chilly breeze, "that your *mamm*'s got Ben watchin' out for her—not to mention his two aunts and his brothers. And the way your Uncle Daniel and Aunt Leah, and the Zooks, and Preacher Tom stood up to Hiram today tells me you Lantzes have nothin' to fear. It'll all work out."

Rachel stood quietly, letting the calm conviction of Micah's words settle her troubled heart. Maybe she *had* been making a mountain out of a molehill . . . again.

"*You* have nothin' to be afraid of, either, Rachel," he continued quietly. "What with your sisters close by, you'll never lack for love or company. And then there's me. Don't think for a minute that I'll let the bishop interfere with a marriage—a family—that's come about as part of God's own plan. Ya believe that about us, don't ya?"

She swallowed hard, still caught up in Micah's unwavering gaze. With his strong arms around her and such intense devotion shining in his eyes, how could she harbor any doubts? "*Jah*, I do believe that," she murmured. His heart beat steadily beneath her head when she laid it on his chest. "There's never been anybody else for me, Micah. I'm mighty lucky that you can see past my frettin' and stewin', ain't so?"

His chuckle rumbled in his chest. "*Jah*, you're one lucky woman, all right," he replied lightly. "And I intend to remind ya of that every chance I get. We've been blessed with each other, so how can Hiram or anybody else spoil a single hour of our life together? We just won't let them."

We just won't let them. Rachel smiled, enveloped in Micah's warmth and strength. If this fine man was for her, who could possibly be against her? *And Lord, if You'll remind me of that, too, I'll do my very best to hand my worries over to You. Thanks for bein' willin' to take them.*

Chapter 18

"Well, Brother, there's not much we can do until help gets here," Ben said with a sigh. "We didn't figure on pickin' up nails in two of the trailer tires."

He slapped his hat against his thigh. Never mind that he'd planned to be back in Willow Ridge by now; it was Wednesday morning and they were only halfway across Illinois. One delay had followed another, and as they waited alongside the highway for the service truck that would bring those new tires, Ben wondered if Miriam was doubting him . . . thinking he wasn't dependable, or that he might not stick around once he got his brothers to their new property.

"Might be a *gut* time for a bite of lunch," Aunt Nazareth suggested. She and Aunt Jerusalem had been riding in Gregg Hatch's van while Ben had shared the extended cab of the pickup that hauled Ira, Luke, and their belongings. "I'll fetch the cooler, Sister, if you'll get out the plates and what-all from the picnic basket. Sure glad we thought to pack extra food for this trip."

Ben smiled ruefully as the two aunts disappeared behind the van. The *maidel* sisters got testy when long hours on the road made their legs stiff, so their little caravan had stopped more often than he'd figured on. Add to that their late start because Polly Petersheim had arrived just as they were ready to pull out—and Polly had always been one to chatter on and on. Ted Murray's pickup drank a lot of fuel while hauling the overloaded horse trailer, so stops for gas had cost them time, too. They'd spent Monday and Tuesday nights at Amish homes where he'd done farrier work in the past, because his brothers' horses needed time out of the trailer to eat and walk around. He knew with a sinking certainty they wouldn't make it back to Miriam's in time for the wedding tomorrow . . .

Ted, their English driver, was talking on a cell phone, so when his conversation ended, Ben asked if he could make a call. He had never used such a fancy phone, so Ted punched in the number Ben hoped he remembered correctly from the Sweet Seasons menu. He got the answering machine and closed his eyes as Miriam's businesslike phone voice told him to leave a message for her café or the quilt shop.

"Miriam, it's Ben," he murmured, wishing this call could be more private, "and we're runnin' way behind—waitin' for two new trailer tires out in the middle of Illinois. I sure hope to make the wedding, but if we don't"—he paused, picturing the disappointment on her sweet face—"I'm sorry. Nothin's goin' right and I wish ya were here with me. Believe the best, all right? Because ya deserve the best, Miriam, and that's who I intend to be for ya."

As he handed the tiny phone back to Ted, they spotted the red tow truck from a tire place they'd passed about twenty minutes ago. *A day late and several dollars short*, he thought as he considered what this stop would cost. Was God telling them this mill in Missouri was a bad idea? Or was the Lord strengthening his younger brothers for the adjustments they faced now that they'd left the only home they'd ever known? One thing was clear: Hiram Knepp would not welcome Luke and Ira to Willow Ridge with open arms, if only because they were Ben's brothers. The bishop would fight the establishment of their mill every step of the way, unless other folks prevailed against his wishes—

Or kept him too busy to be a bother.

"*Denki*," Ben said as Aunt Nazareth handed him a thick ham sandwich. When his other aunt stepped inside the horse trailer with big bottles of milk, loud bleating and the *trip-trap, trip-trap* of restless little hooves made him smile for the first time that morning. Jerusalem Hooley was on a mission, so Hiram had better watch out!

Thursday morning dawned bright and crisp, the perfect October day for a wedding—except that Ben and his brothers weren't here. Miriam gazed toward the road yet again, even though she knew they wouldn't be arriving this early. Ben's voice on the message machine had sounded every bit as forlorn as she had been feeling in his absence, so she told herself to have faith.

Believe the best.

Ben had said they would get here as soon as they could, and he was as good as his word. It would take more than Polly Petersheim's calls and Hiram Knepp's harassment to convince her Ben Hooley was stuck on his old girlfriend or playing on Miriam's affections to get land for his brothers' mill.

Already lights were on in the Sweet Seasons kitchen, where Naomi would be baking the "roast"—chickens baked with stuffing—and peeling the potatoes with Mary, Eva, and Priscilla Schrock. What would she do without such fine friends? Her two brothers, her sister, and their families had arrived yesterday, as well, so the house was noisier and livelier than it had been in years. Rachel's wedding was the first gathering they'd had since Jesse's funeral, and Miriam felt grateful to have family here with her for a joyful occasion this time.

Miriam grinned when a bright red sports car pulled off the road and came toward the house. Who wouldn't feel wonderful-*gut* at the sight of the daughter she'd feared was dead for eighteen years, now coming up the porch steps with a smile brighter than the sun?

"*Gut* mornin' to ya, honey-bunch!" Miriam said as Rebecca hugged her close. "Are ya ready for the big day? You're up before the chickens this mornin'."

"Hi, Mamma! What with uncles, aunts, and cousins here, I wanted to show you what I've drafted—real quick, before things get too busy." Rebecca opened her computer on the kitchen table and made pictures appear on its screen.

"Why, that's the front of the café!" Miriam said eagerly. "And *jah*, there's our menu. I like the way ya put that steam table alongside the words. And—oh my."

After Rebecca tapped a few computer keys, Miriam was gazing at a view of the Missouri River and its rapids, but instead of the grassy banks there stood a quaint wooden mill with a big wheel that slowly turned as the water drove it. Above it all, THE MILL AT WILLOW RIDGE was written in artistic green and rust lettering. "Rebecca, that's quite a sight," Miriam breathed, "but how'd ya know what the Hooleys' mill will look like? And how'd ya get the buildin' in the picture when it hasn't been constructed yet?"

Rebecca smiled sweetly; creating such wonders was second nature to her. "When I asked Micah, he said the plans resemble most classic mills, so I dropped in this image. Once the mill's built, I'll use a for-real photograph."

"Ah. Computer magic."

"*Jah*, that's it." Rebecca closed the laptop and tucked it

into her backpack. "And just so you know, the bishop's webmaster has taken Hiram's photograph off his website."

"Glad to hear it. At least he did what he was supposed to on that account."

Rebecca's eyebrow rose. "Has he been pestering you again? Or has he said Ben's brothers couldn't build their mill?"

Miriam poured Rebecca the first cup from a fresh pot of coffee. "Lo and behold, on Sunday all the members voted in favor of bringin' in the new business, so Hiram had to go along with them," she recounted. "I was mighty surprised at how outspoken folks got after Gabe Glick preached a sermon on the consequences of doin' what ya please rather than listenin' to God and actin' toward the higher *gut* for everyone involved."

"Bet Hiram wasn't too happy about that." Rebecca sipped her coffee and broke off a chunk of apple coffee cake from the tray on the kitchen counter. "Mmmm! Mamma, ya make the best goodies on this Earth, you know it?"

And wasn't it a fine thing that this child, raised by other parents, seemed so at home in her kitchen? Miriam hugged her close. "Let's don't let talk of the bishop spoil our day. Rachel's been waitin' a long time to be Micah's bride—and I hear feet hittin' the floor upstairs. Shall we go see your sisters?"

Miriam put two more mugs of coffee on her tray and preceded Rebecca past the rows of wooden pew benches that filled most of the house's main level. Up the stairs they went, to the adjoining bedrooms Rachel and Rhoda had slept in all their lives . . . but that would change today.

Last week she and the girls had painted the bigger bedroom farthest down the hall for Rachel and Micah . . . and what a bittersweet day that had been, preparing for Rachel to become the woman of this house. Micah had handcrafted a beautiful walnut bed, two nightstands, and a dresser as his wedding present to her. Miriam had completed the top of the Dresden Plate quilt she'd been piecing together these past several months, and now that Eva and Priscilla Schrock had hand-quilted it, the new coverlet graced the bed. So the room, simple yet beautiful, awaited the newlyweds.

Rhoda had redded up one of the other rooms in preparation for Ben's aunts, too. And right now Miriam's sister Deborah and her husband, Wilmer, slept there; her sister Lovinia and her husband, Mose, had a room; her sister Mattie and her husband, Paul, had a room; and all the cousins were bunking over at Leah's house. Miriam had kept the room she'd shared with Jesse, so at least that hadn't changed.

"So Ben hasn't made it back with his brothers?"

Miriam came out of her woolgathering, smiling at the playful tone of Rebecca's question. "He called to say they were havin' one problem after another—nails in trailer tires and such," she replied. "But he'll get here today, whenever he can. Probably not for the wedding ceremony, though."

"I bet he's disappointed about that. Like you are."

When Rebecca slipped an arm around her shoulders, Miriam forgot her fretting over Ben. Weren't there plenty of reasons to rejoice on this day? And her daughters were the three best ones.

Miriam poked her head into Rachel's room and then laughed. The bed was a mess and two nightgowns lay on the plank floor, but the bride had put on her new royal-blue dress and crisp white apron, eager to wear the special clothing she and Rhoda had made a few weeks ago.

"*Gut* mornin', Mamma! And Rebecca, too!" Rachel chirped as she tied her new black high-top shoes. "And ya brought up breakfast? Now this *is* a big day!"

Rhoda came in from the bathroom then, wearing a dress and apron identical to Rachel's. "*Jah*, we're all up before the sun, ready to shine with our own light! Batteries not included—or needed!" With a wide grin, she handed Rebecca her blue dress. "We'll help ya pin that on, and pin your hair back for ya, if ya want."

"Let's see how I do," Rebecca replied.

Miriam slipped into her own room to put on the new magenta dress the girls had made for her. How blessed she was that her daughters were talented in so many ways; so generous and loving. After she pinned the front of the dress, she fastened her V-shaped cape at the small of her back and brought its two halves over her shoulders to pin them at her waist. Her black cape and apron signified that she'd reached forty; no longer a sign that she was in mourning for Jesse, although more than once this past week she'd wished her husband were here to watch this important rite of passage for their dear daughter.

As she reached for her brush, Miriam wondered if Ben would mind the silvery strands mixed into the dark brown hair that fell past her hips—or was it inappropriate to think about him in this bedroom she'd shared with Jesse? She quickly wound her hair into a bun, pinned it into place, and put on a fresh white kapp. No sense in letting her thoughts stray, as this day would require her most focused thinking; she had to get through all the details of church and the big dinner afterwards, with upwards of two hundred family members and friends coming.

When she returned to Rachel's room, Rebecca stood between her sisters, allowing them to pin the Plain dress. Over her shoulders went the blue cape . . . then the white apron, which Rachel pinned in the back. Rebecca wore no makeup today, out of respect for her family, and when her white kapp covered her shorter hair, she turned around.

Oh, Jesse, what you're missin' right now, Miriam thought as she blinked back tears. The triplets linked elbows, and when Rachel and Rhoda extended their arms to her, Miriam stepped into that warm, sweet circle they'd shared far more often since the man of the Lantz family had passed. Miriam knew it wasn't this way in most Plain families, even where the mother and her daughters were close. But today more than ever she craved this physical sign of love and . . . belonging. Where would any one of them be without the other?

Rachel's eyes were shining, crystal blue. "Family . . . *fer gut* and forever—no matter how the names may change," she murmured.

"Family, *fer gut* and forever," they all repeated, huddling until their foreheads met. For a shimmering moment the world around them went still. The people they would see and the food they would serve didn't exist: it was the four of them, as solid as the posts on the walnut bed Micah had made, standing to celebrate their love before Rachel entered into another kind of life altogether—knowing that even then, they would have each other. Always.

"Well now," Miriam whispered. "Everybody'll be up soon. Let's go downstairs to help your cousins with their breakfast and be ready to meet who-all's comin'. And let's promise each other that no matter what the bishop might do or say, this is *your* day, Rachel. And we'll all remember it with the special love we're feelin' right now, in these quiet moments in this fine old house."

As Ted's pickup rounded the curve on the county highway, Ben's heart thrummed: the Sweet Seasons, the smithy, and the big white home back off the road were such a welcome sight! He leaned forward, gazing eagerly at a place he hadn't realized he'd missed so much these past few days. Although a sign that said CLOSED FOR RACHEL & MICAH'S

WEDDING was across the front door, folks bustled in the kitchen as they prepared the feast.

Their driver, too, was gawking. "Wow, judging from all the carriages and tipped-up buggies, there must be a hundred people here!"

"Closer to two hundred, if all of Miriam and Jesse Lantz's kin made it." Ben and his brothers stepped out of the truck, happy to be on solid ground . . . and in the place they'd soon be calling home. They smoothed the black trousers and vests they'd put on early this morning to be properly dressed for the day. "That's the final hymn of the wedding comin' from the house, but we're in time to eat. You and Gregg are welcome to join us," he offered. "There'll be plenty of food, and it'll be the best stuff ya ever put in your mouths."

Gregg came over from his van, followed by Aunt Nazareth and Aunt Jerusalem. "That's the last hymn they're singin'," Nazareth confirmed with a nod. "But we got here in time to help with the dinner, anyway."

"It'll be in that woodworkin' shop over there," Ben said, gesturing to the large metal building on the next spread. "That's where Micah Brenneman'll be workin' on the mill for ya, and his family lives in that house up the way. His *mamm*, Naomi, cooks with Miriam in her café and she's in charge of the food today," he explained. "No doubt they've been hard at it since before the sun even thought of comin' up, usin' the café kitchen's ovens and dishwasher and what-all."

"How nice that the two families live so close." Aunt Nazareth gazed around, taking in Miriam's extensive plowed gardens, the orchard, and the distant trees growing along the river. "What a lovely place! As green as Pennsylvania, but a little more rugged."

"Not every inch of it cultivated or given over to shops," Aunt Jerusalem remarked with a decisive nod. "I can see why Bennie thinks it's gonna be just the right place for a mill."

"*Jah*, I'm likin' the looks of it, too." Luke stretched wearily, yet his smile was wide as he retucked his white shirt. "Ira, we just made it to the promised land, buddy! How about you settle up with Ted while I tether the horses? Best to get the livestock watered before folks come out from the service."

Ben nodded, relieved that everyone felt the same immediate liking for this place that he had. As they'd crossed through central Missouri, his brothers had admired the gentle roll of the hills and the farmsteads sprinkled with cattle, silos, and modest homes. If they could look past the way a certain bishop might behave . . .

But Ben set aside his concerns about Hiram Knepp. If the bishop had nixed their plans while he was fetching his brothers, Derek Shotwell would still find a way to get the mill built. Ben turned to the two English drivers, who were discussing where Ted might stay the night before he started back to Lancaster. "I was serious, sayin' you fellas can stay for dinner."

Ted's eyes widened. "But I don't even know these people! I'd hate to intrude."

"Miriam Lantz and Naomi Brenneman cook for hundreds of folks every day," Gregg said with a laugh. "They'll be so glad you helped these Hooley boys get here, feeding you will be their pleasure. I'll be on my way, though. I live just down the road, and the wife's been expecting me."

Ben and his aunts thanked him, waving as Gregg pulled out of the lot. Ted had punched a few buttons on his phone to find a motel, so he drove off down the country blacktop a few minutes later.

With a tired but happy sigh, Ben strode to the back of the horse trailer to assist his aunts: as *maidels* well into their fifties, they didn't wait around for a man to take care of things. "Keep those little critters corralled in the trailer while I set up the pen over here in the grass," he said over the noise of their bleating.

Aunt Jerusalem and her sister stepped carefully inside the long metal trailer, holding their skirts out to their sides to form a barricade. "*Jah*, you little kids just stay put a few minutes more," Aunt Nazareth baby-talked. "Bennie's gonna set ya up with the best grass you've seen for days."

As Ben grabbed the wooden framework of the portable pen, he chuckled to himself. His brothers had protested, saying four little goats would be more bother than they were worth on the long trip, but Ben's faith in his *dat*'s sisters had prevailed. Knowing Aunt Jerusalem and Aunt Nazareth, they had discussed their plan for these feisty Alpines, and within a few hours they would either win the day . . . or he'd be finding the little kids another home.

He arranged the hinged sections of the pen against the side of the smithy, where the grass was thickest, forming an enclosure by hooking the sections together. A few minutes later the four little goats were trotting around inside it, wagging their tails, as his aunts grinned at them from outside the pen.

"Be *gut* little goats, now," Aunt Jerusalem instructed them.

"*Jah*, no jumpin' the fence or buttin' in on the dinner," Aunt Nazareth added with a laugh.

A loud, ecstatic *whoopee!* made Ben look toward the house. Sure enough, the Knepp twins and Sara had burst out the door ahead of the rest of the wedding guests. "Well, there they are. That's Joey, Josh, and Sara Knepp, the bishop's kids."

Aunt Jerusalem's hands went to her hips in the gesture he'd known all his life. She assessed them, standing beside her sister. "Puh! After keepin' you three wild colts coralled years ago, I don't see much problem handlin' these little whippersnappers."

"*Jah*, bishops' kids tend to be ornerier than most," Aunt Nazareth added as she watched the twins box at each other. "But over our years of teachin' at the schoolhouse, we haven't met one yet who didn't see the light."

"And every one of them joined the church, too," her sister added. "No slackers. No backslidin' into heathen or English ways."

Ben smiled. Well he recalled how these two aunts had corrected him, Ira, and Luke at school—and had then reported to their parents so the discipline would continue after they got home. His *dat*'s sisters had steered many a potentially wayward soul along a higher path, which was precisely why he'd encouraged Nazareth and Jerusalem Hooley to come along for a visit.

But all thoughts of the bishop's rowdy children fled when a familiar figure stood silhouetted in the door of the Lantz home. *Miriam!* His heart sang. *And she's lookin' for me!*

Even from this distance, when Miriam saw the trailer and the five of them between the back of the café and the smithy, her eyes found his. Although the wedding guests were streaming out of the house, visiting on their way to the Brennemans' for the wedding feast, Miriam was striding toward him, her face alight. She hadn't put on a shawl or bonnet, yet the October chill seemed the farthest thing from her mind; in a crisp new dress the color of canned beets, with her black apron fluttering around her legs, she looked like heaven itself.

Ben rushed up the driveway, his heart pounding. "Miriam! I'm sorry we missed the service—"

"Ben! You're finally here!"

He closed the distance between them to grab her in a hug. Miriam's arms went around his waist and he closed his eyes. What sensation was this, that made him forget his exhaustion and frustration . . . forget everything except the

warmth of this woman, the strength of her? "And how was
the wedding?"

"It went fine. But it'll take me a while to call Rachel
Mrs. Brenneman."

And how long before I can call you Mrs. Hooley?

The question nearly popped out of his mouth, but Ben
pulled himself into the present moment again. He wanted to
stand here longer, seeing himself reflected in Miriam's
sparkling brown eyes, but four other Hooleys were watching them—not to mention all the folks coming out of the
Lantz house. He released her and they headed toward his
family, who stood observing them closely.

"Here's Miriam!" His exuberance gave away his feelings
for her, but his aunts and brothers would have to see this
woman for who she was and love her, just as he did. "And
these are my *dat*'s sisters, Jerusalem and Nazareth—"

"So *gut* to finally meet ya! Ben's talked fondly of ya."

"—and my younger brothers, Ira and Luke, of course."

"Welcome to Willow Ridge!" Miriam said. "Every last
family here is excited about ya comin' to start up your mill,
no matter what ya might've heard about our bishop."

His brothers grinned wider than they had for days. "So
it's all set, then?"

"Just need to sign the paperwork with Derek Shotwell
from the bank." Miriam sparkled like the October sunshine
as she looked at each of them. "My Rebecca—raised English, but that's a long story—has started up a website for
ya and has all kinds of *gut* ideas about gettin' folks at the
colleges and towns hereabouts interested in your grains
and flours."

Ben's grin felt lopsided and love-struck, but he didn't
care. "Didn't I tell ya she'd smooth out the path for ya?
Willow Ridge is a wonderful-*gut* place to—"

At the loud bleating from the side of the smithy, Miriam

looked behind the Hooleys. Her eyes widened. "Are those your goats? I had no idea—"

"The aunts thought it only proper to bring a gift," Ben replied with a mischievous chuckle. "And here come Rhoda and Rebecca, the girls who've already been askin' about ya, boys."

Ira and Luke shifted awkwardly, but once the two sisters were introduced around, Ben let the pleasant conversation take its course. He and Miriam led the others past the cleared garden and over the wide lot toward the Brenneman workshop, where the rest of the wedding guests mingled.

Had there ever been a brighter fall day? Had he ever felt happier? Ben glanced at his aunts, who were asking Miriam what-all she'd raised in her garden and if she cooked her own vegetables in the café, while Miriam's two girls chatted easily with his brothers. Up ahead, Preacher Tom Hostetler waved at him . . . he spotted the Zooks and Millie Glick and the Kanagy brothers trundling carts of stainless steel steam-table pans toward the shop, and felt as if he had truly come home after a long time away.

"There's the bride and her groom," he said, guiding his aunts in the couple's direction. "This house is where your rooms are, too, so you'll be in *gut* company," he remarked.

"*Jah*, I can see why ya like it here, Bennie," Aunt Nazareth remarked. "Just *gut*, everyday folks, looks like."

"And this is Rachel—now Mrs. Brenneman!" Ben said as he grinned at the girl in royal blue and white. "And congratulations to ya both. Micah, it's *gut* to see ya again. This is Ira and Luke, of course. Mighty pleased to hear that everybody's in favor of the mill you're buildin' for us."

Micah grinned broadly. His blond hair shone like clean straw beneath the brim of his black hat, and his radiant white shirt was set off by a black bow tie that looked a little snug. "Took some talkin' around Hiram, but ya know what they say," the carpenter replied jauntily. "Ya can't keep a *gut* man down. Or three of them, in the case of you Hooleys."

Another flurry of conversation enveloped them as the young men shook hands and everyone congratulated Micah and his wife. So sweet and fresh Rachel looked . . . Ben could imagine her mother at that age, when she was Jesse Lantz's bride coming from Jamesport to live in this place. And, indeed, as Miriam gazed at Rachel, and then at him, she looked radiant . . . flushed with joy.

Behind her, Ben noted a familiar figure approaching. He stood taller and readied himself. *Lord, I'd appreciate gut words and the best intentions*, he prayed quickly. *We came here to improve our lives and this town, not to divide it.*

"And here's our bishop, Hiram Knepp," Ben announced. He extended his hand, gripping firmly as the bishop scrutinized them all. "My brothers, Ira and Luke—"

"Welcome to Willow Ridge," Hiram said in a formal voice.

"—and these are my aunts, Nazareth and Jerusalem Hooley, come to help us along for a while."

As the two women stepped toward him, Bishop Knepp's lips twitched. "Jerusalem? Now that's the oddest name I ever heard for an Amish woman."

"Only because you've not met the rest of our family." Aunt Jerusalem planted her feet firmly and looked up at the bishop, unflinching. "My twin brother's Jericho, ya see. And then we had Zion—he was these boys' *dat*—and Goshen, Israel, the twins, Judea and Jordan, and another set of twins, Calvary and Canaan."

Nazareth smiled sweetly. "Our younger sisters are Bethlehem, Corinth, and Eden," she continued without missing a beat.

"Our parents thought such biblical places made for names just as proper as the ones so many Plain folks have,"

Jerusalem asserted. "And we weren't in much of a position to argue with that, were we?"

Hiram set his lips in a straight line, as though not to be drawn into this woman's straightforward banter. No doubt he already sensed she was as confident and self-sufficient as Miriam Lantz . . . another one who needed watching. "It's a pleasure to meet you. I need to greet more of Miriam's kin—"

"We brought a gift for ya, Bishop Knepp," Aunt Nazareth said. Her voice and demeanor were generally less direct than her sister's, and she smiled up at Hiram with an almost girlish glow. "But it'll keep until you've got a minute."

"A gift for me?" His eyes widened. "But it was Rachel and Micah who were married."

"We believe in showin' our appreciation up front—payin' our way forward. We want to be *gut* guests while our Bennie and his brothers build that mill for ya." Jerusalem pointed down the driveway, toward the portable pen. "So we brought ya the four best Alpine kids from our goat herd back home. Three does and a buck."

Hiram's jaw dropped. "I breed award-winning Belgians, Miss Hooley. What on God's Earth do I want with *goats?*"

Nazareth blinked, then gazed up toward the sky as though beseeching heavenly guidance. Jerusalem's bosom rose and fell with the deep breath she took. "Beggin' your pardon, Bishop," she said in a teacherly voice, "but maybe ya need a little brushin' up on how to graciously accept a gift. Surely ya don't respond so blunt-like when one of your own flock blesses ya with the fruits of their labor."

For the first time ever, Ben saw Hiram Knepp rendered speechless. He bit back a grin, anticipating his aunt's next volley of staunch Amish education as Josh and Joey raced around a cluster of wedding guests with little Sara toddling after them.

"Dat! Dat! We gotta get on over to the dinner—" one of the boys cried.

"—'cause there's gonna be Preacher Tom's ice cream with the cake!" his twin finished. "And we don't want ya walkin' out before we get some, like ya did at your birthday party!"

Aunt Nazareth calmly reached down to clasp each boy by a shoulder. "And who might you fine fellas be?" she asked in a low voice. "I'm Ben Hooley's Aunt Nazareth, and if you'll tell me your names, why—we might have a surprise for ya. All the way from Lancaster County."

The five-year-old boys came to immediate attention—either out of curiosity or because Aunt Nazareth had them in a firmer grip than their *dat* might imagine.

"I'm Joey, and I'm five!"

"I'm Josh, and I'm the *gut* twin!"

"*Jah*, I can see that right off," Aunt Jerusalem replied as she looked them over. "And I bet your *dat* was just like the both of ya as a youngster, sayin' things were gonna be his way. Apples don't fall far from the tree, ain't so?" Without seeming to look at the girl toddling up to them, Aunt Jerusalem scooped Sara onto one hip. "And you're the little sister, are ya?"

Sara nodded, wide-eyed, sticking her fingers in her mouth.

"That's a perty little pinafore, probably special for today's wedding," Aunt Nazareth added, smiling at the shy girl. "We were gonna show the boys a surprise, but you come along, too. Our goats get on especially well with little girls."

"Goats?" one of the twins murmured, wide-eyed.

"Ya brung us real, live goats?" his brother breathed as he gazed toward the pen. "Nobody hereabouts has billy goats—"

"We *brought* ya some of the cutest little creatures ya ever did see," Aunt Nazareth confirmed as they started down the driveway. "But ya know, they need a keeper. Somebody who'll feed them every day and keep them milked—"

"Me! I wanna do that!"

"No, me! I'm the best one at muckin' out stalls!"

"It may well take *both* of you boys to care for them the way they're supposed to be," Aunt Jerusalem remarked in a firm voice. "But if I catch ya slackin' or not puttin' out fresh water—or treatin' them mean—it's back to Lancaster they go. All of God's creatures need to be cared for every single day . . ."

"We—we'll need to see you at the dinner soon," Hiram called after them. The bishop was watching the little band of Hooleys and Knepps as though he didn't know what had hit him. And when Annie Mae rushed up with Timmy on her hip, as though she'd been searching for her ornery little brothers, Hiram's expression showed nothing short of amazement.

"Who's that with the little ones?" the lanky young woman asked him.

Ben grinned, sensing this was just the beginning of a scheme only Jerusalem Hooley could cook up. "Those are my aunts, come along with us from Lancaster," he replied proudly. "They've been schoolteachers over the years, fillin' in when the younger girls got married. They were tickled to hear ya had siblin's not yet in school—and they'll be pleased to meet you and Nellie, too."

For the first time ever, he saw Annie Mae Knepp smile. And right pretty she was, too. "I'll go along with them, then," she said, "to be sure Josh and Joey don't act up."

"If they do," Ira put in with a grin, "it's for sure and for certain those aunts'll set them straight in a hurry."

"And if ya wouldn't mind sittin' with us at tonight's

supper," Luke joined in, "we'd like to meet your friends and the other single folks around here."

At that suggestion, Hiram snapped out of his trance, but he remained calm. "Well, I do need to speak to a few other folks, and most especially to thank your brother-in-law, Moses Miller, for delivering the first sermon for us. Fine speaker. Excellent message."

Miriam nodded. "*Jah*, he and Lovinia are right there in front of the Brennemans' house," she replied, pointing toward them. "He was wantin' to visit with you, too, Bishop."

As Hiram strode away, Ben felt a flutter in his stomach that had nothing to do with the aroma of baked chicken and stuffing that wafted across the yard. Miriam's eyes were all a-sparkle as she grinned at him. "You're a sly one, Ben Hooley, turnin' your aunts loose on unsuspectin' little boys—and their *dat*."

The three Hooley brothers laughed. They all started toward the cabinetry shop, with the wedding party walking on ahead. "Oh, it's none of my doin', really," Ben replied with a shrug. He glanced back toward the portable pen, where four children were gathered around getting their first lesson from his aunts. "You can take the teachers out of the schoolroom," he quipped, "but you'll never take the *school* out of those two old teachers."

Chapter 19

So Luke Hooley's already pairin' up with Annie Mae, is he? Rhoda pressed her lips together as she looked around the huge room during the noon feast. From her vantage point at the *eck*, the corner table where the wedding party sat, she picked out Ben's brothers as they ate. Ira, the younger one, had darker hair, distinctive eyebrows, and a daredevil grin, while Luke, with his sandy hair and slender face, resembled Ben.

The tables were arranged in a large U-shape along the length of the Brennemans' shop, and with the young men facing the young women, it was easy to observe who was eyeing whom. Her gaze lingered on Ben's brothers, mostly because they were the only fellows she didn't really know in this large gathering. The older folks had eaten in the first shift and then the tables had been reset, so now the couple's younger married friends and the single ones filled the seats. The chatter was loud and happy, filling the high-ceilinged room.

Every last one of the girls gawked at Ira and Luke as they ate their stuffed chicken, mashed potatoes, creamed celery, applesauce, and pie—though Rhoda hadn't tasted much of the special meal. During what should have been a joyous

morning, she had felt . . . left out, even though she'd been at
Rachel's side the whole time. Through the long preaching
service—including Uncle Mose's endless first sermon on
the duties of husbands and wives—she could feel a separat-
ing, like the seam of a well-worn, favorite dress giving way
after many years of constant wear. Even now, Rachel faced
away from Rhoda, visiting with Micah, Katie Zook, and
their cousin Bram Kanagy—the side-sitters to Micah's
right; while at Rhoda's left, Micah's brother Aaron was chatting with her sister Rebecca, who had volunteered to refill
water glasses and platters during the meal. There was absolutely nothing wrong with this scene, except for the way
she felt about it.

Rhoda sensed life was passing her by.

Never mind what Ben Hooley had told her about the
right fellow coming along someday. If everyone else—
including her mother—had found the person who made
them indescribably happy, why hadn't she? And if Luke
Hooley had so quickly overlooked her in favor of flirting
with Annie Mae Knepp, didn't that confirm her own misgivings?

Annie Mae attracted boys even though her father was the
authoritarian bishop of Willow Ridge . . . even though she
was tall and skinny and she squinted a lot because she needed
glasses. Rumor had it that Annie Mae was making the most
of her *rumspringa*, too, running around with Mennonite
Yonnie Stoltzfuz and English boys, after her younger siblings
were in bed—making a reputation for herself that most
mamms warned their daughters against.

Even Rebecca, who would never join the Old Amish
Church, had local fellows smiling at her as she chatted with
kin who hadn't seen her since before she got carried away in
the flood. Rebecca was a good talker, confident and educated
yet respectful of their faith. In her way, she was as much a

queen for this day as Rachel, since so many in Mamma and Dat's families wanted to hear about her return to Willow Ridge after being presumed dead and raised English.

Sighing, Rhoda excused herself. Better to pretend she was going to the bathroom than sit at the wedding party's table with such a pouty frown on her face.

Once outside, Rhoda watched the beehive of activity that involved most of the adults, who were making the wedding a seamless and carefree day for Rachel, Micah, and their friends. Henry Zook, normally behind the butchering counter in the market, and Uncle Daniel, usually minding his sheep or farming, wheeled cartloads of dirty dishes toward the back door of the Sweet Seasons to be washed. Other men stood about talking, enjoying what would be one of the last fine days of fall, while Ben Hooley and Reuben Reihl carried the two aunts' suitcases into the house.

Out of habit, Rhoda wandered to the café and stepped inside. The kitchen was steamy from running the dishwasher. The three Schrocks, Naomi, Lydia Zook, and Aunt Leah were stacking plates and silverware for the supper they would serve later: a lighter meal, yet nearly a hundred family members and young people would remain for the entire day's festivities. Micah's *dat* sat in his wheelchair drying a batch of silverware fresh from the dishwasher, tossing the hot pieces from his towel into the proper bins. Weddings were the only occasions when Amish men helped in the kitchen, doing the heavier work for the women who cooked and cleaned up.

"Rhoda, dearie, how are ya? Everythin' goin' all right at the party?" Naomi wiped her brow, smiling even though she'd been here since four this morning.

"*Jah, jah*," Rhoda hastened to assure her. "Just walkin' around after that feast ya fixed us. The chicken was extra-special *gut*."

"Ah. Makin' room for cake later. And ice cream! Tom must've drained his cows dry and cranked his arm off, judgin' from all the tubs he's put in the freezer." Naomi snatched the towel Rhoda had picked up, laughing. "This isn't your job today, missy! And how's the bride doin'? And my Micah?"

"They're havin' a fine time. With all of us talkin', ya can hardly hear yourself think—but the shop was a fine place for havin' the dinner," she replied. "Awful nice of ya, managin' all the details so Mamma can visit with her family."

"Happy to do it, just like I'm happy my son's married such a fine girl. It'll keep the grandchildren close at hand, too."

Naomi, bless her, had the best of intentions saying that, yet it was one more phase Rachel would be entering, leaving Rhoda behind. Rhoda waved to everyone and then up the lane she started, thinking to talk with her three uncles. Mose Miller, Paul Raber, and Wilmer Byler stood at the corral assessing the many fine horses their guests had driven here. Several of the horses had been retired from racetracks when Amish families bought them and trained them to haul buggies.

The *clip-clop! clip-clop!* behind her made her turn. Here came Hiram Knepp, driving one of his majestic Belgians hitched to a painted blue wagon that shone in the sun. The stallion's harness ornaments glistened as he shook his massive head and came to a halt at the bishop's command. Lo and behold, when Hiram lowered a ramp from the back of the wagon, Josh and Joey dashed down it with a wild whoop, holding large milk bottles with nipples. Nazareth and Jerusalem Hooley, who had Sara and Timmy in tow, followed with two more bottles of milk. The two women were laughing as Hiram handed them down the ramp, as though they'd enjoyed quite a ride from the bishop's stables.

Now, there's a sight! Hiram's steppin' out with his fancy

wagon and tack like he's been showin' off that stallion in a parade.

Her three uncles didn't intend to miss this chance to admire such horseflesh, so they left their spot at the corral fence.

"This one of your studs, Hiram?" Uncle Paul called out.

"Mighty fine-lookin' fella, too," Uncle Mose joined in. "Must stand at least eighteen or nineteen hands."

Hiram patted the huge horse's muscled shoulder. "You're looking at Goliath. His buddy, Saul, is back in the stable yet. Wedding or not, they need some exercise each day."

The bishop turned then to Ben Hooley's aunts. "You ladies know the best method for getting these goats into the trailer, so tell me what to do when—"

"Once the children have fed them, if all of you fellas—that means you, too, Joey and Josh—form a circle around them, we can walk them right on over," Jerusalem instructed them. "As long as you don't make any sudden moves or loud noises, they'll be real happy to move along with ya."

Rhoda leaned against the nearest tree to take this in . . . a scene where the Knepp twins held milk bottles for the scrambling, hungry goats while Nazareth helped Sara and little Timmy feed the other two. Had she ever observed such orderly behavior in this family, even while their *mamm*, Linda, was alive? And had she ever heard the bishop ask women about the best way of doing something? And why, when he had a stable full of draft horses, had Hiram hitched up Goliath in his best tack?

"Well now. This looks interestin'." Annie Mae Knepp sidled up beside Rhoda, observing her younger brothers and sisters—and her *dat*. "Have ya talked much with those Hooley sisters, Rhoda? Real nice, they are . . . volunteerin' to help with those goats, and the cookin', and even sayin' they'd help Joey and Josh learn to write their alphabet so they'll be better scholars when they start school next year."

"*Jah*, they're jumpin' right in," Rhoda agreed. "The way Ben tells it, they came along to keep house for Ira and Luke while the mill gets built, and then they'll head back to Lancaster."

Annie Mae squinted, watching the way Nazareth gently held Timmy over the pen so he could feed a tan-and-white kid. "Oh, I'm hopin' they'll stay a *gut* long while," she murmured. Then the bishop's daughter looked at Rhoda with a wistful smile. "Can ya imagine how wild it's been with Linda gone and Dat out bein' a bishop and tendin' to horse sales and what-all? Nellie and I sometimes talk of walkin' away from it, but she needs to finish school."

Rhoda's eyes widened, but she let the bishop's daughter talk. Annie Mae wasn't going all moony over Luke Hooley, either. She sounded older than Mamma and a lot less cheerful—and who wouldn't, being in charge of the Knepp household?

"The twins never listen to us—do exactly the opposite of what we say—and the two littlest ones are always underfoot, grabbin' our legs and cryin' while we're tryin' to cook and clean up." Annie Mae watched closely as the men, including her brothers and her *dat*, formed a tight line while Uncle Daniel folded back a side of the portable pen.

Then Jerusalem clapped her hands. "Come along, Billy! You too, Pearl and Matilda! Bessie, step lively, now!"

The little goats trotted eagerly into the movable, human circle as it closed around them. They obviously knew their names, just as they knew what Jerusalem expected of them.

Annie Mae chuckled. "And who'd've thought the high-and-mighty Hiram Knepp would be linkin' arms with your uncles, mindin' a woman just like those goats are? Looks like he's playin' ring-around-the-rosy."

Rhoda laughed. It was something to watch, as her uncles and the bishop started toward the back of the wagon, taking baby steps so Joey and Josh could keep up at the back of the circle. "They make a *gut* team, those fellas, when they're all not tryin' to go their own way—like they do at home."

Annie Mae turned to look at her. "And that's the way of it, ain't so? While I'm real happy for Rachel, I'm not so sure I ever want to get hitched," she mused aloud. "I've had enough of a man bossin' me and bein' my constant preacher and— well, maybe I'd see it different if Dat weren't the bishop . . . and if Mamm had been happier."

Rhoda wondered about that. No matter what his position, Hiram Knepp would insist that everyone around him— especially his wife and children—rise to his expectations. It came as no surprise that Annie Mae, known for running around with lots of boys, might not want to marry, but she'd never been one to express her feelings—at least not to Rhoda.

"Probably time to head back inside," Annie Mae remarked, gazing toward the Brennemans' workshop. "That cake your *mamm* made is no doubt the best wedding cake ever, and they say Preacher Tom's made his ice cream—"

"*Jah*, tubs and tubs of it."

"—so let's go enjoy the party!" Annie Mae brightened as they walked. "It's probably gonna be mighty different for ya, now that Rachel will be ridin' off with Micah the next several weekends, to collect their gifts."

"I've been thinkin' about that a lot."

"So what're ya gonna do when you're not workin' at the café? I mean, besides the laundry and housekeepin'."

Rhoda was amazed at how friendly Annie Mae seemed today . . . how she seemed to crave girl talk even though Luke Hooley had asked to sit with her at supper. "I haven't thought much about it. What with winter comin' on, maybe I should start somethin'."

"Do ya crochet?"

"*Jah*, but it's been ever so long."

"For me, too." Annie Mae glanced back and let out an abrupt chuckle. "Would ya look at that! Nazareth's walkin' the kids toward the café door, like maybe they're gonna help the cooks, and her sister's on the wagon seat beside Dat."

Rhoda's eyebrows rose and she turned quickly. Something about the . . . coziness of that couple on the bright blue wagon made her grin. "Now what do ya think of that? Maybe he'll leave Mamma alone now. I mean—well, I didn't intend for that to sound so—"

"Oh, I've never felt sorrier for anybody, the way Dat's made so many scenes about marryin' your *mamm*, and her sayin' right out she's not interested." Annie Mae's expression was thoughtful as they stopped just before going into the party. "Maybe if the Hooley sisters help out around our place—and keep Dat, um—*occupied*—I'll have some time to crochet, like I was sayin'. Nellie makes all manner of crocheted animals, and I keep tellin' her she should ask Mary Schrock to sell them in her shop."

Rhoda blinked. The crowd inside was starting to sing— that was Seth Brenneman's clear, mellow voice leading off. She suddenly realized that after this unexpected chat with a girl she would never have pegged as an avid crocheter, she felt a lot better than when she'd left the shop a while ago. "I like this idea, Annie Mae. Afghans are my favorite project, so maybe I'll make one for Rachel. Let me know when ya want to start."

"I'll do that! Nellie'll be tickled to get out, if—we can come to your house, I hope?"

A smile warmed Rhoda's face. Wasn't it a fine thing to have two girls wanting to come over, hoping she and

Mamma would welcome their company? Suddenly the long winter days ahead didn't seem so . . . lonely. And if Mamma would be spending her spare time with Ben—and Annie Mae was *not* keeping company with Luke Hooley—well, she and the Knepp girls might spend some evenings becoming better friends.

"Let's start this week," Rhoda replied eagerly. "We've got a big basket of yarn stuck away. Just been too busy runnin' the Sweet Seasons and gettin' ready for the wedding to sit around crochetin'."

"I can't wait, Rhoda!"

And wasn't that something? As they went inside and walked down the aisle between the tables, where the boys were singing on one side and the girls on the other, the music swelled within Rhoda and she joined in on the chorus. Rachel's expression welcomed her back—told her she'd been missed. And when she saw Mamma in the back corner singing along, beaming, everything felt right again.

It'll all work out for me, Lord, she mused as her gaze swept the huge roomful of friends. With their faces raised and their voices rising into the rafters, it seemed an almost heavenly place to be. Could angels sing any more sweetly about love and bearing each other's burdens?

Rhoda sighed happily. She felt free again. Contented. And for that she thanked God.

Chapter 20

Early Monday morning, Miriam walked down the driveway holding her shawl around her: the wind was kicking up. The treetops swayed crazily and she hoped it wouldn't be another day when one of their large, old trees fell on something. About three weeks ago when that had happened, Ben Hooley had blown into her life, and with Rachel married now, she had seen enough change for one season. It felt comforting to enter the café's kitchen and get back to her work again.

Miriam paused inside the door. The bakery had been closed for five days, so a long list of orders awaited her, but she allowed herself a few moments to let the kitchen's peacefulness seep into her soul. Bless them, the Hooley sisters were set on being perfect, helpful houseguests, but they tended to take things over, assuming she would welcome their help. Here, she was in control—at least for the next couple of hours before Naomi, Rachel, and Rhoda showed up for work.

Miriam took several pounds of hamburger from the freezer, thinking it would be the perfect day for soup on the lunch menu. As she started large batches of dough for sticky buns and pastries, her body eased into its familiar routine. In the apartment above the smithy, lights came on . . . Ben was taking his brothers to meet with Derek Shotwell today, and the two aunts said they were going to Hiram's first thing, to begin the fall cleaning with Annie Mae.

Miriam chuckled. If Nazareth and Jerusalem Hooley offered to tackle her fall cleaning, she'd be all too happy to let them! The wedding had tired her; the noise and commotion of constant family contact for these past several days had worn her down—which wasn't something most Amish women would notice, as their homes swarmed with children and perhaps three generations every day. Moses and Paul had questioned her need to work so many hours, to the point she'd been glad to see her sisters' families go home. They had no idea how her business had liberated her—or maybe they did, and they hadn't expressed their disapproval directly.

A tapping on the window made her look up. Ben's face was pressed to the glass. He wiggled his fingers, grinning, and that made Miriam grin, too. "Come on in!" she called out.

He stepped inside and inhaled deeply. "How is it that your place smells so *gut* and mine smells like three bachelor brothers are bunkin' there?"

"That question sorta answers itself, ain't so?" Miriam turned the dough out of her mixer bowl onto the floured counter and began to knead it. "And would those bachelor brothers like to eat their breakfast here before they drive to the bank?"

"Don't want to be any trouble, what with you catchin' up on orders—"

"Ben Hooley, when it's *trouble* for me to cook a meal, will ya drop me into my pine box?"

He slipped his arms lightly around her shoulders as she worked, and it felt . . . heavenly. Curious family members had seen her with Ben at various times over the weekend, and to avoid their questions she'd made a point of not seeming overly affectionate or interested in him.

Ben kissed her temple. "Ya must be the most generous, understandin' woman I've ever met, Miriam. Truth be told, the boys were askin' if somebody else could cook their eggs this mornin', as I tend to set the fire too high. Or I get busy makin' the toast and forget to flip them, or—"

"Ya need a woman in your life, Ben." Miriam bit her lip after that slipped out, yet weren't they past the stage of tiptoeing around such a sentiment?

"You're right. Are ya applyin' for that position?"

Miriam raised an eyebrow, pleased to be bantering with him in this way again. "I'd not be your ordinary, everyday wife, ya know. I intend to keep runnin' my bakery and feedin' all manner of other fellas who come here feelin' the same way about my food as you do."

He shrugged playfully. "As long as it's just food you're servin' up, I'll be all right with that. I'll be sittin' alongside those men most mornin's, ain't so? And besides"—he paused until she met his gaze, his golden-brown eyes mere inches from hers—"if it was an *ordinary* wife I wanted, I could've settled down years ago."

Miriam's heart thrummed. She gripped the warm, pliant ball of dough she had been kneading. "I love you, Ben," she whispered.

His smile went lopsided. Then his eyes misted over. "Miriam, are ya sure? I don't want ya thinkin'—"

"Oh, if I was *thinkin'*, I might never follow what my heart truly wanted," she murmured. "But, *jah*, while ya were away I came to realize how much I wanted ya in my life. And with all my family here, askin' about my future and hintin' I should seek out another husband—"

"Don't say ya want me just because your brothers think ya need a man takin' care of ya, Miriam. I'm Amish, *jah*, but I know better than to trap ya with tradition, thinkin' I'll make ya happy that way."

Miriam chuckled as her hands and arms again found the rhythm of kneading the dough. Wasn't it wonderful, the way Ben had figured out so much about her already? "Moses and Paul mean well. They believe family comes first, and to them that implies a house that's orderly; the husband sits at the head of the table and the woman perty much works her day around keepin' him and his kids fed and clothed."

Ben chuckled. "Oh, I'll be wantin' a few other things from ya, too, perty girl."

Tingles shot up her spine. He was standing too close not to notice the gray in her hair and the crow's-feet around her eyes, so maybe . . . maybe she shouldn't worry about those details anymore. Movement outside the window caught her attention and she cleared her throat purposefully. "Company's comin'. Better turn me loose before—"

"Let them see us the way we are, Miriam. There's no shame in showin' affection for a woman ya intend to hitch up with."

"Ya haven't asked me yet." Oh, but that was a brazen thing to say! Yet Miriam playfully held his gaze.

"You're right. I'm gonna keep ya guessin' as to the where and the when," he replied with a chuckle. "We'll let things simmer a bit—"

A knock on the door made them jump, but Ben's arms remained loosely around her shoulders. "Come on in, fellas," he called toward the door. "I've got Miriam all sweetened up, so if ya behave yourselves, she just might cook ya breakfast."

A double chuckle preceded the two younger Hooley brothers through the door. They stopped short when they saw how Ben was holding Miriam from behind as she rolled her dough ball inside a buttered bowl to rise.

"Didn't mean to interrupt—"

"Maybe we should wait for ya to finish—"

"You pups should be takin' notes," Ben said with a laugh. "There's a certain talent to winnin' a *gut* woman, and with all the girls in Willow Ridge ready to check ya out, you'd best be sharpenin' your skills." Ben bussed Miriam's cheek and then backed away. "And what gets you fellas outta bed so early? The birds aren't even awake yet."

"We could ask you the same thing, Bennie-boy," Luke teased. His low voice reverberated with laughter he was holding back. "But *someone* we know lit the lamps while he was primpin' and he was in such a toot to come over here, he left them burnin'. And besides that, the wind's whippin' a tree branch against the wall beside my bed."

"*Jah*, we're in for a storm later," Ira agreed, nodding emphatically. "And a storm's what we'll get before we leave for the bank, too, if the apartment's not redded up when the aunts come over. We'd better fortify ourselves with *gut* food and allow plenty of time for the big cleanup job."

Miriam laughed. At thirty and twenty-eight Luke and Ira had left home for the first time . . . didn't have wives looking after them, but knew quite well what Jerusalem and Nazareth expected. "And maybe you're just a wee bit excited about gettin' your mill business goin' today, ain't so?"

Luke's dimples came out to play when he smiled. He looked a lot like Ben but stood taller and thinner. "And we thank ya again for lettin' loose of some land, too. I was turnin' flip-flops when Ben told me your price—"

"And when we walked the place this weekend, plannin' out where to put the buildin'," Ira joined in, "we realized that Ben hadn't done the place justice. It's real perty in this part of the country, what with the trees turnin' and the river racin' over the rocks."

"We're glad Micah Brenneman's makin' time to get the

place up and enclosed so quick, too," Luke continued. "Once the roof's on and the windows are in, we can live in our new rooms upstairs so you can have your loft back."

"We're askin' Micah to build us some of those rollin' walls, too!" Ira crowed. "Never seen anythin' like that place. Havin' beds that fold up into the wall, and slidin' panels with bookshelves and dresser drawers built in, seem like fine ways to save some space. And we can see he's a mighty fine carpenter, too, before we have him build our mill."

Miriam was nodding as she got a carton of eggs and a package of bulk sausage from the fridge. "Ya couldn't ask for a better fella to do your construction work," she agreed. She formed patties from the sausage and arranged them in her cast-iron skillet. "And if the bishop gets cantankerous about how you're doin' things, or the way you've come here from Pennsylvania to start up, I can assure ya firsthand that everybody else voted for the go-ahead. Lots of folks will benefit from a chance to grow grains for ya, or from havin' more tourists visit their shops when they come to Willow Ridge to see the mill."

They chatted easily as Miriam made French toast from some of Deborah's bread, left from the wedding. It was a fine thing, to have this time with Ben's brothers . . . to smile at facial expressions and gestures she'd observed while getting to know Ben, and to hear their ideas for packaging and selling their grains. Considering it would be nearly a year before their first local crop was available, Miriam was pleased about their confidence—not to mention the financial stability they had established at a young age.

As the four of them ate their breakfast in the dining room, Miriam listened more than she talked. She didn't know of any other young men with such business sense, and the more Ira and Luke talked, the more impressed she became.

Bishop Knepp would have to admit that the Hooleys would be an asset to Willow Ridge.

Miriam got up from the table. "Let me fry up another couple pieces of French toast—"

The jangling of the phone made her glance at the clock. Who would be calling at four thirty in the morning? "I'd better answer the phone first," she called out to them as she passed through the kitchen. "At this hour, it might be an emergency."

Out the back door she hurried, to the little white phone shanty that sat behind the building. Just as it rang for the fourth time, she grabbed the receiver. "Hullo?" she said as she caught her breath. "This is Miriam Lantz at the Sweet Seasons—"

"I need to talk to Ben. I know he's there, so don't try to tell me different."

Miriam's eyebrows rose, and so did her temper. "Do ya realize it's only four thirty in the—"

"Well, if ya have to bang on his door to wake him up, that's only fair, considerin' how he left me in the lurch! I'll wait."

Jah, *and I might just hang up, too*, Miriam thought. She didn't even want to know what sort of lurch Ben had supposedly left Polly Petersheim in . . . but wasn't it time to settle this matter with Ben's old girlfriend, one way or the other? Miriam set the receiver on the tabletop and walked back into the kitchen, crossing her arms against the cold wind. From the doorway she gazed at Ben Hooley, the man she'd just this morning declared her love for. If she'd spoken too soon—if she'd fallen for a fellow who couldn't commit to her and leave his past entanglements behind—well, it was better to find out now, wasn't it?

"Are ya all right, Miriam? Somebody sick?" Ben asked as he rose from his chair. He looked sincerely concerned.

"Polly wants to talk to ya. Says it's urgent."

Ben's face clouded over like the impending storm outside. As he walked across to the pass-through window and into the kitchen, the measured tread of his boots on the plank floor announced his displeasure. "Miriam," he murmured, "I want ya to come with me. I want ya to witness—"

"Ben, this is none of my business."

"Ah, but it is. Polly's tryin' to lasso me from clear across the country, probably thinkin' to make you mad enough to send me packin'," he said in an angry voice. "And it's time to put a stop to such nonsense."

It felt odd to join Ben in the tiny phone shack. When he closed the door, Miriam stood directly behind him as he sat on the old chair to take the call . . . so close she couldn't help brushing against his back. Her heart pounded. Polly Petersheim had a lot more history with Ben than she did, and had apparently felt a spark for him rekindled. And because Polly had been widowed, well—Miriam knew exactly how helpless a woman could feel, and how desperate to see that the livestock and the farm got taken care of, as well.

Desperation drove a lot of lonely women to make decisions—or phone calls—they would never have considered before they lost their man. Miriam closed her eyes as Ben raised the receiver to his ear. *Please help us, Lord, to speak with compassion but to get this settled for sure and for certain*, she prayed. *If You're tryin' to show me that Ben Hooley's not the man for me, I . . . I'll try to understand.*

"Polly," Ben said in a stern voice, "you've got no reason to call here, disruptin' Miriam's bakin' time—"

"Ya told me ya loved me, Ben! Ya said we'd be together forever!" Polly's reply came over the phone. There was no mistaking what she had said, for her strident voice filled the little phone shanty.

Miriam bit her lip. When Ben reached back to grab her hand, she felt him trembling with the effort to restrain his impatience. Or . . . was Polly telling the truth? Expecting Ben to keep his side of a bargain Miriam knew nothing about?

"And we were what, nineteen then?" he reminded her. "We were makin' our plans, like young people do, while your *dat*, the bishop, had other things in mind for ya. And they didn't include a fella without a farm." Ben sighed, gripping Miriam's hand more tightly. "I'm sorry ya weren't all that happy in your marriage, Polly, but like I told ya last week—I've got a new life here in Missouri. A woman I intend to marry, too."

"But, Ben!" Polly shot back, "the only thing that kept me sane while I was with Homer was thinkin' you and I would meet up again someday—"

"And meanwhile, my life has followed a different path." Ben cleared his throat, shifting in the old wooden chair. "There's no doubt in my mind that God has led me here, and that Miriam's the woman He intended for me to make my life with . . . to have a family with. Ya have to accept that, Polly. I'm not comin' back," he said emphatically. "And when I saw ya for those few minutes last week, I never made ya any promises. I told ya how it was, straight-out."

Miriam felt sorry for Ben. How awkward he must feel, dealing with a woman who was weaving a fantasy like a spider spun her web, imagining Ben Hooley's feelings for her hadn't changed as he'd matured. It didn't help that Polly had begun to weep, so now the sound of her anguish filled the space around them.

"I could tell while we were talkin' that ya might need to get some counselin'—some *gut* advice about settlin' your husband's affairs as well as some help for your loneliness and your . . . mental state," Ben continued in a gentler voice. "But that's not help I'm qualified to give, Polly. I'm sorry you're not doin' so well, but you've got a nice home and money enough to keep ya. For that ya should be grateful."

Ben paused to breathe deeply, awaiting what she might say next. When he turned and met Miriam's gaze, she saw sadness and regret in his soulful eyes . . . and she realized that on yet another level, this man was far more understanding and compassionate than many Amish men she knew. She smiled at him, rubbing the tops of his shoulders.

"I'm gonna hang up now, Polly," he said as another of her wails came through the phone. "I wish ya all the best, but please don't call me again. I'm not gonna change my mind. Do ya understand that?"

A long pause followed. Miriam hoped Polly would follow Ben's advice and get some help for her grief and her financial affairs.

"*Jah.* I—I was just hopin' . . . but I won't bother ya again, Ben." Polly sniffled loudly and then blew her nose next to the phone.

"I'll keep ya in my prayers, Polly. Good-bye." Ben laid the receiver back in the cradle with a sad sigh. "Wasn't my intention to drag ya into somethin' so heavy, Miriam," he murmured, "but I wanted ya to see the truth of it, in case Polly keeps callin' to tell ya things are different from what I've just said. I'm sorry about all this."

Miriam wrapped her arms around Ben's broad shoulders and rested her head against his. "Ya handled her real nicely, Ben. I admire that about ya—the way ya don't fly off the handle or expect other folks to see everythin' your way."

He turned sideways in the chair so he could slip his arms around her waist and hold her closer. When he looked up at her, he smiled ruefully. "Will ya pray with me now? I'm thinkin' Polly Petersheim needs all the help she can get— even from halfway across the country."

Nodding, Miriam bowed her head as she kept her arms

around Ben's shoulders. It felt odd to pray in this position, hanging on to a man, yet maybe the power of their prayers would intensify if they lifted up their hearts together. The preachers told young folks wishing to marry that praying together was the most important thing they could do to ensure a stable, happy union . . . so why wouldn't that be true for her and Ben, as well?

After a moment, Ben stirred. When Miriam opened her eyes, he was gazing up at her with so much love on his handsome face she couldn't speak. She could only hold him close, blinking back tears.

"I love ya, Miriam," he whispered. "I hope ya can still believe that."

"More than ever, I do," she replied. "And I love ya right back, Ben."

His sigh joined hers, and then he smiled. "Well, then— better be gettin' ourselves inside or my brothers'll wonder what we're up to. Not that I share every little thing with them, ya know."

Miriam swiped at her tears, chuckling. "Are ya callin' this a *little* thing we share between us, Ben?" she teased.

His laughter filled the phone shanty as he stood up. He kissed her soundly before grabbing the doorknob. "How is it ya always see right through to the point, and then don't let me miss it, Miriam?"

She shrugged happily. Now that this situation with Polly was settled, she felt ever so certain that Ben Hooley was the man she'd hoped he would be. No more wondering about his past. No more letting Hiram twist things around, making her doubt what Ben had told her.

"Will ya marry me, perty girl?"

There it was, the moment every girl dreamed of—the words she'd longed to hear from the man she loved—and the thrill felt no different at forty than it had at eighteen, when

Jesse had proposed to her. Indeed, this moment felt even sweeter because she was fully aware of what marriage entailed. The long-haul reality was a different thing altogether from what a young bride envisioned when she said *I do*.

Miriam hugged him hard. "*Jah*, Ben, I'll be proud to be your wife," she replied joyfully. "And I'll never let ya live it down that ya popped the question in the phone shanty, either!"

He laughed, his body rocking with hers. "Didn't I tell ya the *where* and the *when* were a secret? Goes to show ya that I'm not so *gut* at keepin' things to myself, ain't so?"

Miriam smiled up at him, loving the way his face shone with the same commitment she felt in her heart. "Can we take our time at this now? I can tell ya from experience that courtin's more fun than takin' on the responsibilities of marriage," she remarked wistfully. "Kids Rachel and Micah's age don't appreciate that. So let's enjoy gettin' to know each other better while ya help your brothers get established."

"And while ya adjust to Rachel bein' married, too," Ben agreed. "Somethin' tells me she and her man'll be startin' a family soon. Ya might need to find other help for the café."

"Matter of fact, Naomi and I already have somebody in mind."

"*Des gut*. Because as much as I love the work ya do here," he murmured as he hugged her again, "there'll come a time when I want ya all to myself for a while."

Miriam grinned, feeling as tingly as a newlywed. Was it her imagination, or had the wind died down? Even though the clock might say it was too early for the sunrise, she sensed a glow in the sky . . . a new shine in her life. "*Des gut*," she echoed, "because I want that, too."

Chapter 21

By midmorning, when he and his brothers were returning to Willow Ridge from the bank, Ben couldn't suppress a continuous grin. The meeting with Derek Shotwell had gone so smoothly it was almost too good to be true—which was frosting on the cake, considering how Miriam had agreed to become his wife this morning. As Pharaoh trotted along the county highway ahead of their wagon, the *clip-clop! clip-clop!* of his huge hooves defined the happy rhythm Ben's entire adult life on the road had followed—and now that same cadence made music his heart could dance to.

As they crossed the old one-lane river bridge, Ben tugged on the traces to halt his horse. He and his brothers gazed at the rapids, upstream a short distance. "Well, can ya picture yourselves there on the bend?" he asked them. "It's *gut* that folks'll be able to see the big mill wheel turnin' from the road."

"Real perty spot for it, too," Luke remarked. "The trees hereabouts have some nice color to them in the fall."

"Couldn't have asked for a nicer fella to be doin' business with at the bank, either," Ira chimed in from his seat in the wagon behind them. "He said some mighty fine things

about Miriam and the way she runs her bakery business—
and the way she got the ball rollin' so we could get on with
our buildin' before winter sets in."

Ben's heart hammered. He wanted to shout out about
Miriam accepting his proposal earlier today, yet he also
wanted to let this news simmer . . . wanted to enjoy their
little secret for a while before they turned it loose. "You'll
find no better friend here than Miriam Lantz," he agreed.
"It's just her way to help folks—"

"I'm thinkin' you and Miriam are more than friends,
Bennie-boy! Ya had her smilin' a mile wide this mornin',"
Ira shot back. "C'mon now—tell us what-all ya said to Polly
when she called so bloomin' early."

"*Jah*, I knew as soon as Polly pulled up into the lane back
home that she'd be festerin' like a splinter ya can't pull out
of your finger." Luke, who sat on the seat beside him,
looked at Ben as though he had all day to wait for a full response.

Ben clapped the reins on Pharaoh's broad black back and
they rolled on across the bridge. The wind had picked up,
so the horse moved faster. "I told Polly the way it was—that
I wasn't comin' back for her, no matter how bad she wanted
that. I—I told her to get some help for her grievin', and for
settlin' her husband's affairs, too."

"And?" Ira asked pointedly. "Ya can't tell me that's all
that got discussed in that phone shanty, as long as you two
were gone."

Ben chuckled but kept a straight face. He couldn't keep
his proposal to himself forever, because everyone in Willow
Ridge knew how the two of them had hit it off from the
start. "Miriam and I prayed for Polly."

"Oh, go on with ya!"

"For sure and for certain we did," Ben insisted. He

nodded toward the Sweet Seasons, about a quarter mile up ahead of them. "But Polly's situation is between her and God now, and I'm lettin' Him handle it. By the looks of the buggies at the café, folks are showin' up for lunch. It'll be a *gut* time to get better acquainted with fellas who might want to raise some grains for ya." Ben glanced up at the gathering clouds. "Lots of men without women to cook for them will be there—or single fellas like the Brenneman brothers, who eat there because their *mamm* cooks with Miriam."

Luke turned to raise an eyebrow at their youngest brother. "Did ya hear how Bennie just switched right off the subject of Miriam and the phone shanty?"

"*Jah*, sure did. Are we surprised?"

"Nope. He hasn't changed much, even though he's moved to Missouri."

Ira chortled. "*Jah*, Missouri—the Show-Me State. And I'm ready for somebody to show me some *gut* eats for dinner. That French toast and sausage left me long ago."

Ben pulled off the road and on down the lane toward the Lantzs' barn. "By the looks of those dark clouds rollin' toward us, it's *gut* we got back. Let's pull Miriam's wagon inside and let Pharaoh into the corral."

Between the three of them, it only took a few minutes to park and tend Ben's horse. As they sauntered down the driveway, Ben noted whose horses and buggies were in the gravel lot behind Miriam's café. "Looks like Hiram decided to get his dinner here, too, instead of havin' the aunts cook for him," he remarked.

"Now *there's* another story!" Luke said with a laugh. "And ya can't tell me it's those little goats the bishop was interested in."

"No doubt he's already learned to stay out of the aunts' way when they're cleanin'. No man's safe once Jerusalem and Nazareth get on a mission." Ira sprinted ahead, opening the front door and gesturing for his brothers to precede him inside.

A lot of the usual crowd was there. Ben nodded and waved to several of them: Tom Hostetler, Gabe Glick, and Hiram had a corner table as though they were holding a preachers' meeting. Rhoda grinned at him as she filled water glasses for Nate and Bram Kanagy, while beside that table the three Brenneman brothers were rising to head for seconds at the steam table. Some English tourists filled a long table near the cash register, where Rachel was ringing up Matthias Wagler's bill.

Ben felt deeply, satisfyingly *happy*. It felt good in ways he'd never anticipated, to walk into this place and feel he was among friends, after knowing them for only a few weeks. Nothing sounded homier than the chatter of folks over a meal. Nothing smelled better than home-cooked food, either, and as Ben hung up his hat he glanced at the whiteboard on the wall. The soup he saw cooling in Micah's bowl tempted him with its chunks of hamburger, potatoes, and carrots, but he was hungry for something more filling. Something new and different, to celebrate a morning like he'd never known.

"So tell me about those stuffed shells on the menu," he said as Rhoda came to the table his brothers had chosen. "Don't know what they are, but I bet they're *gut*."

"Oh, *jah*," she confirmed as she set napkin-wrapped silverware in front of them. "Naomi cooked up bulk sausage and mixed it with a couple kinds of cheese. Tucked it into big macaroni seashells," she explained. "Covered it with spaghetti sauce and baked it with more cheese on top."

"Can't argue with that!" Ira said. "Bring me a double order, and some of that lemon icebox pie."

Luke flashed her a big grin. "I second the motion."

"Make it three," Ben added. "Who knew my brothers had such *gut* taste?"

"Be back in a few with your food," Rhoda confirmed. "Ya get salad from the buffet with that, too, so help yourselves."

On the way to the steam table, Luke stopped to shake Micah Brenneman's hand. "So how's married life treatin' ya?" he teased the burly blond. "I'll have ya know the banker gave us the thumbs-up this mornin'."

"*Jah*, the lights are all green!" Ira crowed. "Won't be long before the mill at Willow Ridge is off the paper and sittin' perty on the riverbank!"

"Congratulations!" Micah said, and his brothers all nodded, adding their cheerful remarks. "We've got a Mennonite fella with a dozer and the know-how for settin' the pilin's and pourin' your foundation. I'll tell him you're *gut* to go."

"I'm thinkin' we ought to give these Hooley brothers a big, official welcome to Willow Ridge!" Matthias Wagler called out from the cash register. He began to clap his hands, and the applause caught on like wildfire all over the dining room.

While his brothers stood there, amazed, Ben's heart overflowed with gratitude. He flashed the *okay* sign at Matthias; he had shod the harness maker's horses and had strengthened the axles on the big wagons his brother Adam hauled his painting and flooring tools in. Adam Wagler was a remodeler who often worked with the Brenneman boys, papering, painting, and finishing hardwood floors in the places they built, so Ben sensed Adam would have a hand in the living quarters and the mill's sales room, as well.

Ben also glanced toward the kitchen, tickled to see that

Miriam and Naomi had come to the pass-through window to applaud with their customers. Oh, but Miriam's face had a fine glow to it! She was a woman in love, for sure and for certain. And as he turned further, Ben saw that Tom and Gabe were clapping, too, while Hiram looked on with a nod. When the ruckus died down, they all jumped at a big clap of thunder. The dining room had dimmed with the darkening of the sky and the trees outside were swaying in the wind.

"Well, looks like we're gonna be here for a bit," Bram Kanagy remarked. "The sheep'll go into the barn and I'm not much on walkin' home through the rain."

"*Jah*," Preacher Gabe remarked as he glanced out at the first fat raindrops. "Best to get more pie and coffee and sit tight."

"Pie and coffee!" Luke repeated gleefully as he looked around the dining room. "Rachel and Rhoda, I wanna buy pie and coffee all around, as thanks to these new friends who've made us so welcome. Can ya add that to my tab?"

"*Jah*, I can do that!" Rhoda replied. "I'll bring around a tray so everybody can choose a slice of pie—"

"And what if we put a scoop of Preacher Tom's ice cream on the side?" Rachel suggested. "We had some left from our wedding supper, and it's just too *gut* to be sittin' in the freezer. We've got vanilla and blueberry ripple."

Ira's eyebrows shot up. "Do these folks know how to party, or what?"

Another round of applause broke out—

The slamming of the front door got everyone's attention. In stepped Jerusalem Hooley, wearing a rain-soaked bonnet and shawl—and a scowl that warned Ben she hadn't come to the café for lunch. She looked like a big black cat caught out in the rain. She held a Knepp twin with each hand, and the boys' anxious expressions bespoke a serious situation as they searched the crowd for their *dat*.

Before Ben could walk over to ask about her mission, his aunt spotted Hiram at the corner table. With a purposeful *thunk-thunk-thunk* of her stout heels on the plank floor, Jerusalem made her way between the tables with one boy ahead of her and one behind. "Bishop Knepp," she said in a teacherly voice, "we've got a few things to discuss, and one mighty big question to answer."

Hiram blinked and stood up. "If my boys have found themselves some trouble—"

"Oh no, it's far worse than that," she replied stiffly.

"—we'll head on home to—"

"I'm not goin' out in that rainstorm again to talk to anybody about anythin'!" she declared as she planted herself in front of him. "The change in the weather got the goats riled up, and when one jumped out of the pen, the others followed. Curious creatures that they are, they scattered and explored the stables—"

"They got in with my Belgians?" Hiram's frown matched Jerusalem's now as he leaned down to scold his sons. "I've told you time and again—"

"And you're gonna let me finish what I'm sayin' before ya butt in, layin' blame where it doesn't belong!" she replied sharply. "Goats and horses make natural companions, after all. But when the boys and I went lookin' for the kids, tryin' to round them up before the rain broke, to his credit, your stable manager—"

"Jason?" the bishop breathed.

"—*jah*, Mr. Schwartz came runnin' out to see what the fuss was about, and he helped us gather up the goats," Jerusalem continued. She was building to her climax, and the two boys who held her hands were shifting with their five-year-old excitement and energy.

One look from their keeper made them stand absolutely still again. "We got the three nannies straightaway," Jerusalem went on, "but Mr. Schwartz had inadvertently left a side door of the stable open. Lo and behold, your sons rushed in and found—"

"Billy was standin' in a big black car, Pop!" one of the twins blurted.

"*Gut* thing we got there before he chewed the seat!" his brother added.

"*Jah*, but when we ran at him from both sides, he pooped."

The café and kitchen got totally quiet, except for the fork that clattered onto the dishes Rachel was scraping. Ben bit back a snicker, as did several of the fellows near him. He knew better than to let on that he found this conversation humorous.

Hiram's face had gone deathly pale. He was learning: it wasn't wise to speak out of turn while Jerusalem Hooley was teaching a lesson.

Ben's aunt cleared her throat. Her gaze didn't waver. "To his credit," she resumed in a tighter voice, "young Mr. Schwartz didn't make up any stories by sayin' the car belonged to him, as a Mennonite. And there's no need for you, Bishop Knepp, to explain how you came to be the owner of a black Cadillac convertible, but I do expect to see you on your knees, come the next preachin' Sunday."

Hiram's face went from milk white to raspberry red. "You have no right—you are totally out of bounds, coming here this way to—"

"*Jah*, there's nothin' *right* about it," Jerusalem insisted. She straightened her shoulders, still gripping the twins' hands. "The *Ordnung* expressly prohibits ownership of a car—as you well know, sir—so I consider this one of those teachable moments inspired by God himself."

Jerusalem stepped back, her gaze unwavering. "What have your young sons learned from their discovery today?" she queried in a rising voice. "And what will they carry through their lives with them, Bishop? The image of a father who humbled himself before his congregation and his God to confess his sins? Or the idea that since their *dat* made excuses and felt himself above punishment—or laid the blame on others—they can behave that way, too?"

Ben held his breath. Nobody in the Sweet Seasons moved.

After a moment, Aunt Jerusalem glanced out the nearest window. "Come along, boys," she said in a lower voice. "The rain's stopped for now. We'll get on home to our goats and our fall cleanin'."

One of the twins caught sight of Rhoda, who'd stopped in the doorway with a tray of pie slices. Rachel was behind her with a bucket of ice cream in each hand. He sucked in his breath. "Can we have—"

"*May* we have," Jerusalem corrected him.

"May we please have some pie, Miss Hooley?" his brother hastened to ask in his sweetest voice. He looked hopefully toward Rhoda, so Jerusalem couldn't miss the tempting sight.

Their new teacher smiled but shook her head. "We'll finish your room and have our noon dinner at home with your family," she replied with a pointed glance at Hiram. "Annie Mae and Nellie were bakin' up a nice pot roast—and pie—when we left, remember?"

With that, Jerusalem steered the boys to the front entry again. She nodded at Ben and his brothers, and they nodded back, remaining silent until the door closed. All eyes went back to the bishop, who had remained standing, clenching and unclenching his jaw. As his silvery beard quivered at the end of his chin, it occurred to Ben that Hiram resembled a billy goat himself and it was all he could do to keep from laughing out loud.

But this was no laughing matter. Owning a car was one of the most frowned-upon worldly sins among the Old Order Amish, and Hiram had been caught by his young sons—and called out in front of many of the same people who'd been here when Rebecca displayed the bishop's photograph on his website. What made the situation more interesting, however, was the way Hiram hadn't talked back; he hadn't put Aunt Jerusalem in her place or offered any rationalizations for his behavior. The bishop stood there, staring toward the door. Then he fetched his hat from the peg on the wall.

"We need to call a meeting. Make it this evening," he murmured to the two preachers. Then he took money from his wallet, tossed it on the table, and walked out of the Sweet Seasons without another word.

Gabe struggled to his feet, his face lined with age. Tom rose and fetched the older man's cane and their black hats, and then tossed more money on the table. "Sorry to be leavin' the celebration," he said to Luke with a grim smile. "Guess this just goes to show that ya can't tell what the wind might whip into motion. It didn't toss a tree through Miriam's window this time, but we for sure and for certain have a mess to clean up."

After the two preachers left, conversations resumed among the customers . . . speculation about whether Hiram would indeed confess at a members' meeting this coming Sunday. . . remarks about how Jerusalem Hooley and her sister had taken over the Knepp family while Hiram had put up no apparent resistance.

Matthias Wagler spoke up. "Rhoda, let's bring on that pie and coffee now. No sense in lettin' that *gut* ice cream melt."

Ben and his brothers returned to their table rather than fetching their salad. "Seems like a sign we ought to eat dessert first," Ira remarked as he grinned at the people around him. "So tell me—do you Missouri folks always stir up this much excitement over a meal?"

Chuckles erupted around them. Ben smiled up at Rhoda as she presented the tray of pie, and he snatched a wedge of blackberry with a sugar-dusted crust. He pointed to the blueberry ripple ice cream and Rachel placed a generous scoop alongside his pie. His brothers lingered over their decision until he had to laugh. "This won't be your only chance for Miriam's pie, ya know," he teased them. "We'll most likely eat our dinner here every noon, and there'll be all manner of pies to try, over time. Unless you'd rather have me do the cookin' to save money, of course."

Luke chose a slice of cherry while Ira went for French apple with a streusel topping. "If we get to the point we can't afford the prices on this menu," Luke remarked as he cut his first bite, "we've got no business buildin' a mill here."

Ira let out an ecstatic sigh, closing his eyes. "I don't care if I have to do the dishes to pay," he murmured, "for pie this *gut*, I'd do anythin'!"

"*Jah?* Anythin'?" Rachel scooped the vanilla ice cream they pointed at, grinning at the youngest Hooley. "How about ya ask my sister Rhoda for a date?"

Ira chewed for a moment, while she served ice cream to the Kanagy boys. "Did she make this apple pie?"

"Rhoda's our cream pie girl. Banana cream, coconut cream, chocolate, pumpkin spice, lemon ice box—"

"Oh, stop!" Luke teased. "The poor boy's overloadin' on sugar just hearin' about all those pies he'll have to try."

Rachel shrugged, chuckling. "Maybe you'll be needin' bigger pants then. Rhoda could sew ya up some of those, too."

"I'll think on it," Ira replied. His cheeks were tinged with pink as he mopped up the melted vanilla ice cream with his last few bites of pie.

When Rachel moved on, Ben leaned across the table to chuckle at his brother. "What's this I see? The youngest Hooley hooligan bein' embarrassed about a girl?"

"Ya know better than that, Bennie!" he shot back. "And ya won't catch me kissin' her in the phone shanty, either!"

Ben blinked. Why wasn't he surprised that his brothers had spied on him and Miriam this morning? "Watch out, now. You're settin' yourself up for payback."

"Oh, my word, would ya look at this?" Rhoda had passed around all the pie and returned to the corner table to clear the preachers' dishes. "There's two twenties and a ten on the table here! Their three meals only came to twenty-one—"

"You girls have earned every nickel of that tip, dealin' with Hiram lately," Ben assured her. "Ya work hard here. I hope you'll spend that on somethin' you'd enjoy, Rhoda."

Her face lit up as she considered what he was saying. Was his younger brother paying attention to the way her blue eyes sparkled? To the way Rhoda Lantz moved with such efficiency and had a cheerful smile for everyone?

"I know just the thing, too!" she said as she tucked the money into her skirt pocket. "Somethin' I've been aimin' to make for Rachel. I'll fetch your stuffed shells now. Do ya still want the lemon icebox pie? I saved ya back three pieces."

"*Jah*, bring it on!" Ira replied.

"For sure and for certain!" Luke said as he wiped his last bite of crust through the ice cream puddle on his plate.

Ben glanced at the clock above the kitchen door, amazed that it was nearly two o'clock and time for the Sweet Seasons to close for the day. And what a day it had been! He'd parted ways with Polly Petersheim, proposed to Miriam and gotten an immediate *jah!* and then watched his brothers buy a parcel of land before seeing Hiram Knepp humbled beyond belief by his Aunt Jerusalem. What could possibly top all of that?

He smiled. He had no trouble whatsoever devising ways to make this evening one of the high points of his life.

Chapter 22

As Rhoda hung the damp towels from helping Rachel with the supper dishes that evening, her eyes widened. "Well now, would ya look at this? I figured on Annie Mae and Nellie comin' over to crochet, but who would've thought about the Hooley aunts bringin' them?"

Rachel chuckled. "We should never try to guess what Jerusalem Hooley might do, after the way she cornered the bishop today. Hiram must be stayin' home with the little ones this evenin'. And *that*'s different, ain't so?"

"It'll be interestin' to see what comes of that conversation at the café," Mamma agreed as she watched their four guests come up the porch steps. "Preachin' is at Tom's house this Sunday. We'll have to help him redd up Friday afternoon . . . ask what he knows about Hiram confessin' to the members instead of goin' to the bishop in Morning Star."

"*Jah*, not many folks'll find reason to miss this service, when word gets out about Hiram havin' a car." Micah rose from his seat at the head of the table, a grin tickling his lips. "At least it wasn't Rebecca who caught him this time. He seems to be leavin' you out of it, too, Miriam, and that's a *gut* thing."

Rhoda hurried out to hold the door open for Annie Mae, who was carrying a bulky plastic shopping bag in each hand. All colors of yarn were jammed into the sacks, popping out the tops of them, and the sight made her glad she'd agreed to this crocheting get-together. "Come on in, girls!" she said to Nellie and Ben's aunts. "I've got extra hooks if you two would like to join us."

Nazareth smiled kindly. "I was tellin' Nellie what a fine idea this was. Matter of fact, we've got our own crochet hooks up in the room."

"*Jah*, and after a day of deep cleanin' and settin' that house to rights, a little time with yarn and *gut* conversation sounds mighty fine." Jerusalem Hooley removed her black bonnet and hung it on a peg before doing the same with her sister's. "I suggested to Hiram that this would be a fine time to spend with his younger children, readin' the evenin's devotional and gettin' them all four into bed if Annie Mae and Nellie just happen to be here until after dark. It wouldn't be proper for Nazareth or me to stay over, ya know. Not that we were invited."

Rhoda exchanged glances with the Knepp girls. Their faces glowed with mischief, as though they had every intention of staying until their *dat* put their younger siblings to bed. That would be a rare treat for them.

"This sounds like a hen party I could miss." Micah went for his hat, smiling at them. "I'll mosey over to the smithy and see the Hooley brothers about startin' this mill in a day or two. I'll take care of the horse chores and what-all outside for ya."

"*Denki*, Micah," Mamma replied. "But it's your house now. You're welcome to stay and chat!"

The tall, muscled blond rolled his eyes and blew a kiss to his new wife. "Not sure I could stand all that excitement."

As he jogged down the stairs, he had an air of satisfaction about him, Rhoda thought—just as her sister seemed to be floating on her own little cloud, even after a day of working at the Sweet Seasons. They had all agreed that Rachel and Micah would now spend their mornings together over breakfast before she came in to work. And if business remained brisk as the colder weather came on, it would be a good time to bring in Hannah Brenneman, Micah's younger sister, to clear tables and work alongside her *mamm*.

"Rhoda says she's startin' an afghan," Mamma remarked as she slipped an arm around Rhoda's shoulders. "I think I'll make a few granny squares along with her just to help my fingers recall how to crochet. So what's everyone else got in mind?"

Nellie grinned as they all headed into the front room. "On the way over, Nazareth was sayin' a Friendship afghan might be a fun project, what with all the yarn we've accumulated between us," she recounted. "If we all make squares about the same size, any colors we want, among the seven of us we could make enough blocks for a whole afghan in an evenin' or two!"

"Then one of us could crochet them all together and finish the borders," Annie Mae went on. She sounded genuinely thrilled to be here working on such a project, too. "We could either pass it around amongst ourselves to enjoy—"

"Or we could decide who might like it for a gift," Rachel continued in a voice rising with excitement. "Just so happens we've got three new fellas in Willow Ridge who've got no one to make their place cozy for them, so—"

"Well, that's a fine idea!" Miriam agreed. "And with them livin' upstairs in the mill when it's ready, an afghan would be a real nice present for their new rooms. A perfect way to warm up their first winter in Missouri."

"Or a way to get somebody's attention, ain't so?" Rachel added with a giggle. "Now which of you girls is interested in which Hooley brother? Knowin', of course, that Ben's already spoken for."

"*Jah?* How's that?" Nellie teased. She settled into a rocking chair while her sister took the center of the couch between Rachel and Rhoda, who were watching their mother's reaction to that question. Mamma had seemed especially bubbly today despite the rainy weather . . .

"I've got to tell ya that our Bennie could hardly talk of anythin' besides Miriam and her bakery on our way here from Lancaster," Nazareth remarked with a girlish grin. "And after watchin' the way his old girlfriend was tryin' to grab him back—"

"Now *that* was a scene like I'm hopin' never to see again," Jerusalem declared. "Common sense and a little dignity on Polly's part would've been appropriate."

"It's been such a pleasure to get acquainted with you, Miriam." Nazareth chose a ball of bright blue yarn from the large basket Rhoda had brought out earlier. "And we thank you again for providing us with a room."

"It's yours for as long as ya care to stay." Mamma, too, picked up a crochet hook and plucked a half-used skein of variegated reds, oranges, and yellows from the basket. "I'm sure your family back in Lancaster's glad ya came along to give your nephews a hand—and to let them know what's goin' on, too. That was a big decision for those young fellas, movin' so far away."

"*Jah*, but the right decision, for sure and for certain." Jerusalem nodded decisively. Her fingers deftly formed a loop of brown and she began to cover it with double-crochet clusters. "Truth be told, Nazareth and I figure to stay here and see to the boys' housekeepin' over the winter. Seems a lot more useful than anythin' we could be doin' back East."

"And more excitin', what with watchin' their new mill go up!" Nazareth remarked cheerfully. "They had quite a *gut* business, sellin' their specialty flours and grains back home."

"*Jah*, and the new teacher seems to be handlin' things at the school, so they won't be needin' us to step in anytime soon," Jerusalem explained. "And we've enjoyed seein' new scenery and meetin' new folks, too. Didn't realize how stale we were gettin' until we got out of our own backyard."

Rhoda's fingers flew over turquoise double-crochet stitches as she listened . . . speculating about Jerusalem Hooley's reasons for staying in Willow Ridge. Who would've thought *maidels* their age would seek out adventure rather than stay close to hearth and home, especially in the winter? Or maybe there was more to Jerusalem's plan than she was letting on. Hiram had taken a shine to her from the first time the schoolteacher had corrected him, when they'd met before the wedding feast. Nobody here in Willow Ridge—especially the women—had dared to set the bishop straight about how to raise his unruly children. And who would have dreamed of confronting him about the car he'd hidden away in his stable?

"That's an advantage to bein' unattached, for sure and for certain," Mamma agreed. Her square now had its first three rows; she clipped her yarn and wove in the end before choosing a deep maroon yarn to work with next. "How many rows are we makin' our squares, girls?"

"How about seven rows of color finished off with a row of black?" Nellie suggested. "I've already got five done, so if I work two more in the same red I started with, that'll finish off to a *gut* size."

When Nellie held up the red-and-purple square she'd

worked, they all agreed on that number and compared how their stitch sizes were matching up, so the individual blocks of the afghan would measure the same.

Rhoda finished off her row of turquoise and rummaged in her bag of yarn to choose the next color. "If this is to be for one of the Hooleys, we maybe shouldn't use the pinks and the baby yarns left from makin' booties, ain't so? Don't want it to look girly, or they won't like it."

"And who do ya think we should give this one to?" Annie Mae asked. She held up her square of orange and navy blue. "Or maybe, since this is goin' so fast, we should make one for each of them. It would be a *gut* excuse for gettin' together each week, ain't so?"

"And Dat couldn't argue with the way we're workin' with other folks' welfare in mind," Nellie added with a laugh. "He preaches that at home night and day, after all."

They all laughed, reaching for more yarn or considering how many rows of each color would make their square the prettiest.

Rhoda sat back on the couch. Her fingers had found their rhythm again, so she hardly had to look at what she was doing as she worked her hook around the yarn. She had missed sitting with Rachel and Mamma in the evenings, embroidering kitchen towels and pillowcases, or crocheting this way. They had simply been too busy, what with running the Sweet Seasons all day and then doing the household chores in the evenings. Wasn't it interesting that three new bachelors coming to Willow Ridge had inspired this frolic?

"Annie Mae, I'm sure glad you had this idea," Rhoda said quietly. "It's been way too long since we sat chattin', lettin' our fingers fly while we relaxed."

"You can say that again!" Nellie remarked. "How about if we meet at our house next time, so Dat won't get peeved about us leavin' him with the little ones?"

"*Jah*, we could do that." Rachel finished the black border of her square and plucked at its corners to make the edges straight. "We could keep our finished squares all together and bring them along each time, so when we have enough, somebody can whipstitch them together while the rest of us start on the next afghan. That way, if we can't all show up every time, the rest can keep workin'."

"I think we've just started a crochet club!" Nazareth chirped. "And what a *gut* way to get to know our new friends better! I'm feelin' right at home. Glad you girls wanted us older ones to join ya."

Mamma was nodding, pressing her finished square against the arm of her chair to make it lie flat. She had a secretive grin on her face as she chose a ball of grass-green yarn to work with next. "We still haven't decided who gets this first afghan," she said.

"We could make it a secret contest!" Annie Mae said with a laugh. "Whichever of the Hooley brothers asks one of us for a date first wins the first afghan!"

"*Jah*, that'll work! There'll be a singin' Sunday night— the first one since Ira and Luke came to Willow Ridge. Maybe by then they'll figure out who they've taken a shine to." Rhoda eyed her mother, who seemed to be off in her own little dreamworld. No doubt who Mamma was thinking about, either. "Of course, at their ages, they might not want to join in with girls and fellas who're mostly still in their *rumspringa*."

"Well then," Rachel remarked as she, too, glanced at their mother, "that means they're old enough to meet up with girls on other nights besides Sunday, ain't so?"

"Puh! Don't you girls go thinkin' you've got a corner on the market, far as gettin' fellas to court ya," Jerusalem ventured with a chuckle. "Some of us in this room have been agin' like fine cheese, waitin' for a man *mature* enough to realize we're the best gift God will ever send him!"

"You tell them, Sister!" Nazareth crowed.

Mamma laughed like she hadn't in a long time. "Hear, hear! Willow Ridge has a few unattached men who can probably still be trained up the way we'd want them to go! Feed them enough pie and they'll follow ya anywhere."

Again their laughter filled the front room as their fingers, hands, and wrists didn't miss a stitch. Then Rachel, sitting closest to the kitchen, cocked her head. "Is that somebody at the door? I'll go see."

Rhoda turned to lift the curtain behind the sofa. "Hmm, dark enough that I can't tell for sure," she said as she peered out. "I don't see a carriage."

"Sure hope it's not Dat, come to fetch us home because the twins wouldn't go to bed," Annie Mae said. "I'm havin' such a fine time I could sit here quite a spell longer."

Rhoda smiled. Wasn't that something to hear, from the girl who supposedly sneaked out with the likes of Yonnie Stoltzfuz?

Jerusalem shifted in her chair, chuckling. "Josh and Joey gave me their word they'd go straight to bed—and would help settle the younger ones if they fussed about turnin' in, too. We'll see if the boys get to order those new collars for the goats, with name tags, or if I have to work on them a bit more."

"*Jah*, they weren't keen on writin' their alphabets twenty times today after I caught them shootin' marbles instead of puttin' away their laundry." Nazareth leaned down to pluck a ball of silver-gray yarn from the bag. "They're not bad boys. They just need to be kept busy."

"And speakin' of busy," a familiar voice said from the kitchen doorway, "it looks like quite a sewin' circle we've got goin' here."

"Well, Bennie! How are ya, dear?" Nazareth asked.

"*Jah*, Bennie, ya got here just after we stopped gossipin' about ya!" Jerusalem chortled as though she knew exactly what would happen next. "You and Micah and the boys get that mill business all discussed, did ya?"

Ben entered the front room ahead of Rachel, and Rhoda nipped her lip to keep from smiling; Mamma was grinning like a little girl on Christmas morning as she quickly finished the row she was crocheting.

"Time to set aside the mill business," he remarked as he walked up behind Mamma's chair. "It's a perty night for a ride. I was hopin' somebody special might join me."

"*Jah*, I can do that, Ben." Mamma slipped the end of her crochet hook into her ball of yarn, grinning. "We have our first winner, ain't so? Don't wait up, girls. I'm plenty old enough to let myself in."

Chapter 23

Was there anything more exciting than being picked up by a beau on a moonlit autumn night? The moon, full and round and golden, ruled over a cloudless night sky and beamed down on them as Ben steered Pharaoh over the county highway, away from Willow Ridge. Miriam scooted closer to him, feeling a rush of goose bumps as he put his arm around her.

"And what was goin' on at that hen party, that ya said ya had a winner?" Ben asked playfully. "It looked like one and all were havin' a *gut* time, fingers flyin' almost as fast as the gossip."

"We were sayin' it had been too long since we had our *hooks* out. Makes us sound like a dangerous crowd, ain't so?" Miriam grinned, in too fine a mood to tell everything she knew. "Micah thought better of stayin' around, knowin' he was outnumbered by such ruthless women. And that little bit about a winner?" she said in a mysterious whisper. "Well, that's a contest we crochet clubbers are keepin' to ourselves. A secret yet to be revealed."

"Should've known you'd say that, considerin' my aunts are mixed up in it. Thicker than thieves, those two."

"So where'd ya latch on to this fine courtin' buggy, Mr. Hooley?" she shot back.

"Changin' the subject, are we? We'll see who can keep a secret!" Ben kissed her temple, chuckling. "When Micah thanked me yet again for bringin' my brothers' mill business to his shop, I told him he could pay my commission by loanin' me his fancy new wheels. He said his folks got them the carriage top for their wedding present, but I kinda like open-air rides on a night like this."

"*Jah*. The frost'll be gettin' heavy soon and before ya know it, the snowflakes'll fly."

"Which means you'll ride all snuggled up to me," he replied with a chuckle. "It's been my plan all along to get ya outta the house so's we can talk. Or whatever else comes to mind."

When she lifted her face to smile at him, Ben kissed her gently on the lips. "I've been waitin' for that," she murmured. "It's been a long, long time."

"I'd better do it again, then. To be sure I get it right. Just the way ya like it, Miriam." Ben pulled off to the shoulder of the road and then wrapped the reins around the hook. As he lifted her face between his strong, gentle hands, Miriam felt like a girl in her teens again . . . yet this was like nothing she could ever recall with Jesse. Ben seemed as interested in pleasing her as he was in taking his own satisfaction, and wasn't that a wonderful-*gut* way to romance a woman?

When the lingering kiss ended, Miriam sighed. "I love ya, Ben."

"And why is that? This blew up between us awful quick, and I want us both to be sure we're not rushin' down the wrong road." His face glowed in the moonlight as he gazed at her. "And since I'm not the first fella you've been with, I need to know I'm makin' ya at least as happy as—"

"Oh, don't go comparin' yourself to Jesse Lantz!" she said. "I wasn't yet nineteen when I married him. As I look back, that wasn't nearly old enough to know what I was gettin' into, even though it turned out fine."

"Do folks in love ever really know what they're gettin' into?" he asked softly. "I've met a couple women since Polly and thought maybe they were the right ones, but a few months along the way I was relieved to figure out they weren't—before we made it stick."

"And how is this time different?" Miriam reached for his hand, loving the way it wrapped around hers, so large and strong, without squeezing too hard. Jesse, too, had been a farrier with hands made sturdy from working with horses and hammering out horseshoes on his anvil. Sometimes he'd had no sense of his own strength when it came to touching her.

"Well," Ben mused as he clapped the reins on Pharaoh's back, "for one thing, you've already got a place, and now your bakery business . . . so I guess I'm sayin' you're not lookin' to me to make ya a whole new life. Some women have no idea how they'll get by unless a man comes along to provide them a home and an income. Nothin' wrong with that. It's the way most Amish families are. But—"

"It takes the pressure off ya."

"*Jah*, there's that. It also means you're not hangin' all your hopes on me, sayin' ya love me outta desperation," he said after a moment's thought. "If you'd told me no, ya still have your café and your three girls—and I'm glad they seem to think I'm the sort of fella you should be spendin' your time with."

Miriam smiled. "There were months, after Jesse passed, that I did feel downright desperate," she admitted quietly. "But I've been blessed with opportunities a lot of gals don't get—not to mention three of the best daughters God could ever give a woman. Which brings up somethin' else we need to talk about, Ben. Because the last thing I ever want to do is disappoint ya or . . . mislead ya."

His eyebrows rose expressively. "If you're thinkin' you're too old for me—"

"I can't have any kids for ya, Ben." Miriam closed her eyes, hoping this wouldn't spoil their beautiful evening. "That day Rebecca washed away down the river, I was carryin' my fourth baby. Must've been the strain of hurryin' up the muddy bank with all three of those little girls, scared out of my mind—and then bein' torn in so many directions when Rebecca broke away to chase a bunny she saw ridin' on a log, down the current—"

"Oh, Miriam. That had to be the worst nightmare a mother could ever know." He shuddered, hugging her more tightly. "I'm sorry ya had to go through that—but after all those years went by, ya met up with your lost daughter again. That's a miracle, plain and simple."

What a blessing his words were; what a balm to her soul. And it amazed her how easily she was discussing such an emotional—and intimately personal—subject with this man she'd known for only a few weeks. "I miscarried that day. And then I couldn't seem to have any more children," she continued in the steadiest voice she could manage. "It . . . it came between Jesse and me. Partly because he was grievin' for Rebecca—even though he couldn't put that into words, exactly."

Miriam sighed, wondering if she should share the biggest heartbreak of her marriage . . . or leave it in the past, buried with her husband. "And it was partly because Jesse felt I should've had better control of my girls," she murmured, "and that I shouldn't have come lookin' for him, to warn him that the river might flood while he was fishin'."

Ben considered this, studying her face as though he

couldn't get enough of looking at her. "That's a mighty heavy load to lay on your shoulders, Miriam," he whispered. "And I hope the good Lord above strikes me down if I ever expect ya to bear such a burden. Nobody deserves that sort of guilt."

Her heart throbbed painfully. Yet oh, how wonderful-*gut* it felt to hear a man recognize an inkling of what she'd gone through. She squeezed his hand harder. "I . . . I just don't wanna tie ya down, because most fellas marry to start a family—"

"Ya have a family, Miriam. I have my family, too." He ran a finger along her jaw to make her smile. "We've got way too many blessin's to count, between us, to feel like our life would be lackin' if children didn't come along. Not that I don't intend to try—and try and *try*," he teased softly.

Miriam's face went hot. "Well now," she stammered, "this is the kind of thing younger folks have no idea about when they start out together—"

"Does it bother ya that I've never been married, Miriam? No doubt I'll do things ya don't like, or do things wrong because I don't know any better."

She laughed, loving how the sound floated out into the night as they rolled along the road. "Like your Aunt Jerusalem was sayin' just before ya knocked on the door, ya probably still stand a *gut* chance of bein' . . . trainable."

"Trainable?" he protested.

"And in that respect, it's nice that ya haven't been married, used to the way your first wife did things," Miriam added quickly. "Maybe it's *you* who'll have to deal with a woman who runs her home a certain way because her husband expected it."

"I've got the answer to that."

Ben looked out ahead of them as though watching the road was all he had on his mind . . . as though he expected to give no further explanation of such a statement. For the longest time he ignored the way she squirmed and sighed and waited.

"*And*?" she finally asked, jabbing him in the ribs with her elbow. "Don't think I'll let ya get by with havin' all the answers, Mr. Hooley! I've got an answer to *that*, ya know!"

He chuckled until his whole body shook. "I bet my answer's better."

"Try me! I'll be the judge of that."

Ben gave her the sweetest smile she'd ever seen. "When I was talkin' to Derek Shotwell after we finished the mill arrangements, I asked him about the price of land and the cost of buildin' houses hereabouts."

"But I've got a house. And it's plenty big enough for—"

"And it was Jesse's house. And you've told Rachel and Micah it's theirs now."

Miriam raised her eyebrows. "*Jah*, there's that—not that it's an unusual situation for two or three generations to live together."

"But wouldn't ya like your very own home, Miriam? Wouldn't ya like to have a say in how your kitchen was set up . . . which way your porch swing faced for the best breeze, or the pertiest view?"

Her heart pounded at this possibility. "I . . . I never thought much about it."

"Maybe ya should. I intend to marry only once, Miriam. I'd like my home to be a special place where we can be even happier than kids just startin' out—"

"Instead of livin' in another man's shadow? Or havin' another set of newlyweds in the house?" She smiled. The idea was growing on her . . . glowing inside her. "I like the way ya think, Ben. I'm startin' to see how latchin' on to you is probably the finest idea I've had since—well, since I started up my bakery and café!"

He chuckled. As they rode in silence for a bit, Miriam's mind filled with all manner of possibilities and new ideas. It took an unconventional fellow like Ben Hooley to make her realize how many different ways she could look at her life now, even as she kept her traditional faith and remained close to her girls. "So . . . where were ya thinkin' to build a place?" she asked. "It's been so handy, walkin' down my lane to the shop of a mornin', at any hour I choose to go."

"And ya still could, if my plans work out the way I'm hopin'. It's important for me to stay close to my brothers, too, ya know." Ben shook his head, chuckling again. "And while it's anybody's guess what my *maidel* aunts might do, I can't rule out the possibility that they'll want to live in Willow Ridge. In case ya haven't noticed, Aunt Jerusalem took the bishop's kids under her wing not five minutes after she met them."

"*Jah*. She said those four goats were for Hiram, but it's the boys takin' care of them."

"Oh, that was her plan all along, when I told her the bishop's kids needed somebody ridin' herd on them. She and Aunt Nazareth got a lot of practice at that, bein' schoolteachers—and bein' around us boys when we were little." Ben looked at her, his eyes shining in the moonlight. "But there was no missin' the way Hiram fell right into step when she gave him his marchin' orders, either."

"And who would've thought that would ever happen?" Miriam agreed. "Wouldn't it be a *gut* thing if Hiram got so sidetracked by your aunt that he forgot I was supposed to marry him?"

"I've thought that a time or two lately, *jah*."

Miriam grinned at him, loving the way the moonlight played upon his handsome face. "Do ya really think your Aunt Jerusalem would get hitched at this point in her life? I'm thinkin' she's somewhere near sixty."

"She and Aunt Nazareth don't discuss their age, but *jah*, they're within spittin' distance of sixty. And when it comes to those two gals, I've learned never to second-guess them," Ben replied. "But after all this time of them livin' together—doin' everything together—I don't look for one to get married until the other one's got her *hooks* in a fella, as well."

"Hmm. Maybe I could do a little matchmakin'."

"They got tired of folks tryin' that, years ago, Miriam," he said with a laugh. "But who were ya thinkin' of for Aunt Naz?"

She shrugged, happy to have this little puzzle to work on . . . happier yet to be seated so close to Ben that each time the buggy swayed to Pharaoh's gait, she bumped against him. "Tom Hostetler would be a mighty fine catch—except, until his former wife passes on, he can't marry again. Lettie ran out on him with an English fella early last spring, ya know. Divorced him, she did."

"Divorced Preacher Tom? Why would any woman leave a nice fella like him?" Ben scowled. "He's got himself a real fine dairy operation . . . perty farm, with prime pasture-land for all those black-and-white cows to graze. Nice enough house, from what I saw of it."

Miriam shrugged. "That's what all of us wondered. His married kids are scattered around in other Plain settlements, so his girls look in on him and see that he has some meals, and that his laundry is done," she replied. Her mind raced ahead a bit, matching personality traits between the man and woman in question. "For a while there, we were worried about him. Looked thirty years older, he did, and all tuckered out—like somebody'd been beatin' him down with a big stick."

"He's had a bitter pill to swallow, for sure and for certain.

But it explains why he takes his meals in the Sweet Seasons—
a lot of the time with Preacher Gabe, it seems."

"Gabe's wife, Wilma, is all but bedridden. He takes to-
go boxes home for her most days." Miriam laughed softly.
"The preachin' service is at Tom's this Sunday, so the Brenneman boys will help him set up the pew benches while we
women fix the food for the common meal. Maybe somethin'
along that line fits into Nazareth's schedule . . ."

"Always one to help those in need, Aunt Nazareth is.
Well"—Ben halted his horse, and right there in the middle
of the road he kissed her again—"almost back to your
place, perty girl. And you can bet the curtains'll be a-flutter
with folks peerin' out when we drive in."

Miriam smiled in the darkness as the lighted windows of
her home came into view. She so rarely got out in the
evenings, she hadn't thought about what a comfort that sight
could be—just as it had always made her feel safe to look
out her bedroom window and see the lamps lit over at
Naomi and Ezra Brenneman's place.

Yet Ben talked as if that might change. "So where did ya
have in mind for that new house you're thinkin' about? Ya
wouldn't even have to buy land, ya know. Plenty of room on
our farm for another home."

"When I've got the details worked out, you'll be the first
to know, Miriam." He playfully kissed the tip of her nose.
"But for now, that's *my* secret and I'm stickin' to it!"

Chapter 24

By Friday in the Sweet Seasons, all the talk was about Bishop Knepp's car and how he hadn't been in to eat with Tom and Gabe since Jerusalem Hooley had taken him down a few pegs in front of his boys. Rhoda listened to the menfolk talking about this, not surprised that most of them thought it was Ben's aunt who needed a talking-to: What proper woman would be so brazen as to confront the bishop in public rather than wait until he got home?

Rhoda, however, suspected that Jerusalem was just made that way. The Ordnung was meant to be followed, so it was her natural inclination to keep her students—of whatever age—pointed along the higher path. And while Nazareth Hooley went about instructing folks in a quieter way, she, too, saw that everything was done according to her teacherly standards.

It made for interesting conversation when the two sisters came home from the Knepp house of an evening, although Jerusalem hadn't mentioned Hiram and his car since Monday. She talked as though the four youngest children were her main focus . . . yet Rhoda, Rachel, and Mamma all suspected the *maidel* was carrying a torch for Hiram.

"So, Sister—we'll be back sometime Sunday from the visits out and around," Rachel said as she closed the dishwasher to run it. "We'll be at the Raber cousins' for dinner and stayin' over tonight, then it's on to Uncle Paul's for Saturday noon. I'm sure Uncle Mose will be preachin' in Bowling Green on Sunday, and we'll start home after the common meal there."

"It'll be a long ride back for ya. We'll miss ya, Sister."

Rachel shrugged, but she still had that starry-eyed look about her. "It's not such a bad thing, collectin' our wedding gifts and showin' up at everybody's house as married folks. Adults now, for sure and for certain!"

So . . . if I'm the same age but I'm not hitched, does that mean I'm still a child?

Rhoda bit back this remark. Rachel looked so happy as she sat on Micah's left at the table and as they rode in their buggy, as befit an Amish wife. Micah was in the shop putting the top on his courting buggy to convert it into a carriage, the way most young men did when they married. Like the new beard that framed his face, it was a sign they were husband and wife.

Rhoda stood with Mamma outside the café to see the newlyweds off, waving as the shiny black carriage rolled smartly past them behind Micah's finest bay—a retired racehorse with a proud gait and conformation to him.

"Well, there they go," Mamma murmured. She slipped her arm around Rhoda's shoulders as they went back into the kitchen. "It's *gut* we're goin' to Preacher Tom's to redd up for him after the café closes. And I'm kinda glad the Hooley sisters'll be around for dinner. We won't feel so much like two loose peas rollin' around in a shoebox that way, ain't so?"

"*Jah*, it's different not bein' in the room beside Rachel, and comin' to work without her in the mornin's. But we're doin' what we've gotta do, I suppose."

"Oh, Rhoda, someday it'll be you ridin' off to collect your presents. But meanwhile"—Mamma got a wistful look on her face, like she might cry—"I'm mighty glad to have ya with me yet, child of mine. You're a blessin' like ya have no idea about, every single day."

Rhoda smiled, but it was good that two o'clock was rolling around—and that on Fridays, the dining room usually cleared out a little earlier. By the time she'd wiped down the tables and taken the last English couple's money, Mamma and Naomi were putting away the lunch buffet leftovers.

"How about we take home these green beans and the last of the pork roast?" Mamma asked her. "There's enough for all of us here."

"That'll be easy to whip up after we spend the afternoon at Preacher Tom's," Rhoda replied. "Want me to put it in the fridge at home and meet ya over there?"

"*Gut* idea. See ya in a few."

With the big covered bowl of beans in the crook of one elbow and the plate of sliced pork roast in the other hand, Rhoda walked down the lane toward the house. She saw Ben as she passed the smithy, wearing a safety mask exactly like her *dat*'s; with the welding torch in his gloved hands, he could've passed for her father at first glance—a startling thought. He was forming some ornate curlicues in a wrought iron gate Micah's brothers had brought from the historical home they'd been refurbishing. He was so engrossed in his work, she didn't interrupt him. He looked completely caught up in what he was doing . . . in restoring the beauty of a bygone day.

It was another reminder of how everyone around her had found a purpose for their lives—a reason to work every day at something that was useful and fulfilling. And what was her purpose? As she continued up the driveway without

Rachel, she wondered if she would ever get past this feeling that the other half of her was missing.

When she arrived at Tom Hostetler's, just one farm beyond the Brennemans' on the gravel road, her mood shifted; the lingering aromas of cattle and manure and silage disappeared when she stepped inside the modest white house. Nazareth and Jerusalem Hooley had scrubbed down the kitchen and tossed all the towels in the wringer washer out in the mud room.

"And how's our Rhoda today?" Nazereth asked. Sweat was seeping past the band of her blue kerchief, yet she smiled sweetly. "Busy at the bakery?"

"*Jah*, Mamma made her pies to stock the shelves with at Zook's Market for the weekend, and most of the usual breakfast and lunch crowd was there," she replied as she took up a tea towel to dry the dishes in the drainer. "Not as many tourists, now that school's on and the days are coolin' down. And we can't help noticin' Hiram's not been there all week."

Jerusalem got up off the floor she'd been scrubbing at the end of the kitchen. "Your bishop's finally figurin' out that he might not be able to wiggle out of this business with that black car," she remarked. "Bishop Mullet and Bishop Shetler have both been there for visits, alone and together— and a couple times with Tom and Gabe Glick, as well."

"I hear Wilma Glick took a tumble outta bed in the night, though," Nazareth added with a worried scowl. "Guess Gabe and their granddaughter, Millie, got a driver and took Wilma to the emergency room to check for broken bones, brittle as she is."

Mamma came in through the mud room then, catching the last of that conversation. "*Jah*, they're sayin' she might've punctured a lung when some ribs broke. Poor old thing hasn't been well for so long." She went to check the front room.

"Looks like the fellas got all the partitions down and have us set up with benches and hymn books. And I can't recall the last time I saw this kitchen gleamin' this way. You ladies have been workin' at it awhile."

Nazareth and her sister shrugged at the same time. *Somethin' they've done all their lives, like Rachel and me*, Rhoda thought. "It's what we can do to help out," Nazareth remarked. "It's not easy for a man alone to host the Sunday service—and probably preach one of the sermons as well—while he's takin' care of his cattle chores and the milkin', too."

"Micah's brothers have always set up the pew benches for Tom when it's his turn," Rhoda replied. "And Jonah Zook and Aaron generally come real early in their chorin' clothes to milk on those Sunday mornin's."

"Many hands make light work," Jerusalem quipped. She wiped her forehead against the inside of her elbow and took a long drink of ice water. "What we weren't sure about, though, was the food for Sunday's meal. Should we be checkin' the cellar downstairs—or thawin' somethin' from Tom's deep freeze?"

"All the women bring side dishes for passin' around," Mamma replied. "Naomi and I usually get some sort of meat cooked and sliced up for—"

"Oh, could I do that for you this time?" Nazareth asked. Her grin turned almost girlish. "We've lived in the *dawdi haus* at our brother Zion's for so long, I rarely get to cook, so it'd be a pleasure to contribute that way. Tom seems like such a nice fella—"

"Oh, I've got ya fooled then," a voice teased from the porch. Tom chortled at the surprised look on Nazareth's face as he slipped out of his muddy work boots. "But I can't thank you gals enough for gettin' me ready for Sunday."

He stepped into the kitchen then, gazing around at the

walls and the countertops. "My word. I can't recall this room lookin' so neat and tidy even when Lettie lived here. This is a real big favor you're doin' me. I—I don't know what to say."

"Then suggest what you'd like us to bring for the main part of the common meal." Nazareth folded her hands in front of her, smiling sweetly at him. "Back in our district, we serve a lot of cold cuts. I'm thinkin' ya might eat sand-wiches so often that it's not much of a treat to have the same for Sunday's dinner . . . even if ya don't have to fix them yourself."

When the dairy farmer removed his hat, his wavy brown hair was crushed and damp from the afternoon's work in his barns. Yet Rhoda thought she detected a delight in his eyes she hadn't seen for a long while.

"Truly, Nazareth, whatever ya make'll be a welcome switch from my own fumblin' in the kitchen," he admitted. "I'd even drive ya over to the market if ya give me a minute to find some clean pants. I need a few things there myself, ya see."

"Since you're goin' that direction," Mamma suggested, "could ya pick up the apples and peaches Leah's set aside for Sunday? She's happy to provide the fruit if I'll make the pies. Naomi'll be helpin' me with that at the café tonight—"

"And I'm makin' cinnamon applesauce for Sunday, too," Rhoda added.

"So we can just meet ya there with whatever I find at the market?" Nazareth clapped her hands together. "A pie frolic! And so much easier, workin' in the bakery kitchen where there's room to spread out. I'll see ya there, Sister."

Jerusalem was fumbling in her skirt pocket. "Here—pick me up some fresh lettuce and what-all for that overnight salad we like so well. If there's space in Miriam's fridge, we can make them in salad bowls, all ready to pass around."

"We've got just the bowls ya need and the space to keep them cold for ya," Mamma assured her.

Tom was following this rapid-fire conversation with an awestruck expression. "So—just like that, ya have everythin' figured out for the common meal?"

"That's perty much how it works, *jah*," Jerusalem said with a chuckle. She handed Nazareth a wad of folded bills. "Be generous when you're buyin' those groceries, Sister. Miriam's been takin' mighty fine care of us and it's our turn to buy."

"Consider it done." Nazareth turned to Tom with a sweet smile. "I'll just put on my kapp and write out my shoppin' list while ya find those pants, Preacher. Mighty nice of ya to help us out this way."

Consider it done.

Rhoda had seen Plain women working and cooking together all her life, but with Naomi and the Hooley sisters helping, they had prepared the main part of the common meal for more than 120 folks by eight thirty that evening. Twenty fruit pies lined the back counter of the Sweet Seasons kitchen, while four baked turkeys had been set in the big floor-to-ceiling refrigerator to cool. She and Naomi had peeled and cooked enough apples for a huge pan of applesauce, made with cinnamon Red Hots candies to turn it a pretty shade of pink, while Jerusalem had prepared her layered salad in glass bowls that showed off the rainbow colors of the veggies she'd used.

"See ya tomorrow, Naomi," Rhoda said as their neighbor started for home. "*Denki* for all the help. You're one quick woman with a parin' knife."

Naomi's brown eyes sparkled. "*Jah*, don't mess with me or you're liable to end up in a cookin' pot," she shot back. "Thanks for this peach pie, ladies! The fellas at my house'll make quick work of it."

Mamma gazed around the café's kitchen and grinned. "Not that I'm biased or anythin', but I'm thinkin' this'll be the best common meal we've had in a long time. Smells like Thanksgivin' in here, Nazareth! Sliced turkey'll taste mighty *gut* on Sunday."

"I was tickled to see that Henry had them in his meat case, fresh, for folks lookin' ahead to the holidays," she replied. "Nothin' easier to fix for a crowd than turkey, if ya use those newfangled oven bags."

Nazareth dried her hands with a satisfied sigh. "I'd be pleased to make soup from the broth for our dinner tomorrow night, too, so you and Rhoda won't have to cook after ya work in the café all day."

Rhoda grinned. "An offer like that makes it sound like we've got live-in help! Livin' like fancy folks, we are."

"And if Miriam doesn't mind," Jerusalem suggested, "why not invite the boys to join us? Your turkey chowder's their favorite—"

"And why not ask Preacher Tom, as well?" Nazareth suggested with a coy grin. "He's gotta eat, too. And he must get mighty tired of his own company."

Mamma chuckled as she gathered up the towels and dishrags to take home for the laundry. "If you're doin' the cookin', you can feed whoever ya want, Nazareth."

"And if ya simmer that soup tomorrow mornin', we could take some to Hiram's," Jerusalem remarked. "Those kids'll slurp that chowder right down. Anythin' with cheese makes them line up like piggies at the trough."

Once again Rhoda smiled to herself; consider it done, indeed. With the exchange of a few sentences and a stock-pot of broth left from baking those turkeys, the Hooley sisters had made plans to feed four families. It was easy to see their ulterior motives, too, what with making sure Preacher Tom and Hiram's family were taken care of. And with Ira, Luke, and Ben coming tomorrow night, the matchmaking was in full swing without anyone directly mentioning the subject.

And didn't that mean she would be keeping company with both of the younger Hooley brothers tomorrow night? It was an opportunity not to be missed. "How about if I come in to work early with ya tomorrow mornin', Mamma?" she ventured. "Nothin's better with soup than homemade bread, so I'll make enough for everybody's dinner and to sell in the bakery case. Maybe that recipe with the whole wheat and oatmeal, and the English muffin bread."

The Hooley sisters' faces lit up. "What a feast!" Jerusalem crowed. "There'll be happy faces—"

"And happy fellas," Nazareth added.

"—at the table tomorrow night, for sure and for certain."

Chapter 25

As Miriam started up the lane toward home late Saturday afternoon, the wind whipped at her coat and sent dry leaves into a little whirlwind between the café and the smithy. Where had the autumn gone? In just a few frosty nights the leaves had fallen and winter seemed to be sneaking in early. The past week had ushered in many changes—many things to think about—as the seasons of their lives rolled forward like the wheels of the dozer that was digging the foundation for the new mill.

Hearing the roar of the big machinery, Miriam cut through the apple orchard and walked over toward the riverbank to see what progress they'd made. She stopped, holding her bonnet as the brisk wind whipped around her. The scoop on the front of the dozer was making quick work of the excavation, and the fellow driving it maneuvered effortlessly on the slope as he dumped another load of dark, wet soil off to the side.

What would Jesse think if he saw that gapin' hole in his favorite fishin' spot?

Miriam spotted Ben on the other side of the water and returned his wave. It didn't bother her now to consider her late husband's reactions to these changes on his homeplace; she was living in the present, looking toward a future she'd never dreamed of before the Hooley family had come to Willow Ridge.

Ira and Luke were watching the dozer with excited grins. What an adventure this was for them! The Mennonite fellows who partnered with Micah had told them that one or two warm weeks remained for pouring the footings and the foundation, so the concrete would set up right. Then the building would go up in a hurry. It boggled her mind that the Hooley brothers planned to be in their new rooms by the first of December, while Micah and his brothers would complete the rest of the mill before the New Year.

Miriam turned toward home then, noting how early the dusk fell now . . . how pretty the kitchen windows looked with light coming from them. She opened the door to the most heavenly aroma of turkey and onions and celery, all simmered together. The table was set for eight on a freshly ironed tablecloth she hadn't used for so long . . . plates and silverware were all in place, and bowls were stacked beside the stove, awaiting the soup that would fill them. Voices drifted in from the front room . . . Rhoda and Ben's aunts sat crocheting in there, talking like old friends.

God, I've gotta thank Ya that I can come home to a warm house where dinner's been made and the table's set for friends . . . some we've loved a long time and some who opened our lives and hearts before we knew what-all was happenin'. It's a wonderful life You've given me, Lord.

After Miriam hung up her coat and bonnet, she strolled into the front room. "Well now, what ladies of leisure do we have here?" she teased. "Did the *gut* fairies fix that dinner while ya crocheted more squares for Ben's afghan?"

Nazareth chuckled. Despite the day she'd spent cleaning and making that divine soup before she and Jerusalem took some over to Hiram's, she looked pert and fresh in a dress of jade green. "*Jah*, fairies named Rhoda and Jerusalem whipped up that food, ya know," she replied. "I just sat around twiddlin' my thumbs, waitin' for my date to show up."

Miriam exchanged a grin with Rhoda, who sat on the end of the couch stitching finished granny squares together. "It's true," her daughter said. "Had to be the *gut* fairies who did it, because when I came home from the café, the table was already set. A bowl of baked pineapple was coolin' beside the stove and cherry cheesecake pie was in the fridge."

"Jerusalem loves that for dessert," Nazareth confided, as though her sister weren't in the room. "What she won't tell ya is that she makes one for herself and one for the rest of us."

Jerusalem laughed aloud. "And the other two pies I made have already disappeared—at Hiram's, for noon dinner. My word, but those kids can eat! And by the way, Sister, Annie Mae asked for your turkey chowder recipe."

A knock at the door announced Tom Hostetler, who looked as delighted to be there as Nazareth was to have him. "Brought along some fresh butter," he said as he handed her a plastic container. "Figured you gals could put it to *gut* use. I didn't want to arrive empty-handed, after the way ya got tomorrow's big meal ready for me."

"We'll put it on the table and watch it disappear," she replied.

A short while later, Ben and his two brothers tromped up the steps. They left their muddy boots on the porch and came inside, inhaling as though they couldn't fill their lungs with enough of that aroma.

"I love it when you aunts cook us up a pot of soup! And it's your turkey chowder, too," Luke said.

"And look at what-all else is here." Ira removed his hat and gave it a toss, grinning smugly when it landed on an empty peg on the opposite wall. "Aunt Jerusalem's baked pineapple, and some *gut*-lookin' bread."

"Rhoda made that," Nazareth told him, "and we can tell ya it's right tasty, too."

"Ben, you should sit at the head of this table tonight," Jerusalem suggested, "on account of how ya brought all of us together by sayin' your two aunts should come along for the ride to Missouri. And Preacher Tom, we'd be honored if you'd sit at the other end."

Miriam wasn't surprised when Jerusalem gestured for her younger nephews to sit across from Rhoda, or when Nazareth gravitated to Tom's side, and the spot to Ben's left seemed to have her own name on it. After their silent prayer, Nazareth dipped up the soup while her sister placed the steaming bowls at each of their places.

Miriam rose to carry food, as well, but Jerusalem was having none of that. "This is our treat," she insisted. "You've been on your feet cookin' all day. Let us serve it up so you can sit back and enjoy it, Miriam."

When had anyone ever made such an offer? And hadn't the Hooley sisters worked hard all day, as well? "I—I feel like a queen, sittin' at a table I didn't set and eatin' food I didn't cook," she replied quietly. "Must be true, then, that the *gut* fairies have come to stay at our house. And I'm glad they did."

When she sat down again, Ben squeezed her hand under the table. "We're like one big happy family, ain't so? And it's better chow than what I would've made these fellas eat."

"You can say that again!" Ira slathered butter on a warm slice of the oatmeal bread and jammed it into his mouth as though he hadn't eaten in days.

Luke snickered. "That's the last we'll hear from him. He's too busy feedin' his face to talk to us."

For a few moments they ate in silence, savoring the

warm, cheesy chowder . . . the tangy sweetness of the baked
pineapple . . . the way Tom's butter filled the little pockets
in Rhoda's English muffin bread. Miriam felt herself relax-
ing like she hadn't been able to for months, despite the fact
that she had a kitchen full of company. What a gift their
houseguests had given her, this simple yet satisfying meal—
as well as other folks to enjoy it with.

"So how were things at Hiram's today?" she asked. "I
haven't seen the bishop all week, so I'm guessin' he's preparin' for tomorrow's meetin' after the service."

"It's a different home from when we first took the goats
over." Jerusalem nodded, spooning apple butter onto her
bread. "It's not just the twins who're mindin' their p's and
q's, either. Their *dat*'s spent a lot of time in his office out in
the stable, talkin' with the bishops from Morning Star and
New Haven."

"They'll be with us tomorrow, preachin' and runnin' the
members' meetin'," Tom remarked gravely. "It's not for me
to say how things'll turn out, since the members have a vote,
but we'll be limpin' along without a bishop for six weeks if
Hiram's put under the ban. And I believe he should be."

"Ya think he'll duck his punishment?" Ben asked. "When
we saw that photograph on his website, he got around it by
confessin' to those bishops."

"And now that we've caught him with a car, they're none
too happy with him for doin' that." Despite his serious tone,
Tom raised his eyebrows at the two younger Hooleys. "Ya
should've seen it, fellas. A big old black Cadillac like they
don't make anymore—the kind with a round, spoked case
on the back that holds the spare tire. Cream-colored leather
inside, and the top folded down."

The preacher chuckled as he helped himself to more
pineapple. "It was the kind of car rich English folks drove,
back when I was a young buck—the kind of car that made

ya think *rumspringa* could last forever if ya drove away instead of takin' your instruction to join the church."

Ben smiled as though he understood that sentiment quite well. "Let me guess, Preacher. A perty girl caught your eye and ya figured you'd better come into the fold before another fella latched on to her."

"*Jah*, Letty was the pertiest girl ya ever wanted to see," Tom replied wistfully. "Which partly explains why an English fella drove away with her last February. Men aren't the only ones who like ridin' in fine, fast cars. And women kinda like livin' in a house where ya don't smell the livestock on a hot summer day."

The kitchen went silent for a few moments while everyone ate. Miriam was pleased that Tom, too, had come through a crisis in his life and his heart was healing. Nazareth stood up then, smiling at them. "More soup, anyone?"

"Let me get that cherry cheesecake out of the fridge." When Jerusalem returned with their dessert, she was shaking her head. "As I watched Jason, Hiram's Mennonite stable manager, drivin' that big old car out of the storeroom, I couldn't for the life of me figure why Hiram caved in to that temptation . . . why he thought it was worth the risk of bein' shunned."

"Or why he thought he'd get away with it," Miriam added quietly. "Does that mean he had a driver's license, too?"

"Not anymore, he doesn't." Jerusalem cut the cheesecake with quick, decisive strokes of her knife before she spooned cherry pie filling over it. "I told him I couldn't respect a man who preached at his members about their sins while he hid his own, too proud and pigheaded to confess them. I also told him if there was any way he could be stripped of his position as the bishop of Willow Ridge, it was the chastisement he deserved."

"Several folks feel that way about it. But it won't happen,

of course," Tom remarked. "Once you're chosen by God and the fall of the lot—in the ceremony when that piece of paper flutters from the hymnal *you* picked instead of from the other fellas' books—ya carry that responsibility until ya die or get too disabled."

Ira, who had followed the conversation with interest, grinned mischievously. "So, where'd they park the car? I haven't yet joined the church, so I could take it out on the road every now and again—to keep the battery charged up, ya know."

"Ira Hooley, we'll have none of that talk!" Jerusalem declared.

"A new courtin' buggy is more your speed, dear," Nazareth said lightly. "And your Uncle Israel promised to replace the buggy ya turned over last year, once ya take your vows."

Ben cut into his pie, smiling as though he'd heard this conversation many times. Miriam glanced at her daughter, who was taking in these details with great interest, even though she pretended to be occupied with her last few bites of dessert.

Luke elbowed his younger brother as he set down his fork. "Ya can't win, Ira. Ya might as well declare yourself Amish, like the rest of us. If nothin' else, the girls here'll take ya more seriously—which would be a big improvement over your datin' record back home."

"Puh!" Ira tossed his napkin beside his cherry-smeared plate, his dark eyebrows raised in playful defiance. "I'm meetin' Millie Glick in half an hour. How about *you?*"

"Annie Mae said she'd be real glad to get outta the house tonight, what with her *dat* preparin' what he's gonna say at church tomorrow." Luke smiled at everyone as he stood up. "Real nice of ya to have us over for supper. I'll see ya tomorrow."

"*Jah*, I'll be runnin' along, too. *Denki* for the fine eats." Ira rose, snatching the last two slices from the bread basket. "Real *gut* bread, Rhoda."

As the door closed behind the young men, Preacher Tom scooted back, as well. "Better study the Scripture for tomorrow. What with Gabe's Wilma still in the hospital and Hiram's situation, I figure to be preachin' the first sermon. It's been a real nice evenin', friends." As he put on his hat and coat, he seemed pleased that Nazareth got ready to step outside with him.

When Ben grabbed her hand under the table, Miriam's stomach fluttered. "If ya can wait until I help with the dishes—"

"Go on with ya!" Jerusalem declared as she stacked their soup bowls. "Won't take long for reddin' up because we washed things as we went along. I'll be turnin' in early, so I'll see ya for breakfast, Miriam."

"Tomorrow promises to be a day like Willow Ridge has never seen," Miriam remarked. "We'd all better get our rest, to be ready for whatever happens at the members' meetin', ain't so?"

A few hours later, sleep was the furthest thing from Rhoda's mind. She sat in her nightgown with her brushed hair hanging down her back, gazing out at the vast blackness of fields and farmhouses gone dark for the night. How strange it felt, with Rachel away last night and tonight . . . and how lonely, having no one to whisper with about Ira and Luke.

In the room next door, the Hooley sisters snored so loudly it was a wonder they didn't wake each other. Mamma and Ben sat talking downstairs like a couple of courting kids, so disappearing to her room had been the only polite thing to do—just as her parents had done when she and Rachel sat downstairs with dates. No lamps were lit in the windows above the smithy, which meant Luke and Ira were still out with Annie Mae and Millie.

Annie Mae and Millie! Am I invisible? Nice to have around for makin' bread, but then I'm to clean up with the rest of the maidels?

Sighing, Rhoda crawled under the covers and squeezed her eyes shut. It was silly to pout and throw a pity fit, but it still hurt, how the Hooley boys had tossed off their remarks about their dates as though she hadn't been at the table . . . as though she were blind and deaf and had no feelings.

Rhoda swiped at a tear, peeved at herself now; clueless fellows like Ben's brothers didn't deserve her attention and she shouldn't waste her time being upset over them. "Somebody better than you will come along!" she declared into her pillow.

She swallowed hard. Her shoulders relaxed. That simple statement had made her feel better, so she said it again. "Somebody better than you will come along, Ira and Luke Hooley."

Rhoda smiled in the darkness, promising to keep that affirmation in mind whenever either of them perturbed her again.

Lord, forgive me for sinkin' so low when You've promised to care for me and provide everythin' I'll ever need, she prayed. *Boys will be boys, but You I can depend on. Amen to that!*

Chapter 26

While the sun still slept and the frost made the grass in the center of the driveway whisper beneath her feet, Miriam strode to the Sweet Seasons to fetch Sunday's food from the refrigerators. Ben's brothers were to cart it down the road when they left for the service at Preacher Tom's. As she passed the smithy, the lamplit windows told her the Hooley brothers were up and getting dressed. Who could have guessed the apartment Micah had built for her and Rhoda would be seeing so much use by so many folks?

And I thank Ya, Lord, that Ya brought those brothers to Willow Ridge . . . and I ask Your special blessin' on the proceedin's at today's members' meetin'. Things could get testy if we forget we're doin' Your work while we hear Hiram's confession and decide what comes next.

Miriam slipped into the back kitchen door and flipped on the light.

"Good morning, Miriam."

She yelped and fell back against the door. "Hiram! Ya scared me halfway to Kingdom Come."

"I know you're busy, so I won't take but a moment of your time—and time is of the essence," the bishop added as he rose from the stool he'd been sitting on. "I've been hoping to speak with you all week, rather than catching you at the eleventh hour—"

Miriam remained by the door. Hiram was dressed in his black trousers and vest, wearing a crisp white shirt . . . looking as imperious as he always did at church. He wasn't acting predatory, exactly, but his tone made her wary. "I've been right here, runnin' the café, ya know."

"—but that infernal Hooley woman has been driving me insane," he continued in a frustrated rush. "She thinks I *need* her! Insists I eat my meals at home—"

A smile twitched at Miriam's lips. "So . . . whose house is it, Hiram?"

"—and meanwhile, she's brainwashing my children. The twins and Sara know their alphabet now, so they're constantly hounding me for help with writing everyone's names—"

"And whose children are they, Hiram?"

The bishop heaved an impatient sigh. He gazed at her, so focused on his own thoughts he hadn't heard a word she'd said. "Miriam, these past several days away from you, I've had a chance to consider why you've refused to marry me. I've gone about winning you in all the wrong ways, haven't I?"

This was getting interesting. As the bishop had said, however, time was of the essence. She went to the nearest fridge and opened it. "Hold this, will ya please?" she asked.

Hiram grabbed the door, watching her work. "I understand now why you feel you're serving God by baking—feeding His sheep—and I appreciate how you keep Tom and Gabe and me fed. So if you wanted to keep running your café after we married—"

Miriam removed the platters of sliced turkey, setting them on the countertop quietly so she didn't miss a word.

"—and my offer still stands, to redecorate or even remodel the house to suit you."

She glanced up at him. "It's a mighty long hike from your place to here. My bakin' day starts at three, ya know, and I've always believed a Plain woman should work at home—close to her children."

Hiram raked his free hand through his dark hair. "Then I'll buy a piece of Gabe's ground across the road!" he exclaimed. "I understand that you'd prefer a new home for raising our family, Miriam. Money's no object—surely you know that. You're a fine woman, and you deserve the best."

Oh, but this was making her bubble up with laughter she didn't dare turn loose! She carried the bowls of Jerusalem's layered salad, considering the reasons that might be behind Hiram's new attitude. How long should she let him grovel before she told him she was marrying Ben?

"Maybe I'm seein' things that aren't there, Hiram," she said quietly, "but from the moment ya met Jerusalem Hooley, it looked like ya *wanted* to spend your time with her. Ya certainly did your best to impress her, bringin' that fine wagon and Belgian stallion to take those goats to your place."

He glared, but quickly covered his flare of temper. "Appearances can be deceiving," he replied pointedly. "I soon found out what a bossy, outspoken, overbearing—"

Was he describing Jerusalem, or himself? As Miriam lifted the large stainless steel bowl of applesauce and set it in an empty space near the door, she filed away information that might be useful later.

"—because with you by my side, Miriam, the People would see my willingness to change and become a more . . . humble servant." Hiram sighed, gazing earnestly at her. "Humility has never been my strong suit, I admit. But people *listen* to you, Miriam. They respect your opinion and advice, and if you spoke in my behalf—"

Miriam blinked. Was the bishop asking her to sway the vote at the members' meeting today?

"—they would believe I'm truly a changed man."

She glanced at the clock, motioning for him to let go of the refrigerator door. How could she respond in a way she wouldn't live to regret? Hiram had never taken her rejection gracefully. "I—I appreciate your kind words and generous offers, Hiram. But I can't marry ya."

His jaw dropped. "Why not?" he demanded. "Haven't you heard a word I've said, Miriam?"

Ah, there it was—his usual refusal to accept the word *no*. Miriam almost blurted that she had accepted Ben's proposal, but she swallowed the words. Such an announcement deserved to be made in a time of joy rather than as a comeuppance. She clasped her hands in front of her, looking directly into the bishop's eyes. "I can't marry ya because I don't love ya," she stated. "And ya don't love me, either, Hiram. Not once has that word entered into any of your conversations about marriage."

As he opened his mouth to protest, someone knocked boisterously on the door. "Are ya ready for us, Miriam?" Ira Hooley called out. "Got the cart hitched up for ya."

She had to grin at his fine timing. Had the Hooleys seen the bishop here, or overheard their conversation? "*Jah*, the food's ready to load! Come on in, fellas."

Hiram's face reddened as he quickly leaned forward. "It's up to *you*," he whispered tersely. "The new mill isn't built yet, you know. Cooperation begets more cooperation."

The door opened and Luke Hooley poked his head inside. "Meant to get here a little earlier, but—oh, *gut* mornin', Bishop! Catchin' a bite of breakfast before church?"

Hiram pressed his lips into a line as though he were counting to ten. "My daughter was to be home by eleven o'clock last night, Mr. Hooley."

Ira came in, waving cheerfully as he stepped around Luke to pick up the bowl of applesauce. "*Jah*, we're sorry about that," he replied, "but Annie Mae didn't mention a curfew until nearly midnight—"

"And Millie was pointin' us down so many dark roads," Luke chimed in, "that we had no idea where we were or how long it would take us to get back."

Hiram's eyes narrowed as he gave Miriam a purposeful parting glance. "We'll discuss this later. I have church business to attend to." When he saw the wagon was backed up nearly against the door, Hiram pivoted on his heel and headed through the dining room to go out the café's main entrance.

Miriam gathered bowls of salad into her arms to hand to Luke, waiting until the bishop had closed the door. Then a fit of giggles overtook her, which made Ben's brothers chuckle, too. "*Gut* to see ya, boys. I *so* appreciate your showin' up to help me this way."

"Does that mean we can polish off this fine pie?" Ira gestured toward the counter where the pies were wrapped and ready to go. "Wouldn't wanna take one for the common meal that's already been half eaten, would ya?"

Miriam gaped. She'd been so busy following Hiram's every move she hadn't noticed the sticky spoon and the crumbs on the counterop, next to a peach pie with a large, irregular hole—as though someone had taken a huge bite out of it.

"Well, I'll be—" She let out an exasperated sigh. "*Jah*, ya might as well finish that one off, boys. Looks like a mighty big mouse got in."

"Maybe ya ought to start lockin' up," Luke remarked.

Ira took two forks from the drawer. "Or set a mighty big mousetrap."

* * *

As the women came into Tom Hostetler's kitchen before the worship service, Miriam and Rhoda found places for the food many of them brought. Their platters of sliced turkey and bowls of layered salad had completely filled his refrigerator, so they set Rhoda's applesauce and the incoming food out in the unheated mud room where it would stay fresh on such a cold morning. All was ready . . .

But what would happen if their bishop, Hiram Knepp, was put under the ban?

It was the question on everyone's mind as they entered the house. A cold wind was blowing, so folks didn't linger outside to visit; they put their coats in a back room and then shook Hiram's hand and greeted Jeremiah Shetler and Enos Mullet, the bishops from New Haven and Morning Star. The men entered the huge main room from one side and the women from the other, in lines that went from oldest to youngest. They sat solemnly on the tightly packed pews, silent. Waiting.

Miriam slipped into line behind Leah and Naomi, and they filled in the row behind Ben's two aunts. Gabe Glick, Tom, Reuben, and the bishops entered last, taking their places in the center of the big room. They removed their hats in one smooth, orchestrated motion that had been their tradition since time untold.

But it was *not* tradition, this event they would witness today, watching as their bishop knelt before them to confess his sins.

Or has he wiggled out of it again? Confessed to the other bishops, as he did before? Miriam set aside those thoughts as the men on the other side of the room murmured among themselves, deciding who would be the song leader. The first syllable of the hymn rang out in a mellow, rounded tone that made folks look around to see who that new voice belonged to.

Miriam's body thrummed: it was Ben! Why hadn't she realized he would be a fine singer, considering the rolling cadence of his speech? As always, the bishops and preachers retired into an upstairs bedroom to discuss who would deliver the day's sermons and other matters needing their attention, while the congregation sang for another half hour. As the leaders returned to their pew in the center and the hymn ended, all minds and hearts were focused on what would happen next.

Tom Hostetler rose, looking weighted down by his responsibilities as one of their preachers. "The lectionary lists the eleventh and twelfth chapters of Hebrews as the passages for our consideration today," he began. "These were verses decided upon by the leaders of our Old Order some time ago, yet it's also the topic on all of our minds this mornin'. This is not coincidence, my friends. It is the will of God at work among us."

He paused to draw a long breath. His solemn mood seemed to be affirmed by the looks on the faces he saw. "Every one of us has fallen short of the standards God delivered to Moses—and to us—in the Ten Commandments, just as we have failed to follow Jesus's teachin's about lovin' the Lord and lovin' our neighbors," he went on in a bolder voice. "It is our admission of sin—our conformin' to the faith by way of confession—that keeps us on the narrow way to salvation. Not a one of us can point a finger at our neighbor and blame him or her for what we have done. And not a one of us can claim to be followin' God's will perfectly." Once again he paused to emphasize his next point. "It's not for us to judge who best keeps the Lord's commandments, either. That's a job for God alone . . . and for that we are thankful."

Miriam and many around her nodded. Who wanted the responsibility of declaring Hiram Knepp a sinner? And who, having sinned, wanted to be judged according to the whims and biases of neighbors? She sat absolutely still, following every word Tom spoke. He sounded more eloquent today—more inspired—than he ever had before. He spoke of the faith of Abraham and Moses and Noah, who listened to God's call and believed in it, centuries before Jesus came to bring salvation.

After Tom sat down, everyone knelt on the floor for silent prayer. Then Reuben Reihl, their redheaded deacon, read the Scripture for the day. He was a big fellow, strong from farming and managing his poultry business, yet today he, too, seemed burdened by his calling. As he read the eleventh chapter of Hebrews, he reconfirmed what Tom had preached about the faith of great men and women of the Old Testament. As he made his way through the twelfth chapter, everyone sat a little straighter.

"'For whom the Lord loveth He chasteneth, and scourgeth every son whom He receiveth. If ye endure chastening, God dealeth with you as with sons; for what son is he whom the father chasteneth not?'" Reuben paused, knowing what came next. "'But if ye be without chastisement, whereof all are partakers, then are ye bastards and not sons.'"

Miriam glanced up to watch Hiram's reaction to this passage. He sat straight and tall, yet his face seemed paler. Had the past week of keeping to himself given him time to reflect and repent? Or had he searched the Scriptures and found justification for hiding that car? After the way he'd caught her unawares in the Sweet Seasons kitchen this morning, she wasn't sure what to expect.

Beside Hiram, Gabe Glick slumped with his head bowed. Miriam's heart went out to him; with Wilma still in the hospital, the poor old fellow was surely wishing he were there with her. Faithful to a fault, he was; he'd served as a preacher in Willow Ridge since before Miriam had arrived as Jesse's bride.

"'Furthermore we have had fathers of our flesh which corrected us and we gave them reverence,'" Reuben continued reading. "'Shall we not much rather be in subjection unto the Father of spirits, and live?'"

The deacon read several more verses, slowing his delivery as he reached the end of the twelfth chapter. "'Wherefore we receivin' a kingdom which cannot be moved, let us have grace, whereby we may serve God acceptably with reverence and godly fear. For our God is a consumin' fire.'"

After presenting that grim image for their consideration, Reuben resumed his seat. Then Bishop Shetler from Morning Star stood up. He was a man they saw in the café occasionally. Jesse had known Jeremiah Shetler before he'd become that district's bishop, because Jesse had done a lot of farrier work on the Shetler place. Somewhat younger than Hiram, Jeremiah had a reputation for more lenience when it came to folks installing phones and electricity in their businesses.

Yet when Bishop Shetler glanced at Hiram before beginning the main sermon, there was no mistaking the message he was about to deliver. "'All we like sheep have gone astray,'" he began in a thundering voice. "'We have turned every one to his own way; and the Lord hath laid on Him the iniquity of us all.' Because this familiar verse from the fifty-third chapter of Isaiah reminds us that none are perfect—and because, as Deacon Reihl read, 'our God is a consuming fire,' it's our job to recognize each other's sins when we ourselves are unable—or unwilling—to acknowledge them.

This is a cornerstone of our Old Order faith, and it keeps us strong."

For the next hour he preached on the importance of recognizing worldly sin and the necessity of repentance. Jeremiah spoke without apology or any indulgence for a man who had been chosen by God for the highest level of service. Hiram's name wasn't mentioned, but everyone knew he was the main object of this lesson.

Miriam recalled her own kneeling confession in August, after her daughter Rebecca's reappearance in black mascara and tattoos had caused such an uproar. Hiram had insisted her café business was making her too proud, too worldly. The days leading up to her time of trial had been among the most difficult she had endured since Jesse's passing. She prayed that Hiram would have the grace to face the day's inquisition, just as she had. She truly believed that everything had worked out according to God's will—which was why Hiram didn't own the building that housed her business and the Schrocks' quilt shop.

When Jeremiah's sermon ended, they fell to their knees again as Reuben read a prayer, and then they stood for the benediction and the closing hymn.

Again Bishop Shetler rose. "We call to order a members' meeting for the purpose of discussing and acting upon Hiram Knepp's ownership of a car," Jeremiah said in a solemn voice. "Those who are not baptized members of the faith are excused."

Annie Mae and Nellie Knepp rose, their younger siblings in hand, as did Ira Hooley and other young folks still in their *rumspringa*. Miriam felt sorry for the bishop's girls, for they would bear the brunt of a shunning if the members voted for that as their *dat*'s punishment.

"After much consultation with Enos Mullet and me,

Hiram has agreed to come before you, his congregation, for a kneeling confession. Enos and I were disappointed, however, that he didn't arrive at this decision of his own free will. Your preachers, Tom and Gabe, brought this matter to our attention to ensure it wouldn't slide by."

"Some folks here might not be aware that Hiram came to us earlier," Enos Mullet said as he stood up. Because he had struggled with cancer the past few years, his hollow cheeks and lined face looked as forbidding as the Reaper's. "At that time, he confessed to having a photograph of himself on his website, where he advertises his Belgians. Again, sadly, this admission of worldliness came after someone else saw the likeness of him and challenged him about it."

Several in the crowd looked at each other as though this was indeed the first time they'd heard of Hiram's earlier escapade.

"It's only right that you take these things into consideration as you listen to your bishop's confession and cast your vote as to his penance." Enos turned to look at Hiram. "Are you ready to confess, Hiram?"

With his hands clasped before him, Hiram rose from the bench. His gaze swept the men's side of the room and then the women's, beseeching his longtime friends to be merciful. When he held Miriam's gaze, she kept all expression from her face. He went to his knees then, facing the two bishops.

"Is it true you own an automobile, Hiram?" Jeremiah asked in his sonorous voice. "And is it true that you concealed it, believing no one would be the wiser?"

"Yes."

The two visiting bishops waited, probably for more of a response. Then Enos cleared his throat. "Would you tell us how you came by this vehicle? A customized Cadillac convertible isn't something the average fellow would have parked in his garage. We need to know why an Amish bishop would own one."

Hiram's face went ruddy with suppressed temper. "I sold a registered Belgian stallion to a man in Michigan and he defaulted on his payment," he explained impatiently. "To make matters worse, when I tried to collect the debt, he had already sold the horse. He offered the car for the balance of his payment, and because I suspected this was the only form of remuneration I would receive, I took it."

Miriam pressed her lips into a line. Hiram often used lofty vocabulary when he was talking his way out of a sticky situation.

Jeremiah Shetler's dark eyebrows rose. "And you've kept it locked away all these months? But you've also driven it?"

"Yes."

When a few shocked folks sucked in their breath, Hiram looked up. Judging from the scowls Miriam observed on the men's side of the room, the women probably looked no happier to hear that their leader had not only accepted a car, but had concealed it and taken it out on the roads.

Hiram gazed at her, assessing her allegiance. Miriam gazed back; she didn't condone his mistakes, and she wouldn't fall prey to insinuations that he would hinder the building of the mill. She couldn't imagine that Jerusalem Hooley, seated a row ahead of her, wore an expression that looked any more lenient or loving.

Hiram licked his lips, as though finally realizing his friends might vote to shun him. "I . . . I want to beg forgiveness of my congregation—my extended family," he proceeded in a contrite voice. "I now see that I am guilty of the worldliness for which I disciplined Miriam Lantz several weeks ago. I also wish to apologize to Miriam for the way I have so publicly pursued her and badgered her about marrying me.

"And on a similar subject," Hiram went on before the other bishops could interrupt him, "I wish to apologize to Ben Hooley for my attitude concerning his coming to Willow Ridge . . . and for threatening retribution if he established himself here—with Miriam at his side."

The women around Miriam stole glances at her, and she sighed. She sensed the bishop was voicing his apologies just to sway the vote on his punishment. Wasn't that a shame?

"I also wish to apologize to Tom and Gabe for my arrogance these past couple of weeks. They were doing their duty to God by confronting me about my website photograph and the car I've concealed," he went on in a voice that wavered. "My Mennonite stable manager, Jason Schwartz, has driven the car to his home, so I'm no longer in possession of it. The driver's license I've surrendered is in the glove compartment."

Whispers hissed around the room; a lot of Amish fellows had driven a car during their *rumspringa*, but having a Missouri license meant Hiram had posed for the mandatory photograph on it. Was there no end to the secrets he'd kept?

"Most of all, I owe apologies to my daughters Annie Mae and Nellie for the way I have so often chastised them when the younger children have misbehaved," he went on. "And I wish to express my sincerest thanks to Jerusalem Hooley for showing me how I've distanced myself from my children. She has insisted I remain at home with them more often, to be a mainstay in their lives rather than a father who places other concerns before the raising of his family."

He went silent then, still kneeling before the two other bishops, his deacon, and the preachers.

"Have you anything else you wish to confess to us, Brother Hiram?" Enos asked in his reedy voice.

"Are you insinuating there's more?" Hiram blurted. Then he let out a sigh. "Excuse my cavalier attitude. I'm starting to realize how deeply ingrained my temper and lack of humility have become. I beg everyone's forgiveness and patience as I find my way back to rightness with God."

"So be it." Jeremiah Shetler stepped back, allowing Hiram to rise to his feet. "You may now wait in Preacher Tom's cellar or the mud room—or outdoors—until you're called back in."

All eyes watched Hiram Knepp leave the crowded room. The door from the kitchen to the mud room closed with a decisive *whump* before anyone dared breathe or whisper to each other.

Jeremiah's shoulders relaxed. He looked at everyone as he spoke. "Enos and I have discussed this situation several times in the past week. We feel the *Ordnung* clearly recommends a six-week shunning for owning a car—especially because this sin follows on the coattails of Hiram's having a photograph on his website. Enos and I will share your bishop's duties between us during his time of contemplation and separation. Is there any discussion?"

Tom Hostetler rose, his expression grim. "Gabe here won't mention it, but with his Wilma so ill, he's concerned he won't be around town much to help with any church matters that might arise. And, frankly, he doesn't feel much like preachin' these days," Tom added. "He's also concerned about the hospital bill that's mountin' up, to the point he's sold off a part of his farm to pay it."

Miriam gasped, as did everyone around her. Because most of Willow Ridge's property had been in the same Plain families for generations, it was highly unusual for a man to sell off land rather than pass it on to a son. Poor Gabe looked exhausted from sitting here these past few hours, and he was clearly uncomfortable about having his private affairs discussed.

Enos nodded. "Jeremiah and I will take turns with the preaching, Tom. You won't bear the burden of Hiram's absence alone. And we'll find some help with that money Gabe needs, too. I suggest your scribe for the *Budget* post a request for a money shower."

After a few moments of silence, Miriam felt compelled to stand up. "While shunnin' Hiram is the proper thing to do, it also puts his family in a bad way," she remarked. "To his credit, he's been spendin' more time with his four younger ones, but now he can't eat at their table. And they're not to accept anythin' from him—a difficult concept for little children to understand, especially since they have no *mamm*."

In front of her, Jerusalem Hooley rose, as well. "My sister Nazareth and I have discussed this issue, and—if Hiram's willin'—we can stay at his place to help Annie Mae with the youngsters while Nellie finishes school."

Ben's aunt cleared her throat, as though thinking about how to express the rest of her thoughts. "I feel bad that our adventurous little goats led to all this disruption of Hiram's life, but we Amish believe that followin' the *Ordnung* keeps us strong in our faith—and in our families, too."

"Are there any other concerns?" Bishop Shetler asked.

Ben stood up then, smiling at Gabe Glick before he began. "We knew a fella in Lancaster who got caught with a car, and when he sold it, he donated the money to the district's medical emergency fund," he said. "It's not my place to decide that, of course. But we all know a fella who could use the cash a fancy car like Hiram's might bring."

"Point well-taken." Enos Mullet looked around the crowded room then. "Are we ready to vote? *Aye* means Hiram Knepp is to be placed under a six-week shunning, which will last until the middle of December. *Nay* means we must discuss other options—and in a situation that affects everyone in Willow Ridge, I feel we must have a unanimous decision. Is that agreed?"

Everyone nodded. Most clasped their hands tightly in their laps, awaiting the final outcome.

Wilbert Reihl, the oldest male among them, began the reckoning. "Aye," he said heavily. And on down the pew rows it went, as every man—and then every woman— agreed that Hiram should be shunned. No one sounded happy about it, but this, too, was one of the duties of membership: to ensure justice and conformity to the code of ethics they had agreed to uphold when they'd been baptized into the faith.

Miriam said her *aye* without a moment's hesitation. It didn't sit well with her that Hiram had sneaked into her café to persuade her to derail the vote, and to again propose marriage because it would improve his reputation. The longer she thought about his little speech—and that pie he'd ruined—the more peeved she got.

"We have a decision, then," Jeremiah confirmed. "Will one of you ladies nearest the kitchen bring Hiram in, please?"

Everyone shifted on the benches as Millie Glick rose to fetch their bishop. Miriam bowed in prayer, glad she wouldn't be meeting Hiram's eyes as he entered the silent room. Even the slow, steady tread of his boots increased the tension among them as he stepped forward to receive word from the visiting bishops.

"The members have voted that you are to serve out a six-week shunning, which begins immediately," Enos Mullet announced quietly. "We pray for you, Hiram, as you begin this journey of solitude and reconciliation. As you are not allowed to eat at the same table with other members, you are to leave immediately. I'm sure someone will bring your children home, if they wish to stay for the common meal and the visiting."

Hiram's expression darkened. Without a word, he reclaimed his hat from beneath the preachers' bench and then stalked out. This time the door banged so hard the windows rattled.

"Our meeting is adjourned," Jeremiah announced quietly. "If ever we had a need for a common meal that binds us together in fellowship, it's now."

Chapter 27

Ben hustled with the other men to set up the tables in the area where the service had been held. He wasn't surprised at how they spoke about Hiram's car—all his sinful secrets—in tones of dismay and disgust.

"Guess Hiram won't be ridin' on such a high horse now, for sure and for certain," Ezra Brenneman remarked.

"Almost makes ya wonder what God was thinkin' when He had the lot fall to Hiram years ago, ain't so?" Henry Zook pondered aloud.

"Or, with all Hiram's finaglin'," Daniel Kanagy joined in, "ya gotta ask if maybe he somehow fixed it so he knew which hymnal the marker was in, that day he was ordained by the fallin' of the lot. And I hate it that I'm even thinkin' that way."

"*Jah*, we can only hope bein' under the ban tones him down a notch or two. He's our bishop as long as he lives," Wilbert Reihl stated in his breathy voice. "Sure hope none of our families leave Willow Ridge because they can't trust him."

In his travels, Ben had indeed heard of folks who'd moved from one district to another after personality differences had arisen with the bishop. While it was true the perfect bishop didn't exist, it was a shame when members lost their confidence in the man who served as their spiritual leader.

He stepped out of the way as Rhoda and the two Knepp girls placed bowls of pink applesauce on the tables. It was good to see them working together—the same way they'd been crocheting together the other night. "Say, girls, I'd be happy to take your little brothers and Sara home so's ya can stay with the young people for the singin' tonight."

Annie Mae flashed him a grin. "*Denki*, Ben, but your Aunt Jerusalem's already got that covered."

"She's quick that way, *jah*," he agreed. "And how are ya feelin' about her and Nazareth stayin' at your place while your *dat*'s under the ban?" he asked quietly. "I know from growin' up next door to her, and bein' a scholar in her classroom, that she can be kind of . . ."

"Assertive?" Annie Mae asked with a raised eyebrow.

"Controllin'?" Nellie teased.

"Bossy?" Rhoda added.

"All of those things and more." Ben chuckled at the kitty-cat grins on their faces. "So if ya think she'll be a little more high-handed than ya want to put up with for six weeks—"

Nellie shrugged. "She and Nazareth already have the boys and Sara writin' their letters and spellin' out words by sound. They sit at the table playin' school, except it's real learnin'. So if anybody can teach Dat a thing or two—"

"It would be Jerusalem Hooley," Annie Mae agreed. "And while *we* couldn't point it out to Dat if he was breakin' the rules of his ban, she won't let him get away with anythin'."

"*Des gut* then," Ben replied. "The aunts wanna be useful, and your *dat* and little brothers will give them plenty of chance at that."

As the three girls returned to Preacher Tom's kitchen for more food, Ben followed. He knew better than to get in the women's way, because they were intent on getting the meal served. Aunt Jerusalem was tossing salads while Aunt Nazareth put forks on the turkey platters. He spotted Miriam at the kitchen table, cutting the pies for Naomi to carry out, and made his way among the other women to stand behind her.

"Can I have a word?" he asked quietly.

Miriam teased him with a brown-eyed smile. "Ask me real nice, and ya can probably have just about anythin' ya want, Ben."

He chortled, loving the way she'd kept her sense of humor despite the morning's events. "If it's all right with you . . . shall I make our big announcement? Folks are sayin' so many negative things about Hiram, it might be a *gut* time to offer up a happier subject, ain't so?"

"What a *gut* idea! Our friends'll be glad to hear about us . . . and it means Hiram will be the last to know," she added mischievously. "I didn't tell ya yet, but he was waitin' for me at the Sweet Seasons early this mornin'. Tried to sweet-talk me into marriage again, among other things."

"And what'd ya tell him?"

"Puh!" Miriam resumed her pie cutting as she talked in a low voice. "Said I couldn't marry him because I didn't love him. Almost told him you'd spoken for me, but I thought that information deserved a better time—like now! So see?" she asked brightly. "Ya read my mind, Ben. Ya know me awful well, ain't so?"

Ben grabbed her playfully by the shoulders. "Just you wait, perty girl. I might throw in a surprise or two for *you*, once I start talkin' about our plans."

He returned to the main room, feeling better about this whole day. It amazed him how welcome—how at home—he felt among these folks, and he knew almost every one of them by name already. Ben was pleased to see so many of them talking to his brothers about their new mill, too. Several local farmers had already bought seed for some of the specialty grains Ira and Luke wanted to process, so they were off to a productive start before the building was even constructed.

A few moments later, Jeremiah asked folks to be seated for the meal. By extending Tom's kitchen table with all its leaves, and putting the plates close together at all the tables set up in the front room, the women had found a way for everyone to eat at one sitting. After a moment of silent grace they passed the platters of turkey and the other bowls of food.

Ben had ended up beside his brothers, while Miriam—acting as Preacher Tom's hostess—ate in the kitchen with Naomi and Rhoda so they could refill water pitchers and bread baskets. He rose at his place and, with a big grin, *dinged* his spoon against his water glass. How could he not be delighted, making such an announcement? When Miriam winked at him from the kitchen, his heart fluttered. What a blessing it was—what a joy—to know such a fine woman wanted to spend the rest of her life with him.

"I want to share some *gut* news!" he began as the conversations around the two big rooms ceased. "First off, I want to thank all of ya for makin' me—along with my brothers and my aunts—so welcome here in Willow Ridge. And while it might not be the conventional thing, sayin' this at a common meal, I've never been a fella to stick real tight by convention. So why start now?"

Friendly laughter rose around him. Ira and Luke were watching him closely, and down the table Rhoda's eyes widened, anticipating what he was about to say. He smiled at her, so grateful—to her and to God—that her crush on him had found a graceful resolution without hurting anyone's feelings or damaging her relationship with her mother.

"Lemme guess!" Bram Kanagy called out. "You're gonna park that blacksmith wagon and set up shop permanent-like, so's ya can keep an eye on your brothers."

"*Jah*, they'll be needin' it, too, if they're keepin' company with the likes of Annie Mae and Millie!" Jonah Zook called out.

Good-natured remarks rose around him, with more laughter. And didn't it feel fine that folks here could tease him so freely while saying they wanted him to work among them . . . to live among them?

"The way I see it, that wagon comes in mighty handy, bringin' my farrier work to you instead of makin' you haul your weldin' and horses to me," he replied. "But *jah*, I'll be settin' up shop, too . . . right there at the same forge where Jesse Lantz worked. And I thank Miriam for makin' that possible, and because—well, we're gonna get hitched!"

An "oh!" went up in the kitchen while the men around Ben nodded and murmured "*jah!*" and "*des gut!*"

"Wait'll Mamm hears this!" Ira crowed. "She thought she wouldn't live to see the day!"

Beside him, Luke began to clap enthusiastically. Soon, the applause spread all along the table, and even Jeremiah Shetler and Enos Mullet expressed their congratulations.

"It's Miriam I'm happy for," Preacher Tom said. "Not only is she gettin' herself a fine new husband, but now Hiram'll have no choice but to leave her be. Congratulations to the both of ya—and we're mighty glad ya told us, too. Makes my day!"

Ben beamed, his heart throbbing. He met Miriam's eyes as her friends in the kitchen got up to congratulate her. When the commotion settled, he held up his spoon to signal that he wasn't finished. "It just so happens the parcel of land across the road from the Sweet Seasons—that piece Preacher Gabe sold off—will be the site for our new home," he went on. "Miriam said she wanted to be within walkin' distance of her kids and her work. I'm sure you will all be happy to know that she's gonna run her bakery and café as long as it pleases her."

The Brenneman brothers and the Kanagy boys—and Preacher Tom—resumed the applause. Ben couldn't recall ever seeing a houseful of Plain folks so expressive, or so excited, but didn't this happiness look good on their faces? He smiled at them all. No doubt about it: he'd done exactly the right thing, deciding to stay in Willow Ridge. And he'd found exactly the right woman after years on the road.

"Mostly I want to thank the *gut* Lord for watchin' over me, and bringin' me to this new life," Ben said in a more serious tone. "Okay, I'm finished now. But this is really just another beginnin', ain't so?"

Preaching Sundays were all-day affairs, a time set apart from the work week to visit with friends and family. By the time the women had served a lighter evening meal and then put Tom's kitchen back to rights, it was getting dark. The young folks would start their singing soon, and Miriam was glad the Zooks were helping Tom host the evening's activities. As Ben and his aunts helped load her serving dishes into the wagon, Miriam waved good-bye to Rhoda . . . who was winding a kapp string around her finger, having a flirtatious conversation with Ira Hooley. Jerusalem and Nazareth herded the younger Knepps into their carriage, and off they went to the bishop's place.

"Well, finally!" Miriam whispered when she and Ben stood alone beside the loaded wagon. She tugged him toward her for a kiss. "And aren't you the smarty-pants, buyin' that land across the road from home!"

Ben held her close. His warmth did more than shield her from the chill of the evening breeze: it made her feel secure and oh, so loved. Miriam knew for sure and for certain that never in her life had she felt so happy. So contented and complete.

"Won't be long before that place across the road *is* home," he murmured. "I was real glad when Micah told me he and his brothers could start us a house as soon as they finish the mill. They're welcomin' the work, and—"

"And while it's a sad thing, why Preacher Gabe needs that money," Miriam said, "it was *gut* to hear somebody from outta the district hadn't bought it."

Ben's smile gave her goose bumps. "Did ya hear what ya just said, perty girl? You're talkin' like I've been around Willow Ridge forever."

"*Jah?* Well, startin' now, that's how it's gonna be, ain't so?" Miriam grinned up at him, for Ben Hooley wasn't the only one who could pull a surprise or two. "I know when I want us to get hitched, too."

"Oh, *jah?* You're soundin' awful independent, Miriam," he teased. "Better get that outta your system, ya know, on account of how wives are to submit to their husbands."

"Puh! Ya think I haven't already submitted, just sayin' I'd marry ya?"

Ben laughed so loud that the horses in the corral turned to look at them, their ears pricked forward. Pharaoh, standing closest to the fence, whickered and tossed his fine black head, impatient to be hitched up.

Miriam stood watching Ben . . . the way his body moved so fluidly as he jogged over to the gate . . . the way he and his stallion communicated without the need for words. Within minutes, Ben was helping her onto the wagon seat, and when he'd hopped on from the other side, he kissed her full on the mouth. "Now what were ya sayin' about submission— and a wedding date?"

"New Year's Day." She grinned, nodding emphatically. "*Jah*, it's on a Thursday, the best day for marryin'. But it's a whole new beginnin'—a clean calendar of days to spend any way we want! And I wanna spend them with you, Ben."

Ben's hand went to his chest. "Ya just took my breath away, woman," he whispered. "My heart's poundin' so hard, the skin's pullin' where Pharaoh left his mark on me."

Miriam placed her hand over his, to feel his heartbeat . . . the steadfast love she knew this man would never run short of. "And if ya think your horse marked ya for life, Ben," she murmured, "just wait until *I* get ahold of ya!"

WHAT'S COOKIN' AT THE
SWEET SEASONS BAKERY CAFÉ?

Because I love to cook as much as Miriam and Naomi do, here are recipes for some of the dishes they've served up in AUTUMN WINDS. The weather has gotten cooler in Willow Ridge, so these dishes are a little heartier than some I put in SUMMER OF SECRETS. I read Amish cookbooks and the *Budget*, so I can say yes, the convenience foods you see as ingredients are authentic!

I'll also post these on my website, www.Charlotte HubbardAuthor.com. If you don't see the recipe you want, please e-mail me via my website to request it, plus book-marks, etc.—and let me know how you like them! I hope you enjoy making these dishes as much as I do! Yum!

~Charlotte

Cornmeal Rolls

If you enjoy corn bread and also like soft, satisfying dinner rolls, this recipe's a tasty combination of the two. Makes a wonderful accompaniment to just about any meal!

2¼ C. warm water, divided
⅓ C. yellow cornmeal
¼ C. sugar
3 T. oil
2 tsp. salt
2 pkgs. (2 T.) dry yeast
2 eggs
5 to 5½ C. all-purpose flour
melted butter or margarine
additional cornmeal

In a saucepan, combine 1¾ C. water, cornmeal, sugar, oil, and salt. Cook over medium heat, stirring, until mixture boils, about 7–9 minutes. Set aside to cool for about 5 minutes, and then pour into a large mixing bowl. Meanwhile, dissolve the yeast in the remaining warm water. Add to cornmeal mixture with eggs and mix well. Add enough flour to make soft, pliable dough, then knead about 5 minutes on a floured surface. Place in a greased bowl, turning to grease the top. Cover and let rise in a warm place until doubled, about 45 minutes. Punch dough down and shape into 24 balls. Place on a greased, rimmed cookie sheet, or use a greased 9" x 13" pan. Brush rolls with melted butter and sprinkle with cornmeal. Let rise, uncovered, until doubled—about 30 minutes. Bake at 375° for about 15 minutes or until lightly browned. Remove from pan immediately. Makes 2 dozen.

Apple Crisp

OK, I confess that I make this recipe more for the "crisp" than for the apples! So I tend to put a lot of the oatmeal-butter-sugar topping on the fruit, thinking the oatmeal—as a whole grain—and the fresh fruit qualify this as health food. You decide.

1 C. quick-cooking or old-fashioned oats
1 C. packed brown sugar
½ C. all-purpose flour
1 T. cinnamon
½ C. butter or margarine
3 or 4 large apples

Preheat oven to 350°. Combine the oats, brown sugar, flour, and cinnamon and then cut in the butter until well blended. Set aside. Peel, core, and slice the apples to make 5–6 cups and put them in a greased/sprayed 2-quart baking dish. Sprinkle the oatmeal topping over the fruit, then dig down into the fruit with a spoon to mix in some of the topping. Bake about 40–45 minutes or until fruit is bubbly. Enjoy warm with cream or ice cream. Serves 4–6.

<u>Kitchen Hint</u>: This is also yummy using the same amount of peaches or rhubarb!

Breakfast Sandwich Casserole

Amish folks love their breakfast! And the only thing better than a hearty, mouthwatering hot breakfast is one you can make the night before and pop into the oven when you get up. Talk about a wonderful wake-up call, when your family smells this!

12 slices of bread, any variety
1½ pounds sausage, fried and drained
1 lb. bacon, fried and crumbled, divided
12 slices of sandwich cheese, any variety
1 small onion, chopped
3 C. milk
6 eggs
1 tsp. salt
other seasonings to taste
1 C. crushed cornflakes or similar cereal
2 T. butter or margarine

Grease/spray a 9" x 13" pan. Put 6 slices of the bread on the bottom, then 6 slices of cheese, and cover evenly with the sausage and bacon (reserve about ½ C.). Top with the remaining cheese slices and chopped onion, then with the other 6 slices of bread, like you're making sandwiches. Beat the eggs with the milk, salt, and other seasonings (pepper, dill, parsley are good) and pour evenly over the sandwiches. Mix the cereal, butter, and remaining bacon and scatter this over the top. Cover and refrigerate overnight. Bake at 325°, uncovered, about 50 minutes or until firm. Dig in!

Kitchen Hint: Why enjoy this only for breakfast? If you make it in the morning, it'll be a wonderful-*gut* supper! Make a skillet of fried apples while it bakes, and you'll be set!

Fried Apples

A quick, easy way to enjoy autumn's bounty of apples! Great with pancakes, French toast, pork, or for any meal of the day.

Fresh apples, any variety
1 or 2 T. butter or margarine
brown sugar
cinnamon

Coat a large skillet with nonstick spray. Wash, quarter, and core the apples, then slice them into the skillet to make it as full as you want. Dot with butter or margarine and sprinkle to taste with brown sugar and cinnamon. Add about ½ C. water to the bottom of the skillet and simmer, covered, over medium heat. Stir occasionally to spread the spices and cook evenly. Remove from heat while still firm and cover; let sit until you're ready to eat.

Pumpkin Blueberry Muffins

A wonderful, moist muffin poppin' with blueberries. Amish cooks would use pumpkin puree from their own gardens, but this version works better for most of us.

1⅔ C. all-purpose flour
1 tsp. baking soda
½ tsp. baking powder
1 T. cinnamon
1 C. solid-pack canned pumpkin
¼ C. evaporated milk
⅓ C. shortening
1 C. packed brown sugar
1 egg
1 C. blueberries, fresh or frozen
1 T. all-purpose flour

<u>Streusel Topping</u>
2 T. flour
2 T. sugar
½ tsp. cinnamon
1 T. butter

Preheat oven to 350°. Cream shortening and sugar, add egg. Mix in the pumpkin and milk, then add the dry ingredients all at once and mix well. Combine the berries and flour, then gently stir them into the batter. Divide batter into a sprayed or paper-lined muffin tin. In a small bowl, combine streusel ingredients with a fork. Sprinkle over the muffins. Bake 20–25 minutes or until a toothpick inserted in the center comes out clean. Makes 18 small or 12 large muffins.

<u>Kitchen Hint</u>: I hate to have leftover canned pumpkin, so I use the whole can and double the other ingredients to make 2 dozen muffins at a time.

Ham Balls

This has always been a favorite dish at our church dinners and potlucks. Makes the whole house smell wonderful when they're baking, and goes especially well with sweet potatoes. I buy a lean, boneless ham and ask someone at the meat counter to dice it into chunks (they tell me they won't grind it for me on equipment that's processed other meats).

5 pounds of ham, ground in a grinder or food processor
1 large onion, finely chopped in the grinder or food
  processor

1½ C. crushed saltine crackers
4 eggs
½ C. milk
½ C. cider vinegar
2 T. yellow mustard
Salt, pepper, garlic powder, and dill to taste
1 packet of apple cider drink mix powder

Preheat oven to 350°. Place all ingredients in a large mixing bowl and blend well. Form into 24–30 balls and place in greased/sprayed casserole pans. Sprinkle the drink mix powder over the tops and bake, covered, about 40 minutes. Uncover and bake another 10 minutes or so to brown them a bit.

Yams and Apples

This is a recipe I concocted as another way to enjoy sweet potatoes. The cinnamon and butter make it really satisfying and the whole house smells wonderful as it bakes. To make this a whole-meal casserole, add ham chunks or thin-sliced deli ham.

2 large sweet potatoes
2 large apples (Jonagolds or other firm/tart varieties work well)
Butter, cinnamon, brown sugar

Preheat oven to 350° and spray/butter a 1-quart baking dish. Peel the sweet potatoes and quarter/core the apples. As you slice the sweet potatoes crossways, layer them in the baking dish, then sprinkle with brown sugar. Add a layer of apple slices, and top that with dots of butter and sprinkle with cinnamon. Repeat until you've used up your ingredients, and add more if you wish. Cover with foil and bake about an hour. Serves 3 or 4.

<u>Kitchen Hint</u>: This casserole shrinks as it bakes, so you can heap the bowl high before covering it—to be sure you'll have enough for everybody when they taste how yummy it is!

Loaded Baked Potato Casserole

A surefire potluck pleaser! You just can't beat the combination of sauced meat and cheese. Here's an example of an Amish recipe that uses convenience foods but still tastes down-home good and will fill up the hungriest fellows at your table.

1 28-oz. bag Tater Tots
1 stick butter or margarine, melted
Salt and pepper to taste
1 2.5-oz. pkg. bacon bits
1 C. chopped onion
1 18-oz. container barbecue pulled pork or pulled beef
3 C. shredded Cheddar cheese

Preheat oven to 350°. Spray a 9" x 13" pan and cover the bottom with a layer of Tater Tots. Drizzle the melted butter over the potatoes, sprinkle with salt and pepper, and spread the onions evenly over the top. Cover with half the bacon bits and half the shredded cheese, and then spread the pulled pork or pulled beef over this. Cover with foil and bake about 45 minutes. Top with remaining cheese and bacon bits and bake until cheese is bubbly, about 10 minutes. Dig in!

Kitchen Hint: I have a few Tater Tots left over after covering the bottom of the pan, so I keep them in the freezer for another time. It probably wouldn't hurt to bunch them up more and use the whole bag—might make a bumpier casserole, but who would care?

Fudge Ripple Cake

Call it an indulgent coffee cake or call it dessert, but call it scrumptious!

1 box white or chocolate cake mix
1 box chocolate instant pudding
1 C. sour cream
1 C. oil
4 large eggs
2 tsp. vanilla

Ripple Mix
⅓ C. sugar
1 tsp. cinnamon
⅓ C. cocoa powder
2 C. chocolate chips, divided

Preheat oven to 350°. Spray a tube pan and set aside. Mix the cinnamon, sugar, and cocoa in a small bowl for the "ripple" and set aside, along with the chocolate chips. In a large mixing bowl, combine all the cake ingredients until blended, and then spoon half the batter into the tube pan, spreading it to cover the bottom. Sprinkle most of the "ripple" mixture over this, and 1 C. of the chocolate chips. Top with the rest of the cake batter, and then sprinkle the remaining cinnamon sugar over the top. Bake 50 minutes or until a toothpick comes out dry. Sprinkle with the remaining chocolate chips and spread over the top with a spatula when they've melted. Cool in the pan about 15 minutes and then remove to a serving plate.

<u>Kitchen Hint</u>: If you like walnuts or pecans, chop about a cup of them and divide those between the "ripple" layer and the top of the cake, after you've spread the melted chips.

Apple Walnut Coffee Cake

Wow, is this just the yummiest use of apples there is! Call it coffee cake or call it dessert, but call folks to the table and watch it disappear.

2 C. sugar
1 C. plus 2 T. vegetable or canola oil
¼ C. apple cider
3 large eggs
2 tsp. vanilla
1 tsp. each cinnamon, nutmeg, salt, and baking soda
3 C. all-purpose flour
2 large, firm apples (Granny Smith or Jonathan work
   well), peeled, cored, and sliced (3½ C.)
1½ C. chopped walnuts
Powdered sugar, if desired

Preheat oven to 350°. Spray a 10-inch tube pan (use one that has a removable insert). Stir sugar, oil, apple cider, eggs, vanilla, seasonings, and soda in a large bowl until blended.

Stir in the flour until smooth, and then stir in the apples and walnuts. Pour into the pan, and bake an hour and ten to twenty minutes, until a toothpick in the center comes out clean. Dust with powdered sugar if desired. Cool on a wire rack for an hour before removing the sides of the pan. Cool completely before lifting the cake from the pan's bottom.

Coconut Layer Cake

Coconut lovers, here's your treat! Moist and sweet, this is one of those cakes that adds a special touch to any occasion and deserves a high-quality brand of coconut (I use Baker's). As with all cakes that have cream cheese frosting, store this one in the fridge. You can freeze the leftovers, too.

½ C. butter, softened
½ C. shortening
2 C. sugar
5 eggs, separated
2 C. all-purpose flour
1 tsp. baking soda
1 C. buttermilk
1 tsp. vanilla
2 C. flaked coconut
½ C. chopped walnuts or pecans (optional)

Frosting
1 8-oz. pkg. cream cheese, softened (use full fat)
4 C. to one pound of powdered sugar
¼ C. butter, softened
1 tsp. vanilla
Extra coconut for garnish
Walnut or pecan halves (optional)

Preheat oven to 350°. Cut wax paper to cover the bottom of two round cake pans, then grease/spray the sides. Cream the butter, shortening, and sugar. Add the egg yolks and mix well. Add the flour and soda alternately with the buttermilk and vanilla. Stir in the coconut and chopped nuts. Beat the egg whites until stiff and carefully fold into the batter. Divide the batter into the prepared pans and bake about 40 minutes (center should spring back when you touch it). Cool in pans 10 minutes and remove from pans to a rack to cool completely. Peel off wax paper.

For frosting, mix the cream cheese, powdered sugar, butter, and vanilla until smooth. Frost the top of one layer and place the other layer on it, then spread the frosting over the top and sides. Garnish by pressing extra coconut onto the sides and spacing nut halves along the edge of the top.

<u>Kitchen Hint</u>: No buttermilk? Stir 1 T. white vinegar into a cup of milk and let it sit for about five minutes.

In the story, Miriam baked this as a three-layer cake for Hiram's birthday and for Rachel's wedding. To do that, simply make half again as much batter and frosting: for instance, you would use ¾ C. butter, ¾ C. shortening, 3 C. sugar and 7 eggs, etc. Instead of garnishing the cake with nut halves, you could pipe some of the frosting around the edges with a pastry tube and decorative tip.

Baked Apple Oatmeal

Great to make ahead for a crowd—or make half the recipe, as this serves 8–10 people. I like to leave out the sugar and let folks spoon up as much as they want from the pan before adding the sweetener of their choice: honey, maple syrup, sugar, or artificial sweeteners work well. Have extra milk on the table.

2⅔ C. old-fashioned rolled oats
½ C. raisins
⅓ C. packed brown sugar
1 T. ground cinnamon
4 C. milk
2 medium apples, chopped (2 C.)
½ C. chopped walnuts

Preheat the oven to 350°. Spray a 2-quart casserole or a 9" x 13" pan and mix all ingredients in the pan. Bake uncovered 40 to 45 minutes or until most of the liquid is absorbed.

<u>Kitchen Hint</u>: Serve immediately—or cool and keep covered in the fridge. Keeps for 3 or 4 days, and can be reheated in the oven, covered; or in the microwave, one bowl at a time.

Three-Grain Biscuits

These biscuits offer a tasty alternative for folks who like a serving of whole grains at breakfast. They don't rise as high as a traditional white-flour biscuit, but you'll enjoy the denser texture and nuttier flavor with all of your favorite toppings!

¾ C. whole wheat flour
½ C. all-purpose flour
½ C. whole-grain cornmeal
3 tsp. baking powder

¼ tsp. salt
¼ C. shortening or butter
½ C. old-fashioned or quick-cooking oats
¾ C. milk

Preheat oven to 450°. In a large bowl, mix the first five dry ingredients and then cut in the shortening/butter with a pastry blender or by rubbing with the tines of a fork until the mixture resembles fine crumbs. Stir in oats. Stir in just enough milk so the dough forms a ball and leaves the side of the bowl.

Knead on a lightly floured surface about 10 times. Roll to ½-inch thickness and cut biscuits with a 2½-inch round cutter (or use a drinking glass). Place on a greased cookie sheet, about an inch apart. Brush with milk and sprinkle with additional oats, if you like. Bake 10 to 12 minutes or until light brown. Enjoy! Makes 10–12 biscuits.

Kitchen Hint: You can put the dry ingredients into the work bowl of a food processor and cut in the butter/shortening with the blade, and then add the oats and dribble the milk through the top opening to mix the dough faster—although your biscuits will end up a little heavier. Butter will also make them a little heavier than shortening, but some folks (like me!) prefer that down-home taste! These freeze well.

Boston Brown Bread

This recipe dates back to Colonial times, when refined sugar wasn't readily available. Molasses and raisins make it a dense, sweet, satisfying treat for breakfast—or any time!

Makes nice little sandwiches when spread with cream cheese and cut into squares or "fingers."

1 C. all-purpose flour
1 C. whole wheat flour
1 C. yellow cornmeal
1 C. raisins
2 C. buttermilk
¾ C. molasses
2 tsp. baking soda
1 tsp. salt

Preheat oven to 325°. Spray two 8" x 4" bread pans. Mix all ingredients and divide dough between the two pans. Bake about 40 minutes or until a toothpick comes out clean. Cool for a few minutes, loosen sides, and remove to cool on a rack.

<u>Kitchen Hint</u>: No buttermilk? Pour 2 cups of milk into a measuring cup and stir in 2 T. vinegar. Let it sit about 10 minutes to thicken.

Whole Wheat Banana Bread

This is my all-time favorite recipe for banana bread, so I never make any other kind! The combination of whole wheat flour, butter, and nuts makes a denser, moister loaf that freezes well. Like most fruit-nut breads, this one cuts cleaner and tastes better if cooled completely, wrapped in plastic wrap, and served the next day . . . although we can never wait that long at my house!

½ C. butter or margarine, melted
1 C. sugar

2 eggs
3 medium bananas (1 C. mashed)
1 C. all-purpose flour
½ tsp. salt
1 tsp. baking soda
1 C. whole wheat flour
⅓ C. hot water
¾ C. chopped walnuts

Preheat oven to 325°. Blend sugar into melted butter/ margarine. Mix in the eggs and mashed bananas until smooth. Stir in the all-purpose flour, salt, baking soda, and whole wheat flour alternately with the hot water. Stir in nuts. Bake in a sprayed/greased 9" x 5" loaf pan for an hour and ten minutes—or until a toothpick inserted in the center comes out clean.

<u>Kitchen Hint</u>: This makes a dozen wonderful muffins, too— which shortens the baking time to about 15–20 minutes. Or, for smaller loaves, pour the batter into two 8" x 4" pans and bake about 45 minutes, or until a toothpick comes out clean.

Stuffed Shells

Every time I make this dish for potlucks and receptions I get requests for the recipe! It freezes beautifully and combines a lot of great flavors. Think of it as lasagna in a shell!

1 lb. bulk Italian sausage
1 large onion, chopped
1 10-oz. pkg. frozen chopped spinach, cooked and
   drained/pressed
8 oz. cream cheese

1 egg
2 C. shredded mozzarella cheese, divided
2 C. shredded Cheddar cheese
1 C. cottage cheese
¼ C. Parmesan cheese
Salt, pepper, Italian seasonings to taste
1 box of jumbo pasta shells, cooked and drained
Large can of spaghetti sauce, any flavor

Cook the pasta shells according to package directions, rinse
in cold water, and separate them on wax paper. For the filling, cook the sausage and onion together, drain, and either
chop with a pastry cutter or with a blade in the food processor. Press all the liquid out of the spinach. Combine the meat,
spinach, cream cheese, egg, 1 C. of the mozzarella, the Cheddar, the cottage cheese, and the Parmesan in a large bowl and
mix well. Fill the pasta shells and place in a greased/sprayed
9" x 13" pan; top with spaghetti sauce. Cover and bake at
350° for 45 minutes. Top with remaining 1 C. of mozzarella
and bake uncovered about 5 minutes more.

<u>Kitchen Hint</u>: I usually have an "overflow" pan because it's
better if the filled shells aren't crammed too tightly into the
9" x 13" pan.

Hamburger Soup

This is one of my all-time favorite soups, because you can't
beat the basic meat and potatoes combination. The tomato
juice base packs in lots of vitamins and veggie servings
without adding the calories of a cream-based soup. Like a
lot of soups, this one improves after a day in the fridge, but

if you don't want it sitting around, simply freeze it in 1- or 2-serving portions. Makes a good, quick meal for another day!

1 lb. ground beef
Salt and pepper to taste
2 large potatoes, cubed
3 carrots, sliced
3 stalks celery, sliced
1 large can or 1 quart jar tomatoes (with juice)
2 beef bouillon cubes
1 64-oz. bottle tomato juice
Dill, garlic powder, salt, pepper, to taste

In a 2-quart pan or Dutch oven, brown and drain the ground beef with salt and pepper; set aside and discard the grease. In the same pan, simmer the potatoes, carrots, celery, and tomatoes with the bouillon and seasonings until tender. Add tomato juice and stir in the ground beef. Adjust seasonings to taste and simmer to allow flavors to blend.

Kitchen Hint: If you prefer a creamier soup, as my mom did, shake 1 C. milk with 3 T. flour in a jar until smooth and stir this in after the final step above. Stir continuously to keep the milk from scorching. Freezes well.

Turkey-Cheese Chowder

Here's a tasty, economical way to satisfy a craving for comfort food on a cold day!

2 turkey wings or drumsticks
4 C. turkey broth (from cooking the wings or drumsticks)

1 C. each of diced carrots, potatoes, celery, onion
4 chicken bouillon cubes
2 C. milk
6 T. flour
1 C. shredded Cheddar or Colby cheese
¼ C. butter

In a large pan or Dutch oven, cook the turkey in 5–6 cups of water, discard bones and skin, and cut into chunks. Add the veggies and the bouillon cubes to the broth and simmer until tender, then stir in the cooked turkey. Stir the milk and flour together (or shake them in a jar) until smooth and stir into the hot soup until thickened. Stir in the cheese and butter.

<u>Kitchen Hint</u>: This is also great if you stir in a can of creamed corn. Because this is a milk-based soup, you'll want to lower the heat and stir continuously to keep the milk from scorching on the bottom of the pan.

Overnight Sensation Salad

This is an oldie but a goodie: crisp and crunchy with fresh veggies but topped with just enough bacon, mayo, and cheese to taste sinfully good. You have to make it the day before so it's ready when you are, for any occasion!

1 head of lettuce, broken or cut in pieces
1 red onion, diced
1 head of cauliflower, cut fine
¼ head of red cabbage, cut fine
1 small bag of frozen peas
2 or 3 carrots, halved lengthwise and sliced
1 lb. bacon, cooked and crumbled

2 C. mayonnaise
¼ C. sugar
3 C. Parmesan cheese

Layer all ingredients in a large glass bowl for best presentation—or in a large bowl with a sealable lid—and cover tightly. Chill in the fridge overnight. Toss just before serving.

<u>Kitchen Hint</u>: Don't mix the topping ingredients; just layer them on the salad and let them blend themselves. You can replace part or all of the Parmesan with shredded Cheddar cheese, too.

Baked Pineapple

This side dish, warm and sweet and easy, never fails to get me requests for the recipe. And because it's made with ingredients you have in your pantry all the time, it's a wonderful last-minute addition to just about any meal.

1 large can crushed pineapple with juice
1 egg
1 T. cornstarch
1 T. sugar or equivalent sweetener
Cinnamon

Preheat oven to 350° and spray a 1-quart baking dish. Dump in the pineapple and juice, and then mix in the egg, cornstarch, and sweetener, right there in the baking dish. Sprinkle with cinnamon. Bake about 30 minutes, or until the center is set. Store leftovers in the fridge. Serves 4.

<u>Kitchen Hint</u>: For a little extra zing, add ⅓ C. dried cranberries and/or some shredded coconut!

Colonial Oatmeal Bread

This was one of the first breads I ever made, and is still one of my favorites. It's soft and sweet and chewy—and the kneading works off stress, too!

1 T. salt
2 pkgs. (2 T.) fast-rising dry yeast
4 C. whole wheat flour, divided
2 C. all-purpose flour, divided
2¼ C. water
½ C. honey
4 T. butter or margarine
1 egg
1 C. old-fashioned or quick-cooking oats

In a large mixing bowl, combine salt, yeast, 2 C. of the whole wheat flour and 1 C. of the all-purpose flour. Meanwhile, heat the water, honey, and butter/margarine to 120°, and then add it to the dry ingredients. Mix well. Add the egg and another cup of the whole wheat flour, and mix again. Add the oats and the last 2 cups of the flours to make a warm, dense dough. Knead on a floured surface until smooth and elastic. Let rise in a greased bowl until doubled. Punch down and shape into two loaves, and place in two greased/sprayed 9" x 5" bread pans. Let rise until doubled. Preheat the oven to 350° and bake about 35–40 minutes. Cool in the pan about 10 minutes before loosening the edges to carefully remove the loaves. Finish cooling on a rack.

<u>Kitchen Hint</u>: I burned out two or three mixer motors making bread dough before my husband bought me a big KitchenAid mixer that's built to handle the strain of bread making. Don't even try to use a hand mixer on this or any bread recipes! If you hear your motor straining, or it starts to smell hot, stop the mixer and do the rest of the mixing/kneading by hand.

English Muffin Bread

This wonderful bread tastes like English muffins, complete with all the little crannies to catch your butter, jelly, or whatever you slather on it. Because it's a batter bread, you mix it, let it rise in the pans, and then bake it—no kneading.

5½–6 C. all-purpose flour
2 pkgs. (2 T.) dry yeast
1 T. sugar
2 tsp. salt
¼ tsp. baking soda
2 C. milk
½ C. water
Cornmeal for dusting

In a large mixing bowl, combine 3 C. of the flour, the yeast, sugar, salt, and soda. Heat the liquids together until very warm (120°) and add to dry mixture. Beat well. Gradually add enough flour to make a stiff batter. Butter/grease two 8" x 4" bread pans liberally and sprinkle with cornmeal; rotate and shake to coat all inside surfaces. Spoon the batter evenly into the pans,* butter/grease the tops of the loaves, and sprinkle with cornmeal. Cover loosely with a towel and let rise in a warm place for about 45 minutes, or until loaves are slightly above the tops of the pans. Bake at 400° for about 25 minutes. Loosen sides and remove bread from the pans to cool on a rack.

*<u>Kitchen Hint</u>: This batter is sticky and I find it easier to butter my hands and grab it rather than try to spoon it into the pans. The bread makes excellent toast and even better French toast because it really soaks up the egg mixture!

Welcome to Willow Ridge, Missouri!
In this cozy Amish town
along the banks of the river,
the Old Ways are celebrated
at the Sweet Seasons Bakery Café,
and love is a gift God gives with grace . . .

Summer of Secrets

Summer has come to Willow Ridge, but Rachel Lantz is looking forward to a whole new season in her life—marriage to strapping carpenter Micah Brenneman, her childhood sweetheart. When a strange Englisher arrives in the café claiming to be the long-lost sister of Rachel and her twin Rhoda, Rachel feels the sturdy foundation of her future crumbling—including Micah's steadfast love. As the days heat up and tempers flare, Rachel and Micah will learn that even when God's plan isn't clear, it will always lead them back to each other . . .